A LAST SERENADE
FOR BILLY BONNEY

OTHER FIVE STAR TITLES BY MARK WARREN

A Last Serenade for Billy Bonney

Mark Warren

FIVE STAR
A part of Gale, a Cengage Company

GALE
A Cengage Company

LIBRARY OF CONGRESS CATALOGING-IN-PUBLICATION DATA

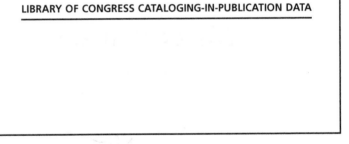

First Edition. First Printing: March 2023
Find us on Facebook—https://www.facebook.com/FiveStarCengage
Visit our website—http://www.gale.cengage.com/fivestar
Contact Five Star Publishing at FiveStar@cengage.com

Printed in the United States of America
1 2 3 4 5 6 7 27 26 25 24 23

To Chatty and her son, Ward
And to Jim Richardson,
for revealing to me how the gears turned inside Billy's head

CAST OF CHARACTERS
A READER'S REFERENCE
LIST OF CHARACTERS

Antrim, Catherine: Mother of "Billy the Kid" and wife to William Antrim. She dies of consumption in Silver City, N.M.T., when Billy is fourteen.

Antrim, Henry: (*See* Billy the Kid)

Antrim, Joseph ("Josie"): Older brother of "Billy the Kid."

Antrim, Kid: (*See* Billy the Kid)

Antrim, William: Stepfather of "Billy the Kid."

Axtell, Samuel: Corrupt governor of New Mexico Territory when the Lincoln County War breaks out.

Beckwith, Robert: A Seven Rivers rancher who joins the Dolan party that besieges the McSween home. Killed in that fight.

Bell, James ("J.W."): Posse man who took part in the Greathouse ranch fight. Deputy sheriff under Pat Garrett. Killed by "Billy the Kid" during his escape from Lincoln.

Billy the Kid: Most wanted outlaw in the history of the New Mexico Territory. Known by the following names, chronologically: Henry McCarty, Henry Antrim, the Kid, Kid Antrim, William H. Bonney, Billy the Kid. Born 1859, died 1881.

Blessing, John: Composer, choral director at San Loretto Chapel, reporter for the *Santa Fe Messenger,* author of the book and musical composition "A Last Serenade for Billy Bonney."

Bonney, William H. ("Billy"): (*See* Billy the Kid) This name is assumed by "Billy the Kid" in the latter part of his life, this moniker likely borrowed from his deceased biological father, whom Billy never knew.

Bowdre, Charlie: Friend of "Billy the Kid" and member of the Regulators.

Bowdre, Manuela: Wife of Charlie Bowdre.

Brady, William: Corrupt sheriff of Lincoln County killed by "Billy the Kid" and the Regulators.

Brewer, Dick: Foreman at Tunstall's Rio Feliz ranch, briefly a constable in Lincoln, and captain of the Regulators. Killed by Buckshot Roberts at Blazer's Mill.

Brown, Mrs. Sarah: Proprietress of a Silver City boarding-house, where the teenaged "Billy the Kid" lives for a short time after his mother dies.

Burns, Walter Noble: Chicago journalist who writes *The Saga of Billy the Kid*, bestseller published in 1927.

Carlyle, Jim: Well-liked blacksmith at White Oaks and posse member killed at the Greathouse ranch fight.

Casey, Mary Richards: (*See* Richards, Mary)

Chapman, Huston: Lincoln attorney who represents Susan McSween after her husband's murder. Murdered in cold blood by James Dolan.

Coe, Frank and George: Cousins who are friends of "Billy the Kid" and ride with the Regulators.

Cosgrove, Mike: Mail carrier in San Miguel County and friend to the Regulators.

Dolan, James: Ruthless businessman of Lincoln County who dominates the economy of the region by assuring that most citizens are in debt to him. Arch enemy of "Billy the Kid."

East, Jim: Deputy under Sheriff Pat Garrett who rides in the posse that captures "Billy the Kid" at Stinking Spring.

Evans, Jesse: Ruthless, violent outlaw who schools a teenaged "Billy the Kid" in the art of rustling. He joins Dolan's mercenaries to become an enemy of "Billy the Kid."

Folliard, Tom: Orphaned, Irish youth who becomes "Billy the Kid's" best soldier. Killed by Pat Garrett's posse at Fort Sumner.

French, Jim: Associate of "Billy the Kid" and member of the Regulators wounded during the ambush on Sheriff Brady.

Garrett, Pat: Sheriff of Lincoln County, killer of "Billy the Kid."

Gauss, Godfrey: German cook for Tunstall's Rio Feliz ranch, acquaintance of "Billy the Kid."

Grant, Joe ("Texas Red"): Braggart, bully, and wannabe bad man killed by "Billy the Kid."

Greathouse, Joseph: Rancher who holds stolen livestock for "Billy the Kid's" rustling gang.

Ham: Jailor for Sheriff Pat Garrett in Lincoln.

Herrera, Maria: (*See* Scurlock, Maria Antonia)

Hindman, George: A member of the posse that kills John Tunstall. Killed in the ambush on Sheriff Brady in Lincoln.

Hudgens, John and Will: Brothers in the posse that besieges the Greathouse ranch.

Hurley, Johnny: One of Dolan's hired guns besieging the McSween home.

Jaramillo, Paulita: (*See* Maxwell, Paulita) She acquires this name after marrying in 1882.

Joseph (José): Errand boy first for the *Santa Fe Messenger* in the territorial capital and then for the Wortley Hotel in Lincoln. A friend to and admirer of "Billy the Kid."

Kid, the: (*See* Billy the Kid) He acquires this moniker early in his cowboying career.

Kimbrel, George: Sheriff of Lincoln County before Pat Garrett. Sympathetic to the Regulators.

Kinney, John: Notorious outlaw leader who joins Dolan's mercenaries to wipe out the Regulators. Wounded by "Billy the Kid" during the Kid's escape from the siege on the

McSween home.

Longworth, Tom: Constable at White Oaks who leads the posse that besieges the Greathouse ranch, where Billy and his gang are holed up.

Martinez, Atanacio: Lincoln constable tasked with serving a warrant on Sheriff Brady for the murder of John Tunstall.

Mason, Barney: Deputy sheriff under Pat Garrett who rode with the Stinking Spring posse.

Maxwell, Deluvina: Cook and devoted friend of Billy Bonney. A Navajo woman who, as a girl, was captured by the Apache and was eventually bought and adopted by Pete Maxwell's father.

Maxwell, Paulita: Sweetheart of "Billy the Kid" living in Fort Sumner.

Maxwell, Pedro (Pete): Protective brother of Paulita and overseer of inherited tracts of land around Fort Sumner.

McCarty, Catherine: Single parent of young "Billy the Kid" until she marries William Antrim.

McCarty, Henry: (*See* Billy the Kid)

McCarty, Joseph ("Josie"): Older brother of "Billy the Kid" before taking his stepfather's name.

McSween, Alexander: Former Dolan bookkeeper and attorney who partners with Tunstall to oppose Dolan.

McSween, Susan: Wife of Alexander and survivor of the siege on her home.

Olinger, Robert ("Big Bob"): Heavy-handed deputy who escorts "Billy the Kid" from Lincoln to La Mesilla and back and then guards him at the Lincoln jail. Killed by Billy during his escape from the Lincoln courthouse.

Patrón, Juan: Respected citizen of Lincoln who runs a store and serves as commissioner.

Peppin, George: Stone mason and builder who serves as deputy to Sheriff Brady. He escapes the ambush that kills

Brady and then takes Brady's position as sheriff.

Pickett, Tom: Outlaw/rustler captured with "Billy the Kid" at Stinking Spring.

Pitts, Edmond: Editor of the *Santa Fe Messenger.*

Raines, Eustace: Rookie journalist for the *Santa Fe Messenger.* Interviews "Billy the Kid" in a Las Vegas, N.M.T., jail.

Regulators, the: Self-organized gang with the mission of avenging the death of Tunstall. "Billy the Kid" plays a prominent role in this group.

Richards, Mary: Schoolteacher of fourteen-year-old "Billy the Kid" in Silver City, N.M.T.

Riley, John: Business partner of James Dolan.

Roberts, Andrew ("Buckshot"): Enemy of "Billy the Kid" and killer of Dick Brewer.

Rudabaugh, David ("Dirty Dave"): Despicable outlaw/ rustler/killer who rides with "Billy the Kid" and is captured at Stinking Spring.

Scurlock, Josiah ("Doc"): Captain of the regulators after Dick Brewer's death.

Scurlock, Maria Antonia: Wife of Doc Scurlock and mother of their ten children.

Sheldon, Lionel: Appointed governor of New Mexico Territory when Wallace resigns.

Truesdell, Clara: Friend who nurses Catherine Antrim during her last weeks in Silver City, N.M.T. She takes in Billy for a short time after his mother's death.

Tunstall, John: Englishman intent on building a cattle empire and competing with Dolan. After being a victim of theft by "Billy the Kid," he hires Billy to work for him.

Waite, Fred ("Dash"): Close friend and comrade of "Billy the Kid" who rides with the Regulators. Part Chickasaw, he survives the Lincoln War and becomes a noted tribal statesman in the Indian Territory.

Wallace, Lew: Union general who becomes governor of New Mexico Territory and bargains with "Billy the Kid" to trade amnesty from crimes in return for court testimony to convict the Dolan faction. He authors the bestseller *Ben Hur,* published in 1880.

Whitehill, Harvey: Sheriff who arrests young "Billy the Kid" in Silver City, N.M.T.

Wilson, Billy: Rustler/outlaw captured with "Billy the Kid" at Stinking Spring.

Wilson, Squire Juan: Lincoln justice of the peace on friendly terms with "Billy the Kid."

1

Blessing's Notes
Coe Ranch
Glencoe, Lincoln County,
New Mexico Territory
Early October 1885

"This country shows no mercy to a young boy on his own With no one to light a candle in the window of a home."

On a quiet summer night at Fort Sumner in 1881, I made a promise to William H. Bonney. We had talked late into the night, each of us sharing pieces of our lives we had abandoned to our past . . . as well as the hopes we held for the future. One minute we were laughing about the foibles of our youth and in the next our hearts had opened to reveal our most fervent dreams. Then, unexpectedly, Billy had stood and slapped his belly with the flats of both hands, saying he was hungry. Two minutes later I heard the gunshots, and I knew he was dead.

Because I was ostracized from the more refined circles of New Mexican society, it has taken me more than four years to begin this journey. And this book. Now, at least, I am in motion. The old wagon road that heads west from San Patricio follows the Rio Ruidoso toward its headwaters in the Sierra Blanca Mountains. Throughout the cool morning I have found the journey by horseback pleasant and the riverine scenery most pleasing to my eye, but now at midafternoon, the gray-whiskered bay foisted upon me by the San Patricio liveryman has developed a troublesome limp.

Dismounting, I check the animal's left forehoof for a crack or a pebble, finding neither. Only when I step back to compare all four legs do I notice the swelling. The horse stands indifferently, awaiting my solution to its dilemma, but all I know to do is treat the injury with a cold compress. To this end I soak my extra blouse in the river and wrap it around the bay's foreleg just above the pastern. After binding it in place with a leather tie cord from my saddlebags, I have no choice but to press on, as the miles ahead of me are less than those I have left behind, and I have brought no provisions for setting up a camp. Walking ahead of the lame animal, I keep a firm grip on the reins and coax the horse on down the trail.

Within an hour I have developed four fiery blisters on my feet, leaving me no choice but to climb into the saddle again. Right away, to my great relief—and, no doubt, to the horse's, as well—I encounter signs of civilization. A cold cigar butt lies next to a metal bucket on a flat shelf of rock jutting out over the river. A fishing spot!

The trail becomes utterly charming as it winds into a confluence with a small wooded canyon. A hand-painted sign assures me I have not gotten myself lost. The canyon is named for the Coe family. It is the Coes I have come to see—George and Frank, cousins who survived the Lincoln County War by getting out of the territory while, as they say, "the getting was good."

My spirits lift now that I arrive at my destination. If I cannot secure another horse for a late afternoon return trip, at least tonight I may have a roof over my head and perhaps a bed separating me from the scorpions, rattlesnakes, centipedes, and sand lice that infest the desert floor. Even the river seems more cheerful here, riffling through a chattering shoal and dancing with shards of sunlight. The sound is like a sustained applause inside a music hall. I can appreciate the Coes' choice of a home site.

Glencoe, as this settlement is called, is scattered throughout the trees in a rather haphazard grid, marking this fledgling outpost as one trying to be progressive and welcoming. It seems too idyllic a setting to find two men who once rode with the outlaw Billy Bonney, but here I hope to find a modicum of hospitality and secure my first interview for the book that I am determined to write. This book was my last promise to Billy.

My rented horse and I move through the autumn shade of rusty oaks, pastel-pink maples, and startlingly yellow cottonwoods that crowd the low ground. It seems remarkable to me that here, seemingly in the middle of nowhere, buildings now reveal themselves, some old and weathered and some so new they still smell of fresh-cut lumber from the sawmill. On the distant hills, where pinyon pines dot the terrain like strategically placed sentinels, cattle nose the rocky slopes for tufts of grass.

Facing the curve of the river is a main house, and behind it are the requisite barn, stables, a smithy jacal, a training paddock, a tool shed, and a large holding pen. A schoolhouse and post office are also evident, standing out front as though announcing this outpost as more than just another hardscrabble village that might blow away on the next dry wind. Here is a nascent community, sinking its roots like the trees, full of hope, and aiming at the elusive dreams of prosperity and posterity.

In addition to its injury, my horse shows a distinct lack of stamina. It has been dragging all of its hooves for the last three miles, but the sullen beast perks up to a limping trot as the trail swings closer to the river. The water runs so clear, even from the road I can spot the dark shapes of trout darting into the shady margins along the shoreline. I seem to no longer control the horse as it steps down into the shallows, just fetlock deep on a gently sloping bed of sand and shale. Just as I question the wisdom of remaining on the animal as it refreshes itself, I hear a man's voice chuckling behind me.

"You rent that nag from Chávez in San Patricio?"

Surprised at the unexpected query, I try to pivot in the saddle without disturbing either the industrious slaking of my horse's thirst or my balance. I see that I am in the company of a less than statuesque farmer in a blue denim coat, mud-stained work pants, rubber boots, and a tan slouch hat. He appears to be not much older than I, but it is difficult to pinpoint his age as the lower half of his face is covered with hair. His eyes burn like hot coals from the shadow of his hat brim. Yet it is his pendulous nose that dominates his face. It hooks downward like a fleshy beak.

"Yes, as a matter of fact, I did," I reply. "It started going lame a few miles back."

The man chortles again. "You mean a few *years* back." He shakes his head and spits to one side. "Chávez would rent a blind mule to a priest if he could."

Tentatively, I lean out to one side to point at the makeshift bandage still wrapped around the horse's leg. "I suppose the cool water might help the swelling."

Now this man props his fists on his hips, arches his back, and laughs outright. "I'd advise you to ease that old girl back up here to high ground before she decides to send you overboard. She's got a hist'ry o' that. I've seen it twice before. Once it was me takin' the bath."

Though the laughing man seems friendly enough, I feel my face struggling with concern and indignation at the same time. "You know this horse?"

My new equestrian mentor lifts both eyebrows like a double sunrise and smiles so that his teeth flash from a gap between his bushy moustache and somber beard. His hazel eyes continue to hold a spark of good humor, but I sense that beneath his neighborly mask he regards me with the healthy skepticism that is part and parcel of this country.

"We sold that shirker to Chávez last spring," he informs me. "He got hornswoggled in the deal, but we owed him that over a damned impotent bull he tried to sell us through a third party."

"Would you be Mr. Coe?"

"I'm one of 'em," he says and jabs a thumb over his shoulder. "Frank's in the barn workin' on the haymaker." He taps the same thumb against his chest, and that's when I notice that his forefinger is missing. "I'm George."

George Coe, indeed. Four years ago, Billy himself told me I would know this man—one of the old "Regulators"—by the absence of that finger. I feel myself warm to George right away, as I know him to have been loyal to Billy. I also know that he is fortunate to be alive, that missing finger being a small price to pay for living through the hell that had once reigned over this county.

Pulling up on the reins, I try to coax the old bay up onto shore before disaster strikes. The mare balks, and I begin kicking my heels into her ribs as instructed by the San Patricio liveryman. I fear I appear as feckless in my predicament as the aforementioned bull.

Coe makes no critical comment as he willingly steps into the water, takes the bay by the cheek strap of its bridle, and walks the animal up onto firm ground. I feel like a child being led on a pony ride at a carnival.

"We got a water trough in the main yard," Coe offers and continues to escort me hand on horse across the yard, as if he fears I might drown in the trough if left unattended.

At our approach a flock of chickens scatters. The birds cluck and squawk in panicked protest and then regroup behind us. An old hound raises its head from the front porch of the house and regards me with minimal interest.

"It's you I've come to see, Mr. Coe," I say. "I am most pleased to meet you."

"That so?" Coe says, receiving my salutations with barely a turn of his head. His voice is matter of fact and, like the dog's insouciant gaze, betrays not the slightest hint of curiosity.

"My name is John Blessing," I explain. "Though for only a short time, I was a friend to Billy Bonney."

Coe stops and the horse with him. Turning to me the man narrows his eyes as he studies me from the crown of my new hat to my button-up shoes. It occurs to me he might be checking my person for a weapon.

"You're Blessing? The newspaper writer?"

"Yes, sir, I was," I say and take the opportunity to dismount. When I turn back to Coe his eyes are focused and alert, seeming to penetrate through my skin in an attempt to examine the soul beneath. "Now I am working on a book. To that end, I am hoping to interview you and your cousin, sir. I want to write the truth about what happened in Lincoln County."

"The truth?" Coe sputters, but this time there is no joy in his laugh. He lets go of the bridle, steps back, and stuffs his hands into the pockets of his coat. "There ain't no truth about the Lincoln Coun'y War. Both sides would say they were in the right. It all depends on who you're talkin' to."

I remove my hat, and the breeze coming off the river cools my scalp like an impromptu christening. I look down at my hat and run my finger along the silk band inside the crown. When I look up at Coe, I try for a deferential tone of voice.

"Billy didn't talk about it that way."

Coe looks off toward the river, his eyes fixed on everything and nothing. "Yeah, well, Billy didn't live long enough to have to learn to get along with his enemies." Pointing with his chin he indicates the trail down which I have just come. "Hell, not long after I moved back to the territory, ol' 'Dad' Peppin and Johnny Hurley come over here to bury the hatchet."

"Peppin's name I know," I announce, sounding, I am sure, like a well-prepared schoolboy giving his teacher the correct answer to a riddle. I want Coe to see that I am no stranger to the players in Billy's story. "He was deputy under Sheriff Brady.

With him the day Billy killed Brady, in fact, and Peppin became sheriff himself. But who is Hurley?"

Coe sucks in his cheeks and lets go with a squirt of saliva that arcs to the ground. "He's one of them that burned down the McSween house. He was against us all the way." Frowning, he spits again and shakes his head. "Don't matter none now. He was kilt over in Chaperito last winter."

While Coe stares across the river, I balance my hat on the pommel of the rented saddle and untie my satchel, which contains my notebook, pen, and bottle of ink. "Mr. Coe, if I could just tap into your recollections for an hour or so . . . it would mean a great deal to me to get your side of things. I know Billy held you in high regard."

Coe bows his head and stares down at the toes of his boots. I assume he is either considering my request or deciding in what manner to run me off his property.

"You were decent to Billy in that newspaper piece you wrote," he mumbles. "Maybe the only one who was." When he meets my eyes, he appears to be relieved, and I wonder if, in these last four years, he has been waiting to tell his story to someone . . . to anyone. Raising that hand with the absent finger, he gestures toward the barn.

"Go on an' stable your horse and give 'er some o' that fresh hay stacked in the back stall. Then come inside an' I'll pour us a drink. Hard to talk about all this without numbin' the brain a little." He starts for the house but stops and turns to give me a shrug. "Better call me 'George.' Too many Coes around here to be usin' the surname."

When I join George in the house, we settle into chairs arranged before his wood heater in the front room. The stove is barely warm. I imagine this is where, at the end of a day, he and his wife talk over the complexities of running a ranch fourteen miles from the nearest town. I can hear someone else in the back of the house—kitchen sounds of pots and lids and rattling spoons—but I feel a tacit understanding that this is to be men-talk in the front parlor.

As George pours two glasses from a dusty bottle, a leaner, slightly older man comes through the front door. He, too, is bearded and has the same beaked nose, but his is thinner like a hatchet blade. I suspect George has sent for the man, because the new arrival shows no surprise at my presence. Without comment he hauls a cushioned bench from the front window. George pulls down a third glass.

"This here is Frank," George offers. "He'll have as much to say about all this as I will."

I stand to shake hands, but before I raise my arm Cousin Frank lowers the bench and straddles it in one motion, as if unannounced parleys like this one might be routine for him. Leaning forward on stiffened arms he bestows a welcoming nod. Lowering myself back into my chair, I realize it is best that we did not complete a handshake, as I had not performed the ritual with George, who probably refrains from such amenities due to his deficit of one finger.

"I read a article o' yours in one o' the Santa Fe newspapers," Frank says. "I reckon you gave Billy a fair shake, which is more'n most writers did." He lifts his drink toward the ceiling. "To Billy, God bless 'im."

We three tap glasses all around. "To the Kid," George seconds.

"To Billy Bonney," I say.

Even though I do not customarily consume alcohol, I throw back the whiskey with a single jerk of my head. I've learned *that* much about New Mexican hospitality. The whiskey scorches the back of my throat as if I've tried to swallow a mouthful of hot desert sand. I clench my teeth to fight back the tears welling behind my eyes, and I manage not to grimace. The three glasses tap down on the floor as though it were a ceremony our trio had practiced for years. The two Coes stare at me, apparently awaiting the commencement of the interview.

"All right," I say and launch into the opening question I had planned on the trail. "In most of the conversations I had with Billy Bonney, he wore handcuffs, and we spoke through the barrier of thick iron bars. Maybe you two gentlemen could tell me more about his personality away from his captors. What was he like when not incarcerated?"

George's body shakes once as he snorts a dry laugh through his nose. "Billy was always Billy. It didn't matter if he was holed up under fire from a posse or talkin' up the young *señoritas* at one of the bailes in Anton Chico or San Patricio." George smiles. "Lord, but that boy loved to dance."

"And sing," Frank adds. He tosses a hand toward his cousin. "Me an' George play fiddle. There was many a night the three o' us whipped up our own fandango and sang up a high time."

"Did he have a favorite song?" I ask.

" 'Turkey in the Straw' for dancin'," George announces without hesitation. "For singin' it was 'Silver Threads Among the Gold.' " George smiles at Frank. "Remember when he taught us that one? We were on a huntin' trip upriver."

Frank coughs up a single chirp of laughter. "That was the night you scorched your new boots by the fire," he says, leveling a finger at George. "Smelled like a polecat, remember? You were so mad I thought you'd shoot somebody."

Here was a memory that brought a scowl to George's friendly face. "It was only one boot, but it was a damned good one. Never could find a match for it." George shows me a contrite half smile. "Don't listen to him. I wouldn't shoot a man over a boot. *I* was the one left the damned thing too close to the fire."

Frank waggles his finger at his cousin. "I don't know, George. You might'a shot somebody. That *was* back in the days you still had a trigger finger."

George leans to me, his eyelids half lowered as he shakes his head. "I was never quick to use a gun."

He holds out his mangled hand and studies it as if it were some kind of unnamed creature that had washed up from the river. Now I have legitimate reason to stare at the altered hand. We're all looking at it, but it is George who seems most amused at its appearance. Rather than thinking about pistols and rifles, I find myself wondering if George can still play a fiddle.

Sporting a crooked grin, Frank points at George. "I know a coupla boys who would argue that claim."

George chuckles as if this kind of bantering is something he and Frank engage in on a regular basis. "Billy *did* have a beautiful voice," George says, getting us back on topic. "He was always makin' us change key . . . until he found the one just right for his voice. He was a high tenor, you know."

Frank purses his lips to whistle a short note of admiration. "The Kid could sing like a choirboy."

Opening my satchel, I prop my ink bottle on the floor next to the woodstove, open my notebook in my lap, and dip my pen. "How did all of you meet?" I ask looking from one Coe to the other, my pen hovering over an unmarked sheet of paper.

Slumping back deeper into his chair George looks to Frank for an answer. Frank, who appears pleased to take center stage, sits up straighter and clears his throat.

"When he was just a boy—maybe fourteen, fifteen . . . right after his mother died—Billy ran afoul of the law over in Silver City, so he sloped over to Arizona Territory for a time. This was before we knew him, but we got the story straight from his lips. He headed over to Camp Grant, where he got into a little more trouble."

George makes a grunt deep in his chest. " 'A *little* more trouble'?" he echoes with a chuckle. His sly eyes angle to me.

"He killed a man over there. Gut-shot 'im."

"It was self-defense!" Frank snaps. "The man was mean . . . a bully . . . and twice Billy's size. Had the boy pinned to the floor while he was a-beatin' on 'im." He points his finger again at his cousin, and I wonder if this habit is Frank's way of gloating about having all his digits. "George, I doubt you'd'a done a lick different yourself."

George shrugs and nestles back into his chair. With a cock of his head, he is all ears again.

"So, the Kid was on the run," Frank continues. "He showed up in these parts over at Charlie Bowdre's place looking for work. Charlie's wife, Manuela, was a native, and Billy could speak Spanish better'n Charlie, so the two o' them—Manuela and Billy—was always chatting up a storm, and Charlie didn't like that one bit. So he brung the Kid down to my place and dropped him off like a stray cat. Charlie rode off and never looked back." Frank shakes his head. "Who woulda ever believed old Charlie would end up riding for the Kid?"

"And dyin' for him," George adds.

The Coes glance at one another briefly, and both go quiet for the time it takes me to finish scratching my notes on paper. Frank swings a leg over so that he sits sidesaddle on the bench. He shrugs and narrows his eyes.

"But, hell, I don't blame Charlie for his cool reception. In those days I didn't have any use for Billy neither. We were all just scrapin' by the best we could, none of us in a position to hire anybody. Besides, the Kid looked so young and frail, I didn't figure him man enough to handle the heavy work needed on a ranch." Frank Coe resorts to a hang-dog expression and stares out the window at the afternoon light bringing a palette of colors to the trees. "I just didn't take the Kid seriously," he confided. Then he huffed a quiet laugh. "But I would learn the mistake in that soon enough."

"It ain't like we turned the Kid away," George adds. "He stayed with us for a while. We all hunted together." He raises one eyebrow. "But, like Frank said, the Kid weren't cut out for ranch work. Not at that time, anyway."

Frank nods. "Billy knew that as well as anyone, so he just up and took off one day. The next place Billy turned up was in the Seven Rivers country. He got mixed up with a bad crowd down there." The pained expression Frank has worn for his introduction to Billy's hard times disappears. Now his jaws clamp like angle iron, and his eyes go cold and hard. "You heard o' Jesse Evans?"

I nod and write down the name. "The outlaw," I say.

"The scum!" George corrects.

When I look up to see if George will expound on Jesse Evans, he turns away, sucks in a long breath, and lets it ease out as a sigh. Swiveling his hand at the wrist he makes a motion for Frank to continue.

"Evans was the worse kind o' man," Frank says in a raspy tone he apparently reserves for his enemies. "He'd shoot your dog just to see if you'd cry." Frank is quiet as I write down this character assessment word for word. "Anyway," he continues, "he was a real bad influence on Billy. Evans took the Kid in and showed him everything he knew about rustling livestock: horses, cattle, goats, pigs . . . it didn't matter. Hell, he'd a stole armadillos if someone was to herd 'em up an' put a dollar value on 'em."

Neither George nor Frank shows any sign of amusement over the image of a notorious outlaw riding for the hills with a herd of stolen armadillos in tow. I keep my face blank and wait for Frank to recommence his story.

"When they stole from the Englishman—Mr. Tunstall—that opened up the ball. Dick Brewer was Tunstall's top man, and Dick acquired a badge and led a posse down to Seven Rivers, arrested every horse thief he could find, and brought back Mr. Tunstall's prized brace of dapple grays. Billy was a-sittin' on top o' one o' them grays when Dick met up with 'im."

George pours himself another drink, raises the glass, and eyes me over the rim. "Dick Brewer . . . now there's a man you oughta write about. You ask me, he was a noble one . . . afraid of no man . . . and yet fair and straight with any stranger he dealt with. And strong as hell . . . built like a Greek god . . . and handsome. Lord, but the ladies gawked at him, and he didn't even seem to notice."

George's face appears to light up with a revelation, and he turns to his cousin. "That there was the turnin' point for Billy. You remember how Brewer treated him like a little brother?" George fixes his intense gaze on me and nods. "That's what turned the Kid around to our side. That was all Dick Brewer, by God."

"Well," Frank says in a tone of disagreement, "him and Tunstall, too. Billy said the Englishman was the only person to ever give him a chance at anything."

"How do you mean?" I ask.

Frank shrugs. "Well . . . I can only tell it to you the way Dick Brewer told me. I guess that makes it hearsay."

I give him an encouraging smile. "I'd like to hear it, if you don't mind. I believe Dick Brewer's word is good enough for me . . . even secondhand."

"Hell, yes," George says, picking up the liquor bottle and extending it to me. I wave it off and avert my eyes by dipping my pen into ink. Frank takes the bottle from George and pours himself a second glass.

"I'll tell it to you the same as Dick Brewer told me," Frank assures me.

2

"THE PIT" COUNTY JAIL
TOWN OF LINCOLN
AND
TUNSTALL RANCH ON THE RIO FELIZ
NEW MEXICO TERRITORY
NOVEMBER 1877

"But if a man lives by his wits and grit and plays the cards he's dealt He just might have what it takes to make that journey by himself."

The hand-dug pit in the new jail building at Lincoln could officially accommodate six prisoners, so said the circuit judge during his inspection of the facility. But anyone who had spent a single night there agreed the hole in the ground was not fit for a feral hog, let alone a human being.

The cold, subterranean chamber measured ten feet deep, its walls lined with heavy timbers and its roof a similar construction, save its trapdoor of thick planks. Slop buckets lined one wall, but they were regularly spilled each time the prisoners were told to haul them up by ladder for the once-a-day "grand empty" and peek at the sunlight. The dark pit was like a cauldron designed to brew diseases, for no man left that confinement in the same health as he had entered.

A deputy tripped the lock, threw open the trapdoor, and knelt with a lantern lowered into the opening. "Back over to the south wall, boys. We're sending a ladder down. Time to stretch your legs and empty your piss pots."

Several deep groans rose up from the cell, as the prisoners began shuffling around in the dark, limited space. Someone stumbled over a bucket and cursed.

"We wouldn't know the south wall down here from a mule's ass," one of the prisoners complained.

Without responding, the deputy lowered the ladder until it was braced firmly on the bare dirt floor. "Every man better come outta there carryin' a bucket; else, you go right back down and miss your outside time."

Obediently, four haggard men scaled the ladder one-handedly as they balanced a chamber pot in the other hand. Last came the Kid. He crawled out ashen-skinned and coughing but still managed to hold a sly smile on his face. When all were assembled, blinking and squinting at their deliverance into the lantern light, they faced three deputies—two Hispanic and one Anglo—each armed with a shotgun and each wearing the determined glare of one who would use his weapon without hesitation. The lantern was hung from a metal hook attached to a wall, where it cast the prisoners' long shadows into a common pool that covered most of the floor.

"Let's go, boys," the Anglo deputy ordered. "You know the drill. Empty out at the privy and then rinse out your bucket at the pump." With the muzzle of his weapon, he motioned toward the building's back door. On cue, the jailor emerged from the front office and unlocked the door. The three officers tightened their grips on their shotguns and snugged the butt ends of their stocks against their shoulders. They stood like hunters expecting a covey of quail to burst from cover in thick grass. As the disgruntled prisoners filed out, each one kept his eyes straight ahead on the back of the man's head before him. No one spoke until the Kid reached the door and stood abreast of the jailor.

"Damn, Lucio, you oughta try an' spend just one night down in that snake hole." Jabbing a thumb back over his shoulder, Billy pointed toward the pit. "You might cultivate a little sympathy for the next man you stuff down in there."

The jailor slowly shook his head, his face as sober as a church deacon's. "Ees the reason I no break the law, Bee-lee."

The Kid smiled, his eyes twinkling with mischief. "Well, at least taste of the damned food you lower down to us. You might be inspired to haul us off to the hotel restaurant for a change." Billy patted his belly. "I think my gut has already died twice. I'm just hangin' on by reserves."

The jailor arched his eyebrows and shrugged. "I got no say in how the jail runs, Bee-lee. I joss open the doors and lock them."

Billy smiled and winked. "I hear you, *amigo*. We all got our jobs to do, ain't we?"

In the yard, awaiting their turn in the outhouse, the prisoners moped around under the watchful eyes of the armed guards, their shotguns now held diagonally across their torsos. The jailor had disappeared back into the building, but now he returned to the yard, spread his boots, and cleared his throat.

"Ho-kay, you men!" he announced in a timid voice. "The constable . . . he need a man to wash the front ween-dows! It geeve that man some time away from the *cárcel*." He raised an arm and pointed back toward the pit.

One prisoner, the biggest of the lot, spat into the dirt and scowled at the jailor. "Tell 'im he can clean his own damned windows." The brutish man gave the others a quick glance, a warning lest someone consider volunteering.

"Hey, *I'm* a damned good window washer!" the Kid announced and broke into the boyish grin that exposed his two crooked front teeth. Ignoring the glare of the others, Billy took a step forward. "Hell, I wash a window, and you can see through it all the way to Mexico."

Lucio looked to the Anglo deputy as if awaiting his approval, but Billy would have none of that. He strode up to the jailor to stand face to face.

"Let's go clean up this town, amigo," Billy said and gave the startled jailor a friendly slap on the side of the shoulder as he walked past him for the building.

Lucio broke into a run and caught up to Billy in time to flatten his hand on the door to the main office. "Don' get ahead like that, Bee-lee," he whispered. "There are some here who would keel you joss for walking through a door."

The Kid feigned a look of shock. "Well, if that's the way it works around here—" Stepping back he bowed and swept a hand toward the door. "After you, *Señor.*" Billy's smile shone bright in the lantern light.

Lucio knocked twice on the door and led the way into the front office. Dick Brewer and another constable were deep in conversation by the gun cabinet. Brewer sat on the edge of the desk, and the constable leaned against the cabinet with his arms folded above the swell of his stomach. Both men turned to the interruption and watched the jailor enter the room. The Kid followed behind him, looking around and grinning as if he were late for a party being thrown in his honor.

"Bee-lee say he wash the ween-dows," Lucio reported in his humble voice.

"Hell, yeah," Billy crowed. "Anything is better than sittin' in that damned dungeon with those whiners." He raised his chin to Brewer. "So, Dick, are you here to retract your accusation against me?" Billy slacked off on his grin long enough to deliver a comic performance of admiration. "It takes a mighty strong man to admit he was wrong, Dick. I'll respect you for it and forgive all this inconvenience to boot."

Brewer got to his feet, took two easy steps toward the Kid, and looked down into the boy's impish eyes. Standing next to Billy's relaxed slouch, Brewer stood half a head taller and straight as a fence post, his muscular frame like an oak next to the boy's willowy stance. For the time it took a wagon outside to rattle across the old plaza, neither man spoke.

"You know, and I know," Dick said in his low, humming voice, "that you stole those dapple grays. You were sitting on top of one when I arrested you."

"Now, Dick," Billy countered, "I walk in here and see you a-sittin' on that desk." He pointed. "But I ain't accused you o' stealin' it, have I?"

Brewer ignored the jest. "We may not have enough evidence to convict you, Billy, but we both know who the thief is standing in this room. I'm bettin' you had a good mother who taught you better."

The Kid's smile snapped like a thread, and his smooth, young face reddened as though he had been soundly embarrassed. Without a word he turned to the front window and chewed on the inside of his cheek as he glared out at the townspeople going about their business.

"You keep on the way you're headed," Brewer continued, his voice now like a priest's inside a confessional, "and we're bound to meet again. When that happens, I may not be so obliging as to follow the law. You understand what I'm saying?"

Billy's eyes darted around in rapid increments as he studied the windows. "I can see this glass does need some cleanin'," he announced to the room. "When can I be shut of this sermon and start to workin'?"

Brewer moved beside Billy and stared at the Kid's face in profile. Billy smiled but would not look at him.

"Those boys you ride with are going to lead you right to hell, Billy."

The Kid laughed a cascade of high notes that sounded almost feminine. Brewer waited until Billy was done, and then he walked casually to the window that offered a view to the south.

"Hell, Dick," Billy said to Brewer's back. "That road to hell is a wide path, and it looks like everybody in Lincoln County is travelin' on it . . . all movin' in the same direction."

As he looked off to the mountains that towered over the town,

Brewer took in a long breath and eased it out. "If that's true," he said, his voice echoing off the window glass in a casual manner, "then maybe what's important is who you choose to die beside."

A subtle change washed over the Kid. Billy said nothing, but the glow of insolence had evaporated from his face.

"You can't be much over seventeen," Dick said, turning to face the boy. "You got your whole life yet to live. Think about gettin' on the right side of things, Billy. Consider working for Tunstall."

The Kid pursed his lips and cocked his head to one side. "Everybody in this county is fillin' his pockets as fast as he can, grabbin' at whatever he can take." He twisted at the waist to sneer at the plump constable standing quietly by the cabinet. "That includes the law, too. Hell, and most of the judges! What makes this high and mighty Englishman 'the right side'? He wants to rob everybody, too, don't he?"

Brewer moved to the west window and looked toward Tunstall's store. Leaning on the sill with stiffened arms, he spoke so quietly that Billy stopped breathing and cocked one ear forward.

"Kid, let me educate you on something: All the troubles in Lincoln County start in Santa Fe. The territorial government is run by a pack of fat, fancy-dressed, back-stabbing liars and charlatans. All over the territory they're snatching up as much land and livestock as they can get their hands on."

Billy spewed air through his lips, summing up his view of all politicians. "I know they're all sonzabitches up in Santa Fe. Same as they are down here." He pointed across the old plaza. "Like that damned Irishman—Dolan—sittin' in his big mercantile up the street. He owns every rancher and farmer in the county." Billy laughed and pointed toward Tunstall's new store. "Now your fine Englishman is tryin' to horn in on that. I guess he wants to own everybody, too."

Brewer nodded. "Tunstall has ambitions, but he's a fair man . . . and generous. Can you say that about Jimmy Dolan?"

Now Billy laughed in earnest. "Hell, no!"

Brewer pivoted his head to Billy. "So, why are you working for him?"

The Kid's frown deepened as he returned Brewer's stare. "I work for Billy. I always have."

Brewer shook his head and moved back to the front window. "You might think you do. Those skunks in Santa Fe have got their claws into Jimmy Dolan, who is a mean sonovabitch in his own right. They're sucking the life out of him. They *own* him. But Dolan can't exist without them. They provide his muscle." Brewer turned, sat back on the windowsill, and folded his arms over his chest. "Like that deviant you ride with." He waited until the Kid dared to meet his eyes. "If you ride with Jesse Evans, you work for Dolan and the Santa Fe crowd."

Billy snorted. "Yeah, everybody's got his favorite angle on the story. How is it you think you know all this?"

Brewer smiled as if he had been waiting for this question. "Tunstall's new mercantile partner, McSween, was Dolan's lawyer and bookkeeper. He knows every little secret about Dolan's business. That's how we know."

Stepping next to Brewer, Billy studied Dolan's store at a distance, his eyes dull with worry and his forehead creased like a fresh-plowed field.

"Maybe I could help you get out of here early, Billy," Brewer said, his voice softened to a personable timbre.

"Yeah?" Billy said, turning to show his smile. "Well, I might not mind *that*! Tryin' to breathe down in that damned pit is like stickin' your head inside a ripe carcass."

"We need more men . . . men with some sand," Brewer said. "We've got to equal their numbers to fight them. But if you sign on with *us* . . . we'll need more than your gun . . . we'll need your loyalty . . . to Mr. Tunstall."

Billy laughed. "I reckon I'd better meet a man before I'll know if I can be loyal to 'im."

"Fair enough," said Brewer. "When you get out of this piss-hole, come down to Tunstall's spread on the Rio Feliz and have a talk with him."

Holding his gaze on the street outside, Billy made a movement with his head that might have been a nod.

"Billy?" Brewer said in such a brotherly way that the Kid turned to him with the eyes of a curious child. "Whatever you decide to do, get some distance between yourself and Jesse Evans. You're just getting your life started, boy. For God's sake, I don't want to have to kill you."

All the innocence left Billy's face when he laughed, but it was not a derisive laugh intended to mock Brewer. The Kid seemed genuinely amused.

"I'd probably not like that much myself," Billy quipped and turned his attention back to the window. "So which of you boys is gonna fetch me some soapy water and a rag? If you're wantin' me to see the light so bad, I reckon we better get this glass clean."

A little over a week later, on a cold windy afternoon, Billy Bonney rode up on the Tunstall holdings by the Rio Feliz. There was no formal house, just a crude log shelter covering a dugout. A stone's throw from the slapdash abode stood a bare-bones pole barn partitioned into stalls. Attached to one side of it was a large makeshift corral of split juniper rails stacked in a zigzag pattern to make a rough circle.

While Billy led a well-muscled, unsaddled blue roan mare by a short rope and hackamore, his personal mount was unspec-tacular—a swaybacked buckskin with a penchant for stamping its hooves and sidestepping when forced to a halt.

Inside the corral, a dozen horses milled about in a tight circle, sending up a swirling dust-devil that was whipped away by the bracing wind. Among them were the two dapple grays that Billy had stolen. He could see that they were the finest specimens of Tunstall's remuda. Just outside the fence, Dick Brewer and another man had suspended their conversation to watch the Kid's approach.

Reining up before them, Billy smiled and pushed his hat brim up off his forehead. The wind flattened the front of the brim against the crown, but the hat held fast to his head. No one spoke for a time, and Billy could see by Brewer's expression that the foreman could probably outwait a cigar store wooden Indian in seeing who would blink first.

"Look at what I found lost out in the hills up on the Ruidoso." Billy turned in his saddle as if to appraise anew the roan he had brought in. "I believe that's your brand, boys." He laughed and pointed to the horse's rump. Still smiling, he tossed his end of the lead rope to Brewer, who snatched it out of the air like the strike of a snake.

"Peace offering?" Brewer asked.

Billy smiled down at his pommel and bounced with a quiet laugh. "Hell, yeah," he said and looked up, "if a free meal comes with that."

Brewer remained stoic. "Are you here to sign on with us?"

Billy gazed off toward the river. "That's the plan." When he looked back into Brewer's no-nonsense eyes, one corner of Billy's mouth lifted, cracking a smile. "That offer still open?"

"Climb down and let's talk," Brewer said and handed the roan's lead rope to his companion.

As the wind snapped at his clothing, Billy leaned back into the cantle of his saddle, swung a boot over his horse's withers, and slid to the ground as lithe as a cat. By the time he had tied off the buckskin to a fence rail, Brewer's friend had done the same with the roan.

"This here is Fred Waite," Brewer said. "Fred, meet Billy Bonney."

Waite stepped forward and offered his hand. The hair spilling out from under his hat was black and shiny as a crow's wing as it jumped around his face with the erratic changes of the wind. His strong, angular face was further punctuated by a thicket of eyebrows, a wide swooping moustache, and eyes as dark as obsidian. These features gave him the look of something half wild, and Billy suspected the man was part Indian. When they shook hands, Waite smiled, and all the natural intensity of his face seemed to channel into a kind of tacit offer of friendship.

"Friends call me 'Dash,' " Waite said, his words slightly clipped like the speech of the Apache scouts Billy had met around Camp Grant.

Billy smiled. "That's what it'll be then. Call me 'Billy.' " When they released hands, Billy cocked his head and squinted one eye. "What tribe are you?"

"Half Chickasaw," Waite replied evenly. "My mother is a full-blood. She married a white man."

Billy grinned, exposing those front teeth that gave him the innocent look of a child. "Me, I'm half Irish."

Waite raised his chin. "What about the other half?"

Billy shrugged. "That's Irish, too. I just don't like admitting it 'less I'm pressed."

Waite laughed. "Long as you ain't related to that damn Irishman Jimmy Dolan."

Billy hissed a series of short bursts of air through his teeth. "If I was, I'd cut out that part o' me, set it on fire, and bury it out somewhere in the desert."

Dick Brewer nodded toward the gun holstered on Billy's hip. "What kind of artillery are you carrying?"

"Colt's . . . a forty-four."

Brewer looked at the boy's saddle rig. "No rifle?"

Billy smiled. "Not at the moment," he replied and hooked his thumbs behind his cartridge belt to snug the rig a tad higher on his waist.

"Let's make sure I made the right decision with you," Brewer said. "Step over here with me away from the horses."

The three men walked together past the pole barn toward the trees that canopied the shoreline of the river. Brewer stopped in the big meadow fifty yards short of the trees, propped his hands on his hips, and looked around the open land. Soon he pointed to the stump of a lopped off juniper twenty yards away. The flat-topped trunk stood less than a foot high, its girth no thicker than a man's lower leg.

"When I tell you," Brewer instructed, "I want you to pull your pistol and shave some bark off that stump before I can—"

Brewer had not yet lowered his arm before Billy jerked his gun and fired three times from a crouch. The reports bled together as a quick chain of explosions that carried away on the wind like a grumbling thunder. The Kid remained frozen in time, his face all business, his attention so fixed on his target that his eyes shone bright as the heads of ten-penny nails. The bark had shattered three times, some of the pieces tearing away and flying off into the grass. Billy straightened, holstered his pistol, and let a little mischief show in his eyes as he smiled at the two men.

"That quick enough?" Billy said, his smile widening.

Dick Brewer laughed quietly and shook his head. "I reckon that'll do."

Waite squeezed the boy's shoulder. "That's some damn good shootin', Kid."

From the dugout a voice called out, and the three men turned to see Tunstall, bare headed, walking toward them through the grass. He carried a Winchester repeater in one hand. His tall boots gleamed with the high sheen of a fresh polishing. Each time the wind mussed his hair he reached up with his free hand and raked his fingers over his scalp.

"What is it, Dick?" the Englishman yelled over the wind.

Brewer started for his employer, and the other two followed. The three men reached the barn just as Tunstall stopped and made a quick turn of his head away from the wind. Blinking rapidly, he set the rifle against the barn, pulled a white handkerchief from inside his coat, and began dabbing at his eye. As he worked with the linen, his other eye inspected the horses tied to the fence.

"Is that my blue roan?" Tunstall asked, a little surprise slipping into his proper English voice.

Billy put on his schoolboy charm. "I returned 'im for you, Mr. Tunstall. I'm William H. Bonney."

As Tunstall squinted one eye at the frail boy, his handkerchief flew from his hand, fluttering on the brisk wind like a white dove diving for cover in the grass. "Oh, bloody hell!" the Englishman hissed. Even as they watched, the white cloth took flight again and leapt another ten yards, where it snagged in a stand of desiccated weeds.

Brewer started for the handkerchief, but Tunstall waved him back. "Oh, don't bother, Dick. Let it go." The Englishman rubbed at his quivering eyelid. "What was that shooting about?"

Waite slapped Billy on the back. "Mr. Tunstall, I reckon this youngster here just passed our job interview."

Up close, Tunstall was no taller than Billy and only slightly heavier. And, like Billy's, the Englishman's soft face showed a rosy hue in the cheeks. Sideburns bordered his weak jawline, and a narrow beard graced his chin. A thin moustache tried to darken his upper lip.

Unlike Billy, the man conveyed a serious nature, as if he were trying to appear older than he was. As he continued to worry his eye by pulling at the lashes, with his other eye he examined the new boy. There was a certain sadness about the man, and Billy wondered if he were homesick for his own country.

"You're the one who stole my dapple grays," Tunstall remarked offhandedly. His good eye angled off toward the fence. "And, apparently, my blue roan mare as well."

Billy smiled down at the ground and brought up his head with a show of bravado. "Well," he laughed, "I wouldn't want to put it that way exactly."

Tunstall did not appear to be entertained by the boy's performance. "Those grays are my best buggy horses," he declared, but his complaint was half hearted. His attention was largely dedicated to removing the grit from his eye.

Billy's brow lowered. "I wouldn't doubt that for a minute, sir. They was both good at mindin' me." Then he broke into his endearing smile. "I'm proud I was able to catch 'em for you after they wandered off."

Tunstall glared at the boy just enough to show that he recognized a lie when he heard one. "If you're going to work for me, son, we'll need to start off by speaking the truth to one another." He held out a small, effeminate hand and waited, letting the challenge stand.

Billy looked down at his own scuffed-up boots and smiled as he compared them to the gleaming footwear before him, but, when his head came up, his face was set with purpose. "I wanna thank you for droppin' the charges against me, Mr. Tunstall. I won't be stealin' from you no more." He took Tunstall's hand and was surprised by the strength in the Englishman's grip. Billy's pale-blue eyes now shone with the earnest light of a child trying to please his father. "You can take that to the bank, sir."

Tunstall stepped back, pulled a pair of suede gloves from his coat pocket, and began pushing his fingers into the leather. "I will take it to the bank, William . . . and deposit it . . . with interest . . . if you take my meaning."

Billy grinned. "Yes'r, I guess I do. Sounds like if I can keep myself in line with your rules, I might be expectin' a pay raise pretty soon."

Tunstall eyed the pistol strapped to Billy's side. "That might depend upon your skill with your revolver," he said.

Dick Brewer spread his boots and crossed his arms over his chest. "He can shoot, Mr. Tunstall."

"On foot or from the saddle," Billy added. "And I can stand up to more than a poor old little tree stump that ain't never harmed a soul."

Tunstall smiled his tolerance of the boy's boast. "You start at a dollar a day, with a bed under a dry roof, and three meals a day. Any raise will depend upon your performance as a rider for me. How does that sound?"

Billy turned to watch the horses moving about in the corral. "Sounds fair." Turning to Dick Brewer, he winked. "But I'll be workin' on that raise from the get-go. See if I can't climb my way up to top hand." He smiled. "Maybe take over as foreman, Dick, should you slack off in your duties." Billy's eyes danced with the friendly jest.

While Brewer ignored the boy's bravado, Tunstall widened his stance, stuffed his gloved hands into his coat pockets, and studied Billy from slouch hat to narrow boots. "You are a bit small to make top hand, William." The Englishman cocked his head to one side. "Can you handle a horse?"

Billy appeared surprised by the question. "Well, let's just see, why don't we?" Peering downwind, he rose up on his toes and sighted the white linen handkerchief still making its way across the field. Untying the blue roan Billy walked the horse from the fence, jumped, and jackknifed his body over the animal's spine. In one easy swivel, he was astride the mare, one hand holding the lead rope and the other clutching a fistful of mane. With a kick of his heels, he barked a wordless command, "Hyah!" to which the mare responded by bursting into a virtual gallop from a standstill.

As Tunstall, Brewer, and Waite watched, the roan tore across the field, throwing up pieces of sod and grass from its hooves, this shrapnel falling in Billy's wake as he swung low on the animal's left side until he seemed somehow to attach to the horse's ribs. Hanging on to the swatch of mane, he took the rope in his teeth and with flawless timing scooped up the handkerchief with his free hand. Holding the linen up like a flag, Billy let out a whoop and waved his prize above him as he coaxed the horse into a turn. Halfway into the semicircle, the rider slipped, tumbled to the ground, and, laughing, rolled to a stop while the roan homed in on the barn, where Waite was able to bring it under control.

Tunstall tapped Brewer on the shoulder and pointed. Billy's arm was all that showed above the grass; it tick-tocked back and forth like an inverted pendulum, the white cloth flapping in the wind.

"Well, he's got heart, don't he?" Brewer mumbled.

Tunstall offered a dry laugh. "Let's hope he has some brains, too."

After brushing himself off, Billy hurriedly walked the handkerchief back to Tunstall. "I do better with a saddle," he said.

The Englishman folded the cloth and put it away. "Yes, I would imagine so."

Brewer leaned against a barn pole and hooked his thumbs over his cartridge belt. "Okay," he announced in a foreman's tone, "now we know who to turn to if we lose any kerchiefs out on the range. Anything else you're good at?"

Billy's cocksure eyes snapped with confidence. "If I ain't good at it, I can learn it. If I can't learn it, I reckon I ain't suited for it. Like bookkeeping or dressmaking . . . that kind of thing. But I figure I can do whatever it is you need. I can ride all over this country and round up cattle for you. Don't matter to me where they come from."

Brewer broke his pose long enough to point at the bony buckskin still tied to the fence. "How're you gonna do all that astride that old nag?"

Billy propped his hands on his hips, his self-assurance seeming to sag as he appraised the horse he had ridden in on. "She ain't much, is she?" he said and hitched his head to one side. "Even my saddle is 'bout wore out."

Tunstall motioned for Waite to bring over the blue roan. When Fred handed the rope to his boss, the Englishman passed it along to Billy without hesitation.

"Take a saddle from the barn . . . one of the new ones. Now you've got a new job *and* a new horse and saddle. Sounds like a good start to me." He arched an eyebrow as if awaiting another chipper reply, but Billy seemed genuinely in awe of the man's generosity. Tunstall picked up the Winchester rifle, muzzle to the sky, and held it out. "Find yourself a scabbard for this." He nodded into the barn. "There should be one in the tack room."

"Forty-four," Brewer said. "Takes the same loads as your Colt's."

Holding the rope and the rifle, Billy stood straighter, gaining most of two inches in height. The longer he eyed the horse and the gleaming rifle, the more his pride pumped through his veins, the same kind of boost that came to him unasked when trouble came knocking.

Tunstall was not through. Reaching into the side pocket of his coat he brought out a compact, nickel-plated revolver balanced in the flat of his hand. "One last piece of equipment. It's a self-cocker. I like my men to carry two side arms. You would do well to keep this one hidden. That will provide you with a

41

way to surprise your enemy, should the occasion arise."

Billy's lips parted in surprise, his blue eyes seeming to catch light from his soul. He openly admired the shining weapon, a Colt's Thunderer, .41 caliber.

"I can provide whatever it is you need, Mr. Tunstall. Presto-changeo! All you got to do is ask."

"What I need," Tunstall intoned like an actor delivering a soliloquy in a play, "is men willing to make a stand against my enemies."

Billy's face took on a look of sheer determination as he combed a strand of the roan's mane to its proper side. "You just point out those enemies, Mr. Tunstall, and I'll do the standin'."

3
Blessing's Notes
Casey Home
Georgetown, New Mexico Territory
January 1886

"When someone reaches out to you to lend a helping hand
Keep that grip just loose enough in case you change your
plan."

Mary Casey's hair is dark and lustrous, tied tightly in back and throwing off sharp glints of light, but I do not have a trained eye to determine if she colors it or if she is younger than I suppose. I put her age at mid-forties, but the gray cast of her skin suggests she is not healthy. Despite her color she is a handsome woman. I've seldom seen more soulful eyes—midnight dark, intelligent, and penetrating. Her stature remains prim and poised, just as Billy had described it to me. Her satin dress is blue and shows off her small waist. The English accent is still evident if you listen for it. This makes me wonder if Billy was, perhaps, drawn to John Tunstall through the memories of this woman, Billy's favorite teacher when he was a young boy in Silver City.

In the quaint parlor of her well-kept house, she sets down a service tray and serves me tea with the options of cream and sugar. A plate of shortbread cookies is placed upon the low table that separates us. A fire crackles in the hearth, and the room is surprisingly free of drafts on this cold day. Watching her float about the room to adjust the curtains and straighten books on her shelves, I can understand Billy's attraction to her. She moves like a tall wading bird prowling through the shallows of a river. It is hard to imagine her upset or scolding or pedantic. Her formidability stems from the proper English manners that infuse her personality.

"So, you want to write a book about Henry McCarty," she says, smiling.

"I do, indeed," I reply. "But I thought he used his new stepfather's name at that time."

When her expression turns pensive, her eyes roll up to look at the ceiling. "Henry tried that name for a time, but when Mr. Antrim disappeared from Henry's life after his mother died, he didn't want the name. 'McCarty' had been his mother's name before she married Antrim. It's the name he asked me to use for him as a pupil in school."

"Did you know the stepfather . . . Antrim?"

She shakes her head. "I never met him." Taking her seat in an armchair across from me, she narrows her eyes and frowns at the floor. "Henry McCarty . . . Henry Antrim . . . William Bonney . . . Billy the Kid," she says, reciting all of Billy's aliases. She produces a sad smile. "He certainly tried to find his name, didn't he?"

" 'William Henry Bonney' was his favorite," I inform her. "That was his *real* father's name . . . according to his mother. She shared that information with Billy just before she died."

Mrs. Casey appears so lost in thought, I am not certain she has heard me. "Well, he'll always be Henry to me. That was the way I knew him."

"What was he like as a student?" I prompt.

She allows a tight little smile that crimps her mouth and pinches a dimple into one cheek. It seems less an affectation than a sign of spunk that lurks beneath her outer reserve. Cocking her head quickly to one side, it seems as if an idea has struck her.

"No different from most boys, I suppose, though he was a

skinny one. His hands were very delicate . . . artistic . . . he loved to take part in the plays we performed." She leans toward me to whisper. "I wanted the children to know about Shakespeare, you see."

After arranging my ink bottle and notebook on the table, I search for my pen in my satchel. "Billy . . . your Henry . . . spoke of you fondly. He was quite taken with you."

Blushing, she absorbs the compliment gracefully. "He was a sweet boy," she recalls. "I was Miss Mary Richards then. Young Henry lost his mother, Catherine, just days after school started that year. He was so distraught. I was told that he and his brother dug her grave, as they could not afford a sexton's fee." Shaking her head, she picks up her saucer and cup of tea and sips without a sound. When she sets the chinaware back on the table, her eyes take on a worrisome slant. "Overnight he became an orphan. Perhaps that was why he attached to me like he did. I felt so sorry for the boy."

"I think he was smitten with you," I say and watch for her reaction. Again that winsome dimple forms on her cheek when she smiles, but she dismisses the compliment with a wave of her hand. She is a cool one.

"Henry was convinced that we were long-lost relatives," she explains, "somehow separated and meant to reunite. We used to look at a map together so that he could point out the proximity of our origins. I was from Southampton on the channel, you see. He would run his finger from there, around Land's End, and on to Ireland to the county where his mother was born." She laughed a solitary note. "It was sweet of him to think we were related."

"Why do you think he believed that?"

For several moments she ponders her answer, then laughs to herself and rises, holding up a forefinger to keep me in my seat. "I'll show you," she says, a twinkle in her eye.

She walks to a walnut secretary with glass cabinet doors closed on sheaves of papers stacked on its shelves. Opening a drawer, she pulls out a small felt box and carries it back to her chair. Seated again, she opens the box to reveal two bright gold coins, each imprinted with a likeness of some royal personage. Leaning forward I make out the profile of Queen Victoria in relief.

The last thing I expected today was some kind of parlor trick, but I am curious, so I remain quiet as she positions one of the coins on the back of her flattened hand. Smiling, she balances the gold piece between us with a look of anticipation, as if I should expect to see the coin leap off her knuckles back into its box.

"Henry taught me this," she explains. As her fingers begin a deft, rippling movement, the coin tumbles obediently across her hand and back. Then, with a fluid movement that escapes my eye, she twists her wrist, grasps the coin in her palm, and holds it out for me. "Can you do that?"

By reflex, my hand almost goes out to receive the offering, but already I am laughing at my ineptness with anything requiring sleight of hand. I shake my head and decline.

"How about this?" she says and takes the coin on her other hand. Only now do I realize that she had performed the first trick left-handed, yet I distinctly remember her pouring my tea with her right hand. Now she repeats the traveling coin trick with her right.

"Impressive," I say, meaning it.

"We're not done yet, Mr. Blessing," she murmurs in a coquettish whisper, and again her tight smile indents a check mark into her cheek. I find myself wondering if she can replicate that fetching dimple on her other cheek as well.

"Now comes the grand finale, sir," she says, batting her long eyelashes in a teasing way. Her face lights up with the adventure of it all, and I can imagine Billy drawn into her enthusiasm to become the schoolteacher's devoted acolyte. As I watch, she balances both coins, one on the back of each hand, each positioned over the index knuckle.

As she begins the undulating rhythm with both hands at once, the coins walk across her fingers in perfect symmetry, tumbling away from one another from index to pinky fingers and then back. The movement is hypnotic. Next she moves the coins in the same direction. I can hardly fathom the coordination needed for such a performance. Finally, she speeds up one coin and slows the other, so that I am lost altogether.

"I am ambidextrous, you see, and so was Henry. It is rare . . . and one of the reasons he believed we were of the same blood."

I nod my understanding to her and think back to the time when I was with Billy in Fort Sumner. When I smile at a memory, she mirrors my smile, leans forward, and touches my knee. At this contact from her fingertips, a palpable energy vibrates like a nest of bees swarming from my knee up into my loins.

"What?" she says, her smile widening as she studies my face. "What are you thinking?"

I had placed my hat next to me on the sofa, but now I casually pick it up and set it down over my privates. "Just a memory about Billy," I say through my constricted throat.

Her fingers press on my knee again and remain there. "Tell me," she says, her eyes shining with curiosity.

The bees return to buzz through my upper leg again. When her hand slides slowly off my leg, I remember to breathe. She clasps her hands together under her chin and tilts her head with a look in her eyes that is either pleading or beguiling. I cannot tell which.

"Oh, please!" she purrs. "I do want to hear it!"

I am beginning to get a sense of the complex relationship

that might have existed between Miss Richards and young Billy all those years ago. It is difficult to imagine any man refusing her wish.

"We-ll," I begin, the word cracking in half as it escapes my scratchy throat, "there was a day Billy was entertaining three young Mexican boys, who had pressed him about his prowess with a firearm. After showing them his two revolvers, he twirled them on his index fingers, a gun in each hand, one spinning forward and the other backward, and Billy smiling all the time as he watched those boys' rapt expressions."

Mary Casey's smile grows wider with every word. "And—?"

"Suddenly the two movements stopped abruptly. The two gun butts slapped into each of his palms with a firm grip. His synchronized control was marvelous. Firing the guns alternately, he caused an old rusted can to jump and jerk its way across the bare dirt yard until it came to rest against a rabbit fence surrounding a vegetable garden. When the can would move no farther, the boys begged him to shoot a bright-red pepper crowning the tallest bush, but Billy refused, explaining that the old can had served its purpose, but the pepper had not yet proved its worth and deserved more time."

I have come to the end of my story, but she looks as though she is still waiting for a clever closing for the anecdote. I realize my tale of Billy was probably a poor choice for a woman, who knows little of firearms. Just to occupy my hands, I pick up my hat and inspect it. Embarrassed at the silence, I set the hat aside and select a cookie from the tray. When I take a bite, a shower of crumbs falls into my lap. I don't know whether to stand up or try to brush the debris into my saucer while seated. Mary Casey appears amused at my dilemma, stands, and begins brushing at my lap with her cloth napkin.

"Let me help you, Mr. Blessing."

What little blood has not surged to my loins rushes to my

face. I take the napkin from her.

"Let me do that," I volunteer, and right away I cringe at the elevated pitch of my voice.

Standing before me wearing a whimsical smile, she props her hands on her hips. "Perhaps you should take those off and let me work on them," she suggests.

Cupping my hand between my legs, I try to sweep crumbs into the bowl of my palm, but all I am accomplishing is a scattering of cookie debris all over her sofa and rug. I'm sure my face is as red as carmine dye. I clear my throat and try to push my voice to a lower register.

"I don't think that will be necessary," I say.

She laughs, and both her cheeks dimple at the same time. Lifting the kettle, she tries to restrain her smile.

"Here, why don't you moisten the napkin with a little bit of water, and then dab it at your trousers? It will pick up the smaller pieces."

I set aside my teacup on the table, fold the cloth twice, and lay it on my saucer. Very carefully she dribbles hot water onto the cloth. When I try to wring out the cloth over the saucer, I nearly scald my fingers, and a little chirp of pain escapes my lips as I drop the napkin and reflexively catch it by slapping my knees together like the jaws of a steel trap. The movement causes an avalanche of cookie dust into the crevice formed by the seal of my legs. I begin the embarrassing process of patting at the crumbs powdered over my crotch. It actually works . . . a little. The smaller cookie dust adheres to the damp cloth, but the larger pieces become mushy and smear on the material. I realize she probably intended me to collect the larger shards first with my fingers.

"Perhaps I should go outside and brush off," I suggest.

"Certainly," my host says. Before I can arrange myself for standing, she pulls an afghan from the chair at the secretary and offers it to me. "See if this will help," she says.

When I stand, pressing a wad of bunched blanket against my groin, I feel like the schoolboy who has popped the buttons on his trouser fly as his teacher tries to assist him and at the same time hold off any laughter from the rest of the class.

"I'll be right back," I say stupidly.

I am certain I look like an imbecile waddling to the front door. She is considerate enough not to follow and merciful enough to provide a conversation starter by calling out from the parlor.

"How did *you* get to know Henry, Mr. Blessing?"

Outside in the cold, with brisk repetitive sweeps by my hands, I brush crumbs from the front of my pants over the edge of the porch. If anyone were to walk by, I'm sure I would look like a man whose trousers had somehow caught on fire. I am grateful that Mr. Casey is not at home to see this spectacle imposed on his wife. Now I worry that I have left the front door open, allowing heat to escape from the house.

"I interviewed him for a newspaper when he was imprisoned in Santa Fe and then again in Lincoln . . . and once more when he was free in Fort Sumner." I announce all this to the neighborhood. After shaking out the afghan, I hurry back inside and close the door. "My editor was disappointed in the article that one of the other journalists submitted, so he sent me to get the story."

"Why you?" she asks from the sofa, where she now sits and plucks up the tiny pieces of my cookie-powdered avalanche. Her face, I notice, takes on an endearing little-girl innocence when she asks the question. Her manner borders on the daring . . . or perhaps mischief. I am quickly learning that interviewing females is a very different proposition than talking to males. After brushing her hands together over my saucer, she sweeps away the remaining crumbs from the cushion and smiles up at me as if we now share some common history beyond our friendships with Billy Bonney.

Standing before her, I am aware of a new aroma in the room. The scent is sweet and tangy. It is similar to some of the expensive perfumes I have encountered at the upper crust social events in Santa Fe. On her secretary desktop stands a small, green, glass vial that was not present before I left the room. Still smiling, she pats the cushion as if I were her pet dog begging for a soft perch.

Feeling my heart start up a pounding that tries to rise into my throat, I sit down and set the afghan on the table. When I turn my head to answer her question, she pivots her entire body toward me, draws up one bent leg onto the seat, and leans an elbow on the back cushion. When she tilts her smiling face to rest against her dainty fist, she looks as though she is posing for a portrait.

"I suppose my editor needed something more than the facts. He wanted a more personal article that dug into Billy's soul . . . to analyze what made him do the things he did."

She nods, her eyes full of admiration. "And he knew you could deliver that?"

"Well, I suppose I was more equipped for that than the first writer."

When she smiles at me now, it is like watching the sun rise. I imagine Billy as a fourteen-year-old boy attempting to coax that same smile from her by his innate charm.

"In what way?" she presses.

I shrug. "I was not a newspaperman at heart. I was . . . I am . . . a composer. I write music. At that time I was conducting the choir at the Loretto Chapel . . . purely as a volunteer. I took the newspaper job for the income. I suppose it was my connection to the church and possibly to the arts that made my editor believe I might elicit something of substance from a poor orphaned boy who was probably going to be sentenced to death."

"I've been to the Loretto Chapel," she informs me, "to see the spiral staircase." She looks over my shoulder and narrows her eyes. "I don't remember any music performed."

"I've had several hymns published," I continue. "And once during the Festival of the Saints, I led our choral group in a musical program at the Palace of the Governors. It was very well received."

Without changing her relaxed pose, Mary Casey leans and touches my forearm with her free hand. I stiffen as though a bird has flown through a window and perched on my arm.

"I'm sure *all* your compositions are beautiful," she declares with confidence.

Unsure what to do or say, I focus on my lap and use my free hand to pick at a few specks of cookie dust still clinging to my trousers. She begins doing the same with the tiny grains dotting my thigh. After plucking at the material three times, she irons out the wrinkles with the flat of her hand and then lets her hand rest there.

"And what about your instrument?" she asks, and with those five words I feel like the champagne bottle that has just popped its cork. Bubbles rise up my spine and lighten my brain with a cool effervescence. "The one on which you compose?" she adds.

I immediately ban the word "organ" from my tongue. "Keyboard," I croak.

Now she straightens and applauds rapidly by hinging her hands at the base of her palms and clapping with only her fingers. In a near paroxysm of delight, she points deeper into the house.

"I have a piano in the library. I would love to hear you play."

"Well," I laugh in a nervous titter, "perhaps after I jot down a few more anecdotes about Henry." I settle my notebook in my troublesome lap and put on my interviewer's face. "You mentioned Henry's brother. Billy never talked about him to me."

Stowing away her pert smile, she picks up her tea but does not drink. Holding it before her she stares into the cup as if her memories float there on the surface.

"Josie was very different from Henry. Even after losing their mother, they seemed not to be very close . . . not the way you expect siblings to be."

"Was he older or younger than Henry?"

"Older," she says. "By about two years. He was not as gifted as Henry. He had no interest in the arts, but he did have a knack for numbers. Rather quiet and unengaging with the other students. When the stepfather abandoned them, Josie began associating with a saloon owner, and I understand he became a card dealer." She tilts her head to one side. "You would do well to interview him for your book."

"Yes, I plan to. I've heard he is in the Arizona Territory, working as a professional gambler. The stepfather is there, too."

Mary Casey's expression hardens. "That stepfather—Mr. Antrim—did those boys no favors. Once Catherine was gone, he wanted nothing to do with Henry and Josie."

"What did the boys do to survive?" I ask.

She frowns and shakes her head. "As I said, Josie, at sixteen, was drawn into saloon life. Henry stayed with different families. First, it was the Hudsons, then the Knights, and then, thankfully, the Truesdells. Clara Truesdell was a saint, good to Henry's mother in her last months, and good to Henry later when he needed it most."

She drinks her tea, leans forward, and sets cup and saucer on the table. When she sits back into the sofa, she has somehow lessened the distance between us.

"The Truesdells ran a hotel, and Henry waited tables and

washed dishes in their restaurant." She shakes her head again, this time in regret. "But it wasn't long before he got into trouble. I heard that he stole something trivial from a local farmer. The sheriff was father to two of Henry's school friends. The punishment he doled out was meant to be charitable, but Henry took it very hard. He was spanked in front of several people, who laughed at the comeuppance. Afterward, Mr. Truesdell expelled Henry from his house."

"Where did he go then?" I inquire.

"He stayed at a boardinghouse. Lord knows where he got the money for that. There must have been some type of barter, like when he worked at the hotel." Her hand returns to my forearm, cupping it like half a manacle laid over my sleeve. "But it wasn't long before Henry found trouble again. Though he did not do the actual stealing, he was a party to a theft at a Chinaman's laundry. This time the sheriff put Henry in the jail."

"This is the same sheriff who tried to be generous to him?"

She squeezes my arm and nods. "By incarcerating Henry, the sheriff was really trying to scare the boy into better behavior, you see. But Henry escaped the jailhouse by climbing out the chimney."

It is difficult to take notes with her hand clasping my writing arm. She leans in and angles her head to read my shorthand, which I doubt very much that she can do.

"That sounds like Billy," I say. "Had anyone ever escaped like that before?"

She gives me a blank look. "I suppose not many people would be slim enough to accomplish the feat, you see. Henry was quite slender."

I lay down my pen and try to ease my arm free of her grasp, but her grip only tightens. "To Billy, it would all have been a series of adventures," I begin to babble. "The planning of the crime, its execution, and then his escape. He was famous for his escapes. There would be many more to come in his life."

"Yes," she whispers in a conspiratorial tone. Leaning closer, she squeezes my arm a little tighter. "I remember reading about them in the newspapers." She shakes her head and maintains a confiding air. "I knew that adventurous part of Henry. He was a voracious reader of those dreadful dime novels. Whenever he was deep into one of those stories, I could see in his eyes that he went about his life craving some kind of excitement."

I pull free of her hand to dip my pen into the ink bottle. "I, too, know that look in his eyes, Mrs. Casey. I saw it the day before he broke out of the Lincoln jail."

"Why don't you call me 'Mary'?" she suggests. Then her large, sensuous eyes fill with a mix of fear and wonder, as her hands come together beneath her chin in the manner of a child saying a prayer. "Did he really kill all those people?"

I seesaw my head from side to side. "He did kill men . . . but probably not as many as you've heard." I meet her eyes. "But you have to understand, it was a war. In those days in Lincoln County there were probably more people who *did* kill than there were those who did not."

Her hand comes to roost on my arm again. "But he was so young to be part of a war." She bows her head as if she might be in need of a shoulder to cry on.

I look at my notes. "Tell me something more about Henry. Something I might not know."

Pushing the misery from her face, she looks up excitedly. "He loved the Mexican culture and made many Hispanic friends in Silver City. Their part of town—Chihuahua Hill—was his favorite haunt. He was always talking about their food, their language, their music . . . and especially their dances. Henry loved them. They called them 'bailes.' "

I jot this down. "I can assure you he never lost that infatuation. Billy became a sort of hero to the native New Mexicans.

He spoke their language as if he had been born among them, and for this—as well as his good manners, good looks, and charm—they adored him. These people were always the dispossessed, the underdogs of the Southwest, and they came to regard Billy as their champion, partly because his enemies were the same as their own."

Grasping at another memory, Mary Casey smiles and revives a single dimple in her cheek. "That's another reason Henry believed we were related. He picked up their language so quickly. He had a talent for that. I am fluent in several languages, you see—German, French, Italian, Portuguese, and Spanish. Henry was convinced *that* sealed the bargain and made us kin."

As I write this down, the simple act of handling my writing instrument jostles an unexpected memory of my own. It is a picture of me watching through the jail bars in Santa Fe as Billy composed a letter to the territorial capitol, asking the governor to remember his pledge for a pardon in exchange for testimony that could help convict Dolan and some of his gang. I had helped with the wording and later had delivered the missive to the Palace of the Governors. I recall walking the letter across the street, my head down as I marveled over the elegant handwriting that graced the cover of the envelope. Had I taken that sample of Billy's cursive script to any renowned graphologist, I doubt that such an analyst could have guessed he was studying the handiwork of a twenty-year-old killer.

"Billy's penmanship was most impressive," I say. "You must be proud of his accomplishment in that area."

Mary Casey closes her eyes long enough to shake her head at my assumption. "I really cannot take credit for that. Henry had already learned his letters from his mother, Catherine. He had the finest hand in my classroom."

She arches one eyebrow and delivers a beguiling expression

that makes me feel like Odysseus being tied to the mast by his crew. "And he could do it with either hand," she adds.

She assumes an earnest expression that mystifies me. Up to this point I have seen little but affectation in her manner, but now I sense some kind of yearning. To avoid her eyes, I look back at my notes and scribble a meaningless sentence across the page.

"Oh!" she chirps, and I look back at her. The surprise on her face is like a photographer's flash. Rising, she holds up that index finger again to keep me seated. "I just remembered," she says, as excited as a young girl about to show off a new dress. She returns to the secretary, where she opens its glass doors. After fingering her way through a pile of papers, she slips out a folded, yellowed foolscap, opens it, and smiles with a look of triumph. "Here it is!" She takes time to scan it alone and then walks it to me, delivering the paper like a formal presentation.

I recognize the flowing script right away. Across the page the words run in arrow-straight lines that appear to benefit from the use of a straightedge. At the bottom of the paper are the words: *Yours faithfully and forever, Henry McCarty.*

"Would you read it aloud, please?" she requests. "I would love to hear it in a male voice."

I set down my pen and settle back into the sofa. "Of course," I say and clear my throat.

Dear Miss Richards,

I don't see how you have the patience to work with all of us children of Silver City. Some of us cannot count even with the help of our fingers and toes, and few have ever pulled down a book except for the purpose of standing on it to reach high enough for the cookie jar. Teaching must be a challenging occupation. Which is why I want to thank you for all you have done for me. Besides my ma, I have had two other schoolteachers, and next to those two you shine like the gold nugget sitting in the sand of a miner's pan. I know we were meant to meet, just as I know that we share two branches on the same family tree. I will always remember you for your kindnesses. Keep practicing with those coins, and maybe one day we will meet again to see who has got it nailed down the best. I would put my money on you.

When I lower the paper, I see tears standing in her eyes. To give her some private time I look back at the paper to admire the beautiful penmanship.

"Just fourteen years old," she says in a whisper, "and just look at the similes. And there is not a misspelled word on the page."

Nodding, I fold the paper, but I am reluctant to hand it back to her. If I can boost the courage for it, I may ask to keep it for the book I will write about Billy.

"He thought highly of you," I offer as consolation for her tears.

Using my arm as a support, she slides closer to me and lowers her forehead to my shoulder. "I've always wondered if I could have done more for him."

She sniffs and I wonder if I can extract my handkerchief from my inside, left pocket with my left hand. I decide not to try.

"What I mean is," she continues, "something that might have persuaded him toward a different outcome." She shakes her head in quick little jerks, as though a palsy has set in. My body quivers with the motion. "He was one of my best, you see, so I necessarily had to spend more time with others who needed extra help. Henry did not appear to need so much from me, not when compared to the rest. Perhaps that was a fatal flaw in my career."

Her guilt seems very real, so I dare to pat the hand gripping my arm. "You should not blame yourself for anything Billy—Henry—eventually did. I would say you were one of the few positive influences in his life." She nods into my shoulder, but I sense that my words do not console her.

"He kissed me once," she admits in a raspy whisper. Her head comes up quickly, as if she is trying to catch my first reaction. I feel nothing judgmental about a schoolboy having a crush on his teacher, but I have to wonder about that equation in reverse. It is not beyond the realm of possibility that this woman's romantic sensitivities had been stirred by the charms of Billy Bonney . . . even at fourteen years of age.

"It took me completely off guard," she goes on. "It was after school one day. He had asked about a poem by Byron. I sat at my desk and looked it up, and he asked me to read it to him. So I did. As soon as I had finished and turned to hear his questions, he was right there leaning beside me, waiting. It was like a trap he had set for me."

She appears mortified when her eyes fix on mine. "I slapped him," she confesses. "I didn't know I was going to do it. I just reacted. I've always regretted it."

"How did he take that?" I ask.

She shrugs her head to one side. "Oh, he said something rather roguish. I don't remember the words exactly. But I'm certain I saw hurt in his eyes."

I remain quiet as I add this vignette to my notes. As I write I wonder how many times Billy had laid similar ambushes on lovely señoritas all over the New Mexico Territory. Mary Casey's head presses into my shoulder again, and her grip on my forearm shifts to my upper arm. Her body leans into mine now, her bosom warm against my arm. We are quiet for so long that the simple sound of our breathing takes on an unexpected intimacy. I perk up my voice to break the spell.

"What about that piano piece, Mrs. Casey? May I play it for

you? And then I should be on my way."

When I start to disengage from her, she relinquishes her hold on me and rises, slipping the folded foolscap from my fingers as she does. I can summon no words as an entreaty for the gift of the letter. At a brisk walk she returns the letter to the cabinet, gestures for me to follow, and leads through a hallway to the next room, where a splendid upright piano stands within four walls of book-filled shelves. It is a Steinway with a burr-walnut case, its front soundboard ornately scrolled with a design of birds on the wing.

"My word!" I whisper under my breath. "Is it in tune?"

"Certainly," she is quick to reply. "In my view, any piano out of tune is on a par with a ship with a big hole in its hull." She takes a lucifer from a small wooden box, strikes it on a rounded river stone no doubt left for that purpose, and lights an oil lamp on the table that sits beside the keyboard. The ivories glow like the smile of a seductress.

"I couldn't agree more," I say.

As she lowers herself into the lone chair in the room, I take my place on the piano bench, throwing out my coattails behind me like a virtuoso about to perform for royalty.

"What shall I play?"

She smiles, but this time there are no dimples. "You choose," she says.

I raise my hands over the keyboard and begin a flowing arpeggiation of notes that leads into an etude by Bach. Only a few measures in, I lift my fingers, and the sudden silence is like a vacuum that sucks all the air from the room. She studies me with an amused look.

"I would rather play you something I wrote for Billy . . . for Henry. May I?"

She appears thrilled. "Of course! Are there lyrics, too?"

"Not yet," I lie.

I am in no way prepared to debut the words that I wrote on the night Billy died. Some of this reluctance is vanity, I admit, as my travels of late have not been conducive to keeping my voice in shape. "Let me just play for you the music. Perhaps you can give me your opinion on whether or not I have captured the spirit of the boy you once knew."

As I begin anew, time seems to stop inside the book-lined room. Mary Richards Casey slips off her shoes, pivots a quarter turn in her chair, and, pulling up both knees to one side, draws her feet beneath her on the seat cushion. She remains as unmoving as the steady flame of the wick. The glow of the lamp converts the space around the piano into a cubicle of intimacy.

I keep the verses spare and unadorned, but when I reach the first chorus, I allow the music to soar with shameless crescendos. Something celestial seems to descend upon the moment, as though my composition has opened up the roof above us to allow an audience of the heavens. The rest of the world melts away.

When I come to the song's end, I continue to press the sustaining pedal into the floor, letting the last notes ascend from the room like the souls of the dead beginning their journey to the other side. When silence takes over, I turn to her.

"It's simply wonderful, Mr. Blessing," she says through a constricted throat. "I don't think I've ever heard anything like it. A little like a hymn but grounded in the realities of life." Tears well in her eyes again. "Did Henry get to hear it?"

I lower my eyes and shake my head. "There was never an opportunity."

As she nods, her upper teeth pull at her lower lip. "He would have loved it," she assures me. "I believe you accomplished your goal. The music captures him perfectly."

I am startled to feel my own emotions prying out of their cage. It seems as though a piece of ice has lodged in my throat, where it presses firmly against the back of my palate. My eyes moisten to the point of blurring my vision. I try to think of something to say, anything that will stuff my raw feelings back into their hiding place in the dark.

"What about the last time you saw Henry?" I ask. "Do you remember that?"

She frowns and touches the tip of a forefinger to her lips. "Well, let's see." Her finger comes down, and the tip of her tongue moves across her upper lip. "After school, on the day before he was arrested by the sheriff, I happened to see him in an alley next to the bakery. He appeared to be cornered by some of the older boys. They were always picking on him because he was so small . . . and because he was quick to be clever with them at their expense. As I approached, the street ruffians scattered, and Henry greeted me with his usual smile as if nothing had happened. When I pressed him about it, he just laughed and said something like: 'Don't you worry about me, Miss Richards. I can always find a way to get out of a fix.' "

"That was true," I concur and stand. "I really must be going now." I pull my watch from my vest pocket and open its cover. "Yes, I am leaving on the stage in less than an hour."

We walk back to the front room, she still shoeless as she follows silently. I pack my notebook, pen, and ink into my satchel. Donning my garments, I walk across the room and then hesitate, facing the front door as I pull on my gloves. When they are snug, I turn back to Mary Casey and am completely surprised to find her face so close to mine that I am engulfed in her perfume. Her lips press into mine, and my reaction is to hold my breath to see what happens next. When she steps back and graces me with a double-dimple smile, I feel my cheeks flush with heat.

"That was my atonement for slapping Henry," she explains. "I hope you don't mind."

I swallow twice, thankful now that I have already mentioned the stage I must catch. "Henry thanks you," I say, lacking any other sane response.

I imagine her telling me next that her husband will be late coming home, but immediately I chasten myself for such a presumption. Perhaps her maternal love for Billy *was* strong enough to warrant that kiss, but I sense no such maternal considerations for me. I offer my gloved hand, and she takes it. We squeeze hands gently, and I waste no time in opening the door.

"Goodbye, Mary. Thank you for a wonderful conversation . . . and for being kind enough to listen to my composition."

"Goodbye, John Blessing. You have made this day a good one for me."

Wearing my perfunctory smile, I back out the door and close it against the cold. No sooner do I turn to descend the steps than I see a thickset man with a full beard approaching up the walkway. He has a flat face and sharp, inspecting eyes capped by dark eyebrows.

"Afternoon, sir," he greets me without the least sign of curiosity.

I know from photographs inside the house that this is Mr. Casey. He bustles past me without any inquiry about my presence at his house with his wife.

I feel a wave of relief that I am leaving this town without a confrontation with an enraged husband who believes I have wronged him. Oddly, I feel as much allegiance to Billy in this matter as I do to my own moral standards. And yet, as I make my way to the stage depot, I cannot help but imagine Billy Bonney laughing and giving me a rascally wink for my good fortune with his Miss Richards. Perhaps I am even one up on him, since I did not receive a slap for my passive part in the affair.

4

BROWN'S BOARDINGHOUSE
SILVER CITY, NEW MEXICO TERRITORY
SEPTEMBER 1875

"Hold dear your mother's lullaby; it's all that you have left She
loved you more than life itself until her dying breath."

It was Mrs. Sarah Brown's habit to launder her tenants'
bedsheets on Fridays, but on this week in late summer she had
promised to escort her pastor's ailing wife to Hudson's Hot
Springs at the end of the week, which was why on a Thursday
she made the rounds through her house collecting linens. When
she reached Henry Antrim's room, she did not bother to knock.
The boy ought to be in school, and if he wasn't, she planned to
dispatch him in that direction without delay. Pulling out her
master key she unlocked the door, walked straight to the bed,
and began stripping it.

Mrs. Brown operated her boardinghouse with a standard
policy of respect toward her boarders' privacy, but she could
not help but look around at the disorder of the room. It was no
surprise to her that a fifteen-year-old orphaned boy would show
little efforts toward keeping a neat living space, but she felt an
enhanced duty to keep a sharp eye on Henry. Not only because
he was without a parent to guide him, but more so because she
held a certain distrust toward the glib youngster who was
charged with keeping her firewood pile stacked high, the porches
swept, and the windows regularly washed. She had to carp at
him constantly about his chores.

Once the rumpled sheets had been removed, it was evident

that something was mounded under the mattress. Lifting it she felt her breath catch. Sitting atop a bundle of colorful clothes and a plaid blanket—all folded and none of which she had ever seen—lay a heavy gray revolver with a smooth white handle that cast glints of light like mother of pearl.

"Lord in heaven!" she said aloud, her voice harsh with disapproval.

Without delay she marched down the stairs and out the front door to throw out a peremptory command at the first idler she might spot. Her surprised victim turned out to be the gimp-legged stable hand who cleaned out the stalls at the livery, where she had rented a wagon for the trip to the springs on the next day.

"You there! Go down and fetch Sheriff Whitehill for me! Tell him to come straight away!"

The man paused in his limping gait and stared at her with a stupid frown pinched on his face. Turning his gaze to the front door, he, no doubt, wondered what crime might be in progress inside the boardinghouse.

"Go!" she barked, and he did.

When Harvey Whitehill arrived, his seldom-seen gun strapped to his ample waist and his badge shining in the morning sun, Mrs. Brown was pacing on the front porch. Together they climbed the stairs to Henry's room, where the landlady stood aside with her arms folded beneath her pendulous breasts as she glared at the bed. She had left the mattress half pulled off the bed frame, leaving the cached items in full view.

Without speaking, the man scowled at the weapon for a full ten seconds before carrying his grim countenance to the woman. "Charley Sun's laundry was broke into a few days ago. Said someone took two pistols, some of his customers' clothes, and several blankets. Altogether, about two hundred dollars' worth."

He eyed the items on the bed again. "Looks like this is part of it." When he turned back to Mrs. Brown, she was still glaring at the contraband and shaking her head. "Henry in school right now?" he asked.

Mrs. Brown kept shaking her head. "Who knows where that boy is?"

Whitehill moved to the bed and picked up the revolver. Setting the hammer at half cock, he opened the loading gate and rotated the cylinder through five clicks.

"Fully loaded," he reported and closed the gate. He lowered the hammer, set it at the first click, and stuffed the gun into the front of his cartridge belt. "I'll keep this for now," he said and looked around the disheveled room. "Did you find another gun?"

"I haven't looked," she told him. "Maybe you should do that."

He nodded and panned the room again. "Maybe I should."

Walking around the perimeter of the bedroom he casually peeked into the clothes cabinet, sorted through the few items on the shelves along one wall, and rifled each drawer of a tall chest near the window. Lifting a dime novel from the dresser, he read its cover and dropped it back.

Watching the man's half-hearted search, Mrs. Brown made a muted grunt in her chest. "It appears that beating you gave the boy did not have the desired effect."

He turned quickly to her. "Wasn't a beating. Was a spanking."

She produced a tight smile. "Well, whatever it was," she said and swept an open hand toward the stolen goods, "here we are again."

Whitehill propped his hands on his hips and nodded. "Here we are again," he echoed, his tone aggravated.

Staring out the window, Mrs. Brown tightened her lips, making crimped crease marks around the perimeter of her mouth.

"He's been spending a lot of time with that older boy, George Schaefer. I don't trust him any farther than I could throw my bathtub." She pointed out the door. "He has a room down the hall, you know."

Whitehill presented a sour expression. "That slacker is a known thief," the sheriff growled. "Calls himself 'Sombrero Jack' down at the Orleans Club. He gets drunk every Saturday night and usually ends up in my jail." Whitehill took in a deep breath and purged it. "I'd better have a look at Schaefer's room, too."

Finding no evidence in Sombrero Jack's quarters, Whitehill and the landlady walked the hallway back to Henry's room, where the sheriff stood in the open doorway and frowned at the pile of stolen items. "I want you to let me know when Henry or Schaefer comes in." He turned to her to make the request official. "Send someone to my office right away, do you hear?"

When young Henry returned to the boardinghouse that afternoon, he wore the light-blue shirt, denim trousers, and soft moccasins that he regularly wore to school. Mrs. Brown sat in the front room with a book open in her lap. He had never seen the woman sit still for more than a few seconds at a time, unless she was entering figures in her ledger.

"You want me to start the windows today?" Henry asked.

Closing the book, she stood and set the book on her secretary. It was a Bible.

"No, I need you to run down to get Sheriff Whitehill for me."

Henry waited for more, but the woman began straightening things on the desk that did not appear to need straightening.

"What for?"

She flashed an angry look his way. "Just get him for me, would you?"

Ten minutes later Henry scuffed up the stairs to the upper

floor, the sheriff and a deputy right behind him, and the landlady trailing all of them. When they entered the room, the boy showed no surprise at the colorful clothes stacked on the slats of the bed frame.

The deputy walked around the bed, spread his boots, and smiled down at the contraband. "Well, looka here," he said.

"I have the gun back at my office," the sheriff informed the boy. "You want to tell me about this?"

Henry grinned and looked the sheriff in the eye. "Not really."

Whitehill's jaw knotted. "This is not a joke, boy. It's damned serious this time."

Henry's eyebrows lifted, and his hands slipped into his trouser pockets. He managed to drop the smile, but still his eyes danced with mischief as he looked at each of his accusers.

"This could go hard on you, boy," Whitehill warned. "You'd better tell me all about it."

"What's to tell?" Henry replied in his carefree way. "I don't know nothing 'bout it."

The sheriff gave him a hard look, one eye squinting as if over a rifle sight. "I figure this is more than a one-man job. Does George Schaefer play into this somewhere?"

This seemed to catch Henry off-guard. The boy shifted his gaze to the window and stared out at the rooftops.

"No, I stole it all myself," he declared, convincing no one in the room.

"Henry Antrim!" Mrs. Brown scolded. "Your mother taught you better than that! God rest her soul! Catherine would be wailing in her grave if she knew what you were up to! Stealin' and lyin' like this!"

The boy looked at her quickly. "My name ain't Antrim . . . it's McCarty."

Whitehill waited, but Henry would say no more. "All right, son," the sheriff growled. He took a step closer to the boy and pointed. "Pick up that evidence and go with my deputy down to the jail." He turned to bark at his deputy. "Lock him in a cell, J.B."

Henry's face hardened. "Are you gonna whip me in front of the whole town this time?"

Whitehill gripped Henry's upper arm and forced him to the edge of the bed. The boy bent and took the load in his arms.

"We already tried that, didn't we?" the sheriff scoffed. "This time I'm taking you before a justice. If he binds you over to the grand jury, you'll have a three-month wait for the judge. That's three months behind bars, son."

When the deputy led Henry away, the sheriff approached the landlady. "Any sign of Schaefer?"

Mrs. Brown shook her head and moved to the window, where she stared down at the street. She watched the deputy jostle Henry like a puppet as they walked toward the jail, the man's hand clamped on the back of the boy's neck.

"Henry is a handful," she admitted, "but he doesn't have anybody. Who is going to post his bail?"

Harvey Whitehill stepped beside her and looked out at the traffic below. "I'm not gonna hold him in jail that long. I just wanna scare him . . . knock him off this path he's on."

"Well, somebody better," she ordained. Turning to the sheriff, she frowned. "Should I hold his room for him?"

Whitehill took in a deep, wheezing breath through his nose and exhaled. "Yeah, hold it. I'll see can I get our church to pay for it 'till he can get back on his chores."

When she began straightening up the bed mattress, he spoke to her back. "Let me know when Schaefer shows up." Then he walked heavily out of the room.

After Henry's first night in jail, the sheriff ambled into the cell-block and leaned into the barred door of the boy's cell. "Did the jailor bring you some breakfast?" Whitehill asked, his tone authoritative but friendly.

"I guess you could call it that," Henry replied. "I tried to offer it to the two rats that live up in the ceiling, but they turned it down."

Whitehill nodded at a familiar complaint. "There ain't much to commend about a night in jail, Henry. Ninety nights can be purely miserable."

Henry looked around at the dirty walls and floor of the jail. The place was less than a year old but appeared not to have been swept out in months. The bed smelled like a pair of worn-out socks pulled off of a dead man.

"It ain't so bad," Henry said, putting a little melody into the assessment. " 'Least in here, I won't have to do any schoolwork."

Whitehill narrowed his eyes. "I thought you liked school."

Henry smirked. "I like my teacher. It's two different things."

The sheriff bobbed his eyebrows once. "Thought you'd wanna know . . . about your friend Schaefer, alias 'Sombrero Jack.' " Whitehill injected a healthy dose of sarcasm into the assumed name. "We got wind o' the fact he's carryin' a new pistol and sportin' new clothes. All of it matches what was taken from Charley Sun's place. We know Schaefer was in on this with you."

"So?" Henry said.

"So," the sheriff continued, "he snuck into his room last night, cleaned out his belongings, and skipped out of town. Looks like he's left you to face the judge all by yourself." He watched Henry's face try to hide any disappointment. "If he was the one did the stealin', this could go easier on you with the judge. Anything you wanna tell me?"

"Yes, sir, there is," Henry announced. "Your jailor won't let me out to stretch my legs." He gestured to the interior of his cell. "There ain't room enough in here for a man to get any exercise. Can I at least use that space there where you're standing? If I can't walk proper on a reg'lar basis, I got a leg that stoves up on me and burns like the dickens."

Whitehill looked around at the corridor running between the two rows of cells, finally settling his gaze on the fireplace at the back end of the building. "If it's exercise you're wantin', we might even let you cut a little firewood for that hearth, seeing as how you'll be with us into winter." He checked Henry's face to see if his words had made an impression, but the boy's pleading eyes waited for an answer. "All right," the sheriff said through a long exhalation. "I'll tell 'im to let you walk out here in the corridor once a day. How's that?"

"Can we start now, sir?" Henry asked, his demeanor now as close to contrition as the sheriff had seen in the boy.

Whitehill pushed himself away from the bars. "Don't see why not." He squared himself to his prisoner and crossed his arms, each hand snug under the opposite armpit. "Then maybe we can have a talk about Schaefer. How does that sound?"

Henry stared unblinking at the sheriff. "Give me an hour, and then there'll be plenty to talk about. I'll promise you that."

Whitehill nodded. "That's what I like to hear." He started out of the cellblock and spoke over his shoulder. "I'll send in the turnkey; then I'll be back for that talk in an hour."

Just minutes after the sheriff closed the heavy oak door to his office, the jailor entered and gave Henry an oblique glance of disdain. "So, ya sweet-talked your way out into the room, did ya?"

Henry shrugged. "I don't figure I'll trouble you much more than this."

The man frowned through the bars as he worked the key in the lock. He looked like he wanted to ask a question, but, after opening the cell door a few inches, he shrugged and walked back the way he had come.

"Thank you for your hospitality," Henry called to his back.

The jailor made no reply. He left the cellblock and slammed the door. The sound of the locking bar made a loud *clack* as it slid into place. To Henry it was the toll of the Liberty Bell.

In less than an hour, when Sheriff Whitehill entered the cellblock, he stopped after two paces and felt a cool, tingling sensation ripple across the skin on the back of his neck. He stepped into Henry's open cell and crouched to look under the bunk. Then he walked back into the corridor and hurriedly looked into each of the other cells. Turning a full circle, he studied the ceiling from corner to corner.

"What the hell!?"

Rushing into the office he barked at the jailor, "Where is he!?"

Slouching in a chair tilted back against a wall as he read the newspaper, the man paled and sat forward, righting the chair as the legs tapped down. Slack-jawed, he stared at his boss.

"Where is who?"

Without answering, Whitehill stormed outside, looked up and down the street, and then circled the building. On the second circuit he stopped in back near the privy and jerked his head in every direction. Finally, he squinted toward the top of the jail building.

"Señor Sheriff!" a man called from behind him. "*¿A quien busca?*"

The sheriff turned to the voice and recognized the Mexican stone mason who was working on one of the churches on the east side of town. Lowering a heavy, flat rock into a cart, the man kept his eyes on the distraught lawman.

"Did you see a scrawny kid come this way?" Whitehill yelled, his voice hoarse with anger. "*¡Un prisionero!* Maybe fourteen, fifteen years of age. He wore a light-blue shirt."

As he looked west, the mason dusted off his hands before him with brisk swipes of his palms. When he turned back to the sheriff, he raised his chin toward the top of the building.

"*Sí*. He come from the cheem-ney, Señor. I think maybe he clean it for you." Then he raised an arm and pointed west. "He go that way."

Sheriff Whitehill cursed and glared at the vacant lots behind the buildings of Main Street. He saw no one. When he heard the Mexican quietly laugh, he looked back at the mason.

"Hees shirt no blue anymore, sher-reef. It mostly black . . . from the cheem-ney."

Whitehill's first impulse was to run and collect his deputies, set up an organized search, and throw the scoundrel Henry Antrim back behind bars. But the futility of the exercise already haunted him. The boy had made a fool of him and his staff, and the sheriff had every reason to believe that this embarrassment would only get worse. The urge to chase the boy drained out of him on the spot. Cursing again, he scuffed his boot heels into the dirt as he marched back toward his office.

"Goddamn kid!" he hissed under his breath.

5

BLESSING'S NOTES
SILVER CREEK SALOON
MOGOLLON, NEW MEXICO TERRITORY
FEBRUARY 1886

"Forget me not, my bonny child, for I will soon depart I am
crossing to the other side so hold me in your heart."

After the stage stops in the narrow canyon where the camp
called Mogollon has sprouted like a row of weeds, I stretch my
legs by walking just off the main thoroughfare, which is a river
of mud topped by a light rime of snow. The day is cold and the
sky overcast in leaden gray. I crave a cup of coffee for its warmth
more than anything else. There is no restaurant in the primitive
village, only a crudely constructed land office and one log house
with a sign advertising cheap provisions and tools. All the rest
of the businesses lined up are canvas tents, several with lawyers'
shingles hung outside their door flaps.

The remainder of the camp consists of every manner of
makeshift hovel—lean-tos, dugouts, and tarpaulins stretched
over pole frames—all lined up along the creek to accommodate
the miners, who have swarmed into the area like flies drawn to
a fresh carcass. For as far as I can see up and down the stream,
I am witness to an army of rubber-booted, determined men
swinging pickaxes and sledgehammers into the shallows along
the rocky creek bed. Seeing a hand-painted sign with possibilities, I gravitate toward a large tent saloon, but I hold serious
doubts about coaxing hot coffee out of a bartender.

The dingy saloon consists of a crude bar—thick rough-cut
planks propped upon large barrels standing on end—and a

dozen wooden crates evenly spaced around the tent to serve as tables for customers. The seats surrounding these crates are simple four-legged benches hacked out of juniper. Oil lamps hang from the tent poles, but none are burning. The only light penetrating the interior comes from the tent's entrance, where the door flaps are tied open, allowing a cold draft to compete with the pulsing wood heater centered in the room. The liability of juniper splinters convinces me to stand at the bar, where a customer in a red and black plaid flannel jacket leans on the bar planks and stares into an empty glass.

Another man—short and stout and sporting a thick moustache—appears from the dark of a back corner and walks behind the bar to intercept me. "What's your pleasure, sir?"

Before I can answer, the man beside me snaps out of his stupor to smile at me. "Well, hello, dude! I ain't seen clothes that clean in months."

This is not the first time I have endured *that* sobriquet. Even Billy referred to me as "dude" on several occasions, but the term never carried the tone of condescension coming from his friendly tongue.

"May I have some hot coffee, please?" I ask the bartender.

My neighbor laughs. "Now there's a damned missed opportunity. You're in a saloon, dude. Put some fire in your belly, for God's sake!"

My instinct is to continue to ignore the man . . . that or politely ask him to mind his own business, but good timing intervenes when someone calls out behind me. "Mr. Blessing?"

Turning, I recognize the stage driver standing in the doorway, a large wrench in one hand and a grease-stained rag in the other. He stares directly at me.

"We're gonna be laid up here for repairs. Stage cracked a wheel rim."

I feel my stomach begin the slow burn of dread, for I know

there cannot possibly be a hotel in this dismal place. "How long?" I ask, trying to hide my annoyance.

The coachman shrugs. "Coupla hours, maybe. Blacksmith is already on it." He gestures toward me with the wrench. "We'll let you know when we're ready to pull out for Tombstone."

As the bartender pours my coffee, the customer next to me continues to smile his amusement. "Tombstone? Why the hell would anyone wanna go there? Miners are strikin' . . . the damned mines are floodin' . . . some o' the saloons closin'. Ain't a lick o' work to be had there." He snorts. "I just come from over there. Ask me, the town'll be dried up inside a year."

I consider not replying to these unsolicited remarks, but the bartender sets down my coffee and fixes his attention on me as if he, too, is expecting my answer. After sipping from my mug, I place it back on the bar and try to hide my displeasure at the stale brew.

"I am not traveling there for the mines. I am seeking an interview with a man who is said to be there."

The customer perked up at this. "Interview? What . . . you looking for laborers or somethin'?"

"No, sir. I am a writer. I'm working on a book. I'm looking for a particular man."

The man leans one elbow on the planks and studies me. "Well, hell, tell me who it is you're lookin' for. I might can tell you if'n he's still there."

I turn to him and match his pose by leaning my elbow on the bar. "Joseph Antrim. I believe he is a gambler. Did you frequent the sporting dens?"

My would-be informant pushes out his lower lip and shakes his head. "Never heard o' him," he reports and goes back to brooding over his empty glass. Then he surprises me by slapping his palm down on the bar. "But since I tried, how 'bout you standin' me a drink?"

The bartender slings a rag over one shoulder and steps closer to me. "There's a Antrim right here in Mogollon." He points out the door. "Works a claim up at the mouth of the canyon where the creeks come together. Don't know his given name. Kinda quiet and keeps to hisself."

"How far is it?" I inquire. "I don't have a horse."

The bartender shrugs. "It ain't a far walk . . . quarter mile or so. Just follow upstream and ask somebody up that way."

I consider the information long enough to know I cannot pass up the opportunity. If it is Billy's brother, I certainly don't want to be traipsing off to Arizona Territory looking for him.

"How much for the coffee?" I ask.

The barman waves a hand at the air between us. "Aw, it's two days old. I should be payin' you to drink it."

Because I have already fingered a coin out of my pocket, I drop it on the rough countertop. "In that case, why don't you give this gentleman his pleasure. Will that cover it?"

The barman shrugs. "Close enough," he says and picks up the coin so deftly, his movement suggests a sleight of hand that reminds me of both Billy and Mary Richards Casey.

"Hey, thank you, dude," says my fellow customer, his manner now entirely friendly.

I button my coat front and wait for the bartender to meet my eyes after pouring the man's refreshment. "If the stage driver looks for me, could you let him know where I am?"

"Yep," the man says and corks the bottle. "I'll tell 'im."

Pushing against the wind I walk beside the muddy road that leads out of the camp, passing the crews of men working their excavation sites. A light flurry of snow blows into my face, and I clutch my coat collar against my throat. Beyond a copse of bare trees, I spy what must be the canyon from which the tributary creek flows. Off in the distance only one man is visible to me along this stretch of the stream. Wiry and industrious, he is busy chiseling away with a mason's hammer at a large boulder. He works at a pile of scree before the dark mouth of a cave.

Even when I am within speaking range, he does not notice my approach, and so I have an opportunity to study him. Ten paces away I stop. His demeanor, I would say, is driven. Because he is hatless in his work, I can see that he is mostly bald. For this he compensates with a heavy beard. Wearing a ribbed sweater, canvas pants, and thoroughly scuffed leather boots, he appears to be one of those men who is well-accustomed to working outside no matter the weather. There is an inexplicable aura about the man that suggests he is a loner.

"This claim is taken," he says without turning. "Move on." When I hesitate to gather words of introduction, he lowers the hammer to his side and fixes his gaze on me. His eyes are the no-nonsense eyes of a man who assays the worth of everything he encounters.

"I'm looking for Joseph Antrim," I announce.

His eyes narrow; otherwise, nothing else about him changes. There is a haggard look about this man, as if he has endured the failures of prospecting for too long.

"Who are you?"

I tug down on the brim of my hat in the standard gesture of greeting. "John Blessing, sir. I am a writer. Would you know where I might find Mr. Antrim?"

For the uncomfortable lapse of time that he stares at me, the sound of the creek behind me seems to grow louder. A spit of snow swirls chaotically in the air around us. The wind blows in erratic patterns here at the mouth of the canyon.

"*My* name is Antrim. But I'm not the one you're looking for."

"May I ask which one you are?"

He scowls toward the camp, his face harder now. "William Antrim," he finally says.

The wind surges, and I almost lose my hat. The quick move I make with my hand to the crown of my hat, I realize, is ill-advised. Some men might reach for a weapon at such a gesture, but Antrim appears resigned to tolerate whatever transpires around him. He moves not an inch. I can see no pistol on his person, but I have learned not to make assumptions along that line. Pressing my hat down on my forehead, I take two steps closer to preclude yelling over the wind.

"You're Joseph's father?"

The man's face shudders once with a subtle wince. "I ain't nobody's father."

Hearing the defensiveness in his voice, I realize to whom I am speaking. "What about 'stepfather'? Are you *that* William Antrim?"

His eyes angle away quickly, and his lips press into a hard line. When he returns his gaze to me, resentment boils off his face.

"What is it you want?"

"I am on my way to Tombstone to interview your stepson Joseph. The bartender at the saloon informed me that a man named Antrim works a claim up this way. So—" I shrug, leaving my explanation open-ended.

Antrim sets his hammer on the boulder and shakes his head. "He's not in Tombstone. He's moved on to Colorado some-where. If he owes you money, that's between the two of you. I've got nothing to do with his affairs, do you hear?"

I hold up both hands, palms out, and I attempt a friendly smile. "No, it's nothing like that, sir. I just want to talk to him."

Antrim's facial features clench like a fist as he shakes his head. "Well, I can't help you. I don't know where he's bound, and I don't expect to see him again."

Smiling, I lower my eyes, trying to make the man feel less threatened by my questions. When I bring that smile up to him again, he looks annoyed that I am still standing before him.

"Perhaps I could talk to you then?" I say, trying for the appearance of an offhanded notion. I reach to a pocket for my notebook and pen, but I realize I have brought neither. Both are packed in my valise, loaded atop the luggage deck of the stagecoach and lashed down beneath a canvas cover.

Antrim watches my movement and scowls. "What about?"

"Your other stepson . . . Henry."

Now he gives me a withering glare. "I have no other stepson," he says with finality.

I temper my reply with as much kindness as I can muster. "But you did once, sir."

I wait, as we seem to have entered into a staring contest. For the first time since arriving at his claim, I hear a slow steady drip of water coming from inside the dark mine behind him. Antrim picks up the hammer again and presses his free hand to the bear-sized boulder he had been working on. He concentrates on the rock as if he can feel the value of the ore through his fingertips.

"He's dead," Antrim barks.

"Yes, sir, I know. Might I ask you a few questions about him?"

Still staring at the rock, he shakes his head. "Got nothing to say about that."

I nod as if I might understand, but all I can think about is the limited time I have before the stage will depart with my luggage. I press on.

"I interviewed Henry in the jails at Santa Fe and Lincoln. Then I spent some time with him in Fort Sumner. The young man I got to know was—"

"A thief and a murderer!" he interrupts, challenge written all over his weathered face.

I cannot, of course, deny those charges. "But, Mr. Antrim, no man is just one thing."

"That was two things!" he argues. "A thief *and* a murderer."

"Yes, sir, but—"

He points vaguely with the hammer in the direction of the tent town. "Let me tell you about the last time I saw the boy. I was prospecting over in Clifton. That's in Arizona Territory. He showed up there after breaking out of the jail in Silver City. I talked to him about five minutes at the mine I was working. Then he traipsed off to my lodging and stole some of my clothes and a pistol."

"Why did he seek you out, sir?"

Antrim's mouth curls into a crooked sneer. "Money. What else?"

"Did you give him any?"

He averts his eyes and shakes his head. "There was none to give. So he just stole what he wanted. That's the way he was. There never was a way to handle him."

I want to ask this man about his abandonment of both boys after the mother's death, but I know that such a query would end this conversation. I store that one away for a time.

"Did you give Henry any counsel in this last meeting?"

"Yeah," he huffs in a humorless laugh. "I told him to stop using my name. Prob'ly used it to cause me problems." Antrim appears disgusted at the memory and points again with the hammer. "He ended up over near Fort Grant at that filthy hog ranch just outside the military reservation." He gives me a self-righteous smirk. "You know what a hog ranch is?"

"Yes, sir . . . an establishment for prostitutes."

Antrim makes a disgusted face. "He partnered up with the worst kind of people. He always did that. He earned quite a reputation over there for stealing horses. Even stole government-issued mounts and tack from the soldiers."

I nod to show that this is no surprise to me. "Did you also know that he attempted to work as a cowhand? He was hired by the likes of Henry Hooker and John Chisum, among other big ranchers. Then he was the cook for the Hotel de Luna."

" 'Cook'!?" Antrim huffs. "About all he could cook up was trouble. And that's what he did over there. He killed an unarmed man in cold blood in a saloon brawl. Gut-shot him, stole a horse, and ran off."

"A horse he returned to its owner," I clarify.

Keeping sharp eyes on me, Antrim rotates his head a few inches away so that he is studying me from an angle. "You seem to want to defend the boy for all his sins. Why is that?"

"Well, as you say, he was just a boy in those days. Henry had very few people to stand up for him. I'm just trying to balance out his story by learning the rest of it."

Antrim frowns off at the distance, apparently annoyed at my answer. Then his steely eyes fix on me again.

"Why? Why do you want to dredge all this up now? I spent years trying to get shed of all his shenanigans. It was the first time in my life I'd been ashamed of my own name." Antrim tilts his head to one side. "Who are you, Mister Blessing? What's your game?"

"I'm writing a book about your . . . about William Bonney, sir. I just want to—"

He points the hammer at me, and the tension in his muscles causes his arm to shake as if from a palsy. "I do not want to be a part of any book, do you understand?" He glances down the road and sweeps the back of his free hand toward me as if I am a bothersome fly. "Just go back to wherever it is you came from and leave me alone."

So faced with the end of this interview, I unleash my parting salvo. "I understand you did not attend the funeral of your wife, Catherine . . . Henry's mother. And that you gave the boys up to various trustees . . . in a word, you 'abandoned' them. Do you not think this might have some bearing on why Henry chose the path that he did?"

Sulking now, Antrim stares at the boulder in which he currently places his hopes. "Every man chooses his path," he quips and turns hostile eyes on me. "I gave those boys a roof over their heads, three meals a day, and even some carpentry training! If they didn't want to follow my lead, don't you try to judge me over it!"

I try to keep my voice casual. "My understanding is that the boys' mother, Catherine, supported them by her laundry business in Silver City . . . until she was too sick to work, that is."

Turning his back on me, he strikes a half-hearted blow, sending a spray of grit that scatters on the rocky ground. When he begins working in earnest, it is as if I am no longer present. He looks exactly as he did when I first approached. The snow has escalated to a steady fall, and the rocks here begin to resemble icing-topped buns in a bakery window.

"Just so you know, Mr. Antrim," I say to his back, "when Henry killed outside Fort Grant, that man he shot was a blacksmith who weighed almost a hundred pounds more than your stepson. He was a known bully, and Henry was his favorite victim. He was beating on the boy while sitting astride him, pinning Henry's arms with his knees as he slapped the boy mercilessly and laughed. This blacksmith might have killed him had Henry not worked an arm free and managed to pull a gun. Several of the witnesses said the boy had no choice."

Antrim ceases his hammering and turns to me. "Well, that's something I never taught the boy. I've never killed a man in my life, not even in the war." He starts to turn away again, but he is not through. "I can't even keep count of how many men he killed. One of them was the sheriff of Lincoln County."

I nod. "Sheriff Brady was as corrupt as any of the Santa Fe Ring. It was he who was responsible for murdering your stepson's employer, a man who treated Henry like a son."

Antrim glares at me, moving his knotted mouth from side to side as if he wants to spit. "You've got an answer for just about everything, don't you?" Extending his arm he points the hammer at me again, and this time his arm is steady. "I don't want you writing about me, do you hear? Just go away and leave me alone!"

I tip my hat and turn to go, but after two paces over the rock-strewn ground I feel the need to further capitalize on this moment. It is not likely that I will cross paths with William Antrim again. Abruptly, I turn and raise my voice to be heard over the wind.

"When you heard about him being killed by Pat Garret, did you feel anything at all?"

Antrim stops working again, turns, and considers me with a tired expression. "Why should I? He brought nothing but shame to me. He went out there alone to fight against the world . . . break every law . . . and fill up a graveyard in the process."

I say nothing for a time, letting the wind howl between us like a muted scream from the underworld. Antrim takes the lull as a cue to get back to work.

"He was the beloved son of the woman you married, Mr. Antrim. I think Catherine would have wished him a better chance at a good life under your guidance. But you weren't there. You were gone prospecting."

Without turning to me he replies, "Think what you like. I don't care." Then he stops working, wipes his mouth with his sleeve, and leans on both arms against the boulder. "They were *never* my sons . . . *neither* of them. Especially Henry." Now he eyes me with an unexpected calm. "You can't know what I'm talking about, because you're on some kind of crusade, son. You want to glorify Billy the Kid? Go right ahead, but leave me the hell out of it."

Laying the hammer on the rock, he pulls a pair of leather

work gloves from under his sweater and begins tugging them on.

"I'll tell you this, Mr. Antrim," I say, surprised at the calm in my own voice. "Something Henry said to me once. He said the time when Catherine needed you most, sir, was after she died. She counted on you to take care of her boys."

He turns his back on me and resumes his chiseling. It is clear that we are done exchanging words. I start the march back for the camp to collect my belongings from the stage and make arrangements for passage back to Las Cruces. There I will board a train headed north. There are friends of Billy's I need to see.

6

TUNSTALL'S RIO FELIZ RANCH
LINCOLN COUNTY,
NEW MEXICO TERRITORY
FEBRUARY 18, 1878

"So keep one eye upon the trail and one eye behind your back
You can live your life just like a king, but watch that one-eyed
jack."

Carrying his overcoat under one arm, Tunstall emerged from
the dugout and strode through the lunette of sandbags his workers had stacked as a defense around the front of the crude
abode. It was rare for him to go armed with a pistol, but today
his Colt's revolver was holstered at his waist for all to see.
Without slowing, he slipped his arms into the coat and buttoned up the front against the cold. Behind him came old
Gauss, the German cook, hatless and still wearing his greasy
apron from breakfast.

Pulling his wool fowling hat down over his brow, the Englishman approached his men at the pole barn as they prepared for
the trip to Lincoln. Dick Brewer was saddling Tunstall's favorite
bay, as Fred Waite readied the wagon for hauling supplies. Billy
entered the corral to cut out the seven horses and two mules
that Brewer had pointed out for their journey. Three other hands
stood by their mounts in casual conversation, checking the loads
on their revolvers, and stuffing rifles into saddle scabbards.

"Hold up on that, William!" Tunstall yelled into the corral. "I
want to talk to all of you before we get started."

Astride his blue roan, Billy sidled to the fence, and all
gathered there for a meeting. Gauss, now wearing a worried

frown, stood a little apart from the others, untied his dirty apron, and slung it over one shoulder. Folding his arms over his chest he appeared to regret leaving his coat inside.

With a smart, military-like widening of his stance, Tunstall clasped his hands behind his back and looked each man in the eye, saving Brewer for last. As was his habit, he cleared his throat for his speech.

"I suspect Sheriff Brady is sending a posse here today to collect my livestock," he began in his formal way. "As you know, Dolan has filed a civil suit against me for ten thousand dollars, something he trumped up with the judge in Mesilla. Now they have filed an attachment on my property and a portion of my livestock."

"What?" Waite moaned.

"We expected something like this," Brewer said. "This is a war, boys."

Billy's face sharpened, his eyes full of fight. "We'll give them some game, Mr. Tunstall! You want to fort up here or make a stand up on high ground?"

Tunstall eyed the boy with appreciation but shook his head. "We're not going to be here. I understand Dolan has raised an army of over forty men from Seven Rivers."

"That'll mean Jesse Evans and his outlaw trash," Waite said.

"Precisely," Tunstall agreed. "I'm not giving them any excuse to open hostilities with us. Especially here at the Feliz, so far from witnesses." He nodded toward the corral. "There are nine animals here that are not part of that claim. They are legally exempt, and I don't want them lumped in with the others. Dick and I have decided to drive them to Lincoln by taking a wide arc out by the Hondo. We'll camp there tonight. Once we get to Lincoln I'll present papers to a friendly judge—someone who is not in Dolan's pocket. I'm leaving the cook and his helper here. The posse will not bother two old men."

All the hands turned to look at the old German. "Let's hope not," Gauss muttered.

Brewer raised his chin to Billy. "Let's get the remuda started. You need some help in there?"

Billy's mood changed as quickly as the snap of his fingers. He smiled, and the twinkle in his eyes was like a playful wind rippling over water.

"Not me, nobleman. I'll have 'em out pronto. Presto-changeo!"

Billy leaned in the saddle, and the roan pivoted in a tight turn. Weaving through the animals, he herded the appointed livestock toward the gate. When Brewer swung the gate open, the horses spilled out of the enclosure with the mules following behind them. Billy spurred the roan and gained their flank to turn them toward the river. Tunstall, Brewer, and the other hands hurried up on horseback to assist, as Waite brought up the rear in the wagon.

Gauss watched them get the animals under control and move out onto the trail. Though shaking now from the cold, he propped his hands on his hips, looked north, and scanned the horizon for a full minute. Finally, he walked back to the dugout, shaking his head all the way.

After only a mile into the journey, Waite's wagon struggled with the debris from a rockslide. Turning the wagon back toward the main road to Lincoln, he continued alone. The horsemen with the remuda, now making better time, reached the Hondo in early afternoon, so they decided to push on a few more miles before making camp. An hour later, where the road crested the last hill before the Ruidoso, the men up front with the livestock—Tunstall, Brewer, and two others—slowed the herd before the animals could smell water and bolt. Billy and one other of the crew had hung back several hundred yards, keeping an eye out on their back trail.

Tunstall's horse suddenly shied when a flock of turkeys burst out of the brush and started for the river. A dozen birds retreated through the pines in a chaotic zigzag, and then, unexpectedly, they settled to a slow walk, weaving through the scrub and scratching for food.

"Would that I had carried my fowling piece," Tunstall muttered.

Dick Brewer slid his rifle from its scabbard and offered it to his employer. "Try this, sir."

Taking off his overcoat, the Englishman chuckled. "No, no . . . I'm no good with that. Why don't you boys see if you can bag one of the birds? We'll take it into Lincoln and make a gift of it to McSween's cook."

The three drovers headed off into the pines. They had not been gone two minutes when shots rang out from somewhere behind the remuda. By the time they had returned, Billy and his companion were galloping toward the remuda. Hot on their trail were more than twenty riders, all with guns drawn as they pursued.

Hurrying back to Tunstall, Brewer and his companions yelled out to the Englishman and rode hard for high ground, where a boulder field spread out over the upper part of the slope.

The Englishman frowned and tried to look two ways at once. "What is happening!?" he muttered to himself.

"Follow us, Mr. Tunstall!" Dick Brewer yelled back to his employer. "There's cover up this way!"

By now Billy had closed the distance and could see the confusion on Tunstall's face. "Skin out, Mr. Tunstall!" Billy advised as he reined up. "There's too many of 'em for us." As his friend thundered past to follow Brewer, Billy reached out to slap the rump of Tunstall's bay, but the horse had begun sluing in a nervous circle. Billy wheeled his horse around and dug in his spurs to head for the boulders. "Follow me, Mr. Tunstall!"

"But who is it?" Tunstall called back, squinting at the oncoming riders. But Billy was out of earshot, quirting his roan, hellbent on gaining the high ground.

Recognizing several faces in the advancing posse, Tunstall draped his overcoat across the pommel of his saddle and raised an arm high, as if the simple gesture might defuse the moment. He kicked his heels into the bay's flanks and started for the intruders at a walk, all the while calling out to them in his high English voice.

Fifty yards up the hill Billy scrambled off his mount and led it behind a low boulder—a shield of rock little larger than his horse. Brewer had dismounted behind a similar outcrop just a few yards away. Squinting back in the direction of the herd, both men leaned against their boulders with their Winchesters poised to shoot.

"Where the hell is Tunstall?" Brewer snapped.

Billy peered down the hill. "Shoulda been right behind me!"

Dick gnashed his teeth and bobbed his head around, trying to see movement below. "I can't spot him for the trees!"

A gunshot broke the silence, echoing up from the road and running the course of the canyon. Billy's horse nickered and stutter-stepped in the rocky ground.

"Goddamnit!" Brewer hissed.

From behind them one of the other hands called down from higher up the hill. "They've kilt Tunstall! I'd bet my wages on it!"

Billy started to mount.

"Wait! Stay here!" Brewer commanded, his arm extended and his hand flattened, palm out, toward Billy. "Let 'em come to us! We'll kill more that way!" When he lowered his arm, he added in a whisper, "Before they kill us."

Another shot was fired and filled the canyon. Billy and Brewer just stared down the hill, each man's face hard and shining in the sun.

"What're they doin'?" someone called from upslope.

Brewer did not answer. His gaze remained fixed on the stand of pines that blocked their view of the activity below.

"We ain't goin' down there?" Billy asked.

Dick Brewer shook his head. "If Tunstall is dead, I want to live long enough to kill every man in that posse. We don't stand a chance on open ground against those numbers."

When a third report rippled through the canyon, Billy closed his eyes and gritted his teeth. "Hell on a biscuit!" he spat and glowered at Brewer. "Ain't we gonna make no show here?"

"No, we ain't!" Brewer ordered. "Sit tight, Billy!"

They waited as the afternoon light threw long shadows toward the river and ushered a coolness into the canyon. The colors on the hillside around them softened, and the cold began to creep into every man's bones. With his rifle propped against the boulder, Billy squatted beside his horse and impatiently turned the cylinder on the revolver Tunstall had given him.

"Damnit, Dick!" Billy hissed. "I'd rather ride into a firestorm of bullets than hide in these damned rocks another minute!"

Brewer continued to scan the trees. Uphill, the other men talked in low conversations from their hiding places, their whispers like a bothersome pebble in Billy's boot.

"They ain't comin'!" Billy announced. "Ain't got the sand for it!" Standing, he pocketed the pistol, snatched up the Winchester, and stamped some life into his cramped legs. Looking up he spotted two vultures wheeling high in the sky. After leading his roan into the open, he mounted and propped his rifle butt on his thigh with the muzzle pointed up. Brewer said nothing. He simply nodded to the boy, mounted his own horse, and waved for the others to follow.

The posse was gone, as was the remuda. In the road lay two

corpses—Tunstall's and his prized bay's. The Feliz crew dismounted and stood around the bodies. John Henry Tunstall lay hatless on his back, his eyes closed, his blouse glistening with blood high on the chest. His forehead was a mass of gore from an exit wound above an eye. Beneath his head his overcoat was neatly folded as if the man had decided upon an impromptu nap in the road, except that no man could have slept through such a bother of flies. Some of Tunstall's hair on the "pillow" showed signs of powder burn. The stench of burnt hair was still evident.

Next to the Englishman, the elegant bay was sprawled out on its side, motionless and glassy eyed, its fine mass of muscle now reduced to nothing more than deadweight. Flies crowded around a dark hole beneath the animal's ear. Scrape marks in the sandy soil showed where Tunstall had been dragged to his final repose, giving the scene the macabre appearance of two bunkmates lying side by side.

No one spoke for a time, as the Feliz men stood helpless around the two bodies. Finally, Brewer removed his hat and swatted it against his leg.

"Anybody recognize any faces in that crowd?"

"I saw Jesse Evans and a couple of his boys," Billy reported. Then he pointed. "What's that under the bay's head?"

Brewer squatted by the animal and swept back part of the dark mane that partially covered a rounded edge of thick cloth. He looked up at the others with a question in his eyes.

"It's Mr. Tunstall's hat," he said softly.

"That s'posed to be a joke?" Billy hissed.

Billy dismounted and walked five paces away from the bodies. Gazing off to the southeast, he saw where the tracks of the remuda turned back toward the direction whence they'd come. When he spun around to his friends, all the boyish light had drained from his face. He pointed to the man and horse whose deaths had been reduced to a charade.

"We'll return that joke ten times over," he promised with a little snap in his voice.

Pivoting to Tunstall, Brewer reached to the Englishman's revolver and tugged it from its slender holster. He held the muzzle under his nose and frowned.

"Been fired," he reported. Holding the frown on his face, he opened the loading gate and turned the cylinder a full revolution. "Two spent cartridges."

"He never pulled his gun," one man said, "not while I was here."

Billy approached and squatted alongside Brewer. "What do you figure, Dick?"

Brewer stood and kicked at a stone in the road, and it rolled away ten feet, coming to rest in one of the many boot prints notched into the sand. "A man who gets shot out of the saddle doesn't take time to holster his gun," Brewer replied. "They must have finished him off with his own gun. The horse, too." Brewer looked down at Billy. "Why would they do that?"

For a time no one spoke. Down the hill the shoals of the Ruidoso made a soft shearing sound, a whisper that seemed appropriate for the dead.

Billy stood, gripped the horn of his saddle, and swung up in one easy motion. "Guess that's part of the joke, too, I figure," he said. "We'll keep a tally and make good on the score."

No one offered a reply to this.

"What do you wanna do, Dick?" asked one of the boys.

Brewer stared at the lifeless body of the man who had named him foreman. "Let's get him covered up." Dick walked to his horse and untied the blanket rolled behind his saddle. "Here, lay this over him."

Two of the boys spread the blanket over the man who had held the promise of all their future plans. They moved with an atypical gentleness, as if taking care not to awaken a sleeping man.

"We need to get word to Mr. Tunstall's partner in Lincoln," Brewer said. "I want McSween to start proceedings on making out warrants for every man responsible for this . . . starting with Sheriff Brady." Propping his hands on his hips Brewer looked north. "But we'll need to do it on the sly. Lincoln could be a hot place for us right now."

"I'll go," said Billy. "I like a hot place."

Riding through the night, Billy saw no one on the journey north. Swinging east of Lincoln he followed the Rio Bonito upstream to the flats north of town, where the natives had irrigated the floodplain for their vegetable gardens. Crossing the Bonito in darkness, horse and rider climbed the slope behind McSween's home, passed quietly through the trees, and came up on the open end of the U-shaped adobe complex from the rear.

After rousing the domestic help in their sleeping quarters, Billy—with hat in hand—stood before Alexander and Susan McSween, both wrapped in robes over their nightgowns as they huddled by the smoldering hearth in their parlor. The room was cold. The old Mexican woman, who cooked, managed their chickens, and tended to odd jobs about the *hacienda*, lighted a lamp on the mantle and stoked the fire into a blaze. A wisp of smoke escaped from the fireplace and hovered at the ceiling like a low stratum of clouds.

"How did it happen?" McSween whispered, his eyes brimming with tears, his face paler than usual.

"Brady's posse ambushed us on the Ruidoso. They shot Mr. Tunstall twice, once in the chest and then looks like they finished him off at point-blank range . . . in the back of the head."

"An execution!" McSween gasped, his face contorted with

the horror of it all. He sat on a wood bench before the hearth and turned his teary eyes to the flames licking through the logs. "Poor John!" he moaned and lowered his face into his slender hands. Shaking his head back and forth, McSween groaned until his voice cracked into a high keening sound. When he spoke again his words came out muffled by his palms. "I can't believe he's gone."

Billy looked to Mrs. McSween to see if she might comfort the ailing attorney, but she appeared more angry than shocked. With her arms folded across the front of her robe, she glared across the room at the front window, her jaws clenched as though she had taken a hold of something and was not going to let go.

"If Dolan is the devil," she said in a clear and condemning voice, "then Brady is the right hand of evil."

McSween's head came up quickly. "Brady was here in town this afternoon. I saw him."

Billy hissed through his teeth. "It don't matter where he was. *He* was the one sent 'em."

McSween's teary face wrinkled. "But how could they just open fire on John?"

Billy huffed a dry laugh. "Whenever Dolan needs a favor, the damn sheriff clicks his heels and curtseys. They both wanted to see Mr. Tunstall dead and said as much. I heard 'em."

Susan McSween dropped heavily into a cushioned chair and slapped her forearms down on the armrests. "They hold the same sentiment for us," she said.

Her husband seemed not to hear her. He stared across the room as if deep in a daydream.

"What about John's body?" he said from his trance. "What will you do with it?"

Billy moved to the window and looked out on the quiet village. Down the street at Dolan's store, a light shone in a window on the second floor.

"I reckon our boys will get hold of a wagon and bring 'im here to Lincoln." Billy closed the curtain and turned. "Brewer wants a coroner's report . . . something official."

"Tell them to bring the body right here," Susan McSween ordered. "We'll hold a wake in this parlor and let everyone see what it means to be an enemy of James Dolan."

Lawyer McSween blinked rapidly and looked at his wife. "Here?" When she gave him a cold eye, he began to nod. "Yes, of course."

"Brewer wants you to take out warrants for the men in Sheriff Brady's posse," Billy said.

McSween's face tightened with worry. "But who will serve them? Brady certainly won't!"

"We'll get the constable to do it," Billy said coolly.

McSween's brow creased like a wicker basket. "Martinez? He won't go up against Brady."

Billy's nostrils flared. "He'd better. Else the killin' around here will start with *him*."

McSween lowered his head and ran his fingers through his hair. "Well, I can see the justice of the peace tomorrow. Then I'll talk to Martinez."

Susan McSween stood. "Have you eaten?" she asked Billy.

Billy shook his head. "I've been in the saddle all night. I could use a bite. Mostly I need a bed. I'm plumb wore out."

Mrs. McSween walked quickly to the door that led to the east wing of the building. "Consuela?" she called.

Without waiting for an answer, she stepped back to the hearth and laid a hand on her husband's shoulder. His body made a little jerk of surprise, and he tried to cover it by hugging himself against the cold in the room.

"There's nothing to do tonight, Alex," she said. "Come back to bed. We have a busy day tomorrow." Turning to Billy she added, "Consuela will fix you a meal and show you to a bed."

"Yes, ma'am."

McSween pushed up from the bench like an old man and followed his wife out of the parlor. Billy moved back to the window and parted the curtains to see that Dolan's building was dark now.

"Sleep tight, you damned sonzabitches," he whispered into the window. "This town will get lit up like Christmas tomorrow."

Hearing a quiet footfall behind him, he turned to see the white-haired Mexican woman drying her hands on a small towel. "*¿Quiere algo de comer ahora, Señor Bee-lee?* I make you tortillas, yes?"

Billy nodded. "*Sí . . . gracias.*"

The old woman waved for him to follow. "Come," she said and began shuffling back down the hallway toward the kitchen.

After unbuckling his cartridge belt, he slung the rig over his shoulder. Then pulling the Thunderer from his pocket, he recalled the day Tunstall had presented the pistol to him, explaining that he needed two-gun men riding with him. And the Winchester, too. And the horse and saddle. Four substantial gifts from the Englishman, all presented on Billy's first day as a Tunstall employee.

The sour feeling that had been nagging at him on the long night ride to Lincoln now became fully blown. He had used neither gun to help his benefactor today. Like all the others— even Dick Brewer, for God's sake—he had run for cover. That fact stuck to him like a spiny bur.

"There'll be a new game tomorrow," he muttered, "and hell to pay."

He started for the kitchen, walking lightly to keep the ring of his spurs to a minimum inside the house.

7
BLESSING'S NOTES
WAITE RANCH
CHOCTAW NATION, INDIAN TERRITORY
APRIL 1886

"There are men who live for evil and will steal away your life
And other men will stand by you and fight until they die."

Fred Waite is a darkly handsome man. His strong jaw and high cheekbones subtly reveal his native heritage, but I can see how his unkempt hair, bushy eyebrows, and full drooping moustache might have served him well as a passport into Anglo affairs when he lived in Lincoln County. Billy had told me Waite was only part Indian, with the other parts being a combination of "jackrabbit" and "pure gold." I am not certain what he meant by either term, but I took both to suggest endearing assets for the man.

Waite's eyes are friendly and full of compassion as he shakes my hand. I suppose I have Billy to thank for that. However, I have no trouble imagining this man's gaze all business as he sights down a gun barrel to end another man's life.

"I remember your name, Mr. Blessing. I read an article you wrote in the newspaper about Billy. Must have been four or five years ago . . . right before Garrett killed him. I believe you were the only reporter in those days to give the Kid a fair shake."

We stand at his front gate. To my left, across the much-trodden yard, I see a modest barn with a gambrel roof. Beyond it stands a clapboard house nestled into the shadows of a grove of tall spindly trees that are just beginning to leaf out. Between the two buildings, a neatly constructed fence encloses a motley cluster of horses, perhaps forty or fifty, all of whom appear content to stand in the sunlight on this cool spring day.

At the center of the yard a windmill towers over the homestead, its blades turning with a smooth humming sound but for the sharp punctuation of a rhythmic *clack* with each revolution. The place smells of cured hay, manure, and woodsmoke.

"So you are Choctaw?"

Waite closes the gate, and we begin to walk together for the house.

"I'm Chickasaw. But it suits me to live here for now." He points past the barn to a notch between two low hills in the distance. For as far as I can see the land is covered in the shimmering green of new grass. "I was born not too far from here."

"Billy told me you were the educated one among his friends," I say. "Where did you receive your schooling?"

He chuckles to himself. "Well, yeah, I went to college, but let's not forget Mr. Tunstall," he says. "*He* was the educated one. Myself, I finished up school in Saint Louis." After several more paces he turns to me quickly. "But there's different kinds of 'educated,' you know. Dick Brewer knew more about most subjects than most of us." He hitches his head, and a pained look flashes across his face. "Now *there* was one damned good man."

I can hear the same awe and respect in his voice that I remember from interviewing George Coe. For the second time in this project, I regret not being able to talk to Brewer. His death must have been an incalculable loss to the men who rode with him.

"And Billy, by God!" he adds, his voice now lively with a different kind of admiration. "Billy was smart as a whip. That boy found more ways to spring himself from a trap than a wily old lobo." Waite surprises me with a hearty laugh. "I believe he could've talked his way out of a hailstorm." He looks at me quickly. "Did you ever see his handwriting? The Kid could've worked in a monastery and put the other scribes to shame."

"Yes," I agree. "I posted some letters for him from jail."

When Waite smiles, his teeth contrast brightly against his dusky skin. Gradually his smile fades, and I remain quiet to see where he takes the conversation.

"Billy and I aimed to start up a ranch together. Mr. Tunstall was going to set us up over on the Hondo with some of his herd . . . just so he wouldn't have all his eggs in one basket, so to speak. Billy and I had big plans to make it bigger and better than the Feliz ranch."

We gain the house and climb the front steps to the porch, where a clothes wringer and basin lie disassembled on the wood planks. A heavy box of tools sits nearby. Waite opens the door and sweeps a hand into the semi-dark room. As soon as I enter, I smell pipe tobacco. Against the wall to my left an elderly man sits on a bench. He is motionless and his skin so dark he almost disappears in the crepuscular light of the house. Across the room a few red coals pulse in an open hearth.

Waite rattles off something in a choppy language that is foreign to me. The old man says nothing but inspects me with curiosity.

"This is my uncle," Waite explains. "He speaks only Chickasaw."

I nod to the man, but he merely stares at me through the pipe smoke, as if he believes himself to be invisible. Following my host into the next room, I find myself in a spare kitchen dominated by a still-warm cookstove and an open cupboard of mismatched dishes and cups. A small table and three chairs take center position in the room. At one wall a pitcher pump is mounted on a counter and next to it a stained porcelain basin. Spread across the countertop are a dozen unwashed potatoes, none much larger than a hen's egg.

Waite wraps his hand in a soiled rag and lifts a kettle off the stove. "How about some coffee, Mr. Blessing?" With his free hand he waves me to a seat.

Setting my satchel on the table, I take one of the chairs. "Please call me 'John.' I doubt I am much older than you." I smile at his hospitality. "Coffee would be splendid."

As Waite prepares our refreshments, I study the room more closely and spot a rifle propped between the cupboard and back door. I cannot help but wonder what part that weapon might have played in the Lincoln County War. When Fred Waite places a cup before me, I snap out of my reverie and smile my thanks. He sets down a cup for himself and takes a third into the front room. No words pass that I can hear. When he returns he is empty handed.

"Sorry, but we've got no milk right now. We do have some sugar."

I sample the coffee and find it offers a surprisingly tasty yet mellow flavor. "Thank you. This will be fine." When I set down my cup, I lean forward to examine its tawny color. "What is it? It's very good."

"Persimmon seed," he informs me. "Something the Chicka-saws drank in the old days . . . before they were pushed out here to a place no white man wanted to live."

I offer a grim face and nod. I start to tell this man about the newspaper article I wrote on the Indian removal—the one my editor refused to run—but the idea strikes me as too self-serving. I sip the coffee again and try to compare the taste to something else in my experience, but I fail. From my satchel I extract my writing paraphernalia.

"I'm curious," I begin. "Billy always referred to you as 'Dash.' Why is that?"

Waite smiles broadly, and again his teeth flash whitely below

his moustache. "They all called me that. I'm fast on my feet."
He shrugs. "At least I was. I've probably lost a step or two."
Slouching back in his chair, he turns his cup with one hand in a
slow spin on the table. He watches the motion in a distracted
way and pushes his lower lip forward. "Guess I'm getting pretty
civilized these days." He sits up and leans toward me, his
forearms sliding on the tabletop. "I've got aspirations with the
tribal government. I spend a lot of time reading and writing
now."

I lift my eyebrows and nod my approval. "So, you've become
a statesman."

"More a 'tribes-man.' Mostly I read the law. I'm going to see
what I can do for the Chickasaw Nation."

Not only do I like this man . . . now I admire him. I think
now I might understand Billy's description of Dash Waite as being "part jackrabbit" and "part pure gold." I sip my persimmon
coffee and glance again at the rifle by the door. Setting down
the cup with barely a tap on the table, I settle my voice to a
somber tone.

"As I wrote to you a few weeks ago, I plan to write a book
about Billy. May I ask you some questions about the old days in
Lincoln County?"

Waite nods. "Ask away."

"You were with John Tunstall when he was killed, correct?"

Waite's mood changes immediately, and he stares into his
coffee. "No. I started off with them that day . . . driving the
wagon . . . but I had to turn back for the main road. The way
they were taking was too rough on the axles. But I know
everything that happened. Billy told me every detail."

I open my notebook, remove the cap to my ink bottle, and
assume the interviewer's pose. "Tell me this," I begin. "Do you
feel that Mr. Tunstall's murder was the tipping point for Billy?
In your view, is that when he became 'Billy the Kid'?"

Waite thinks about his answer for a time. Then he crosses his arms on the table, each hand clasping an opposite elbow.

"Funny thing about Billy," he began, "people started calling him 'Kid' because he was so young and skinny. He had small hands and feet, and his voice lacked any depth. But Billy never really had much of a childhood. Not for long anyway. He had to fetch up to manhood before he should have. A lot of grown men underestimated him for that. You see, he kept a youthful spirit—the way he acted and talked and danced with the girls— but beneath all that he was tough as rawhide. A man might go up against Billy thinking it was a boy to be dealt with, but when Billy pulled his gun, he was a seasoned killer and thought nothing of sending to hell any man who had wronged him or his friends."

I dip my pen and begin taking notes. When he sees that I lag behind in the transcription, Waite is kind enough to slow his narrative.

"He never knew his father, you know," Waite continues, "and his mother died when he was still a boy. He had a stepfather for a time, but the man took no interest in Billy. He just walked away when Billy's mother died. Must've been a cold bastard."

I write and, in keeping with professionalism, keep my assessment of Antrim to myself.

"Here's how I see it," Waite said, getting back to his story. "When Mr. Tunstall took in Billy to ride for the Feliz, I think Billy felt like he had a father for the first time . . . even though Tunstall was only the same age as me. He had a way about him . . . something about being English, I guess you'd say. Formal and businesslike. And he *was* the boss. In addition to a job, he gave Billy a horse, a new saddle, a Winchester repeater, and a new model Colt's—a double-action. Billy prized them all. It was like he had inherited them from royalty." He smiles at the memory. " 'Course Billy already had a way with horses, and he knew how to shoot any kind of weapon you put in his hand, but he groomed that horse, soaped that saddle, and oiled those guns like a soldier. He would do anything for Tunstall."

Waite sips his coffee, stands, and sets the cup next to the kettle on a cooking plate of the stove. Turning, he points at my cup.

"Warm that for you?"

I lift my cup and swallow the dregs. "I'm done, thank you."

"So, to answer your question," Waite goes on, returning to his chair, "Tunstall's death cut Billy to the bone. While it made some people more fearful and careful—like McSween, the lawyer who had partnered up with Tunstall—it made Billy bolder. He was always devil-may-care, you know, but, after Tunstall's death, I don't think Billy cared any more whether he lived or died." Waite frowned and seemed to listen to the echo of his own words. "Except that he wanted to live long enough to kill everybody responsible for John Tunstall's murder."

He watches me write down his words. That was something Billy used to do: look through the jail bars at me with his head tilted just so as I scribbled my shorthand notes.

"When Tunstall's body was hauled into Lincoln, Mrs. McSween had us lay him out on a table in her parlor. I'll never forget seeing Billy take his turn at viewing the body. His hat was in his hands like he was asking a señorita to dance. His hair was mussed and his face smooth as a schoolboy's. But what came out of his mouth sounded like a quiet, soul-less curse rising up from the grave of a man buried alive." Waite clears his throat, and when he speaks again his voice carries the edge of a rusty blade. " 'Before I die,' Billy swore, 'I'll kill as many of those sonzabitches as I can find.' "

Fred Waite is quiet for a time, no doubt remembering the moment. "That parlor was already quiet, but after Billy made that oath . . . I could hear my own heart beating in my chest."

Rising again he uses the rag to grip his coffee cup. He raises it to his lips, carefully tests it, and returns to the table. "Then the strangest thing happened. Who should show up at that wake but Dolan's new business partner—a man named Riley. He was so drunk he could hardly make it through the door. I thought Billy might kill him, and, if not that, Dick Brewer might tear his head off his shoulders. But Riley started crying. I'm not sure he knew what he was doing, tell you the truth. He was either the scared-est man I ever saw or the most contrite. Billy made him empty his pockets, and the man complied without argument. From inside his coat, he laid down a small ledger with some posted letters inside. While Billy braced him, I sorted through his belongings and decided to keep the book and its contents. When Riley left without his papers, he was none the wiser."

Waite shakes his head and then fixes his gaze on me, eye to eye. "Those papers gave us about everything we would need to put Jimmy Dolan and Sheriff Brady away in jail for larceny . . . and maybe the county prosecutor, too . . . if we could find a judge who had not been bought off by Dolan's crowd."

"Were you able to get warrants for them?" I ask.

Waite nods. "Justice of the peace issued them . . . a dozen or more. Billy and I went as deputies with Constable Martinez, warrants in hand, down to Dolan's store. We knew Brady was there. What we didn't know was how many men he had with him. *They* were waiting for *us,* guns out. Brady took our weapons, arrested us, and marched us to the pit." He shakes his head and looks right through me to the past. "That was a damned lot of crow to have to swallow."

Waite sucks in his cheeks, accenting the angles of bone under the skin. "He marched us down to the jail in front of a big crowd, prodding us all the way with Billy's prized rifle . . . the one Tunstall gave him. We were left down in that hellhole for three days. Long enough to miss Mr. Tunstall's funeral. He was buried behind his store." Waite pauses to stare out the window. His jaws knot repeatedly like a heartbeat. "That really burned us up. When we got released, Brady refused to return Billy's Winchester rifle. When asked, Brady said he didn't know anything about a rifle."

Waite's brow tightens, and he fixes steely eyes on me as if he has come to an important decision. "That right there," he whispers and points a finger at me. "That might be the moment that Billy stepped off the edge. I don't think anything in the world was going to stop him from killing Brady. But Billy was smart, and he knew to bide his time to get it done right."

"What did you do next?" I ask.

Waite raises his forefinger between us, a signal for me to sit tight. Rising from his chair he walks into the front room, where I hear a drawer slide open. When he returns, he wears an expression on his face that seems a mix of pride and deliberation. Sitting again, he sets down a badge on the tabletop, a simple silver shield bearing one inscribed word: *Deputy.*

"That same justice of the peace appointed Dick Brewer as special constable, and we were all his deputies. There were about fifteen of us. The Feliz crew plus any friend of Tunstall we could find who could handle a gun."

"Can you give me their names?" I ask.

Looking doubtful at my request, Waite stares at the badge for several seconds. "I guess it doesn't matter to anyone anymore." His head comes up, and his eyes glaze over as he assembles a list. One by one, he gives me over a dozen names, spacing them so as to give me time to write. Only a few of these names are known to me, reminding me that the Lincoln County War had drawn so many fighters, I doubt any historian will ever assemble the complete story.

He picks up the badge and turns it in his hand. As he reminisces, a little twist of fire turns in his dark eyes.

106

"We called ourselves 'the Regulators.' " He glances at me. "Billy's idea."

"And what did you do?" I inquire.

He sets the badge down slowly, quietly and gives me a tired look. "We started killing every man we could find who had ridden with the posse that murdered Tunstall."

I swallow involuntarily. "How did you know who rode in that posse? Weren't the Tunstall men taking a defensive position on a hillside when he was killed?"

Waite curls one corner of his mouth and angles his eyes toward the window. "Old Gauss, our cook back at the ranch, he saw all of them when they came by the Feliz earlier that day. Because of him, we knew every man's name who came looking for us. From that point, our plan was simple. Whenever we found someone on that list, we killed him."

"You didn't try to make arrests?"

Waite stares at me long enough to make me feel I should think through my questions before I ask them. "No," he says in a flat tone. "We did not."

I tread carefully into my next remark. "But you were the law then."

Waite snorts a loathsome laugh. "So were those men who killed Tunstall."

He must have seen by my expression that his answer does not satisfy me. He shifts his weight in his chair.

"Look, we knew if we brought our prisoners into Lincoln, Sheriff Brady would whitewash the whole thing and set them loose."

I feel the skin on my face tighten. "So you just killed them without a trial?"

He flattens his palms on the table, splaying the fingers wide, and then he rises. "Come with me outside. I want to show you something."

I follow him across the yard to the barn, where he turns the latch on the tack room door and steps inside. After lighting a lantern, he kneels before a dust-covered chest and raises its lid.

Without turning his head, he calls to me, "Come in here and look at this, John."

When I enter the small quarters, I smell the tang of leather and saddle soap in the air.

"I don't know why I kept this," he says and stands holding a package wrapped in oil cloth. Setting it on the workbench he begins the unwrapping process, peeling back the layers with a delicacy that reminds me of a doctor removing a bandage from a patient's wound.

I am surprised to see a thick wool hat, olive green, its brim extending no more than two inches from the soft crown. It has been flattened on its side from storage. On one edge of the brim a blackened half circle surrounds a small erose tear with edges charred to a crust. The side of the crown nearest the tear is stained to a dark rust-brown. With great care he picks up the hat and holds it between us in both his hands.

"This was Tunstall's," he says quietly. "He was wearing it when they killed him." He shrugs. "I guess I just needed something to remember him by. Or maybe to remind me of that day . . . to justify all that we did later."

Waite stares at me, I suppose, to see my reaction. When he turns the damaged side of the hat toward me, I almost take a step back.

"The bullet just clipped the brim there," he explains. "Those are powder burns around the hole. The deep black there on the edge is where the material caught fire." He pointed at the discolored part of the crown. "There was a lot of blood. Most of this came from his horse. They folded Tunstall's coat like a pillow and put it under his head. After they killed the horse, they put the hat under the bay's head. We figured that was their idea of rubbing the whole thing in our faces."

I try for a stoic expression, but my proximity to the gruesome relic makes me feel queasy. "Why are you showing me this?" I ask.

He nods at the hat. "For powder burns in that tight a cluster . . . and for the wool to catch fire . . . the shooter had to be no more than a few inches away. After they shot him off his horse, somebody stuck a gun to the back of his head and just killed him easy as you please . . . the way you might shoot a rabid skunk."

I hold the question on my face and look into his dark eyes.

"I want you to picture that," Waite implores me. "Taking a gentleman's life that way. If you can put yourself in that place at that time, maybe you can see why we went on a rampage and shot Brady to pieces."

Studying the hat again, I force myself to imagine Tunstall lying face down in the dirt, his body already in shock from a mortal chest wound. I see the killer's eyes shine with satisfaction as he delivers the *coup de grace*. Feeling my legs go weak, I put a hand on the workbench.

"If you can see all that," Waite says quietly, "maybe you can understand Billy a little better. For me it was losing my employer. For Billy it was like losing his grip on the hand that was rescuing him from falling off a cliff."

"Yes," I whisper. "I think I can understand that."

Waite begins swaddling the hat inside its wrapping. "It took him three years to hit bottom, but the Kid was falling all that time. But you got to hand it to him . . . he sent a few men to hell first."

I watch his hands fold the cloth with tenderness. "Weren't the rest of you falling, too?"

"Certainly," he said without hesitation. "Some had a shorter distance to fall—Dick Brewer, McSween, Tom Folliard, and

Charlie Bowdre—God bless their souls." He hitches his head to one side. "Some of us just got out before our time was up."

He shows me the saddest eyes I have ever encountered on a man's face. Or perhaps it is regret I see. Waite nestles the package into the chest and closes its lid. He stands for a time, gazing down at the big wooden box before he speaks.

"Yeah, some are gone . . . and some of us pulled out to have some kind of life." He turns those melancholic eyes on me again. "I'm still not sure which of us are the lucky ones." He shrugs. "We carve out a life for ourselves, and then we're gone. But I guess Billy will live on forever."

I memorize these lines so that I can duplicate them in my notes later. Fred Waite has probably struck upon a thought-provoking truth. It is my fervent hope that I play some instrumental part in that legacy.

8

MAIN STREET, TOWN OF LINCOLN
AND
BLAZER'S MILL ON TULAROSA CREEK
LINCOLN COUNTY,
NEW MEXICO TERRITORY
APRIL 1–3, 1878

"O, Billy, *mi compañero*, you were always quick to smile You laughed right in the devil's face and charmed him with your guile."

Rain on the last day of March had left Lincoln's main thoroughfare a muddy mess for the first of April, which is why the five men making their way east from Dolan's Store walked the middle of the street, taking advantage of the slight berm left there between the natural flow of two-way traffic. Leading the group, Sheriff Brady carried a Winchester rifle in one hand. His revolver could be seen only as a lump on his side under his overcoat. The other men—apparently serving as his body-guards—carried rifles, too, yet none seemed alert or concerned about their surroundings as they kept up a running conversation among themselves. The long shadows cast behind them followed the group like flat black serpents slithering over the shining street.

It was still early morning, the chill in the air bracing. Only a few other citizens moved about the town. As the entourage of lawmen came abreast of McSween's adobe, a woman walked briskly from the house across the street and called out to Brady. The sheriff made his way to her, tiptoeing through the mire at the edge of the street. The deputies slowed but continued east into the sun.

After a brief exchange with the woman, Brady picked up his

pace to catch up with his protectors. Joining their ranks again in front of Tunstall's Store, he followed behind his men.

Less than a half hour earlier, when Brady had entered the Dolan building, Billy Bonney, Fred Waite, and four other Regulators had slipped from the back of Tunstall's Store to hide in the corral that attached to the east side of the mercantile. Notably missing was Dick Brewer, who had not been included in their plans. As the bulk of the Feliz men crouched behind the adobe wall, Billy ran lightly through the gate to the front corner of the building to keep watch.

Fifteen minutes later, when the Kid hurried back in the same stealthy gait, the gunmen raised their rifles before them, muzzles to the sky. "He's comin'," Billy reported. "And that goddamned George Hindman is with him in a tan coat and dark hat. Be sure an' hit him, too. He was with them that killed Mr. Tunstall."

A cascade of quiet *clicks* ran through the group as hammers were cocked on rifles. Just inside the gate, Billy turned beside Waite and dropped to one knee, his movements quick and silent, his concentration complete. Letting the four deputies pass by, he leveled his rifle and waited, as still as a cat just before pouncing on its prey. As soon as Brady's bulky silhouette hove into view, Billy pulled off the first shot. From the corral a barrage of gunfire followed, the fusillade echoing through the town in a startling chain of explosions.

Sheriff Brady sat heavily in the mud as if his feet had been jerked from beneath him. With his torso upright and his legs splayed out before him, he moaned, "Oh, Lord!" Shot at least half a dozen times, he looked down at himself, trying to appraise the damage to his body. Then his head came up and turreted slowly, as though he was now trying to orient himself. Just a few yards away George Hindman lay prone, squirming in the street and screaming. The remainder of the deputies had run for the sparse cover available: behind trees and fences, in drainage ditches along the side roads, and around the corners of houses.

When Hindman continued to cry out for help, a businessman ran from a building and got the deputy to his feet. Together they started hobbling toward the safety of the old courthouse.

"Now *there's* a man with some sand," Billy laughed, but he set his gun sights on Brady again. The sheriff had propped the butt of his rifle in the mud, bracing himself to stand. "That's my Winchester!" Billy whispered to Waite. "That damned sonovabitch!" He fired, levered another round, and fired again. The other Regulators joined this second volley with six, seven, eight shots, the roar of the reports almost deafening.

Brady fell on his side, his head turned so that his face slapped into the mud. His bullet-riddled body lay motionless, and no sound issued from him. Further east down the street, Hindman was hit again and suddenly became deadweight to his rescuer. Abandoning his burden, the citizen tried to run, slipped in the mud, and went down. Clawing his way on all fours, he gained the refuge of the bench in front of the old courthouse and lay flat in the weeds.

Smoke hung in the corral, so thick it looked like a brush fire had been recently doused. In this lull of the ambush, Billy stood and started at a trot toward the street.

"I'm gettin' my damned rifle back," he called over his shoulder to Waite.

"Billy!" Waite objected, his voice a rasping whisper of urgency. "No!"

One of the other Feliz boys—Jim French—started after him. "I'll cover the Kid! You boys cover me!"

As soon as these two reached the street, someone opened up on them from behind a house on the south side of the street. A bullet hummed through the cold air like an angry hornet, just nicking Billy's jacket. The second gouged the cartridge belt at his hip and whined away in a high-pitched whirr. The reports came at spaced intervals that suggested a patient marksman at work. The third bullet plowed through French's left leg, turning him back for the refuge of the corral.

"Billy! I'm hit!"

Without retrieving his rifle, the Kid joined the retreat, following French's lively limp back into the alleyway beside the Tunstall Store. The other Regulators were already mounting their horses, readying for their escape.

"Somebody out there is making it hot for us out on the street," Billy warned. "Jim took one in the leg! Use the back gate, and ride like hell!"

Dash Waite swung up into his saddle and tried to settle his nervous horse. "You're not hit?" he called to Billy.

Billy mounted. "That joker put a burn in my cartridge belt." He laughed. "I'm lucky my ammunition didn't start popping like a string of firecrackers."

"I can't ride!" French yelled angrily. He was still afoot, bent forward, holding his reins in one hand and pressing the other to his thigh.

"Well, I know you can skip by the way you skinned outta there," Billy replied. "See can you get back into the store. Maybe they can hide you there."

"We'll take your horse," Waite called out. "So they won't know you stayed behind."

The ambushers streamed out of the corral and skidded down the hill to the Bonito, where they splashed through the stream in a bright spray of sunlit water. Sluing right on the flats beyond, they rode into the sun. Waite led French's mount with Billy right behind. When they veered south and picked up the main road, a few shots rang out from various positions along the street behind them, but none found their mark.

Regrouping at Brewer's ranch on the Ruidoso, the assassins of Brady and Hindman perched on chairs, benches, barrels, and crates as they ate venison steaks, potatoes, and jars of cooked peaches—that last delicacy from a horse swap Brewer had made with Charlie Bowdre's wife, Manuela. Bowdre, himself, had joined the crew, as had George Coe and a few other boys who had taken the "Regulator's oath."

Charlie Bowdre was a quiet little man who could get feisty in a fight. As a neighbor of Brewer's, he had chosen the farmer's life, growing corn, raising cattle, and breeding horses, all with the help of his Hispanic wife. When he had signed on as a rider for Tunstall, he necessarily slacked up on his home duties, but of late he had begun to feel anxious to get back to his wife. On this day, however, he was especially vocal and took his place at Brewer's table alongside the men who had killed the sheriff.

"I'd'a liked to a' seen the expression on the sonovabitch's face when he sat down in the mud," Bowdre commented. "That crooked Irishman has took up too damned much room in this county for too long."

"Well, let's see," Billy said, pulling on his chin. "I'd say he looked 'bout like any man who'd just heard his name whispered in his ear by ol' Scratch himself."

"Same for Hindman," Waite offered. "I do believe the coroner will have to change ol' George's trousers before the funeral."

George Coe hitched his head with a rueful pinch in his eyes. "Me and Hindman helped dig a well together one time over in White Oaks. Too bad he got swept up in all this."

"*He* made the choice to ride with the posse that murdered Tunstall," Charlie Bowdre quipped.

"Hell, yeah," Waite agreed. "They both signed their own death warrants."

"You're damned straight they did," Billy chirped up.

Everyone in the room knew that these appraisals were meant for the ears of Dick Brewer, who never would have agreed to an ambush on the main street of Lincoln. Dick chewed on a chunk of meat and stared down at his plate, his jaw knotting like the working parts of a sewing machine. After swallowing, he looked squarely at Billy, who sat on the corner of the firewood box and, with his elbow crooked before him, scooped up peaches from his plate with a spoon.

"It wasn't the right way," Dick said in a low monotone. "What you did was no different than what they did to Mr. Tunstall."

Most of the men present found anything to look at other than Brewer, but Billy met Dick's gaze, pursed his lips, and let his eyebrows rise. "That's sort o' the point, Dick," Billy replied easily. "Hell, if it hadn't a' been such a hornet's nest out there, I woulda folded Brady's coat and stuffed it under his head for 'im."

Now all eyes angled to Brewer, who returned his attention to his plate and, with his mouth set in a grim straight line, shook his head. "Eventually, this war is going to be decided by how many people are swayed to one side or the other." He looked up to show his disapproval to Billy again. "You might have swayed a lot of people the other way."

The Kid set his plate on the stack of logs beside him, and then he wiped his hands on the front of his trousers. "Well, we'll just sway 'em back then. Why don't we ride back into Lincoln *pronto*, kill Jimmy Dolan, and mount his head on a flagpole. That oughta make us a lot o' friends. Just about everybody in the county owes him a pound of flesh."

"More like twenty pounds," Bowdre corrected.

Brewer made no reply.

"Dead is dead, Dick," said Billy. "It's done now. Let's move forward. What's next?"

Brewer gave Billy the solemn eyes of a preacher. "There's more to it than just killing, Kid. I want to have *right* on our side. Don't you?"

Hiding his smile, Billy looked down at his hands splayed over his knees. When his head came up, his expression mirrored Brewer's.

"After what they did to Mr. Tunstall, I figure we already got *that*. Main thing I want on my side"—he slapped his holster—"I already got right here. Loaded with six warrants."

Brewer closed his eyes for the time it took to suck in a deep breath.

"What *are* we going to do, Dick?" Waite asked.

Brewer pushed his plate forward, dropped his forearms on the table, and made eye contact with each man present. "I got word that some of the men we have warrants for are hiding out on the Mescalero reservation. I want to ride over that way and smoke 'em out."

Billy stood and slapped his holster again. "Now you're talkin', Dick."

In the quiet that followed, Fred Waite cleared his throat. "I got some bad news from McSween." Everyone in the room focused on Waite as he cut worried eyes to Brewer. "The governor has revoked your appointment as constable. He even stripped the title from the justice of the peace who appointed you. That means none of us can wear badges."

Brewer nodded. "I know that already," he said in an even voice.

Bowdre spewed air with a flutter of his lips. "The gov'nor is in Dolan's pocket."

"I know that, too," Brewer replied in his calm way.

"So what do we do?" Waite asked.

Brewer raised his fingertips off the table and tapped them back down on the wood. "We ignore it. We keep doing what we're doing. Like I said, we ride for the reservation and find these men."

Billy made a little dance step in place, his boots delivering a flurry of smart taps on the floor. "Let's go now!" the Kid said, his fever up.

"You boys'll lay low for a day," Dick ordered. "There will be men looking for all of you. They might come here, and I want to be the only one here when they do."

"Maybe we should stay with you, Dick," Waite offered. "You might need some help."

Brewer shook his head. "I don't want my place shot all to hell." He picked up his plate and hesitated. "You boys can go up to our old hunting camp up near Apache Summit. I'll meet you there day after tomorrow . . . before noon."

While all the other men seemed to mull over the idea, Billy accepted it gleefully. "Hell, yeah! We'll have us a high ol' time up on the mountain!"

Brewer bobbed his plate toward his guests. "I figure three of you to heat some water and wash all these dishes. That'll square us for the meal." He jabbed a thumb toward the kitchen. "There's a slop bucket in there for my pigs."

The men continued to look at one another, but now there were no smiles.

"Well, which three?" Bowdre asked.

Brewer shot a casual glance in Billy's direction. "How about the three youngest? That sounds about right to me."

The older men turned to grin at Billy. Without missing a beat, the Kid began rolling up his sleeves.

"Hell, I think I'll just volunteer. I doubt any of these ol' roosters know how to clean a plate anyway . . . not without using their tongues."

"The Kid wants to be back there where those peaches are hidin'," Bowdre said. "He just about cleaned us out one night when Manuela was crazy enough to ask him to stay for supper."

The Kid pointed at Bowdre. "That was one peachy night, Charlie." He picked up his plate and started for the kitchen, already whistling the tune he would keep up throughout the chore.

They built the campfire big, adding so much wood that the flames jumped higher than a man's shoulders. The night air was cooler on the mountain, but every seated Regulator had removed his coat to use as a cushion against the cold stony ground. The blazing fire sufficed to comfort them outwardly as the liquor they consumed warmed from within.

It was their second night at the camp, and the mood was celebratory and raucous. Exaggerated retellings of the ambush in Lincoln became more colorful, with all parties claiming to have put the killing bullet into Brady or his deputy. As the laughter and braggadocio escalated, Billy, who did not drink, grew quieter and smiled at the revelers.

The group's illuminated faces danced with grotesque shadows as they howled at the rotation of performances. Everyone had some aspect of the killing to act out—the most popular being Sheriff Brady's sit-down in the street after the first volley.

"Oh, Lord!" one of the men wailed and sat down hard on his bedroll. He clapped both hands to his heart and turned a surprised expression to his comrades. "How can this be? My term as sheriff is not yet up, and I ain't stole all the taxes I need for my retirement!" When he flopped over to play dead, the circle of spectators roared their approval. All but Billy, who stood back from the light holding in one hand the rifle that Dick Brewer had loaned him.

"Hey, Kid," George Coe called out in his chuckling voice. "Try some of this. It'll scratch a lucifer to your bones." He held up a bottle of whiskey and shook the contents.

Billy smiled. "Got all the fire I need right here, George." He raised the Winchester, and its side plate flashed with a glint of light from the flames. Holding his smile, Billy added, "Don't you boys think you oughta keep your hardware handy? There ain't no tellin' who might pop outta the dark up here. I'll bet this fire can be seen all the way to Las Cruces."

Coe leaned to one side and farted. "Got all the firepower I need right here!" he crowed, mimicking Billy by clipping his words the way the Kid did. The crowd roared.

Taking the performance in good humor, Billy smiled downslope where the horses had been picketed on a long rope in a stand of young oaks thirty yards away. All rifles save his had been left in their saddle scabbards. Cartridge belts and holstered pistols hung on pommels and tree limbs.

"You boys are new to this killin' business," Billy explained in that offhand way that meant he was laying the groundwork for a joke. "I'd hate to see you end your careers so soon."

"There ain't nobody would come after *us*, Kid!" Coe asserted. "We own this mountain tonight! Right, boys?"

"I wish those sonzabitches would try!" Waite hooted.

Billy picked up a hollowed log from the fuel pile. "Hey, George!" Billy laughed. "Show us again how Brady planted his britches in the mud!"

Coe pushed himself up and began going through the pantomime. Billy propped a hand on his hip and casually freed up four live shells from the cartridge loops on his belt. When the crowd's laughter crescendoed, he laughed with them and inserted the handful of bullets inside the cavity of the log. Balancing the piece of wood just so, he stepped forward and set it carefully in the flames.

"Damn, George!" Billy said, pouring on his admiration, "and you weren't even there!" He stepped back and clapped. "Now show us Hindman!"

Coe's comrades pushed him back to his feet. "Yeah, George! Do Hindman for us!"

By the time George had fallen and gone into his pretended death throes and crying for help, the boys were laughing so hard they were in tears.

The explosion seemed to shatter the very air around them. Sparks flew up in a shower and fell over the crowd. Every man was jolted back a foot or two as if by the impact of the blast. Then all was still, as the Regulators stared wide-eyed into the dark.

Before anyone could speak, another round went off. Then two more. The mighty warriors of the Feliz crawled all over each other trying to get to the copse of oaks where the horses were tethered.

The first man to arm himself was Fred Waite, who levered a round into his Winchester and crouched in the trees. When the others had done the same, they saw Billy still standing at the fire, his arms folded over his chest, his lips pursed as he whistled an Irish tune from his childhood. His roguish eyes were as bright as a pair of lighted candles.

When Billy could restrain himself no longer, he burst out laughing in his high tremolo. "Well, boys, you're a damned sorry bunch o' soldiers. I thought you'd kill each other tryin' to get to your shootin' irons." He smiled and shook his head. "It's best you learned this little trick up here instead o' in the thick of a fight."

"You did that, Bonney?" one of the men called out.

Billy sat by the fire and stretched his legs out before him. "You can thank me for the lesson tomorrow when you've cooled off." He took up whistling the song where he had left off.

"Damned smart-mouth Kid!" someone muttered.

George straightened and laughed. Then he turned his back to Billy to face the other men.

"He's right, and you all know it," Coe said quietly. "We might as well swallow our pride, boys, and take the lesson to heart."

Grumbling, the men began scuffing their way back to the fire, their heads hanging like whipped dogs. Waite stepped beside George Coe and huffed a quiet laugh.

"Hard to stay mad at Billy," Dash said.

Coe laughed and shook his head. "Look at him," he said, nodding toward the Kid. "His smile conquers us every time."

When Dick Brewer joined them at midmorning, he brought with him Josiah Scurlock, whom all the boys called "Doc." With these two added to their numbers, the Regulators descended into South Fork along the banks of Tularosa Creek. When they approached the cluster of buildings that had sprung up around Blazer's sawmill, Brewer sent Billy to the Indian agent's house to ask about getting a noon meal for his men. Bowdre was dispatched to the small post office to see what information he could gather about which men were in the area. The rest led their horses into a high-planked corral to be fed and watered out of sight.

Because the hostess in the agent's house allowed no weapons inside her home, Brewer stationed Scurlock outside, while the others gathered around a long table in the communal dining room. Frank Coe, who had arrived earlier and was waiting for a home-cooked meal, greeted his friends and started into his familial banter with his cousin, George.

"Boys," Billy announced, "it's a good thing we got here when we did. Frank's been known to polish off a side of beef when he eats by himself."

The good-natured conversation continued as the hot dishes

were delivered to the table by the hostess. Then the riders got serious about eating, and the clink of silverware and porcelain pitchers became their common anthem. Partway through the meal, Doc Scurlock stuck his head inside the door, and all paused in their eating to turn to the interruption.

"You know an Andrew Roberts?" Doc asked, his question directed to Brewer. "Just came in on a mule and asked if he had any mail at the post office."

Dick Brewer frowned and set down his fork. When the others quieted, Bowdre pushed back his chair and stood, his dead eyes fixed on Brewer.

"That's 'Buckshot' Roberts. He was with the posse that killed Tunstall."

Brewer wiped his mouth with a cloth napkin and dropped the linen into his plate. "I have a warrant for him in my saddlebags."

Scurlock arched both eyebrows above his thick eyeglasses. "He's totin' a Winchester like it's bolted to his hand."

"Well, let's go unbolt it," Billy suggested.

"He won't go easy," Waite murmured. "He an ornery son-ovabitch."

"Good!" Billy said. "All the more reason to put him under the ground."

Frank Coe stood, his napkin still tucked into his collar. "He knows me. I might can get him to surrender." He turned to Brewer. "Whatta you say, Dick?"

Brewer thought for a time. Then the woman serving food opened the kitchen door, hesitated with a platter in hand, and returned to her cook without a word.

"Go talk to him, Frank," Brewer said, his answer cool and deliberate, as if the voice of reason had entered the room.

Frank Coe walked to the post office and met Roberts as he exited the building. Roberts clutched his rifle in his right hand on the narrow neck of the stock, three fingers inside the lever, one inside the trigger guard.

"What are you doin' over this way, Roberts?" Coe greeted.

Roberts's eyes narrowed and scanned the yard before fixing a sharp gaze on his neighbor. "I'm headed out of this country . . . for good. Already sold my ranch. I was expecting the check in the mail, so—" Leaving the rest unsaid, he looked toward the big house. Already he appeared savvy to the situation. "You alone here?" he asked with an edge to his voice.

Coe opened his coat to show he carried no weapon. "Listen . . . I come out to talk to you friendly-like. Brewer and his boys are here. They've got a warrant for you. I want to give you a chance to go with them peaceable. Can you do that?"

Roberts raised the rifle and took a left-hand grip on the forestock. "Is the Kid with 'em?"

Coe inhaled deeply, looked down at his boots, and exhaled. Smiling meekly, he nodded.

"Can you surrender to Brewer?" he urged. "I'll stand by you . . . won't let nothin' happen to you."

Roberts made a single firm headshake. "Ain't gonna happen. The Kid will shoot me on sight. I heard about Brady and Hindman."

"I'll talk to the Kid," Coe promised.

"Yeah . . . and you can talk to the wind while you're at it."

"Please," Coe pleaded. "I think we can avoid any shooting."

Roberts's face hardened. "You can't promise that, Coe. What I can promise *you* is I won't go down easy."

Frank Coe stuffed his hands into his trouser pockets and shrugged. "I'd hate to see it come to that. Won't you talk to Brewer?"

"Not a chance in hell."

Charlie Bowdre appeared from around the corner of the postal building, his revolver leveled at Roberts's chest. Behind him came Scurlock, George Coe, a smiling Billy Bonney, and two other Regulators. Nothing changed in Roberts's expression. It was as if he expected this.

"That's enough talking from the sonovabitch," Bowdre snarled. "Drop your damned rifle!"

"This ball has opened, ladies," Roberts replied and went into action so quickly that Frank Coe stumbled backward a few steps. Three shots exploded in a tight cluster. As Roberts jerked backward into the doorjamb, Bowdre and Doc Scurlock went down. George Coe fell to one knee, holding his right wrist with his left hand, his right forefinger replaced by a crimson stub. Roberts fired twice again, as fast as a man can clap his hands, and another Regulator went down. Billy skipped sideways to take cover behind the building. When George Coe followed him, Roberts fired at him twice, missing with each try.

A gray cloud of smoke hung across the front of the building. Taking advantage of this cover, Billy eased out from behind the building and, seeing Roberts backing across the street, grabbed Bowdre under the armpits and dragged him to safety.

"Goddamn! He's a fast bastard!" Bowdre gasped. "Did you get him?"

"It was too hot for me out there," Billy laughed. "I skinned out." He searched Bowdre's body for a wound. "You took it on your belt buckle, Charlie! I don't see any blood." Billy peered out at his two comrades lying in the dirt. The one farthest away was breathing heavily as he stared up into the sky. The other was Doc Scurlock, who lay on his side holding his leg. "He lit us up, all right!" the Kid said and lifted his own arm, craning his head to inspect a fresh tear in his jacket at the elbow. "He liked to a' got me, too!"

Shot through his rib cage from side to side, Roberts seemed to be working on sheer willpower as he backed toward Blazer's adobe office. He fired back at Billy's corner of the building until the rifle's hammer snapped down on an empty chamber. Roberts turned and managed to stumble into the one-room building. Right away he piled a bed mattress across the doorway as a barricade.

When Brewer ran up to Billy and saw his men in tatters, he got angry and snapped at the Kid. "What the hell happened!?"

"That ol' cuss made some show," Billy replied and pointed across the road. "He's shot through, and now he's holed up in that adobe. Unless he's carryin' extra cartridges in his pocket, he's all done with that Winchester." Billy shook his head once in wonderment. "He 'bout licked us to a finish, Dick."

Brewer knelt to examine Bowdre. "How bad is it?"

"Charlie fell into a piece o' luck," Billy laughed and pointed to the dented belt buckle. He patted Bowdre's shoulder. "This ol' boy wasn't ready to cash in."

Brewer looked at the two men still lying out in the open. "Help me get those two back here."

Together, Brewer and Billy rushed out and dragged the wounded to the safety of the side of the building. By the time they got both men settled, Frank Coe came toward them at a run from the back corner of the building.

"George is hurtin' something fierce!" Frank said in a rush. "He got his finger shot off!"

Scurlock turned to Coe's voice and grunted through clenched teeth. "I guess you didn't talk the sonovabitch into surrenderin'." He pushed up on an elbow to examine his bloodied leg. "That damned Roberts is quick as a rattlesnake."

Brewer stood and glared at Roberts's impromptu fortress. "Four men down!" he hissed. "I'm going to kill that bastard if we have to tear that place apart brick by brick."

Billy stepped closer to Brewer and studied the open ground between them and Roberts. "That jaybird is prob'ly dyin' in there right now. Why don't we just let him?"

Cursing under his breath, Brewer hitched up his rifle and started running toward the back of the mill house. "Come with me!" he called over his shoulder.

When Billy rounded the last corner, he found George Coe leaning against the building, his face contorted in pain. George was using the front of his blouse as a compress to stanch the flow of blood from his right hand.

"Lost my damned trigger finger!" he growled.

Stopping to help George, Billy untied his silk scarf and offered to bandage the man's mangled hand. As he wrapped the wound, he checked on Brewer, who had nestled in behind a log pile at the front corner of the building.

"I never saw a man use a lever-action rifle that fast," Coe said.

"He slipped a sour apple into *our* pie, didn' he?" Billy replied as he tied off the scarf. He checked on Brewer, who was peering over the wood pile, keeping watch on the doorway of the little adobe. Just then Dick brought up his rifle, took aim, and fired. Immediately, he ducked down and crouched behind the logs, waiting.

Keeping low, Billy approached the captain of the Regulators and squatted behind him. Brewer levered a round into his rifle and turned back to whisper. "You're sure he's out of cartridges?"

"I ain't sure o' nothin', Dick, 'xcept we got us a load of misery from that jasper."

Brewer frowned as if this was not what he wanted to hear. Slowly he rose up again to peek over the logs. Billy strained to look through a gap in the wood pile and found a small opening that allowed a view of the doorway of the adobe. Even across that distance he realized he was looking at a man's head canted over the muzzle of a rifle.

A plume of smoke blossomed, and the sharp report of a rifle was followed by a buzz that tore through the air. Brewer's head snapped back, and his body seemed to come unhinged as he fell backward. George Coe came running in a crouch and knelt beside Brewer's limp body.

"Oh, Lord, no!" George cried. "Not Dick!" Tears filled his eyes as he stared at the vacuous hole in Brewer's eye socket.

Billy pulled Coe by the arm and coaxed him closer to the building. "Stay back, George. We've already lost enough soldiers today."

Both men stared down at the stillness of their captain. The brightness of the midday and the blue of the sky were like a show of God's indifference to the petty ways of men. From the other side of the building, shots rang out, and pieces of the adobe's doorframe splintered. Roberts answered these reports with his own.

"Looks like that damned ol' rooster has come up with another rifle," Billy said.

"He was the best of us," George said, his gaze transfixed on Brewer's ruined face.

Billy leaned back against the building, rested his head against the boards, and closed his eyes. "That he was," he agreed, his voice barely a whisper.

Coe cradled his mauled hand against his chest and grunted at the pain of moving it. "What are we going to do about Roberts?"

Billy opened his eyes, took his friend's wounded hand, and checked the bandaging. "Looks like the bleeding has stopped. We need to get you and the others to a doctor." Glancing through the logs at the adobe, Billy put an edge to his voice. "We'll leave Roberts where he is . . . to die slow . . . and alone. Maybe he's earned that much."

9
BLESSING'S NOTES
SCURLOCK HOME
ACTON, TEXAS
MAY 1886

"The señoritas danced with you and they loved you by and by
As you high-stepped to their music with that twinkle in your
eye."

I have been warned by everyone who knew Doc Scurlock that he will not talk of his old days in Lincoln County. Which is why I wrote to him not about Billy Bonney but about a poem he had penned and managed to get into print through a newspaper editor who owed him a gambling debt. In 1883 "By the Grace of Her Husband's Demise" was first published in the *San Angelo Messenger,* but it was picked up later by the newly founded University of Texas and presented in a short-lived literary journal. Heaven knows why.

The poem, I am sad to say, is dreadful, borrowing heavily from the phraseology of Whitman, but in the end pretentious, desultory, and disconnected. It is a circuitous journey without a destination. And, worse, it changes horses in every stream it crosses—from first person to second person to third, from present tense to past and to future. Even the rhyme scheme fluctuates. Reading the poem feels like wearing a different kind of shoe on each foot. Still, I have virtually memorized the piece in order to be well fortified for my interview.

But who am I to label anyone "pretentious." In my letter to Scurlock, I revealed myself as a composer of music, which is true. My reason for contacting him, so I wrote, is to consider using his words as lyrics to a song of my design. This claim, of course, shames me, but I know of no other way to gain passage through his door. How I will segue from iambic pentameter to gory gunfights I haven't a clue. As Billy once told me: "Once you go ahead and step off the cliff, you'll get a better view of where you oughta land."

After pushing through an angry west Texas wind, I arrive at the Scurlock domicile in a two-seater buggy rented from a livery in Granbury. It seems more fitting that a musician would travel this way rather than astride a saddle. As I climb down and tether the horse to a hitching ring bolted to the gate post, I remind myself one last time: *Do not call him "Doc."*

Carrying my satchel of writing materials, I climb the steps to the porch of a handsomely built wooden house with a fresh coat of whitewash. I rap on the door and wait.

If I had not been prepared by a description of my interviewee, I would take the man who opens the door as a mousy accountant . . . or possibly a preacher of the meekest stripe. His large sweeping moustache only serves to further dwarf his small stature. His wet hair is combed flat against his skull and tops off at my eye level. He cannot weigh more than a one-meal-a-day schoolboy. He squints through spectacles that appear to be cut from the bottoms of Mason jars. And his ears! Immediately, I am reminded of a joke Billy Bonney shared with me about this man: *"Doc Scurlock cannot leave home during a high wind for fear of being carried off to parts unknown. He is the envy of vultures all over the New Mexico Territory."*

"Josiah Scurlock?" I say, doing my best to hold my gaze on his magnified eyes and away from the wingspan of his ears. "I am John Blessing, the composer, late of Santa Fe. I wrote to you about a visit?"

Scurlock smiles, and now I see the rationale for his mammoth moustache. Again, my self-discipline is called on for diplomacy. The man's lower incisors are completely missing, leaving a dark gap that tries to lure my eyes toward his dental embarrassment. The story must be true that these teeth were shot out over a card game in Mexico. I can only wonder how a man lives through such an ordeal. I find myself wondering if there is an exit scar on the back of his neck.

"I've been expecting you, Mr. Blessing. Come in out of the wind."

There is a soft rounding out of his words that, by my ear, puts his origins in the Deep South. His enunciation suffers only slightly from his reduced tooth count. As I enter the front room I find a dozen children, variously aged, seated on benches set up like church pews. A map of the world and various charts and unframed illustrations hang on the walls, and an impressive set of leather-bound encyclopedias stands like a squad of soldiers at attention along a shelf. Next to these books are a scattering of bleached animal bones and skulls.

All the young ones are turned in their seats staring at me with curious eyes. I notice that most are mixed-blood *Mestizos*. In each lap is a slate marked with chalk scribbles, and I realize that I have interrupted a schooling session.

"It appears I have come at an inopportune time, sir," I say, purely out of social obligation. I certainly do not wish to repeat this journey into west Texas, unless perhaps the devilish wind were to be at my back next time. "Are you holding a class here, Mr. Scurlock?"

He offers a modest shrug. "It is an informal affair. We're studying Dickens. I fancy myself a teacher of sorts." He smiles at the front row of students. "Five of these are my children, so they have little choice in the matter."

When his smile expands to include his eyes, he laughs, and I can see that his humor is genuine. He strikes me as a loving father.

131

He gestures toward the hallway leading to the back of the house. "We can talk in my study. Let me just get my wife to take over here." He turns to his students. "We'll continue with Mr. Dickens tomorrow. Mrs. Scurlock will commence with your language lessons now."

He turns to fetch her, but a young, long-faced, Hispanic woman appears unbidden from another room. Her dark hair falls well below her shoulders. By her youth and by the way her devoted eyes fix on Scurlock, I assume she is one of his students until I notice that she is with child. Her serious face breaks into a smile that suggests a hidden warmth. Holding that smile she glances at me only briefly, and in that fleeting inspection, I sense an ineffable connection with her. Before her she holds a tray with two filled glasses.

"I thought you and your guest might enjoy some sweetened lemon water, Josiah," she says in that lyrical accent that marks her as one who has mastered English but enlivens it with traces of her own heritage. Looking past us at the children she arches both eyebrows. "And if all of you do well with your lessons today, I will bring in a treat for you as well."

The children begin to murmur among themselves. Scurlock takes the tray from her.

"Thank you, dear. Mr. Blessing, this is my wife, Antonia." He touches his fingertips to my shoulder. "Mr. Blessing has come to talk to me about my poetry."

Mrs. Scurlock holds out her hand, palm down, and I realize she expects me to bow and kiss the backs of her fingers, but I am unprepared for such a formal show of etiquette in the presence of a former gunman from the Lincoln County War . . . who happens to be her husband. I quickly grip the proffered hand and rotate it into an acceptable handshake. Surprising me, she adds her other hand to our clasp, enclosing my hand in both of hers.

"Welcome to our home, Mr. Blessing."

Again, I see in her eye some cryptic message that baffles me. Withdrawing my hand, I turn to Scurlock and attempt to get down to business.

"I promise not to take up too much of your time," I say. This lie is one I have become quite adroit in delivering to my interview subjects. As usual, I rationalize it on the spot. All for the sake of my book.

Scurlock leads the way down a twilit hallway and turns left into a room where the afternoon rays of the sun stream through a window at an angle that slices the study into contrasting portions of light and shadow. There are no revolvers or rifles adorning the walls. I had hoped for a show of some weapon or other remnant of his past as a possible entry into a conversation about Lincoln County. The walls on three sides are lined with books, meticulously stacked and free of dust. The fourth wall displays a parade of photographic portraits, all mounted inside frames. I step to the gallery with optimism, but the images reveal nothing of a New Mexican past. Portraits of individual children and group family poses are all I find.

"You have an impressive family, Mr. Scurlock," I observe.

"And more on the way," he says proudly. He sets the tray on a desk and pulls a straight-back wooden chair from behind it to face the only other chair in the room, the latter a cushioned armchair next to a small table supporting an oil lamp. He offers me this soft perch as he picks up the glasses and places one next to the lamp. I sit and settle my satchel in my lap.

"So, what compositions have you published?" he asks as he lowers himself into his chair, his refreshment in hand.

"Mostly chorales for churches. I had one piece performed by a chamber group in Santa Fe. It was a special performance for the governor."

Something changes in Scurlock's eyes as he pins me with his

stare. "Which governor?"

"Governor Sheldon," I say truthfully. By the steely blue of his gaze, I have the distinct notion that if I had answered "Axtell or Lew Wallace," Scurlock might have pulled a pistol from his pocket and shot me dead. Instead, he relaxes and raises his glass to me.

"Congratulations. I know how gratifying it is to have your work shared with the public."

I lift my glass, and we toast the arts. The tartness of the drink is like a slap to the face, but its sweet aftertaste lures me in for a second indulging. Scurlock downs half the contents of his glass, exhales in a rush, and sets his glass on the floor.

Straightening, he says, "You mentioned in your letter that you want to put my words to music. To what purpose? Would this be something you would perform for a governor? Or might you publish this to go aborning into the world?"

Returning my glass to the table, I bob my eyebrows. "One never knows. It's a tricky business. I'm no Stephen Foster, but I really do not aspire to be. My music is, perhaps, more classically designed. Still, I would not mind some degree of popular appeal."

Scurlock nods. "Well, I don't know what a poet can expect from this world, unless he somehow strikes a chord with the people. You're a composer. Maybe you can supply the chord."

I smile and offer my humble opinion. "It really is a roll of the dice. We can slave over our work and craft it just so, but it comes down to the eye or the ear of the person to whom we present it. Tastes are fickle. One man might laugh at our works, while another is awed to tears."

"Do you have a favorite piece of music?" he asks and cocks his head.

Immediately, several compositions by Bach come to mind, but I grasp this moment as an opportunity to draw something from him about Billy Bonney.

" 'Silver Threads Among the Gold.' That's one that appeals."

Scurlock threads his fingers together in his lap and smiles down at his hands. "I know it well," he says and looks up at me. "Had a friend who used to sing it all the time."

"Oh?" I reply, hoping to sound casual. "Who is that?"

Scurlock pushes out his lower lip and shakes his head. "No one. He's gone now."

In a back room of my mind, I scramble for the right words to keep this inquiry alive. "It's an example of a successful collaboration," I recall. "Hart Danks wrote the music. His lyricist, Rexford, was a poet." I am quiet for three beats as I summon my courage. "They say it was the favorite song of Billy the Kid."

Looking away from him, I pick up my drink and take several swallows. When I set the glass down and face him again, he is waiting for me with leaden eyes. Though I can hear the collective voices of the children down the hall as they decline a verb in Spanish, the silence in the study is suffocating, as if we are holding our breath, staring at one another at the bottom of a lake.

"Why are you here, Mr. Blessing?" he says, his voice so calm as to be menacing.

I slump back into the chair cushions and take in a deep breath. I feel like a man just defeated in a high-stakes card game. Scurlock exhibits the patience of a mountain lion waiting to see if the rabbit will run. I flatten my hands on my satchel and dive in.

"I'm here for Billy Bonney," I admit and then quickly add, "I was his friend."

For five heartbeats, I wait to see if I will be tolerated or kicked out of his home by the seat of my pants. Scurlock is absolutely still, but I imagine his working parts wound up inside him like the jaws of a steel trap. When he stands, his chair almost tips over.

"You may leave now, sir," he says, his voice flat and peremptory.

I close my eyes long enough to nod. I feel like a child caught in an ill-conceived prank.

"Mr. Scurlock," I begin in a pleading voice, "I am trying to do something good here."

"Get out!" he says, raising his voice a notch.

I lock eyes with him, trying to match his resolve. "You were captain of the Regulators after Dick Brewer's death. You were Billy's leader. Surely you—"

"Out!" he shouts, his voice now like the bark of a dog.

Gathering my satchel, I push myself up from the chair and resort to my most earnest entreaty. "Someone needs to speak for Billy Bonney, Mr. Scurlock. It seems that his enemies are having the final say in his story. He was—"

"A crazy kid who murdered at the drop of a hat!" he interrupts, completing my sentence in a hard monotone. "Now you listen to me. You made your way in here as a charlatan. How do you want to leave? As an upright liar or a prone one?"

Lowering my eyes, I nod again. "I'll go. I'm sorry to have wheedled my way in here on false pretenses. I thought that once I explained to you—"

"You thought wrong!" he growls in a low murmur that feels even more menacing than his abrasive bark. But it is I who am the dog. With my metaphorical tail between my legs, I walk out of the room, turn down the hall, and, without so much as a glance at the students, pass through the classroom. Quietly I open the front door, step out into the wind, and ease the door shut.

By the time I store my satchel away, gain the driver's seat, and turn the buggy around, I hear a voice and turn my head to see Mrs. Scurlock walking at a fast pace from the back corner of the house. She holds her pregnant belly as she hurries toward me. I pull up on the reins and check the front porch, half expecting to see Doc Scurlock appear with a shotgun.

When she reaches my buggy, she glances back at her home and then surprises me by climbing into the limited storage space behind the seat, where she plops down as though I am expected to smuggle her and her unborn child out of Texas.

"Drive down the street past the old adobe *carniceria*," she instructs me. Seeing the confusion on my face, she points down the road and translates. "The old meat market." When she draws her knees to her swollen belly and wraps her arms around her shins, I see no recourse but to comply.

As soon as we stop past the empty adobe, she climbs over the seat and settles next to me. She is most agile for a woman in her condition. Our hips and thighs press together in the confined space, but she seems not to mind.

"You do not remember me." She phrases this not as a question but as fact. "I was Maria Antonia Herrera . . . half sister to Manuela, Charlie Bowdre's wife. We met in Fort Sumner. It was at the cemetery when they bury Bee-lee. I was there to visit Paulita when they keel him."

A picture wells up from memory. I had stood over Billy's grave, one of very few Anglos to attend the service. Though only a few feet from Paulita Maxwell, Billy's sweetheart, I'd made no intrusive attempt to talk to her. I had started walking back to my room when a thin Mexican girl with shy eyes ran out to me and pulled on my sleeve.

"Maria! Yes, I do remember! You were the one who thanked me for coming. You were the only one who would speak to me."

"*Sí*. I was visiting from Texas," she says and shrugs. "The Mexican people who loved Bee-lee . . . they were not inclined to be friendly to any white man that day." She surprises me by laughing quietly. "And now here I am running after you again . . . this time to explain to you about my husband."

"Explain what?" I ask.

"I know Josiah got angry with you. You must understand that he does not want to be the man that he was. And he wants no one to know of his past. He has 'burned all the breedges' as the *Americanos* say. He has new dreams, and the old days could prevent him from reaching those dreams." She laughs again. "It seems I am always apologizing to you for the behavior of others."

"Why is that? Both times you could have let me disappear without explanation."

She clasps her hands together in her lap, intertwining the fingers. Looking down, she slowly opens and closes her fingers like the wings of a dying butterfly.

"Because you were good to Bee-lee, yes?"

"Well, I was his friend, but—"

"I was in love with Bee-lee," she says quietly and then looks at me with a timid smile. "All of the girls were." She raises both her eyebrows and shrugs. "I think all the men know this, too. They are jealous. I know Charlie felt that way when he was alive. He did not want Bee-lee spending time with Manuela."

Leaning forward, I tie off the reins to the brake handle. Then I prop my elbows on my thighs and nod my understanding.

"I wrote to Manuela after Charlie was killed," I confide, "both to express my condolences and to ask for an interview. But she did not reply."

"She was angry with *everyone* over Charlie's death. Not just Garrett. She blamed Bee-lee, too. She knew you took Bee-lee's side of things. She wanted no part of that."

"Why did she blame Billy?"

She shrugs her head to one side. "Because he was so *ligero* . . . how do you say it . . . 'cavalier' about life . . . always smiling and laughing? Manuela saw Bee-lee as being careless with Charlie's life, too."

I turn to her. "Then why did all the other girls like Billy?"

She is quiet for a moment as she looks off to the horizon. Then she offers a single whispery laugh.

"Because he was so cavalier . . . always smiling and laughing," she repeats. Now she turns to me with a coy smile. "And so handsome." Her face turns confiding. "Sometimes it is a man's smile that makes him handsome. Even with those two teeth a lee-tle bit crooked." She makes her faint, airy laugh again. "Those teeth endeared him to us. He was like a little lost boy, and we all wanted to take care of him."

She looks off to the plains that roll away to the west. "Bee-lee always laughed when he danced, and we señoritas loved to dance with him. Even though I was so young, I think he bring out the *madre* in my soul."

The wind makes her loose hair stream forward like a black flame engulfing her face. Combing the strands from one eye she gives me a cautious look.

"Did you know that Charlie made a deal with Pat Garrett?"

"What!?" Her words open up a cold, dank cave in the pit of my stomach.

"It is true. He asked Garrett to leave him alone. Charlie was ready to get out of the territory. Manuela made him promise it to her *and* to the sheriff."

"Do you mean that Bowdre gave up the Kid?"

She frowns. "What does this mean: 'gave up'?"

"Did he betray Billy?"

She shakes her head vehemently. "Charlie would not do that. He was joss thinking of his wife, and he was ready to put all the kee-ling behind him. Ever since he was shot . . . and the belt buckle saves his life . . . Charlie believed his luck was running out."

The wind has its way with her hair again, and she waits it out. Both of us stare off into the distance. With the grit of sand accumulating on my neck I consider pulling my hat from beneath my seat, but it would only blow away.

"It looks like you and Josiah have made a good life here in Texas," I say. "I'm happy for you." I turn to her and watch her continue to hold her hair back away from her ear. "I apologize for coming here with a hidden agenda. I'm simply trying to learn all I can about Billy. I am compiling notes for a book I want to write. I want to tell the story that explains why there *was* a 'Billy the Kid.' "

She nods. When she speaks again her voice can barely be heard over the wind.

"Of course, if you want to know about the soul of Bee-lee, you will need to talk to Paulita. She knew him, perhaps, as no one else did. He was the love of her life."

"After the funeral, I sent a message to her room that I would like to talk, but her brother, Pete, asked me to leave Fort Sumner. Actually, he told me to leave. He said she would talk to no one about Billy. That the rumors about them were untrue. He told me if I wrote anything about her, I would face a lawsuit for liable."

Maria offers a wan smile. "She found herself in an awkward situation that made her brother very angry."

"The pregnancy?"

Maria eyes me carefully. "You knew?"

I nod. "Billy told me."

Maria frowns. "She did not want the baby to be cursed by the scandal of being a . . . *bastarda*. She started looking for a husband as quickly as she could."

"Are you saying Billy Bonney has a child?"

Her eyes close, and she shakes her head. "The baby never breathed. It was a girl."

For a moment I imagine Billy smiling and laughing as he dandles a child on his knee. Then the picture comes apart to be replaced by the image of Billy in his stockinged feet, lying dead in a dark bedroom.

A bony, copper-tan dog trots across the road in front of us and begins sniffing around the abandoned meat market. It goes about its business as if we are not present.

"Paulita was like Josiah," Maria continues. "She had no wish to drown in her past. That kind of notoriety, she told me, can destroy a woman's life. She needed to move on."

I frown. "You say 'she *was* like Josiah.' Does that mean she might feel differently now? Might she talk to me?"

Maria Antonia Scurlock gives me the knowing expression that only a woman can deliver. "There is no *bastarda*. And though she did find a husband a few years later, it is not a good marriage. Her husband is not loyal to her. Maybe she talks to you now . . . out of spite."

She climbs down from the carriage and stands facing me. The wind pushes her hair across her face. For a moment she looks like a masked highwayman, only one eye showing through the dark storm of her hair.

"If you see her," she calls over the rush of the wind, "give her my love. Tell her I miss her."

"I'll do that," I say and slip the knot from the reins. "Good luck to you and your family." Giving the horse a light tap of leather on its rump, I head west with the wind thankfully at my back.

10
McSween Home
Lincoln, New Mexico Territory
July 1878

"Until you learn the difference you don't have to be afraid You
just keep that pistol loaded and you'll hold the world at bay."

Through a network of comrades across the trans-Pecos territory, word reached Doc Scurlock that over forty mercenaries
were coming up from Seven Rivers to wipe out all that was left
of the Tunstall contingency. These gunmen were the vilest that
New Mexico had to offer, and some from Texas, including a
gang under the notorious criminal John Kinney, who may have
been the worst of the lot.

There could be no doubt where the funding for this army
was coming from. Jimmy Dolan had to reach deep into the
pockets of his failing business, but such was the logic of a man
so driven by violence. In addition, he had called on the com-
manding officer at Fort Stanton just several miles down the
road. Pulling all the strings at his disposal, Dolan demanded
that federal troops intervene in the affairs of Lincoln, not only
for the safety of its citizens but for the welfare of its businesses.
It seemed not to matter that Congress had just passed the *Posse
Comitatus* Act, preventing the U.S. Army from interfering in
civilian affairs, including the jurisdictions of sheriffs, constables,
or any other lawmen.

The response by Scurlock's Regulators was to enlist as many
locals as possible to take up arms and join their cause. In just a
matter of days, sixty Regulators were barricaded at strategic

points throughout the town. When the invaders arrived, skirmishes broke out everywhere.

Billy Bonney was among a dozen gunmen holed up in the McSween house. One of those was a new recruit, a tall red-headed boy who had latched onto Billy like an acolyte to his priest. Like Billy, Tom Folliard was an Irish orphan. Determined to be a warrior of note, he took every opportunity to prove himself to Billy.

After days of fighting, the windows of the McSween adobe compound had been reduced to rectangular rims of broken glass. Gunfire had riddled the upper third of the walls inside, splintering cabinets, gouging paintings, and tearing apart bookshelves, leaving shards of glass, paper, adobe, and wood splinters strewn over the floor. This beleaguered group was trapped, but they gave back as good as they got.

Those confined to the house received their first hint that other Regulators around the village had abandoned the cause when the number of the Seven Rivers boys surrounding the U-shaped hacienda appeared to double. When the soldiers arrived and set up a cannon pointed at the house, the situation began to look pointless to McSween. When he finally broke down, losing all resolve, the pall that had hung over the trapped household now seemed to fall over them like a smothering blanket.

For reasons unknown to them, the cannon had not been put to use. Still, McSween, virtually useless and ready to surrender, demoralized everyone in the house. All save Susan McSween, who grew angrier by the hour. And Billy, whose fighting spirit appeared to feed off of the tension. Several times during the ordeal, the Kid coaxed the lady of the house to sit at her pump organ and play accompaniment to the songs he requested. By the gusto of his singing and by his winning smile, he even drew in a few of the boys to add their voices to the musical festivities.

It was a strange counterpoint of themes: celebration inside the house with death lurking just outside every door.

"Billy don't know quit," Folliard assured McSween's new clerk, a New York City student who had never experienced frontier violence firsthand. "He'll come up with somethin'. You wait an' see."

On the fifth day, Dolan grew impatient. It took several tries and multiple buckets of coal oil, but the attackers finally set a sustaining fire to the structure. Once it was roaring, the occupants were forced to retreat deeper into the east wing, moving room by room. The heat was horrific and the smoke choking. Crouching low to the floor, Billy summoned all to him in the kitchen to give instructions.

"We can squirrel out o' this skillet. I got a plan that might work if we time it right."

McSween was close to tears. "I want to take my family out and give up!"

"That's *primera parte*," Billy agreed and looked at Mrs. McSween. "Ma'am, it's best you surrender 'cause the rest o' us are gonna hot-foot it out o' here. It's gotta be hard to skedaddle in a dress. You'll need to take your children and sister out under a white flag."

Alex McSween appeared mortified. "What about me?"

Billy showed the lawyer a hard smile. "If you think they'll let you give up, go ahead."

"What do you mean?" McSween chirped.

Billy gave the man a doubtful look. "You really think Dolan will let you live?"

McSween's brow lined like a rutted road. He looked at his wife but said nothing.

Billy pulled a white kitchen rag from a drying bar and tossed it to Mrs. McSween. "You need to get your family together and go out the front now. Hold up that flag and surrender to whoever's in charge of those soldiers. You goin' out on the street side will help us with the second part." He turned to Folliard. "Tom, you already heard the plan. Help her to get out the front, and then you skip back here with us pronto for the break."

Susan McSween kissed her husband and enfolded her children like a hen gathering her chicks under her wings. When Folliard led them down the hall toward the parlor, Billy put a hand on McSween's shoulder and squeezed to give him strength.

"Here's how it'll go," Billy continued, his eyes dancing now with excitement. "It's gettin' dark now. Me and Tom and you boys—" He pointed at two fellow Regulators and the clerk. "We're gonna bolt outta this door like jackrabbits and skin out through the gate." He turned to the clerk. "Can you run? You'll be the first one out."

"Why me?" the boy asked.

Billy hitched his head and winked. "First one's got the best chance. Nobody will be expecting you. We'll be right on your tail. So, what about it? Are you quick?"

The clerk swallowed, looked at McSween's misery, and then turned back to Billy. "I will be tonight."

"What about the rest of us?" McSween whined.

Billy leveled his finger at the lawyer. "After we go, wait exactly fifteen seconds. Then run for the gate out back. That will give those boys out there time to empty their guns at us as we scramble down the hill, cross the river, and scatter out on the flats."

"Where should *we* go?" McSween begged.

Billy pressed his lips together tightly and nodded as the answer to the question came to him. "They'll prob'ly go after us . . . at least to the edge of the drop-off. Stay on this side of the river . . . close to the buildings. See can you get down to the Ellis store. Maybe they can hide you down there."

When the time came to open the door, Billy had to use a towel to turn the hot doorknob. Pushed out by Billy, the clerk sprinted out into the yard, now bright from the flames leaping from the roof of the building. Billy and Tom were next, followed by the other two Regulators.

As soon as the clerk reached the gate, gunfire exploded from the back end of the yard. The clerk went down like a sack of grain. Jumping over his body, Billy and the others started a dash for the trees, but when Billy recognized John Kinney near the McSween's chicken house, he stopped, took aim with his pistol, and fired off a round that caused Kinney to lurch backward and throw his hand to his face. Folliard took a stand next to Billy, and the two poured more shots into the crowd around Kinney.

"Let's go!" Billy yelled, and the two friends followed the other Regulators, skidding on their boot heels as they scraped down the slope toward the river. When they bottomed out, Folliard splashed through the water, climbed up the other bank, and turned to see Billy hesitating on the south bank.

"What're you doin'?" Folliard whispered across the narrow stream.

"Go on ahead and see can you pinch us a coupla horses." Billy pointed. "There's a contrary old Dutchman keeps a remuda at the base of that mountain." He shifted the aim of his finger east. "I'll meet you at the little crook in the river right past that orchard."

"What're you gonna do?" Folliard pressed.

"Just go on and do what I say. I'll be there."

The boy lit out across the flats in the night, weaving through the dark shapes of juniper trees that dotted the valley bottom. Billy turned around to see a surreal orange glow lighting up the trees between him and the fire at McSween's. The ribbon of forest next to the river was cast in stark black silhouette. No one had followed them down the hill. At least a minute had passed since they had escaped the mad volley that had ripped through the air all around them. All was quiet now up the hill.

After pushing fresh loads into his pistol, he scaled the incline. When he was close enough to see the fence and the clerk's still body, he knew something was not right. The smoke from the burning building had swirled low and hidden the kitchen door, but Billy could make out McSween and the others in the shadows just outside the door.

"Jesus!" Billy hissed under his breath. "You missed your damned chance."

Just as those dark shapes began to venture out toward the gate, the surrounding gunmen opened up with a deafening barrage of rifle and pistol fire that riddled the adobe at the back of the house. McSween retreated back into the shadows, and the others followed.

When the gunfire stopped, McSween's voice called out in a high tenor that cracked on every other word. "This is Alexander McSween talking! I'm surrendering! I'm coming out! For God's sake, don't shoot me!"

True to his word, with his hands held high above his frazzled hair, he stepped out of the cloud of smoke into the fire-lit yard and moved cautiously toward his enemies. From the doorway four others followed his example. Then a shot was fired from somewhere, and right away a dozen more rounds erupted from the attackers. Even with raised hands, every man in the yard was cut down.

Billy watched McSween's body long enough to be sure he was dead. "You were just too well dressed for this party," he whispered and quietly started back down the hill. When he was halfway to the river, a riot of celebratory voices rose up from McSween's yard. The Seven Rivers boys sounded like a drunken crowd in a saloon, reveling over a round of free drinks.

"Sing on, you sonzabitches!" Billy muttered. "Pretty soon I'll teach you how to sing a dirge."

The siege at McSween's was thenceforth called "The Five Days War," and it marked the promotion of Billy Bonney to leader of the Tunstall loyalists. Doc Scurlock and Charlie Bowdre had called it quits and retired to their families at Fort Sumner. Though now reduced in number, the Regulators remained a hard-riding gang of brigands raiding the ranches allied with Dolan and stealing as much livestock as their party could handle.

Just to spite the enemy, some cattle were driven off into the brush or onto a friendly party's land. But all the horses were kept. Horses could be moved more quickly from one hiding place to another until they could be sold to the right buyer. Billy Bonney slipped effortlessly back into his former occupation as a full-time thief. The only thing different now was the level of his notoriety. Whenever the newspapers reported the revival of his criminal activities across the territory, they now referred to him as "Billy the Kid."

After Billy and the boys sold off a herd of horses in Tascosa, Texas, the Coe cousins struck out for Colorado, declaring their intent "to go straight." They might return, they said, once all the hatchets of the Lincoln County troubles were buried.

Dash Waite headed north to the Indian Territory to disappear inside the Choctaw nation. Others returned to former residences or previous jobs in Texas and Kansas, anywhere that put Lincoln County in their distant back trail. With Tom Folliard in tow, Billy rode back into the New Mexico Territory flush with money and with a smile on his face. He wanted nothing more than to see Paulita Maxwell . . . and to settle accounts for John Tunstall.

11
BLESSING'S NOTES
MAXWELL QUARTERS
OLD FORT SUMNER,
NEW MEXICO TERRITORY
JUNE 1886

"O, Billy, take the best of her and hold your head up high She taught you your good manners, but you'll still have to survive."

I have been loitering in Fort Sumner for days, waiting to get word from a paid informant, who is keeping an eye on Pete Maxwell so I know when he is away from his rooms in the old military compound. The last time I had stood face to face with Maxwell, he had casually picked up a shotgun to underscore the gravity of our conversation, so, naturally, I want to avoid the man. He did not strike me as particularly violent, but one never knows when family honor is at stake. He had made it very clear to me that he would not stand idly by if someone contrived a scandal that linked his sister, Paulita, to Billy Bonney.

Having breakfast at a cantina on the other end of the compound, I see my paid informant appear in the doorway and look anxiously around the room until his eyes fix on me. Without delay he approaches my table, stops, and removes his sombrero, which he holds before his midsection like a shield.

"Señor," he begins in a whisper, "Pedro . . . he go to Puerto de Luna today to make the sale for cattle. He comes back tonight."

I motion to the chair across from me. "Sit down."

He scans the room, as though considering the prudence of accepting my invitation, but then he sits and plops his hat in the empty chair beside him. When I push aside the plate of eggs

149

and fry bread to lean closer to the man, his longing eyes follow my unfinished breakfast.

"Who is left at his quarters?" I ask.

"*Su hermana,*" he replies. When I shake my head, he translates, "His sister, Paulita."

"Alone?"

"*Sí.* I think so."

As I stand, I loop my satchel strap over my shoulder, dig into my pocket, and bring out a clip of folded bills. Counting out our agreed amount, I place the money on the table before him. Then I peel away one more bill for the meal and leave it by the plate.

"Why you go see Paulita?" he asks, now squinting at me with a hint of suspicion.

I sit back down. "To talk to her about Billy Bonney."

He closes his eyes and shakes his head. "Thees I was afraid of." He leans in and looks deep into my eyes. "Is bad idea, Señor. She no talk about Bee-lee."

"You knew him?"

He waves a hand through the air, seeming to include all in the café. "We all knew him." Shaking his head again, he holds his gaze on me. "You only make her angry. No one talks to her about that." He grimaces. "And Pedro . . . if he find out—" He leaves the rest unsaid.

"Which is why I have hired your services over the last three days." I nod at the money laid in front of him. "I tried once to see her and was turned away. It's worth another try."

He shrugs as if dismissing me to a fate I have foolishly orchestrated for myself.

"You have been a big help," I say and rise again. "Thank you."

After staring at my plate, the man looks up at me. "You no finish to eat, Señor?"

I hesitate, not wanting to misconstrue the man's meaning and insult him, but there is no mistaking the yearning in his eyes. "Please, help yourself."

He stuffs his pay inside his blouse, reaches for the unfinished plate, and carefully sets it before him without a sound. At the door I glance back to see him hunched over, scraping the remains of my breakfast into a blue bandana.

It takes me less than two minutes to reach my destination. As I pass through Maxwell's gate and gain his porch, I hear a female voice humming inside a room to my left. Pausing to listen, I recognize the tune, and a wave of hope surges inside me. The simple melody of "Silver Threads Among the Gold" floats from an open window. I approach and listen through two verses of the song.

Perhaps, I convince myself, I have caught the obstinate Paulita Maxwell in a felicitous mood. I fervently hope my informant's facts are correct about her brother. Even though five years have passed since the Lincoln County troubles, I believe that an Anglo could still disappear in this sleepy Spanish village without leaving a clue as to his demise.

Not wanting to intrude on her privacy through an unconventional portal, I back away from the window to knock on the closest door. The humming stops, and footsteps approach the open window. The woman who leans out through the curtains has a full face just shy of plump. Hispanic features show on her face, but there is something else there, too—a hint of ethnicity for which I am not qualified to interpret. As she leans on the sill her arms appear strong yet smooth and feminine. Her eyes show no challenge at my presence, only the melancholy sag of one who has learned to live with her disappointments. I brace myself for the possibility of immediate eviction from her porch.

"Yes?"

"Hello," I say, and the subdued tone of my voice surprises

me. I did not want to be taken as an upbeat salesman, but neither do I mean to alienate her with the performance of a beggar. "Mrs. Jaramillo?" I inquire with an earnest smile.

"*¿Sí?*" Her brow creases to insist on an explanation for my presence.

I take off my hat. "My name is John Blessing." Glancing down at my shoes, I prepare myself for defeat. When I look up at her, I feel all my preparedness for this moment fade along with my smile. "I—"

" 'Blessing,' " she repeats. "You wrote the article about Bee-lee . . . the one that was kind."

I don't try for modesty. It would never sell here.

"Yes," I say. "Though I knew him only a short time, he was my friend." It seems this description of my relationship with Billy Bonney has become my rote response, yet it still contains the simplest truth I know.

"And you were his," she assures me, her expression now softening. I am so stunned as to feel lightheaded. She inspects the plaza behind me as if making sure we are alone, and then she nods toward the door. "I will come around."

Her footsteps circle through the house, and the door opens. Her smile is sad but welcoming. Stepping aside she swings the door wider.

"Come inside," she says ever so softly. "I have made fresh coffee."

"I would love some. The brew at the cantina left much to be desired."

She laughs quietly and closes the door. "Bee-lee used to say it tasted like the puddle left by a horse." She walks me deeper into the house. "Of course, he used more explicit words."

"I'm sure," I chuckle.

She stops and I with her. "Do you know what I said to *that*?" she says.

I smile and shake my head.

"I would say . . . 'and how would you know that, Bee-lee?' "

I chuckle again and nod.

"And do you know what *he* said to *that*?" she adds.

As I shake my head again, she makes a little flip of her hand from the wrist, as if fanning away a bothersome insect. It was something that Billy used to do.

"He would say . . . 'don't ask questions with answers you don't want to hear.' "

This time I laugh outright and try for something clever. "Well, I suppose a man can get quite thirsty between watering holes out on the desert."

She scrunches up her face into a comical scowl and shakes her head with tight little jerks. "Not that thirsty, let us hope."

Clasping my hands together before me, I cock my head and allow her to see my delight. "You're not at all like I imagined you would be, Mrs. Jaramillo."

She arches an eyebrow and shrugs. "Oh, I probably am," she admits. "But today is a good day." She makes a gesture with her head toward the back of the house. "I have the quarters to myself for most of the day. My brother is away on beez-ness."

"And here I am trespassing on your freedom," I offer, finding myself willing to abort my mission at the slightest prod from her.

Closing her eyes, she shakes her head quickly again. When she opens her eyes, I am surprised to see tears clinging to the lids like beads of water about to drip from a tree branch.

"I am thinking a lot about Bee-lee today," she confides.

I nod and look around the room, giving her time to compose herself. When I turn back to her, I see that the tears have left shining track marks down her plum cheeks. She stares at me with such facile sincerity that I find myself surrendering to complete honesty.

"I would love to talk to you about him. Would that be all right?"

Her moist eyes narrow as she gazes out the front window. "Does this mean you will put my words in a newspaper?"

"No. I am working on a book. I will use your words but reveal your name only if you give me permission," I assure her. "But, regardless, I want very much to learn more about Billy Bonney. I can always use your insights without revealing my source."

As she nods, fresh tears replace the vacated ones. She points over a low table to a sofa next to one wall. It is crudely put together and cushioned by a folded red blanket laid over a latticework of loosely woven ropes. Its coarse wooden frame shows the purple heartwood of split juniper.

"Please have a seat, and let me see about the coffee."

After she leaves the room, I drop my hat and satchel on the sofa and tour the walls, examining the homey items hanging there: portraits, a varnished wooden cross, a row of hats on a rack, books with Spanish and English titles, and a colorful tapestry that hangs from wooden pegs. No image of Billy here. But I did not expect to see such a thing in Pete Maxwell's abode.

When I sit on the sofa, the rope hammock beneath me groans with sharp little *ticks,* the sound like the cocking of a dozen pistols. I realize that beyond the wall and hallway behind me is the bedroom where Garrett killed Billy. A chill passes through me, rippling up my spine like ice water defying gravity.

My host returns with two ceramic mugs, both of which she sets on the low table before my shins. She pulls a chair to face me across the table. When she sits, we both lift our mugs and sip at the same time. I set mine back on the table, but she cradles hers in her lap.

"I visited Maria Herrera recently . . . in Texas. It was she who suggested I try to visit you again. Mrs. Jaramillo, I—"

"Please call me 'Paulita.' I grow weary of that surname. How is Maria?"

I drink more coffee and think about my answer. "Happy enough, I would say. She has five children and another on the way. She told me she misses your company."

Paulita lowers her eyes to the cup in her lap. "They were wise to go when they did." When she partakes of her coffee again, I summon the will to pry open the door she has cracked.

"Why did you and Billy not leave? It seemed inevitable what would happen if he stayed in the New Mexico Territory."

"Of course it was!" she snaps. "How could it end any other way?" She appears to hear the harshness in her voice, clears her throat, and starts again in a mellower tone. "Some have said that Bee-lee simply tried to fulfill that destiny . . . as if he had no choice."

"But you don't believe that," I venture flatly.

She shakes her head. "Bee-lee believed no more in destiny than he did in the good intentions of the *politicos* in Santa Fe. He knew that he 'made up his life on the fly.' That was the phrase he would use. He once told me . . . it goes something like thees: 'Living here in this territory is like riding a horse stolen from the devil's remuda . . . and fighting it all the way . . . just trying to hold it on the straight and narrow.' "

I consider opening my satchel for my writing supplies, but I feel the gesture would be somehow insulting. "So, why do you think he stayed too long?"

She gives me a crooked smile. "I know what everyone says . . . that it was for me. But I begged him to leave. I would have gone with him anywhere . . . to start over in a new place where no one knew him." She begins to shake her head slowly. "That last night . . . we talked about Chihuahua . . . but we did not know that it was already too late." She sweeps a hand toward the wall behind me. "Pat Garrett was right here . . . waiting for Bee-lee."

155

She stares at me for a time, her dark eyes seeming to penetrate to my soul. "You were here that night. I remember he talked about you."

"Yes," I say. "I was here." I point west down the plaza. "Staying in the soldiers' old barracks a few buildings down."

She nods. The silence that takes over the room is like a fragile rime of ice. I smile just enough to let her know that we share a common loss.

I clear my throat and keep my voice personable. "After the two of you were together that night . . . in the orchard . . . Billy and I talked for a while. He wanted to go to Mexico with you. He told me that."

Her sad smile remains in place, but her eyes appear to take on a hint of jealousy. "You were the last friend he saw that night." She turns her gaze to the window, and her expression softens. "He liked you. I think you were good for Bee-lee." She shakes her head. "But I don't think you understand Bee-lee's love of this land." Her gaze returns to me, inspecting me as if plumbing the depths of my ability to understand her words. "Bee-lee was swept up in the noisy part of New Mexico. That is how he is remembered by most. But he loved the gentle side of this land: the native people, our culture, our food, our music, our dances . . . our way of life." When she turns toward the window again, her profile is near angelic. "He became one of us, you know."

"I *do* know," I agree. I lean forward and turn my coffee mug in a slow circle on the table. "And I know you wanted a new life . . . for the two of you." When I look up at her, I see tears forming in her eyes again.

"Three of us," she corrects. "Maria told you, I suppose. I was carrying Bee-lee's child."

I look down at my coffee and nod. "Actually, Billy told me."

Sitting back against the sofa I am resigned to let her speak of this or not.

"The baby was steel-born," she explains quietly. "It was a girl. Bee-lee wanted to name her 'Catherine,' after his mother. Our little one came at the end of that summer when Bee-lee was killed." She breathes through her mouth as she continues to stare out the window. "It was, of course, a point of contention with my brother. He never approved of Bee-lee. And he despised my pregnancy. He was actually relieved when my baby arrived dead. He believed God had killed the child in the womb to spare our family name." Her eyes search mine with a heavy longing. "Can you imagine thinking such a thing?"

"I am sorry, Paulita."

For a time, she alternates sipping her coffee and staring out the window. "Bee-lee would have been the kind of father to spoil a child." She smiles. "But it would have brought out the best in him."

"Just like you did," I am bold to say. "He told me that himself."

Showing no surprise, she nods. "Yes, I know. He told me many times, and yet I knew it even before he realized it." She shrugs her head to one side. "I know he had other girls. They all loved him. How could they not? But I knew what we had was the gift that God gives only once."

I wait as she basks in the remembrance of her love. I can hardly believe that I have somehow, perhaps inadvertently, slipped past all the much talked about defenses she has employed to distance herself from journalists.

"All the writers who came to you," I begin, "they said you denied the whole affair . . . that it was nothing more than silly gossip invented to add a tragic romance to Billy's story."

Her mouth crimps into a knot of displeasure. "That was my brother's will. He forced me to say what I did. I was just a girl, and he was like an overbearing father. I never confided anything to him, but somehow he knew. I suppose a love conceived by God cannot be hidden." She lifts her chin in defiance. "Later, I married to get away from here." She looks at me quickly to read my reaction. "I know," she says, sighing. "That is a foolish reason to take a husband."

"Why are you here now . . . back at your brother's home?"

"I have many relatives and friends here. I have missed them." She picks up my mug and stands. "May I warm this for you?"

"Please."

While she is in the kitchen, I stand to stretch my legs and return to the photographic portraits on the far wall. Close to the window, on a small shelf by itself, a tintype tilts on its free-standing frame. Leaning closer to the image I recognize the very man who had repulsed my efforts to interview Paulita Maxwell after Billy's death. Pedro "Pete" Maxwell looks quite different wearing a smile. Next to him, sporting a similar expression of satisfaction, stands former Governor Axtell, the top-ranking official of the New Mexico Territory throughout most of the Lincoln County War. I realize now that, in the photo, the two men are standing in the Palace of the Governors in Santa Fe.

"My brother was not above consorting with the vile and corrupt," Paulita says behind me. I turn and take the coffee mug she offers. "Apparently, he has no shame."

"I knew the governor through my newspaper work," I say in a tone that suggests I have shaken hands with the devil. "He was a smooth one. I was never so happy as to see Axtell *axed* by President Hayes."

She scowls at the tintype. "Look at them. Two of a kind." Then she huffs a laugh. "Axtell was never for the people. He was interested only in filling his own pockets."

I cock my head just so and attempt to clip my words just as Billy did. "Crooked-er than the hind leg of a crippled ki-yote."

She smiles at my pitiful impersonation. "Yes," she says, and her eyes are still smiling over her cup as she drinks. Lowering her cup, she fixes her condemning gaze back on the photograph. "But the man who replaced him was, in his own way, no better."

"Well, he wrote a fine book," I contend, "but he was certainly no friend to Billy."

"Lew Wallace has no honor," Paulita declares in a menacing monotone. "He made a deal with Bee-lee, and then he broke his word."

"Yes, I know all about that. I was with Billy when he wrote to Wallace from jail. In fact, I posted a letter for him."

Disgust takes over her face. "Wallace, too, cared nothing for New Mexico. He just came here to go through the motions of his job while he wrote that book." She sets her jaw at a formidable angle. "He could have saved Bee-lee." Turning away, she returns to her chair and sits. I follow and take my place on the creaky sofa.

"Do you understand what it took for Bee-lee to try and make peace with Dolan?" She looks at me, expecting an answer.

"I can only imagine," I say.

She turns her head to the window and narrows her eyes. "Wallace called for all men in Lincoln to lay down their weapons and stop the fighting. Bee-lee and the ones who rode with him came into Lincoln and shook hands with the devil, himself— Mr. James Dolan. Dolan had all of his trash with him—his hired thieves and murderers. They all agreed to a truce and made a pact that no one of them would ever testify against any other. It was, perhaps, the hardest thing Bee-lee ever did here in the territory." Her eyes film over with tears. "And he did this for me. I asked him to do it."

I nod. "That was admirable of him."

"No. It was foolish. It only led to more trouble. And it was my fault." She makes a scornful smile and shakes her head. "After they shook hands, Dolan took the crowd into a saloon and bought drinks for everyone. Bee-lee, of course, did not drink, so he was the only one there who was thinking straight. Right in front of everyone, Dolan picked a fight with a lawyer—a man named Chapman—who had worked against him in a court proceeding. Dolan and his men tried to force Chapman to dance, but the lawyer would not lower himself to the indignity. And for his principles, this man—not even carrying a gun—was shot dead."

I nod. "Billy told me about it. This was the murder that Billy told Wallace he would testify about in court . . . to get Dolan prosecuted. In exchange, Wallace promised amnesty."

Paulita tilts toward me to drive home her point. "Yes, Wallace promised. Bee-lee testified, and, in so doing, he broke the oath he had agreed to with Dolan. And then Wallace turned his back on Bee-lee. The famous man who wrote the book about the Christ was a hypocrite and a liar."

"And Billy Bonney became the most wanted man in New Mexico," I say, stating the obvious. "Not only by the law . . . but by Dolan's mercenaries."

The skin on her face tightens. "It all could have ended there," she says in a steely voice, "if Wallace had kept his word. More than two hundred indictments were brought against the Dolan men." She shakes her head. "Two hundred!" she repeats and fixes her sad eyes on me. "And all dismissed, or misfiled, or pardoned . . . all but one."

"Billy Bonney's," I say.

Closing her eyes, she inhales deeply and lets her breath ease out. "If there *is* a road called 'destiny,' that was when Billy began to travel down it."

"Like a moth circling closer to the flame," I venture.

She wrinkles her face and shakes her head. "I would not

compare Pat Garrett to a flame. He is too dark." She glances at the wall behind me. "That is why Bee-lee could not see him that night." She gestures toward the window. "There was a full moon. I remember it well." Scowling, she glares at the wall behind me. "But inside that room, there was too much darkness . . . both from Garrett and from my brother."

A silence settles around us in the room. Outside, two men can be heard laughing somewhere down the road. Then their voices fade as they move away from us.

"Billy and I were talking together in the soldiers' bunkhouse," I whisper. "This was after the two of you had met in the orchard. He left me to get something to eat. I heard the shots, and somehow I knew. I'd never felt such loss in all my life."

She wears a sad smile as she nods. "It was the same for me. Somehow *I* knew."

Three loud knocks rattle the door. For just an instant, Paulita and I look at each other like conspirators caught in a secret rendezvous. She rises and starts to say something to me. Instead, she raises her chin and walks to the door with the nobility of a queen. When she pulls the door open, I see a short, stout Mexican man removing his wide hat. His chest is broad, and his thick hands show a history of manual labor. His bronze and rugged face is marked by a pale scar on one cheek.

"Señora?" he says, looking past her to steal a look at me. "*¿Está todo bien?*"

"*Sí*, Marcos. *¿Por qué me estás preguntando esto?*"

Folding her arms before her, she presents a formidable barrier, even when viewed from the back. The man frowns at me, but Paulita's stoic demeanor draws his attention back to her as if she has cracked a whip.

"I have a guest! *Un invitado!* What is it you want?

The man turns his hat by increments before him, like a wheel tentatively rolling, going nowhere. "*El jefe . . . él dice que nadie debe molestarte.*"

"No one bothers me, Marcos. When you go back to the corral, I would like you to bring in the blue roan for saddling."

"*¿El qué?*"

"*El azul roan,*" she instructs.

Wearing a troubled expression, he shifts his weight from side to side. "Señor Maxwell . . . he say I no let you ride alone."

"I *want* to ride alone," she announces. "And I *will!*"

From the sofa I can't see her face, but I see the man flinch.

"Señora, *por favor*—"

"Marcos," she interrupts, "do you know who is in charge here when my brother is gone?"

When his face contorts into a mask of wrinkles, she speaks again more sharply in their native tongue. I assume she is repeating the question. Marcos props his big hands on his hips and looks away to one side, his eyes glazed over as if seeing nothing. When he turns back to her, he appears desperate.

"Señora, when he come back, he be the *jefe* again, and he fire me. We ride now, *sí?* I have *mucho* work to do before the *jefe* return."

She stares at the miserable man for three more beats and then turns to me. "Mr. Blessing, I must take some herbs to a woman who lives near the river. It appears I must go *now*. I am sorry."

Standing, I loop my satchel strap over my head and do my best to hide my disappointment. "You have been very kind, Paulita. It has been a great pleasure to talk with you." She waits for me at the door, where we shake hands.

As I exit the building, I am surprised to see my rented horse saddled with my valise lashed behind the cantle. Stopping on the porch, I try to sort out my confusion. Not only has someone retrieved my horse and tack from the livery but also packed the belongings I had left in my rented room. For an answer I look to the hired hand, who stands by the gate waiting for me.

"You still owe the innkeeper," the leathery man says. "You are paid at the stable."

Feeling violated, I walk toward him at a crisp pace. "How do I know you collected all my things in my room?"

One of his big hands takes an iron grip on my upper arm, and he escorts me rather roughly to my horse. "You no come back," he growls in a sandy whisper. "*¿Comprendes?*"

"Marcos!" Paulita calls in a sharp tone. "This man is my guest!"

I try to jerk my arm free, but this brings no results other than a bright pain that sears to the bone from elbow to shoulder. This man, Marcos, has clearly run out of patience. He fairly lifts me into the saddle onehandedly.

"Marcos!" Paulita snaps, her face now inflamed with color.

"Señora Paulita," Marcos says, raising his voice. "I will have our horses here *en dos minutos*. We leave then for the Pecos."

Fuming, she stares at the man as he turns my horse to point north toward the room I had rented. "Mr. Blessing?" she calls out. "Use anything you want from our conversation, do you hear? Anything! And my name with it!" She raises a hand. "Good luck to you!"

Marcos hands me my reins and looks up at me with the eyes of a rattlesnake. When he speaks through his teeth, his lips barely move.

"The only luck you need is if you come back here." And with that final advice, he slaps the rump of my mount, prompting the horse to jolt into a startled run. It is an ignominious exit I must endure, but I am leaving Fort Sumner with much more than I had hoped for.

12

SQUIRE WILSON'S JACAL
AND THE PATRÓN STORE
LINCOLN, NEW MEXICO TERRITORY
MARCH 1879

"O, Billy, *mi amigo,* can your soul be really saved? They say
you killed for pleasure and then spat upon their graves."

Sitting in one of the three straight-back chairs that had been
brought over from the courthouse, Governor Lew Wallace
crossed one leg over the other, sipped his coffee, and looked
straight ahead at the rough boards on the far wall of the crude
jacal that attached to Justice of the Peace Wilson's adobe. With
only one lamp burning, there was more shadow than light in
the simply furnished room. The governor's face showed a bright
coppery line etched along the craggy angle of one cheekbone.
Even when relaxing in a chair, with his low brow, sharp eyes,
and aquiline nose, he displayed the fierce look of a predator.

"You know him," Wallace said, his stiff beard bobbing with
each word. "Do you think he will come?"

Old Judge Wilson settled into a second chair next to the table
with the lamp, leaving the third and final chair conspicuously
empty. "I think so . . . unless, of course, he encounters one of
Dolan's men somewhere out there. If so, he may suspect a trap."

Wallace coughed up a quiet laugh from deep in his chest.
"So . . . he can trust thieves and murderers like Jesse Evans but
not his governor?" He drank more coffee, pulled his watch from
his vest pocket, and pried open the cover with his thumb.

"I dare say Bonney never trusted Jesse Evans either,
Governor," Wilson argued. "Even when he rode with him. You
have to understand, Billy is not like Evans or Kinney or any of

164

that class of cold-blooded killers."

Wallace turned scornful eyes on the justice. "You don't consider assassinating a sheriff . . . from ambush . . . on the main street of Lincoln . . . to be cold-blooded murder?"

The old man raised his head as if he were to deliver a verdict at a trial. "On the surface, perhaps. But keep in mind that Sheriff Brady orchestrated the foul murder of John Tunstall." Wilson nodded once, as though convincing himself that his words had merit. "Tunstall had been good to the Kid . . . and the Kid has always been loyal to the Englishman."

Wincing at the justice's impromptu editorial, Wallace glared at his host. "You do not sound much like an officer of the court, Mr. Wilson."

Wilson shrugged. "And, with all due respect, sir, you have not lived in Lincoln."

The governor uncrossed his legs, letting his boot hit the floor with disapproval. "No one in this territory has reason to doubt my word, sir. I dare say I have a reputation to uphold."

Squirming in his seat, Wilson cleared his throat. "You have to remember, Governor, our previous territorial executives left much to be desired in the area of trust."

When Wallace made no reply, Wilson leaned on the table and began needlessly adjusting the wick on the lamp. "You know, Governor, some men come into office with the daunting task of filling the big shoes of their predecessor. In your case, I think you're going to have to show people that your shoes walked right over Axtell to get where you are."

Wallace frowned at the metaphor. "You think I should have blood on my boots? Is that it?"

The old adjudicator lifted his eyebrows. "You got *that* when you walked into Lincoln." He hitched a thumb toward the main thoroughfare. "Probably been as much killing out on that street as you saw at Shiloh."

Wallace gave the man a tired look. "I can assure you not."

"Well, maybe not. But that's the way it feels to us here in Lincoln. It's different when it happens in your own front yard."

Two quiet raps sounded at the door. Wilson looked to the governor for instructions, but Wallace kept his gaze fixed on the door.

"Come in!" Wilson called out.

For several seconds nothing happened. Then the latch tripped, and the door swung open a scant few inches.

"Somebody wanna tell me who's in there?" a whispery voice said.

"It's Squire Wilson, Billy," the justice announced. "And the governor. No one else."

The crack in the doorway remained unchanged. "I'd like to hear it from him, if you don't mind."

The governor appeared to be irritated about talking to a door. "I'm Lew Wallace," he snapped, his voice chiming with the rarefied importance of his office. "Governor of the New Mexico Territory."

A sharp tap started the door into a slow swing on its hinges. All that could be seen from inside the room was the barrel of a Winchester repeater pushing the door and widening the dark entrance way. Then the rifle retreated out of view, and footsteps could be heard scuffing in the sandy soil outside. The faint outline of a man could just be made out where he had backed up to peer into the room from the darkness.

When Billy entered the *jacal,* his rifle was leveled in his right hand and his revolver in his left. Using his boot, he closed the door. His eyes jumped by increments as he inspected the interior of the room. Then he pointed with the rifle, letting it swing in an arc toward town.

"Anybody else know we're here?"

"No, it's just the three of us," Wilson assured him. The old man stood and extended an arm toward Lew Wallace. "Billy, Governor Wallace has come in good faith."

Billy laughed. "Good to know there's still some o' that goin' 'round."

Wallace remained seated as he studied the boy from slouch hat to scuffed boots. When he looked into Billy's blue eyes, Wallace's face hardened.

"I'd like to have this talk without a gun pointed at my head."

Billy maintained his pose as he raised his chin toward Wilson. "This on the square?"

The justice positioned the third chair for Billy, turning it to face the governor. "It is, son. We're here to talk."

Wilson sat. Billy remained by the door.

After leaning his rifle against the wall, Billy holstered his pistol and stepped to the back of the vacant chair. Setting his hands on the backrest and leaning on the chair, he faced Wallace.

"You want me to testify against Dolan, right? Well, I want to hear it from you face to face: I get a full pardon for anything you think I might've done in the past. Is that about it?"

Wallace stood and approached until the empty chair was the only thing between them. "That is exactly it," the governor said. "Help me with your testimony, and you will go scot-free."

Billy narrowed one eye and tilted his head. "And you'll put that in writin'?"

"I will," Wallace replied. "It will be an official notice of amnesty. You can carry it in your pocket."

Billy held out his slender hand. "Will you shake on that?"

Wallace appeared amused by the formality, but he clasped the offered hand and pumped it once. Then the governor returned to his chair and sat. Billy pointed at Wilson, causing the old man to sit up straighter and widen his eyes.

"You remember this. You're a witness to this agreement.

¿Comprendes?"

"Indeed I am a witness," the justice assured him. "Now can we get down to business? I don't like late meetings like this in the dark. I should be in bed."

Billy lifted the chair, spun it a half turn, and straddled it, all in one smooth motion. Stacking his forearms on top of the backrest, he gave all his attention to the governor.

"So, tell me how this will work."

Wallace hooked one leg over the other and clasped his fingers together around the top knee. "You say that you were there when Chapman, the attorney, was killed?"

Billy nodded. "Just about as close as I am to you right now." He pointed over Wallace's shoulder. "Right out there in the street."

Wallace pivoted his head a few degrees, looking at Billy from an angle. "And you say Dolan murdered him?"

"You're damned right I say it! It's what happened! With Jesse Evans and Billy Campbell bullyin' the poor man, Dolan shot him from so close it set his shirt to smolderin'!" Billy turned to Wilson to finish his report. "Then Dolan led all of us up to Mc-Cullum's for drinks. Inside he gave me a little Smith and Wesson pocket pistol . . . tol' me to put it in the dead man's hand . . . to make it look like self-defense."

Wilson produced a grim smile. "That sounds like Dolan. He wanted you implicated."

"And did you take the gun?" Wallace asked.

Billy scowled. "I took the gun, yeah, as a reason to get outta there. But I didn't go near that dead lawyer. By then that whole crowd was loco on hooch, so we skinned out . . . me an' Tom Folliard."

Wallace unclasped his hands long enough to point a finger at Billy. "If you'll testify to that in a court of law, we can put Mr. Dolan right where he belongs."

Billy's brow tightened as he looked from one man to the other. "Well, how're you gonna keep me from gettin' killed durin' all this?" He flung an arm toward the sleeping town. "If I stand against Dolan in court, there's fifty men out there who'll be after my hide."

"We'll arrange an arrest," Wallace said. He uncrossed his legs and sat forward, his hands propped on his skinny knees and his bony elbows pointing east and west. "It will be for appearances only . . . we'll ask Sheriff Kimbrell to do it. Can you yield to him?"

Pushing out his lower lip, Billy thought for a moment and slapped his fingers on the back of his chair with a snappy rhythm. "Yeah, I can trust Kimbrell. But I'm not goin' back down in that hellhole of a cell again. The Lincoln jail's not fit for any kind o' man, no matter what he's done. Besides, if Dolan's men were to break in there, I wouldn' stand a chance. I'd be caught like a 'possum in a trash barrel."

Wallace nodded. "We'll make other arrangements. I've seen the jail pit, and I agree. It is unconscionable."

The three men stared at one another, Wallace wearing a haughty frown with his head held high, Wilson slouching as he pulled at his whiskers, and Billy astride his chair like a horseman on a pony with no go. The quiet of the room was absolute but for the soft wheeze of Justice Wilson's breathing. Outside, the broad valley of the Bonito was so still that the light chirr of crickets seemed less a sound than a texture of the night.

"One more thing," Billy said as he pointed a forefinger at Wallace. "I want a pardon for Tom Folliard, too." When the governor hesitated and exchanged a glance with Wilson, Billy added, "It's both o' us or nothin'."

Wallace straightened his arms and sat erect. "All right. Agreed."

Billy nodded once and smiled. "All right then! So, how do we get this ball rollin'?"

Wallace leaned back in his chair with a sober expression. "First of all, I want no one to know about our meeting tonight. To that end, we'll set up the arrest away from Lincoln. Where did you ride in from today?"

Billy hesitated, looked down at his boots, and rubbed the back of his neck. "San Patricio," he said finally and checked Wallace's face for the trust he needed.

Wallace nodded once. "All right, in three days we'll send Sheriff Kimbrell there to collect you and your friend. Meanwhile, we will select a place here in Lincoln where the two of you will be under house arrest. I will make sure you have plenty of guards to protect you."

"How many is 'plenty'?" asked Billy.

Wallace appeared irked by the question. "As many as the sheriff can muster, I suppose. Three or four? I don't know."

Billy laughed. "In that case, Tom and I will hold on to our guns while we're in custody. I don't mind dyin' in a standup fight, but I won't be shot down like a mad dog chained to a tree."

Wallace allowed a self-righteous smile. "Any other mandates, Mr. Bonney?"

Billy stood and cocked his head to one side. "I got to know I can depend on you to deliver what you say."

Wallace stood, gripped the front hem of his vest with both hands, and straightened the material with a smart snap downward. "I am the governor of the territory, son."

Billy showed him a crooked smile. "Yeah . . . well . . . that's why I'm askin'."

Wallace sniffed sharply. "I will have to trust you to do what you say . . . and you must trust me." When that assessment got no response from the boy, Wallace put some iron in his voice. "Can't you see I'm trying to cut out all the corruption from our territorial government?"

Billy held on to his smile and tilted his head to one side. "I'm just tryin' to understand what you could lose in all this if it don't go the way you say. I know what I'll lose."

Groaning with the effort, Wilson pushed himself up from his chair. "Billy, President Hayes himself revoked Axtell's position and gave it to Governor Wallace to clean up Santa Fe and Lincoln. If we can't trust that . . . then Lord help us!"

Billy backed to the door and picked up his rifle. "I ain't so sure the Lord even knows where Lincoln County is." He looked from one man to the other and then settled his gaze on Wallace. "Guess I'll have to depend on you to be a stand-up man."

Standing erect, the governor hooked his thumbs in the pockets of his vest. "So be it."

After the Kid had slipped out into the dark, Wallace and Wilson stood for a time, their eyes fixed on the closed door. Billy's footsteps moved away from the *jacal* toward the rear of the courthouse. When there was nothing more to be heard, Wallace turned to the justice.

"Well, what do you think?"

Wilson exhaled a long sigh. "I think we'd better make sure this plan works as you've laid it out. Otherwise, there will be hell to pay."

Wallace snorted. "The devil's due. I faced it many times during the war."

"Well," Wilson said, lifting the lamp and carrying it to the door, "I guess it's good you've had the practice, because this here is a war, too."

Wallace lifted his coat from the back of his chair and crossed the room to stand by Wilson. "So I keep being told," he said and pushed his arms into his coat sleeves. "Better snuff that light before we go out."

★ ★ ★ ★ ★

In four days' time Sheriff Kimbrell and three deputies brought Billy Bonney and Tom Folliard from San Patricio into Lincoln under cover of night. As pre-arranged, they housed the two "prisoners" in a supply shed attached to the Patrón house. There the two detainees enjoyed gracious meals, free cigars, and daily poker games with the staff and friends of the casa. Only one deputy kept watch outside, a man Billy considered merely an expendable watchdog. If an attack came, Billy knew, it would begin with a single gunshot directed at this guard. The warning shot would suffice, giving Billy and Tom time to take their planned defensive positions.

Two days into their layover at the Patrón casa, in the late afternoon, Billy whistled a tune as he cleaned his .44 revolver at the table that served for meals and cards. A single lamp lighted the windowless room. Folliard forked strips of meat from a skillet he had set over the coals of the brazier Patrón had supplied. Taking a seat at the table, Tom ate and watched Billy run a rag through the chambers of the Colt's cylinder.

"Billy," Tom said around a hot mouthful. He sucked in a sharp intake of air through his mouth, trying to cool the food before chewing. "No offense to your music tastes, you understand, but you *got* to learn another song. I believe you come close to wearin' that one out."

Still whistling, Billy continued his work as if he had not heard. When he had rubbed a light sheen of oil over the exterior of the cylinder, he set it down and narrowed his eyes at the Colt's strapped to Folliard's side.

"Tom, when're you gonna replace that damn pistol of yours?"

Folliard had started to stuff more meat into his mouth, but he froze with a look that bordered on indignation. "Hell, it's the same as you carry! What's wrong with it? I like it." He frowned down at his gun and carried that frown back to Billy. "It ain't never failed me yet. Why mess with somethin' good?"

Billy smiled and ran the rag along the frame of his pistol. "Yeah, I like my song, too." He picked up his place in the song and whistled as he set the cylinder inside the frame.

A hard knock on the door turned their heads. Billy laid down his Colt's revolver on the table, wiped his hands with a clean cloth, and pulled his backup pistol from his belt.

"You got comp'ny!" someone called from outside.

Recognizing the deputy's voice, Billy rose. "Well, send 'er in!" he returned happily.

The lock *clacked.* Governor Wallace entered the room and closed the door behind him. Billy and Tom stared at the man as he studied the perimeter of the room.

"It looks as though you are well provisioned," the governor observed.

Billy pocketed the revolver and smiled at Folliard. "Tom, meet the gov'nor."

Wide eyed, Folliard stuffed a piece of meat into his mouth and, wiping his hands on the sides of his trousers, stood. "How do, sir?"

Wallace nodded and sat in one of the chairs at the table. After glancing at the array of disassembled parts of the gun spread out on the newspaper, he cleared his throat and arranged the front of his coat to hang evenly at his sides.

"How are you men holding up here?"

Billy sat. "We're gettin' fat an' lazy, Gov'nor, but I reckon I shouldn' complain. I'm gettin' rich playin' poker with young Tom here." He laughed. "Or at least I would be if he had any more money to lose."

Wallace ignored the jest and brought out writing paper and pencil from the pocket of his coat. "Let's get started with our business," he huffed. "I want to get some information from you about a few things."

Tom settled back in his chair and fairly sat at attention. Billy gave him a wink.

"One—" Wallace began. "I want to know about the routes that are used by Jesse Evans and his gang for spiriting away stolen cattle through the Seven Rivers area. Two, I need the names of every man who rode in the party that killed Tunstall. Three, I want the names of other men who were witness to the Chapman murder." With the fourth ultimatum, he turned hard eyes on Billy. "And last, I'll need to hear all the details about Sheriff Brady's death."

Billy smiled throughout the listing of demands and began a performance of his own. "Like I told you, Tom, we can speak freely with the gov'nor here, 'cause he's gonna give us our amnesty on paper." As he said this, he angled his eyes to Wallace. "Only trouble is . . . we ain't seen that paper yet." He pointed at the sheets Wallace had placed on the table. "Maybe they're in that stack there?"

Wallace frowned and shook his head. "I cannot issue such a document until I receive all the information satisfactory to our arrangement. The sooner I get what I need, the sooner you get what you need."

Billy crossed his arms. "Well, let's get to it, presto-changeo! Where do you wanna start?"

They conversed into the night, their muted voices punctuated from time to time by Tom Folliard's laugh whenever Billy donated a joke to Wallace's somber interrogatives. The governor took notes with his spine erect and chin up so that his eyes had to angle down sharply to follow his scribblings across the page.

Just as the subject turned to the shooting of Brady, a small band of musicians struck up a quiet performance outside. After a brief introduction by guitar, violin, and *guitarron,* a somber tenor voice sent Spanish lyrics aborning in the night.

"What the devil is that?" Wallace said, twisting in his seat.

Billy listened for a time. "Well, that one is about a horseman who crosses this broad prairie every night to be with his *amor verdadero.*" He smiled. "It's one of my favorites."

Tom squinted one eye. "His '*amor*' what?"

Billy tapped his fist to his heart. "His true love, son." He turned to smile at Wallace. "That's our lullaby, Gov'nor. We got one last night, too."

"You arranged this?" Wallace asked, his face drawn with disapproval.

Billy laughed. "No, sir, not me. I still got friends here, you know . . . most of 'em Mexican." He spread his hands with the obvious. "It's one o' their admirable traits. Wherever there are Hispanic folks, there's gonna be music."

Wallace closed his eyes and shook his head. "We agreed you would be anonymous here."

Billy shrugged. "I reckon it's better to be anonymous *with* some music than *without* it."

Wallace collected his papers and stood. "We'll finish this another time. I don't like the idea of drawing attention like this." He put away the papers and hesitated. "It's taking time to arrange all the indictments," he said over the music outside the door. "We have over a hundred already. Three of those are against Dolan himself."

Billy's face sobered, his dark-blue eyes hard as ice. "And you'll be there alongside us when we testify, right?"

The music outside came to an end, and the silence was like a stage curtain opening on the governor's answer. "Yes, of course, I'll be there," he said and sniffed.

Billy raised an eyebrow. "And when do we get that amnesty paper?"

"First things first," Wallace reminded, as he walked to the door. There he knocked for the guard and turned back to the young outlaws. "After your testimony, we'll draft the papers."

He stuffed his hands into his coat pockets. "You'll just have to continue to trust me, gentlemen." The lock tripped, and the door opened. "I must go now. I'm meeting with the prosecutor."

Wallace was halfway out the door when Billy called his name. The governor stopped with an impatient tic pulling at one corner of his eye.

"You're not goin' to tell those musicians to cease and desist, are you? It gets a mite lonely shacked up in this place. It's 'bout all we got to keep our spirits up . . . 'specially for Tom . . . now that I won all his money in poker."

Wallace thought about it for two seconds. "If you want the music . . . so be it." And with that he left.

When they heard the lock turn in the door, Billy sat and resumed his work on his gun. Folliard watched him set the base pin and secure the cylinder.

"You think he'll stick?" Tom whispered.

Billy spun the cylinder through a flurry of well-oiled *ticks*. "There ain't nobody else with the sand to testify. I reckon that's why he'll stick with us."

Tom leaned forward, propping his forearms on the table. "He won't really look us in the eye 'less he's demandin' something from us. You notice that?"

"Yeah, I know." Billy laid down the pistol and stared at it. "But he's all we got." Showing none of his usual swagger, he looked up at Tom. " 'Least he's fought in a war. That oughta stand for somethin'."

Tom frowned. "But Wallace was a general, wasn' he? Don't that mean he watched all the fightin' from a distance?"

Billy conceded the point with his own frown. "I reckon so."

Folliard leaned in closer. "So why trust him, Billy?"

The Kid laughed. "Well, I gave my word, Tom." Shaking his head, he picked up the pistol and pushed it into its holster. "I saddled this crazy mustang. Reckon I'll have to ride 'er out.'"

Tom leaned low and craned his neck forward, trying to get into Billy's line of vision. "You don't owe Wallace nothin'. You can crawfish on a gov'nor easy as you can somebody like Jesse Evans."

Billy conjured up a weak smile. "It ain't my word to Wallace I'm talkin' 'bout. I promised Paulita."

Folliard pushed back from the table and stretched by arching his back, his fists reaching for the ceiling. "You reckon we'll get out of this alive?"

Billy's smile turned sly. "Ain't none o' us can do that, Tom. Just take 'er a day at a time."

Outside, the music started up again, a livelier tune with a melody that jumped around like a basket full of crickets. The singer's voice swept out all the gloom Wallace had left in the room, and Billy began tapping a boot to the tempo.

"Son, I need to hunt up a *baile* soon. It's been too damned long since I danced." He pointed at Folliard. "I still got to teach you how to step to a fandango with the señoritas."

Tom held up his hands, palms out. "You might as well try to teach a rock how to swim."

Billy laughed. "Hell, you can skim a rock across the face of a pond, can't you?"

Tom laughed and began stamping his boots, turning a circle on the floor as if he were making up for a lifetime deficit of dancing. Within seconds after he started whooping, a loud thumping sounded on the door, and the music stopped.

"You boys all right in there?" the deputy called out.

Billy cupped a hand beside his mouth to yell to the guard. "Ask those boys out there if they know how to play 'Silver Threads Among the Gold.' "

After a few moments the guitar strings strummed the familiar chords of the song's introduction, and soon the singer's soulful voice joined in, delivering the lyrics in English. Billy stretched his legs out straight, laced his fingers behind his head, and closed his eyes. Breathing open mouthed he looked as though he were inhaling the music. When the song came to its end, he raised his hands above his head and applauded.

"*¡Excelente!*" he called out. "*¡Juéguenlo una vez más, mis amigos!*"

This time the musicians played a slower version, the lyrics sung in Spanish. Billy shifted over to his bunk, lay on his back, and again closed his eyes.

"How come you like that song like you do, Billy?" Tom asked.

Without opening his eyes, Billy answered in a whisper. "You ever listen to the words?"

Tom frowned. "Sure . . . I guess. Ain't it just about gettin' old?"

Billy nodded. "That and still lovin' your woman . . . who is gettin' old, too."

The creases in Folliard's brow deepened. "What's so special 'bout gettin' old?"

Billy laughed quietly to himself. "Did you ever think we might not ever get there, pard? Might be we'll never find out what's special 'bout it."

When Billy said no more, Folliard raised the shield on the lamp and blew out the flame. He moved to his bunk on the opposite side of the room and lay down. His pistol and rifle lay beside him on the covers.

"Sleep light, amigo," Billy said. "We'll see if we can't make it to another sunrise and get at least another day older."

13
Blessing's Notes
Picacho Road, Southeast
of San Patricio
Lincoln County,
New Mexico Territory
July 1886

"But now I know your story and the justice that you sought You
may have been the only one whose soul could not be bought."

Picacho lies about twelve miles below San Patricio. Travelers by
horseback regularly make the trip in a half-day's ride, I am told.
But not I. Just an hour into my journey, without any warning,
my rented horse drops dead beneath me, and I am barely able
to pull my feet out of the stirrups in time to prevent being
pinned under the weight of the sudden corpse.

There is no feeling quite like having your horse go lifeless
underneath you as you perch upon its back. The experience
brings to mind the hangman's trap door falling away to the
weightless world beneath the boots of a condemned man.
Thankfully, no rope was noosed around my neck, and I was
able to squirm free during the collapse, though not gracefully I
am sure. In my acrobatics to reach safety, I have wrenched my
back and either broken or severely bruised my leg on the small
boulder upon which I chanced to land.

With the horse expired, I feel utterly alone. I sit for a while in
the dirt and gravel and decide to look beyond my own injuries
to consider my deceased travel companion. All at once I feel a
combination of guilt, empathy, and panic. I suppose I should
take some comfort in knowing that the animal need never again
carry the weight of a human being. For a beast of burden, death

is its emancipation proclamation, and if there is a place in heaven for these animals, I wish for them a room with a good view over the punier creatures called "men," who will be stabled in countless purgatorial stalls, no doubt, as they await judgment.

I feel utterly stranded. I have never considered such a twist of fate happening to me in my travels. What do people do in such a situation? I suppose this is why so many frontiersmen lead a pack horse loaded with supplies. In a pinch that extra animal could be promoted to top honors as a saddle horse.

Good fortune is with me. The rattling sound I hear down the trail smacks of divine intervention. The numbing vibration that has invaded my body from tailbone to shoulder blades is still humming when I spot a spring wagon drawn by two rusty-hued horses. A lone man sits upon the buckboard handling the reins. In the bed of the wagon a large wooden crate is lashed down by a network of ropes.

I do not try to rise. It is obvious the driver sees me and my dead horse blocking the road, as his face is lined with worry, and already he begins to pull back on the reins. When he stops, he leans forward, props his forearms on his thighs, and stares at my predicament.

"Was that animal shot?" he asks.

I push myself up on my feet. The buzzing inside my bones crescendos, but I mask the pain, not wanting this man to think any less of me than he already might. Apparently, my leg is not broken. Looking down at the deceased horse, I shake my head.

"It just died. I don't know why."

My savior has a friendly face, just starting to grow prematurely flaccid. A full tawny moustache almost hides his neighborly smile, but his eyes more than compensate with an amicable glow.

"Is it *your* horse?" he asks.

I shake my head. "I rented it at the livery in San Patricio."

"Chavez?"

"Yes. As far as I know, his is the only livery in town."

The driver's head bounces once with a quiet laugh. "Don't worry about it, then. Most of his nags are at death's door. If you press it, you can get your money back." His expression turns curious as he jabs a thumb over one shoulder. "You headed for Picacho?"

"I was. I suppose now I'm going wherever you are going, if I might impose on you."

"Glad to have you," he says in good cheer. "I get tired of my own company. Nothing new to talk about with yourself, you know. Name's George."

"John Blessing," I return.

He ties the reins around the brake handle and groans as he climbs down. "Let's see if we can get that saddle off 'er. We'll pile your gear in the wagon."

"Easier said than done" would be the appropriate phrase for this interlude. It takes us the better part of an hour to undress the animal, this project eventually requiring the use of his animals in rolling the corpse to free up the tack. With the task complete and my belongings loaded in the bed of the wagon, my new friend climbs up to his seat and unwraps the reins.

"What about the horse?" I say. "I don't know the protocol. Are we expected to bury it?"

"No, sir," George replies without a hint of sarcasm. "We leave her for the buzzards and ki-yotes." He considers the corpse, fills his cheeks with air, and expels it. "It would take us half a day to dig that hole, and what for? Ki-yotes would dig 'er up tonight anyway."

I frown at the poor animal. "It seems like there would be a horrific stench."

George chuckles. "You'd be right there. But you know how it

is . . . all things must pass."

Indeed, I think to myself as I look at the massive corpse. With George's few words serving as last rites for the poor animal, I climb up onto the board seat next to him.

"So are you headed to San Patricio?" I ask.

"Yep," he says and points to his freight. "Got to deliver these clothes to my wife's sister." George laughs. "I've outgrowed most o' my clothes, and now my brother-in-law wants them." With a light tap of the reins on the horses' backs, he starts us in the direction from which I have come. George shakes his head. "What the hell would men be without horses, I'd like to know?" The philosophical question does not burden him for long, as he points high into the northern sky. "Here they come. See there?"

I follow the aim of his finger and spot five dark shapes wheeling high above the land, like little flecks of charred paper swirling in a gentle vortex of wind. The circling vultures appear to be on the prowl, methodical and ominous in their silent hunt for carrion.

"Ever smell one up close?" he asks.

I wince and look at him. "A rotting horse?"

"No," he chuckles. "A turkey vulture." Again he blows air from inflated cheeks. "Hoo-whee! You'll not likely forget it if you get the chance." He seems to be talking from experience. "So, what is it you do?" he asks.

"I'm a writer. I'm working on a book about this territory."

He turns to study my face in earnest. "What did you say your name was?"

"Blessing . . . John Blessing."

His attention on me is so complete now that I look forward at the road up ahead, as if I may be of some help navigating.

"You're the one wrote about Billy Bonney in the newspaper a while back," he says.

"That's right," I say, feeling his gaze on the side of my face like the radiant heat from a stove.

"Well what are you doin' headin' down to Picacho?"

I lean in to speak over the jangle of the harnesses, the rattle of the wheels, and the thump of the horses' hooves in the sandy road. "I was hoping to interview a man there . . . a Judge Kimbrell."

He beams at me. "I'm George Kimbrell!"

I am astounded at my luck. "The same George Kimbrell who was sheriff in Lincoln?"

"The very same," he assures me.

By reflex, my hand moves to my satchel for paper and pen. "This is wonderful!" I blurt out. "It appears my horse died for a good cause."

Kimbrell narrows one eye. "I wouldn't put too much stock in the sacrifice of a poor old nag, Mr. Blessing. We would have met anyway . . . just a little farther down the road."

I feel my face redden. "Of course," I mumble. "I didn't mean to—"

"I'm pleased we crossed paths, however it happened. I remember your article about Bonney. I'd say you went beneath the Kid's devil-may-care smile and got to the heart of him."

"So you liked him?" I ask.

Kimbrell smiles. "I think everybody who met the Kid on friendly terms liked him." He nods at his assessment, but then his smile dissolves. "Except maybe Lew Wallace, that is." Beneath his moustache his upper lip curls to a sneer. "I think the great general must have sat down on his own sword after the war. He was a stiff sonovabitch. Thought he was walking around with his head a coupla feet higher in the air than the rest of us."

I hold up my writing utensils. "Do you mind if I write down some notes?"

Kimbrell shrugs. "Write away!" he laughs. "If you can manage it." As if to punctuate his challenge, one of the wagon wheels drops into a hole and jars us so that I lose contact with my seat for an instant.

"Judge Kimbrell, I do want to hear about Wallace, but first tell me a little about your relationship with Billy Bonney."

"This is going to go easier if you'll just call me 'George.' " His smile is endearing. "Can I call you 'John'?"

"Please do," I insist.

He flips both wrists and sends a double wave of leather rippling down the reins. The horses perk up their ears and pick up their pace but only for about ten strides. Then they settle back into their previous relaxed gait.

"Well," George begins, "I was for Tunstall from the start. Dolan and Brady had the people of Lincoln County under their thumbs, and it looked like Tunstall might save us from them. He was going to give us another option for merchandise and credit. I was glad the Englishman had the grit to challenge Dolan, but it was pretty clear from the outset which one was going to be the last man standing. I've never met a man more ruthless than Dolan."

Another wheel drops into a deep rut, and the lurch of the wagon sends my pen streaking down the paper to render a lightning bolt of ink running from Dolan's name. I can't help but wonder if this might be some kind of metaphysical symbol sent from the universe.

"So, yes, my sympathies were with the Regulators," he goes on. "As sheriff, I gave them as much of a wide berth as I could get away with. And, truth be told, I liked Billy Bonney a great deal. I played cards with him and Tom Folliard about every other night when they were detained at the Patrón house all that time they were waitin' for their trial."

"You were the one who captured Billy and brought him in, correct?"

Kimbrell chuckles to himself. "Well, I wouldn't say 'capture.' It was all a put-up job, you know. The governor gave me my orders and I followed them. Billy put up just enough resistance to make the arrest look legitimate, but once he was housed at Patrón's, he was a guest and as gentle as a lamb."

"Did you sit in on any of his meetings with the governor?"

He shakes his head. "Nope. Guess I wasn't important enough. But I met with each of them alone enough times that I'm satisfied I know exactly how those confabs went."

"Why did it all backfire?" I ask.

Kimbrell's friendly face darkens, and a sneer makes one side of his moustache twitch like the tail of a cat. "Wallace promised this, and Billy promised that," he says through clenched teeth. "Billy followed through. Wallace did not."

"Tell me about that," I prod.

He coughs up phlegm and spits it off to his side. "Well, Billy testified in court about Dolan killing the lawyer, Chapman. And he told all about the ambush on Tunstall and who was there doing the killin'. He spilled the beans on Jesse Evans and John Kinney and a lot of other riffraff that once infected this land. Wallace promised to pardon Billy in return, but he didn't."

"Why did Wallace go back on his word?"

Kimbrell scowls at the world. "Guess we'll never know that. He just up and left at some point during the trial. After he departed, the prosecutor laid into Billy with a vengeance. He picked apart everything Billy had sworn to, finally summing up the Kid by saying, 'A liar once is a liar a hundred times.' That really burned Billy up." Kimbrell narrows his eyes. "Tell you what I think. I think Wallace and the prosecutor worked the whole thing out between 'em. I don't think Lew Wallace ever intended to see Billy Bonney out loose in the world again."

Kimbrell is worked up now, his face red and his breathing labored. He stares straight ahead and clenches his jaw.

"All those indictments . . . over two hundred of them . . . and they were all dismissed . . . except for the ones against Billy." He spits off to the side. "There was a federal charge for the killing of Buckshot Roberts, on account of it happening at the Mescalero reservation. But Billy's lawyer proved it didn't happen within federal boundaries, and the case was thrown out. So then, they tried him for killing Sheriff Brady in Lincoln. As soon as Billy saw which way the wind was blowing, he did exactly what Wallace did. He just disappeared . . . him and Tom Folliard. They were only under house arrest, you see, so it was an easy task to slip away."

We roll along for a time without talking. The horses seem to be dedicated to the same easy walk. George digs a packet of tobacco from his shirt pocket, offers me some, which I decline, and partakes deftly using only one hand.

"You were the sheriff," I remind him. "Did the court expect you to go after Billy?"

" 'Course they did. And so I gathered up enough deputies to make a big show if it and took off as the dutiful sheriff pursuing a man I knew had been wronged by the governor himself. Well, one man that accompanied me in that posse was the prosecutor's hired gun, and he made me push things a bit. He got word that Billy was holed up at a big, two-story, abandoned house about six miles below Lincoln, so we surrounded the place and dug in for a long fight. I had men especially assigned to watch each of the doors and windows, and, when night came, we took turns at those posts so the guards would be alert."

I hear a low grumbling deep in my companion's chest, and I realize he is laughing.

"The next morning, we got no return fire," he continues. "When I yelled out for Billy, I got no reply. After a few hours of waiting, the man who had led us there got impatient and broke in through a window. We waited, expecting to hear gunshots any moment, as the man went room by room through the house. After a half hour, that uninvited posse man came striding out of the door, mad as a wildcat with a stick poked in its eye. 'He's gone!' he yelled, and some of us boys looked at each other and smiled."

Now George's grumbling laugh escalates to a steady chuckle. "Well, I remembered an old story I had heard about the Kid escaping from a jail when he was just a boy. So I went inside, lighted a lamp, crawled into the cold hearth, and stuck my head up the chimney. Sure enough, you could see scuff marks all over those sooty rocks. I'm betting the Kid looked like a Alabama darky 'bout the time he broke free at the top. It's no wonder we didn't see him. He woulda been black as the night. Prob'ly dropped off the house on the one side that had no windows. We had nobody watching there."

"Was that it?" I ask. "Did you stop chasing him?"

"That was it for me," he replies. "Billy and Folliard mostly stayed away from Lincoln. I reckon that was a favor to me. But they joined up with some reprobates and started rustling livestock again." He turns to me to check my reaction. "Ever hear of Dirty Dave Rudabaugh? Billy Wilson? Tom Pickett?"

"I met them all at the Santa Fe jail when I interviewed Billy. I must say Rudabaugh made my skin crawl."

George shakes his head in disgust. "Billy should never have partnered up with those buzzards. He told me one time, 'George, those boys were a mite dark for my taste. Can't say I ever really lined up with 'em, but they served a purpose . . . at least I thought so at the time. The truth is . . . those boys dug a deeper hole for me.' "

I write as fast as I can on the bouncy wagon. When I finish, I offer my own assessment.

"Billy said when they were on the outlaw trail, he would never sleep within thirty paces of Rudabaugh . . . and, even then, never with his back toward the man."

Kimbrell's mouth puckers as if he'd bitten into an unripe lemon. "Dave Rudabaugh was the worst kind of human being. The kind that makes you wonder why God would make such a man." He nods to the south, where the mountains of Mexico stand in a faint pink haze in the distance. "Just a few months ago, so the rumor goes, Rudabaugh was killed in a saloon in Chihuahua. I hear they hacked off his head with a machete, stuck it on a pole, and displayed it like a memorial in the center of town for all to see." He nods to me sharply. "That there tells you a lot about that man."

"So, you didn't go after Billy again?" I say.

"Nope. I wasn't sheriff much longer anyway. At the next election Pat Garrett rolled over me like a herd of hungry cattle headed for the feed lot. The higher-ups in Santa Fe wanted Billy the Kid gone for good, so they pulled some strings down here to get me ousted from my position." George shrugs at the memory. "And rightfully so. My heart was no longer in it. And Pat Garrett was probably the right man for the job. As soon as he pinned on the badge, it was just a matter of time for Billy."

Again we rattle along on the bumpy road without conversation. I try to imagine myself at nineteen, making a deal with the territorial governor, and being double-crossed in the bargain. It has been my experience that a young man does not forget a betrayal.

"You know?" says Kimbrell, his voice now almost whimsical. "If there ever was something like fate or destiny, it might have shown its face right there in that moment. Pat Garrett and Billy Bonney were going to cross paths at some point. They were like a couple of mountain lions claiming the same range for their hunting grounds. One was seasoned and single minded. The other was young but quick and full of tricks. The only question was: which one would prevail?"

"Whom did you bet on?" I ask.

George raises his chin and gazes off at the horizon. "I've never bet on such things. But I know what you're asking." He turns to me and winces. "Garrett can be a grim hunter . . . very businesslike. I would not want him after me. I knew him then almost as well as I knew Billy." Kimbrell looks down at his team of bays and shakes his head. "I don't think there was anyone to doubt that Garrett would kill Billy." He pivots his head to show me the pitiful smile of a complicated apology. "I guess I knew Billy's days were numbered." He turns back to his horses. "And my guess is . . . Billy knew it, too."

"Then why do you think Billy stayed around for that appointment?" I ask. "All he had to do was leave the territory."

Kimbrell studies the horizon as though some possession of his has been lost out there for years and he is still looking for it. "I asked my wife that question," he says in a dreamy voice. "She's Mex'can. Got the same name as Billy's girl—Paulita. They knew one another, so—" He maintains his glassy stare, but I don't believe he is seeing anything of the landscape. "I think he made this place his home. He wasn't going to let anyone run him out of his chosen place."

"So it was pride? That unspoken competition that exists between some men?"

Kimbrell shakes his head. "No, not that. For Billy, it was not about Garrett at all. It was about this land and the people who really belong on it. He loved the Mex'cans, you know."

I take my turn gazing at the horizon. Those mountains to the south have darkened a shade, now approaching violet. I imagine being a nineteen-year-old boy . . . without a family . . . carving out a place for myself in this hard land. When I spot a grassy plot of low ground near a creek, I imagine Billy stopping there to let his horse graze and drink. I see him dismount, splash a little water on his face, and then stretch out on his back on the grass to stare up at the sky. He is in no hurry. He has no destination. He is just being in the moment. A traveler free of obligation. An interloper accountable to no one. Exempt from time. A man simply but fully engaged in the act of being alive.

When I look up to see what Billy might have seen, the simple act of tilting my head back to inspect the heavens makes me wonder if God ever looked down on Billy Bonney and offered him the hand of mercy. Perhaps he did. Maybe that explains all those against-all-odds escapes he pulled off during his career.

When I look back at the grassy spot by the creek, he is gone. Like a ghost slipping into the scrub brush . . . leaving no trail. But the place is still charged with his presence. Perhaps the whole territory is. Maybe it is because he stayed and didn't run that this place he called home embraced him just as he embraced it. Perhaps his ghost will always ride these trails.

"Do you miss him?" I ask. "Do you miss seeing Billy?"

Kimbrell glances at me briefly, as if to see if my question is sincere. "Sure, I miss 'im." He looks down the length of the long canyon that the road follows. I sense that he has more to say, so I remain quiet. "But I feel like I still see 'im sometimes . . . just cresting a hill before going out of sight . . . or moving through the shadows down by the river . . . or across a room full of people at a baile." After a long pause, he turns his head to me. "Sounds crazy, don't it?"

I smile and shake my head. "No, it doesn't. It's not crazy at all."

14

Bob Hargrove's Saloon Old Fort Sumner, New Mexico Territory January 1880

"Oh, Billy, *el chivato,* when they look into your eyes They don't see the killer who will cut them down to size."

When Billy Bonney walked into Hargrove's with five men from the Chisum ranch, the Kid was smiling like the coyote who had invited the rabbit into his lair for dinner. Just a few nights prior, Billy had stolen livestock from Chisum, and now a free round of drinks was to be his unspoken penance for shaming these cowhands as ineffectual guardians of the herd.

"Belly up to the bar, boys, and name your medicine," Billy announced. "First dose is on me." He laughed as he dug into a pocket. "But the joke's on you," he muttered.

Young Jack Finan frowned as he leaned on the bar. "I heard that, you damned buzzard. Was that a confession?"

Billy stacked a small tower of coins on the bar. "Hell, Jack, you oughta know me better'n that. I don't believe in confessions . . . to any man . . . startin' at the bottom with governors."

Finan shook his head with the hopelessness of staying angry with the Kid. "You're still a damned buzzard, but I don't mind drinking if you're payin'."

"Well, I'm glad to hear that, Jack." Billy laughed and pointed at Finan's holstered pearl-handled revolver. "That fancy pistol o' yours could put the fear o' God into a man."

Finan smiled down at his gun and patted the side of his holster. "Cost me a month's wages. Mail ordered it right from the factory."

Billy hitched his head to one side. "Well, she's a beaut. And I know she shoots straight. I watched you boys engage in your little shootin' match this mornin'."

Finan frowned. "You were there watchin' us? Why didn' you come down an' join us?"

Billy shrugged. "I heard your shots and came over to spectate." Billy's smile widened. "Never a good idea to go rushin' in on a bunch o' disgruntled drovers who just been rustled."

Finan raised an eyebrow. "Guess I won't ask you how you knew that."

When the bartender stood before them, Finan and the other four herders ordered a beer. When the barman turned expectant eyes on Billy, the Kid waved him away with a friendly smile.

"Hell, Bob, you know I ain't old enough to drink." Billy laughed and turned back to Finan. "That was some fine shootin' I saw you perform out there, Jack."

Finan showed his teeth in a rare grin and leaned in to whisper. "Won five dollars off these boys." He jerked his head toward his companions.

Touching two fingertips of one hand to the brim of his hat, Billy offered a modest salute. "And well you should have. By my count, those boys hit everything *but* that tin can with twelve rounds. You stepped up and hit it three times outta three."

A rough hand clasped Billy's shoulder and turned him. The Kid's gun appeared in his hand like the flip of a card, even before he faced the man who had grabbed him. There stood Joe Grant, a foul-mouthed blowhard and bully who liked to call himself "Texas Red." It was obvious he was drunk, his grip on Billy's shoulder more for balance than aggression.

"I hear you're buyin'?" Grant said, delivering an alcoholic breath that covered Billy's face like a rag soaked in coal oil.

Billy smiled. "You must'a heard wrong, Red. I owe these boys here, you see." Billy's smile remained in place, but his eyes hardened to blue ice. He pressed the muzzle of his gun into Grant's belly and cocked the hammer. "I don't owe you a fat pig's fart."

Grant—trying to sober—let go of Billy and tottered on his own. "Easy now, son," he said with a nervous laugh. Propping his hands on his hips above his cartridge belt, he looked around as though someone might tell him how to react to the insult of Billy's gun. In his weaving, Grant's eyes focused on Jack Finan's new sidearm.

"By God, that's a handsome weapon, boy! Where the hell'd you git a hold o' somethin' that fancy?"

When his beer arrived, Finan turned his back to Grant and leaned both forearms on the bar. "Bought it," he said over his shoulder. "From the factory." Raising his mug, he sipped at the head of foam spilling over the brim.

"I might like one o' these for myself," Grant brayed. "That's a Smith and Wesson, ain't it? Lemme have a look-see."

Finan set down his drink and faced Red. "You've already had a look." He raised his chin toward the back of the room. "Why don't you go back over there to your friends."

Grant rocked back on his heels and held up his palms as though to fend off trouble. "Hey," he fairly sang out, "I'm just bein' friendly." Smiling, he glanced at the dark muzzle of Billy's gun that held steady on his midsection. "Sure, I'll just go sit down and admire your gun from a distance. Will that be all right with you?"

Finan's reply was to swivel back to the bar and raise his glass. Billy did not move.

Grant's smile seemed to compress his entire face as he poked at the air, repeatedly pointing a finger at Billy. " 'Member what I tol' you yesterday? That holds for today, too."

When the drunkard stumbled away to his table across the

room, Billy lowered the hammer of his gun, turned, and watched Grant in the big mirror hanging behind the bar.

"Damned no-good drifter," Finan said quietly. "Never known him to hold a job more'n a week." He turned his head to Billy. "What was it he said to you yesterday?"

Without taking his eyes off the mirror, Billy curled his upper lip. "Came up to me out of the blue, grabbed my arm, and said, 'Twenty-five dollars says I kill somebody today before you do.'" Billy turned to Finan. "My advice? Don't enter into any negotiations with Texas Red Grant, financial or otherwise. He's a unpredictable cuss."

Finan finished his beer and leaned an elbow on the bar to address the other Chisum hands. "Hey, boys, don't you think young Billy here owes us maybe *two* rounds for our trouble?"

"I was thinkin' three!" one man replied with a poker face.

Billy leaned over the bar to show his smile. "Boys, you can order all the drinks you want." He patted the bar twice next to his stack of coins. ". . . Until that runs out," he added. His eyes danced with a mischievous blue light. "Then you're on your own."

Billy smelled Texas Red's stale breath and sweat-soaked shirt before he saw that the drunkard had returned. Wearing a garish smile, Red took a quick step back, both arms extended before him, one hand gripping a Colt's peacemaker and the other holding Jack Finan's pearl-handled Smith and Wesson. Finan could not resist looking down at his own empty holster. Red chose this moment to cock both guns, and as he did a smile stretched across his face to expose a crooked row of yellowed teeth.

"You damned thievin' sonovabitch!" Finan said in a seething voice.

"Well, now, Mr. High an' Mighty," Red crowed, "all I did was ask to see your damned shooter."

Jack Finan's jaws knotted. "So now you're stealin' a man's gun?"

Putting on a show for the saloon crowd, Red pretended to be offended. "Don't git your trousers all in a twist, boy." He squinted at the borrowed gun. "It's the Schofield model, ain't it?"

Finan's fists clenched at his sides. "Yeah, it's a Schofield." Jack's voice lowered to a menacing monotone. "I don't like bein' without a gun, goddamnit!"

Texas Red laughed. "Well, hell, that's easy. Here go." Easing toward Finan, he lowered the hammer on the Colt's and stuffed it into Jack's holster. "Now, everybody's happy, see?"

" 'Cept you got my Schofield," Finan reminded.

Billy reached to Finan's arm and tried to turn him toward the bar. "Let it go, Jack. It's just temporary. Let me buy you another drink."

When Finan would not be turned, Billy squeezed tighter until Jack was forced to look at him. "Just let it go for now, Jack. It'll be all right. You got my word."

The Chisum boys leaned in to talk to their friend, and the tension at the bar eased up. Still smiling and wielding the Schofield, Texas Red backed toward his side of the room.

"Hey, Billy," called out one of Finan's friends, "is that a free second for all of us?"

Billy laughed. "Sure . . . why not?"

As the mugs were refilled, Finan leaned both elbows on the bar and glowered at Billy. "You're sayin' you trust that damn Texan to return my gun?"

"Hell, no," Billy whispered, "but I know he's itchin' to kill somebody, and I was tryin' to help scratch you off that list."

Finan's eyes glowed in the dusky room. "I'll *have* that goddamn gun back. It's mine!"

Billy nodded his understanding. "Let me handle this, Jack. I never could stomach a bully, and I reckon this one is overdue a lesson in manners." Billy gestured to the bartender. "Bob, I'm payin' for this round, too." He dug into his pocket and slapped down six more coins. "And bring me one, will you?"

Bob Hargrove frowned at Billy. Then he shrugged and pulled a clean mug from the shelf.

"Well, how the hell're *you* gonna get it back?" Finan whispered to Billy.

Billy leaned in close until their elbows touched on the counter. "Listen, after you showed up these boys with your shootin' this mornin', I didn' see you reload. Did you?"

Finan frowned down into his beer and thought for a time. "No," he said in a firm tone and raised his head to look into Billy's eyes. "Why?"

"You're sure?" Billy said softly. "You didn' replace those three you fired off?"

Jack shook his head with certainty. "My cartridge belt was empty. I was gonna reload later and fill the belt loops, but I forgot to dig out the box of shells from my saddlebags."

When Hargrove brought the full mug, Billy picked it up and spoke out of the side of his mouth to Finan. "Stay here. I'll be back with your gun."

After sauntering across the room, Billy stopped a few paces away and watched Texas Red as he displayed the gun and boasted about its future in his hand. The three other men at the table had thrown in their cards, and now they were tolerating Red's performance. A fifth chair was unoccupied.

Smiling, Billy raised the beer mug like a toast to Grant. "I sold off thirty horses today, and I got more money than a man oughta have. How 'bout I sit down with you boys for a few hands?" He gestured with the mug toward the empty chair. "You mind?"

Grant hesitated but gradually worked a smile back onto his

face. "Sure, sit down, Kid. We'll see how your luck's holdin' today." He set the Schofield on the table but kept his hand on the pearl grips.

Settling into the chair, Billy reached across the table and set the mug of beer before Grant. "There you go, Red. Never let it be said Billy Bonney refused a man a drink."

Grant lifted both eyebrows and considered the peace offering. Grunting his acquiescence, he picked up the mug with his left hand.

"I'll take your drink . . . *and* your money," Red laughed. "Deal 'em up, boys." Then he took a long draw on the beer and set it down. "So, tell me, Kid . . . who've you killed lately?"

Billy shrugged. "Well, if you believe the newspapers, everybody who expires in Lincoln County dies by my hand. Even if they fall off their roof while nailing up a shingle or get mauled by a bear or die of consumption. I'm the culprit."

Texas Red laughed heartily and wagged the shiny Schofield at Billy like a scolding finger. "I guess if you're a killer, they're gonna call you one."

Billy laughed. "Sure, why not?" He pointed at the Smith and Wesson. "I guess if I had a gun like that, I could double my numbers. Whatta you think?"

Red held the Schofield muzzle up before him and rotated it to admire its construction. "Maybe I'll use this to beat your numbers, Kid. Whatta you think of that?"

Billy shrugged. "Well, if you're bound to outscore me, at least let me hold that new shooter for a bit. I wanna be able to say I held Texas Red's Schofield in Bob Hargrove's Saloon at Fort Sumner in the winter o' 'eighty."

Giving Billy a sidewise glance, Grant worked up a sly smile. "I don't think so."

Billy leaned in close and whispered. "I ain't askin' any more o' you than you asked o' Jack over there." He tilted his head toward the Chisum boys. "Besides, I hear pearl grips are cool to the skin . . . never slip in your hand." He smiled. "Just ten seconds. I wanna see if it's true."

Grant narrowed his eyes. "I'll need some collateral for that."

Billy's gun appeared suddenly, as if it had been in his hand all along. Balancing it in the flat of his palm with the handle extended forward, he offered it to Grant.

"Collateral," Billy quipped. "There you go."

Texas Red took the proffered pistol with his left hand and held it pointed at Billy. Reaching toward Billy, he set the Schofield on the table.

"Ten seconds," Red reminded and cocked the hammer on Billy's Colt's.

Ignoring Red, Billy conjured up a look of wonder as he lifted the Schofield with both hands, balancing the gun as if it were a cup of coffee filled to the brim. He flipped the weapon over to see it from both sides. Pursing his lips, he let out a low whistle of approval.

"She's a beaut, all right," he said. Raising the gun next to his ear, he closed his eyes and touched the tip of his tongue to his upper lip. "Let's see how the working parts sound," he suggested and set the hammer at half-cock. After rotating the cylinder through three crisp *clicks*, he opened his eyes and smiled as if he had heard three perfect notes plucked from a harp. "Ticks like a banker's watch!" Billy said. He lowered the hammer and set the pistol back where Grant had laid it down. Billy gestured toward his cocked pistol in Texas Red's hand. "How'd that'n o' mine sound to you?"

"Good," Red said and grinned. He lowered the hammer on Billy's gun and picked up the Schofield. Handing Billy's gun to the man next to him, Red said, smiling, "Here's the collateral back to you. I'm gonna ask Stubbs here to slip it into your holster, if you don't mind."

Billy winked. "That'd be right as the rain, Red."

The man named Stubbs appeared uneasy about the transaction, but he stuffed the gun into Billy's holster without incident. Then he scooped up the cards, stacked, and shuffled them. After two shuffles and a cut, he began to deal in a fluid motion, sailing the cards to each man's place to make five discrete piles.

"Well, Red," Billy said, sitting back to slouch in his chair, "it's a damned nice *pistola*. Smooth action . . . good balance . . . pearl grips." The Kid took on a concerned expression and shook his head. "Too bad it's gonna be an unlucky gun for you."

Red's face closed down. "What the hell does that mean?"

Billy shrugged. "It just ain't gonna work out for you . . . that's all."

Still holding the Schofield, Red glowered like a jowly wolf. "The hell you say, you snot-nosed kid. I could spill your brains all over this saloon right now."

Billy appeared to be genuinely amused. "Well, I doubt you're quick enough," he said and slid both hands back until only his fingertips touched the edge of the table. All the humor drained out of Billy's face. "But you are welcome to try, Red."

Grant held the Schofield steady, his thumb wrapped over the spur of the uncocked hammer and his fingers wrapped in a death grip around the pearl handles. He sat absolutely still, but he appeared to be wound up inside like a spring.

"Are you tryin' to push a fight with me, Kid? 'Cause if you are, I'm the right man for it!"

Billy snorted. "You might be the right man, Red, but"—Billy raised a hand to point at the Schofield—"that's still the wrong gun."

Several people seated around the room stood and backed away to be distant spectators. When the men at Red's table quietly rose and moved toward the front of the saloon, the room seemed transformed into the stage of a theater, the two seated men now like actors in the final scene of a play. The saloon was so quiet that the pounding of a hammer could be heard from the blacksmith's jacal far down the plaza.

Billy idly tapped a finger on the table three times as he watched Grant weigh the odds. The Schofield still remained uncocked.

When Billy burst out laughing, Red jumped as if he'd backed into a hot stove. "Hell, Red," Billy chuckled, "I was just testin' you."

Grant frowned with a questioning look. "Whatta you mean by 'testin' '?"

Looking around the room to share his smile, Billy raised his voice loud enough to be heard by every man in the saloon. "Oh, I was just tryin' to prove ever'body wrong."

Red's frown deepened. "How do you mean?"

When Billy faced Texas Red again, he cocked his head at an angle. "Why, Red, they say you ain't got the sand to throw down on a man if he's face to face with you." Billy smiled with the wonderment of a child. "Damn if they didn' have you pegged. And to top it off, you stole another man's gun." He tapped the finger three more times on the table. "Why, here I am callin' you a damn thief and a coward . . . and my hands are on the table." Billy nodded toward the revolver in Grant's hand. "And there you are holdin' that fine gun and still you can't find the nerve to use it." Billy tilted his head the other way. " 'Course, that's a lucky thing for you . . . since that's an unlucky gun far as you're concerned."

Grant's face darkened. "Why do you keep sayin' that?"

Billy turned to his friends at the bar. "This sonovabitch has got no show!" he announced. Looking back at Grant, Billy pushed back his chair and stood. He leaned on the table, his hands splayed flat on either side of the cards that had been dealt him. "Guess your so-called reputation has just took a lickin', Red," he said quietly. "Too bad. Now ever'body's gonna know what I've known all along . . . that your hot air comes outta your mouth no better'n it comes outta your arse."

Grant was a pot about to boil over. His thumb remained frozen on the hammer.

Billy straightened, propped his hands on his hips, and smiled. "Either use the gun or lay it on the table, Red."

With his free hand, Texas Red picked up a half-full bottle of whiskey and hurled it across the room toward the front door, where it crashed into the wall above the coat rack and sprayed whiskey and shards of glass over the garments hanging there.

"Well." Billy laughed and half turned toward the men gathered by the door. "At least we know he's hell on a whiskey bottle."

One of the spectators laughed, and then a new silence entered the room, as if the Grim Reaper, himself, had pushed through the door. Billy turned back to Red, and the two stared at one another for five long heartbeats.

"Always easy to spot a coward," Billy said quietly. "He's usually the loudest man in the room." Turning, he started back for the bar.

The sound of Red cocking the Schofield was, for Billy, like the starting signal for a horse race he had arranged, placed heavy bets on, and fixed. Someone called out Billy's name from the bar, but the Kid was already spinning, his gun out and cocked, his movements so fast that the dull snap of Grant's gun was hardly noticeable as the hammer dropped on a spent cartridge casing.

Red's face compressed into a web of creases, and his eyes widened. Just as he cocked the pistol again, Billy's gun roared, transforming the saloon into a flashpoint of violence. The report had barely blossomed through the room, when another followed . . . and then a third. Texas Red Grant collapsed backward, tumbling out of his chair and sprawling across the floor, his unseeing eyes fixed on the ceiling.

Billy checked the room for dissenters, but no one dared speak. Stepping around the table he knelt and picked up the pearl-handled Schofield lying on the floor next to Texas Red's body. Rising, Billy stood over the body and looked down at the expression Red had chosen to carry with him to hell.

"I've been there too often for you, Red," Billy remarked casually.

Returning to the bar, Billy set the Schofield on the countertop next to Finan. "Oughta be more careful who you loan that to, Jack."

Finan swallowed and cast a worried glance at the Texan's lifeless body. "Reckon I will," was all he could say.

One of the other Chisum boys slid closer on the bar. "You outfoxed him good, Billy! That ol' boy's been beggin' for it for too long."

Billy looked back at the crowd of men examining the body. "It was a game of two, and I got there first . . . that's all."

The bartender approached with a doubtful look. "You gonna just leave him there?"

Billy smiled. "Wasn't plannin' on takin' him home with me, Bob."

The barman frowned. "Well, what am I supposed to do with him?"

Billy scanned the wall above the mirror and pointed to a bare spot. "Why don't you mount him there? That might look good. 'Course, you'll need to find a taxidermist willing to take on the job. I think we already established that Red was full o' hot air."

Finding no humor in the reply, the bartender glowered at the men going through the dead man's pockets. "We need a damned lawman in Fort Sumner," he complained.

Billy slapped his right hand over his heart and feigned an

injured look. "Now that purely hurt, Bob! How would that work for me?"

The barman waved away the question with his hand. "Aw, you always find a way to weasel out, don't you?" He flipped a towel over his shoulder and came around the bar in a plodding walk. Joining the crowd at the other side of the room, Hargrove started barking orders for carrying the corpse out of his saloon. Billy tipped his hat to his friends.

"*Adios,* boys, I've got an appointment with some livestock down on the Pecos."

When Billy started away, Jack Finan touched his arm and stopped him. "You reckon you could have your appointments with some other rancher for a while? You're makin' us look like a bunch of mooncalves holdin' the short end o' the rope, Billy."

Billy's front teeth showed when he smiled. "Why sure, Jack. You're not even on my list . . . not for a while, anyway." He nodded to the Chisum group. "Stay sharp at night, boys. You never know what's comin' at you outta the dark." He pointed at Finan's holstered pistol. "Don'cha forget to reload now." He hitched his thumb back toward the men hoisting the dead body. "You can ask ol' Red there . . . could be the difference in walkin' outta a saloon or bein' carried out."

When Billy left Hargrove's, one of the Chisum hands leaned into Jack Finan. "The Kid is crazy as a one-winged goose."

Finan huffed a laugh. "I'd rather have 'crazy' as a friend than an enemy." He turned to show the gravity on his face. "Wouldn' you?"

15
BLESSING'S NOTES
ROCA AMARILLA HOTEL
WHITE OAKS, NEW MEXICO TERRITORY
AUGUST 1886

"O, Billy, *el bandito*, now they're calling you 'the Kid' And saying that you killed a man for every year you lived."

Tom Longworth is a lumbering, broad-shouldered specimen. Billy once told me the man could fill an open doorway and easily block out the wind. His size may explain why he was elected constable of White Oaks back during the Lincoln County War. His was the kind of weight citizens wanted to see thrown on the side of the law.

At midday we sit at a table in the restaurant of the hotel where I am staying. The only other customer in the room is a young California engineer, whom I met in the hotel lobby yesterday. He is occupied with his meal and a book that lies open beside his plate.

"Yeah, I met the Kid a few times," Longworth explains in his deep, empty-whiskey-barrel voice. "He was just another hard case who drifted from town to town, hung out with the wrong people, and stole anything that wasn't nailed down. Those boys he rode with—killers like Dave Rudabaugh and Jesse Evans—they were the scum of the earth." His face cringes with a remembered thought. "They kilt a man's dog one night . . . just for sport. Those two put down twenty dollars each on a bet whether or not the man would cry."

I open my notebook, dip my quill, and poise pen above paper. "As I understand it, you led the posse that caught up to them here in White Oaks."

"Well," Longworth says and points down the street with a thick forefinger, "it was at the Greathouse ranch, a few miles down the Las Vegas Road. Those boys had been stealing horses all over our part of the county. We knew Greathouse did business with them, so we surprised them there." He pauses here to smile and take his due. "There were posses all over the Pecos country, including some from the Texas Cattleman's Association, all hunting the Kid and his gang, but it was us that first ran 'em to ground."

He traded his prideful smile for a thoughtful purse of his lips. "There was snow that day. Bonney's boys were holed up in the house, which was pretty well built to stand off a fight. And they were almost twice our numbers, which is why I left my party and came back to town to round up some more men."

"You left?" I blurt out, unable to hide my surprise. I'd never heard of a lawman in charge of a posse who left his deputies in the field. Even *I* knew the job of messenger should have been doled out to the least needed man in the group.

Clearly troubled by my tone, he shifts in his chair. The table wobbles back and forth from the weight of his meaty arm.

"I knew just about everybody in White Oaks, so I knew the right men to enlist," he says, more than a little defensive. "And, besides, I left my posse in capable hands."

The waiter approaches, and we temporarily abandon our roles as interviewer and interviewee to sort through the choices for our meal. I settle on rice and beans with a topping of sautéed onions, peppers, and tomatoes. My guest orders a T-bone steak. When the waiter retreats to the kitchen, I jump right in to revive the momentum of the conversation already begun.

"Whom did you leave in charge?"

Longworth gives me a disapproving glance, as though he does not care to name names. But, after an appropriate show of reluctance, he spills the beans, so to speak.

"Well, there were the Hudgens brothers and Jim Carlyle. Jim was our blacksmith in those days. Everybody thought highly of him, and I knew my deputies would follow his orders."

" 'Carlyle,' " I repeat, the name dredging up from my memory of obituaries. "He's the man who was killed in that mix-up."

" 'Mix-up'!" Longworth scowls as he throws the phrase back at me. "It was a case of those damned thieves going against the truce they had called!"

Just to mollify him, I nod as I write down his outburst word for word. I remind myself that a good interviewer remains objective and unbiased.

"So you were not there for the tragedy that followed?"

"No, I was not!" he growls. "I can't say that I would have handled it like Jim did, but I'm sure he thought he was doing the best thing. It was certainly a brave thing—laying off his arms and going inside the house to negotiate."

I wonder how many times this man has defended his actions about that day. His reply seems well-oiled and confident.

"I got the full report later," he assures me, "so I can tell you exactly what happened." His chair groans as he settles back to relate the story. He has performed this narration quite a few times, too, I suspect.

"We had a stalemate going. Shots were fired by both parties to no effect. Then Bonney sent out Greathouse to deliver a message about wantin' to see any warrants we might have."

"And did you have warrants?" I ask.

Longworth appears displeased at my question and waves it away with a bloated hand. "Once Greathouse was free of the house, he begged us to keep him among the posse because he was afraid of Rudabaugh and the Kid. He claimed he was a victim in the whole affair . . . that he'd been forced to hide stolen livestock in his corrals." Longworth laughs quietly. "Well, my boys didn't buy that, and neither did I. I could see this was going to come down to a show of force, so that's when I went for help."

"Why did you have no warrants?" I try again.

Longworth puts on a sour expression and dismisses my question with a shake of his head. "After I left, somehow or other, Bonney convinced Carlyle to come inside the house and parley under a white flag. Said he'd talk surrender only to Jim. So Carlyle went inside. He was in there for an hour. When our boys started yelling for Jim to come out, Rudabaugh yelled back at them, but there was not a word from Carlyle. Some of our boys figured they'd cut Jim's throat."

"But he was shot, wasn't he?" I say.

"The story gets pretty muddled here," Longworth hedges. "You can get five different versions of the facts from five different people who were there." He raises his blocky fist and extends a big index finger to point at me. "Here's what I figure happened: Our boys kept Greathouse as a hostage to balance out Carlyle's gamble to go into the house. Once he was in there, they made Jim drink liquor until he couldn't think straight. We know that because he reeked of whiskey when we buried him. Jim was not knowed to drink more'n a beer or two."

Longworth shakes his head again, his face sagging with disapproval. "Then somebody on our side fires off a shot." He looks at me quickly. "To this day nobody will own up to it." He inhales deeply through his nose and expands his chest. Staring out the front window, he exhales, and, as he does, regret seems to pour out of him. "I reckon Jim thought our boys had killed Greathouse. So, naturally, he figured Bonney or Rudabaugh would kill him to even the score. He musta took off running for the window 'cause he came barreling through it headfirst, hands tied behind his back, pieces of glass and wood flying all over the place. He landed face down in the snow, scrambled to his feet, and tried to run for cover. My men didn't know what to think at first. Before they could react, Bonney's gang gunned Jim down. Shot him in the back."

When I finish jotting down his words, I close the cover on my notebook and temper my voice to prevent his flying into a rage. "I've heard another version from people who were there."

Longworth waves away whatever perspective I might offer. "I told you there are plenty of other ways that day was described. What I just told you is based on the best evidence available." He points at my notebook, jabbing at it three times. "You write it the way I told you," he orders and gives me a look I will not soon forget.

"One of my sources," I begin in my most courteous tone, "a man in your posse, admitted your men believed Carlyle to be one of the rustlers trying to make a break from the house. They did not recognize him with his head down to suffer his impact with the glass. So they opened up on Carlyle, not knowing who he was. He was shot three times. Those bullets entered from the front, I am told."

Longworth appears to have heard this version, but now he will not look me in the eye.

"What happened next?" I ask. "Why were Bonney and his men not taken?"

Longworth shrugs. "What happened is . . . night rolled in. I was late getting back to the Greathouse ranch because I couldn't find all the men I needed. When I did return, half of the men I'd left there had just wandered off and gone home. Those damned boys in the house had slipped away, too."

"So it was all for nothing that Jim Carlyle died," I dare to say.

Longworth knots his mouth and pushes it to one side of his face. "Seems that way, don't it?" Breathing harder through his nose, he shows his anger in the deepening color of his skin.

"Our boys were so upset about Carlyle, they burned down Greathouse's place." He shakes his head. "If they'd just done that a few hours earlier they could have had the Kid and Rudabaugh and that whole God-forsaken bunch . . . either in chains or burnt to a char."

He stares out the window. "But, no, Jim didn't die for nothing. When people found out how Bonney's boys shot him in the back while under a flag of truce, that's when the territory really turned against those damned thieves. The newspapers were howling about the murderous, back-shootin' 'Billy the Kid.' They wanted to see the boy fitted with a hemp necktie and hanging from a cottonwood tree. About then, Pat Garrett pinned on a badge and had the governor prodding him with a hot running iron. This put Garrett in a fever to catch the Kid."

Our food arrives, part of which is a basket of hot biscuits nestled into a thick yellow cloth to keep them warm. Longworth tries to appear casual as he slices open a hot biscuit and begins slathering it with butter.

"So, who were your sources?" he asks.

"What do you mean?" I say, pretending not to understand his question. I spread a napkin over my lap, scoop up a spoonful of food comprised of each part of my order, and fill my mouth. The tripartite tastes comingle nicely on my tongue.

Longworth also feigns indifference. He takes a bite of the biscuit, and suddenly most of the crusty disk is gone. After sopping the scrap of bread into the steak juice standing on his plate, he leans forward and finishes off the biscuit.

"Who gave you that version of what happened at Greathouse's?" he asks again.

Dabbing at my servings with my spoon, I make an effort to keep my face unreadable. "I have those interviews in another notebook, I'm afraid."

He offers a tight smile. He knows I am lying.

"And I have heard Bonney's side of it," I add. I take a mouthful and speak around my chewing in true frontiersman style. "He told me the only man in that house mean enough to shoot Jim Carlyle would have been Dave Rudabaugh, but he swore Rudabaugh didn't do it. He had no reason to lie about it to me, because Billy has no allegiance to Rudabaugh. And, besides that, when Bonney shared this with me, he was in jail and scheduled to hang. He had no reason to lie."

Longworth saws at his steak with his table knife and smirks. "I guess I know what story Billy Bonney would tell." He forks a juicy chunk of meat into his mouth and chews it into submission. "Only thing wrong with it is . . . that ain't how it happened."

After he swallows, he downs half a glass of water and then wipes his napkin across his mouth. "And even if it was true," he says, carving off another corner of steak, "it's too late now. We already got the truth we needed." He stops the knife work to glare at me with the authority of his old constabulary position. "And, by God, that oughta make Jim Carlyle rest a little easier."

I am not sure Carlyle would agree about the machinations of his martyrdom, but I nod and decide to move on to another subject.

"The newspapers all over the territory seemed to band together then," I observe. "Starting with that incident at the Greathouse ranch, Bonney got nothing but bad press."

Longworth sets down his knife and fork and glares at me. "And why not? Mister, if you'd lost a remuda of horses . . . or fifty head of cattle . . . or your favorite dog . . . to that bunch of scoundrels, maybe you could feel what the rest of us around here experienced. Bonney was nothing more than a dirty, conniving brat who stole from or murdered people who were just trying to make a honest living."

I look into this man's angry hazel eyes and try to plumb the depths of his soul for the genesis of his hatred for the Kid. "That wasn't your dog that was killed, was it, Mr. Longworth?"

He shakes his head. "That ain't the point." He cocks his head to look at me from an oblique angle. "You seem to want to defend the Kid . . . as if he was important somehow."

"Did you know he was an orphan? He had no one to—"

"Lotta people are orphans," Longworth interrupts. "Hell, my grandmother was one. But she didn't wreak hell across the countryside stealing and killing."

I start to debate that point, but I close my mouth when his big forefinger comes up and hovers before me. "You say you wanna write the truth about Lincoln County, but you don't wanna hear it. I don't know what your game is, but I'm gettin' mighty tired of it." He points at my notebook as I scratch down his last words. "How do I know you're writin' all this down the way I'm sayin' it?"

He plucks up my notebook and spins it around to read. By the frown on his face, I assume he can make no sense of my shorthand techniques.

"What the hell is this?" he growls. "Chinese?"

"Mr. Longworth," I say as I take back my papers, "I assure you I would never misrepresent your feelings."

He pushes his plate aside, bangs an elbow down on the table, and points that lethal finger at me again. "See . . . that's what I'm talkin' about. These ain't my feelin's. They're the facts."

I manage a professional smile. "Like you said earlier, sir, there are always different versions to the same story. The accounts of eye witnesses at the same crime always differ. I'm trying to collect them all for a better picture of what really happened." I push my plate aside, lean in, and plant both my elbows on the table. "Bonney wrote Governor Wallace after the fiasco at Greathouse's place. He explained his side of it and said the newspapers had it all wrong."

Longworth hisses a laugh through his teeth. "Yeah . . . and Wallace knew just how to reply to that letter. He put out a five hun'rd-dollar *re*-ward for the Kid."

Though sitting, I stand my ground. "The governor betrayed Billy after a deal was struck in good faith."

Longworth smiles at my expense. "The Kid has really got your head in a cloud, don't he?" His eyes narrow with a question. "What is it you hope to get outta all this, Blessing? Do you think you're gonna rewrite the story of Billy Bonney and get yourself a big goddamned name out there in the world, where people read about other men's lives but don't know how to lead one on their own? Ain't that what writers provide for such people?"

Longworth butters another biscuit and takes a voracious bite, leaving a thin quarter moon of bread in his hand. A sickle-shaped crust. He chews with his mouth open as he glares at me. This man's manners and speech begin to suffer as he grows more hostile toward me. This hypocrisy seems to fuel my own self-righteousness to the point of confidence in my perspective.

"There are a number of people who see Billy as a savior," I rebut in a level voice, ". . . someone who stood up to the corruptions that spilled out of Santa Fe."

Longworth laughs. "That'd be all the dirt-poor people who didn't own nothin' worth stealin'." After finishing off biscuit number three, he wipes his hands together over his plate. "I guess you've had a lot o' book learnin', and people who keep their nose in a book gen'rally think they know a lot more'n they really do." He slides his plate of food back in place and continues his assault on the steak I have bought him. "You can read fancy words about the great wars o' hist'ry, but you can't know what it's like to shiver half froze through the night as you outwait your enemy, who is intent on shootin' your brains out as soon's you let down your guard."

He puts down his fork and knife and holds up two big fingers. "Two o' my men suffered frostbite that night at Greathouse's. Later, when Garrett's men tracked the Kid to Fort Sumner in a damned snowstorm, I hear a few fingers and toes were lost on that forced march."

"Were you with Garrett then?" I ask.

He gouges a piece of steak with his fork and hurries it to his mouth. Chewing aggressively, he shakes his head.

"I was constable here . . . not a sheriff's deputy. Wasn't my job . . . unless the Kid and his crowd came back to White Oaks." He wipes his mouth with his napkin. "But Jim East was a friend of mine. He told me all about that campaign, including the trip out to Stinkin' Spring. Snow almost up to the stirrups. Jim said it was so cold they had to bunk up double at night just to stay alive." He laughs. "Ever'body except Garrett. Nobody would sleep with him."

"Perhaps it was an odd number of men," I suggest.

Longworth glowers at me, and I half expect the man to slap me. "Weren't nothin' odd about those men!" he says in a menacing tone. "They were doin' their duty as lawmen."

"I merely meant that their total—"

"I know what you meant! You ain't never been so cold that you prayed your blood wouldn't freeze, have you?" He snorts. "Hell, you wouldn'a lasted half a day with that posse."

Unable to argue that point, I lower my eyes.

"Garrett was the right man for the job," he admits. "He lured Bonney and his boys into Fort Sumner and surprised them."

"That's when they killed Tom Folliard," I recall.

Longworth makes a dismissive sound deep in his chest. "Woulda kilt the whole bunch except that a thick fog ruined their plans." He shrugs. "No matter. Garrett caught up to 'em at that stone house at Stinking Spring."

As I write I raise my free hand to slow him down. "About

that," I say, "I have a question." I catch up in my notes and look him squarely in the eye. "I know Charlie Bowdre had just recently made some kind of deal with Garrett. And yet, when Bowdre walked out of the building that morning to check on the horses, Garrett shot him dead without warning."

Longworth shrugs again. "They all thought it was Bonney . . . on account o' Bowdre and the Kid wore the same kind o' hat."

I begin to write again. "So Garrett had no intention of arresting Billy," I deduce. "He was there to execute him." I look up to see the ex-constable shrug yet again. He starts buttering biscuit number four.

"Ever'body was wantin' the Kid dead, from the gov'nor on down." Longworth gives me a tired look. "And, as far as Bowdre goes, he shouldn'a been *with* the Kid. He told Garrett he was gettin' out and had cut all ties to Bonney. But there he was . . . holed up with the others like a nest o' rats." When he snorts, his head bobbles up then down. "Bowdre made his choice. He shoulda got out when he said he would."

I lay down my pen to show him that what follows is off the record. "If you had been in charge of that posse—the one at Stinking Spring—would you have felt comfortable shooting Bonney on sight . . . without giving him a chance to surrender."

Longworth looks at me as if I have recited a love poem. "Mister, holdin' on to Bonney was like tryin' to carry a handful of sand in your fist while you swim across the Pecos. I would have been happy to squeeze off a shot and put an end to that boy's party. And I wouldn'a lost a minute o' sleep over it."

After storing my notebook inside my carrying case, I cross my arms and try to appear nonjudgmental. "But what if all your loathing of Bonney is rooted in Jim Carlyle's death? And what if, as some men say, Bonney's men were not Carlyle's killers?"

The big man stands, wads up his napkin, and drops it in his plate. "You ain't listened to a damn word I've said, have you?"

Braving a smile, I spread my hands, palms up. "Mr. Longworth, I am only trying—"

He points that big bludgeon of a finger at me again. "You're tryin' to squeeze something sweet outta a sour lemon. You wanna make up some fancy story that favors the Kid and all he done. Yet you ain't never seen his victims, I bet."

He starts to walk away but turns back to the table to wield that finger yet again. "If you'd'a knowed Jim Carlyle, you wouldn' dream o' glory-fyin' Billy Bonney."

In a ludicrous attempt at matching Longworth's hulking pose, I stand. "I have heard nothing but commendable traits concerning Mr. Carlyle. I have no doubts he was an upstanding man. Certainly, he was courageous to remove his weapons and walk into the Greathouse stronghold to discuss terms of surrender with his enemies."

Longworth appears confused at my change in direction. Frowning at the remains of our meals, he clicked his teeth quietly, the sound like a telegraph clerk tapping out a terse reply.

"Jim Carlyle was a damned good man," he sums up. Idly, he picks up another biscuit. Number five.

Even though I never met the esteemed Mr. Carlyle, I nod in agreement. "Did you know Dick Brewer?" I ask.

His eyes quickly angle to me and pinch with suspicion. Meanwhile, that fifth biscuit is casually lowered into his coat pocket.

"Sure, I knew Dick. No finer man came to this country."

"What about Tunstall? Did you meet him? Or Alexander McSween?"

Longworth shakes his head. "Never had no dealin's with either man." He shrugs. "I heard Tunstall treated his hands fair." He huffs a quiet laugh through his nose. "McSween was a lawyer and, for that reason alone, prob'ly ought not to a' been trusted."

"These were men whom Billy Bonney looked to for guidance," I say, feeling much like an attorney making his closing arguments. "When you are an orphan, such relationships can take on immense importance. Billy saw each of them die . . . unjustly. Along with Charlie Bowdre and Tom Folliard."

Longworth takes a step toward me and leans in closer to put me in his shadow. "Look, dyin' is what men do in a war. Ever'body who got into this difficulty knew *that* goin' into it."

When I start to rebut, he raises the mighty finger.

"I'm done with this little interview," he growls and nods toward the table. "I appreciate the meal, but I can see we got nothin' else to say to each other." Looking down at my notebook he seems to engage in a staring contest with my shorthand notes. He gestures toward the papers with a fling of his hand. "If you use my words in whatever it is you're writing, be sure you get it right. If you put your words into my mouth, I'll be lookin' you up right quick, do you hear?"

Because he continues to glare at me, I assume his question not to be a rhetorical one. "I hear you, sir. I assure you I would never do that."

After another few pounding heartbeats under his scorching inspection, I have no choice but to blink. When I do, he turns and walks out of the restaurant, slamming the door behind him. I look around the room. The California engineer is gone. His table still shows the spoils of his meal. When I take my seat again, I discover the biscuit basket on my table is empty. I'm certain there had been one left, which I, myself, had planned to eat. I never saw Longworth pick it up. Number six. But take it he did.

When the waiter leans out through the kitchen door, he eyes

me expectantly. "Is there anything that you need?" he inquires. "Tact," I reply. "Maybe a little tact."

16
City Jail
Las Vegas, New Mexico Territory
December 1880

"They needed to condemn someone and wrap him in a myth
To glorify the capture of the men you're riding with."

When Pat Garrett and his entourage came down the icy main street of Las Vegas on the day after Christmas, word spread quickly as to whom the sheriff had brought in under arrest from Stinking Spring. The name "Billy the Kid" was on everyone's tongue, and a growing crowd of spectators braved the raw weather, stepping out of shops and saloons, lining the boardwalks in their shirtsleeves. Some cheered and congratulated the law officers, while others stood quietly with grave expressions.

Billy stood in the transport wagon and waved to the citizens running up to gawk at him. He smiled and bantered as if he were the guest of honor at an impromptu parade. The other three prisoners remained seated, hunkered down against the cold and bouncing along as the wagon rattled over the frozen ruts in the road.

"How did they catch you, Bee-lee?" a young, wide-eyed Mexican boy wanted to know. "Were you not napping with one eye open thees time?"

"I drew the low card this time, *mi amiguito*," Billy replied, laughing at the lapse of vigilance that had delivered him to this moment. "I guess the joke's on me."

"How'd they take you, Kid?" someone asked.

Billy leaned on the side rail of the wagon and adjusted his

voice to a storytelling timbre. "It was cold as hell, and we were holed up in the old Perea house at Stinking Spring. We coulda stood 'em off, but the posse employed a foul tactic, if you ask me." He lifted his arms to shrug but his wrists were chained to Rudabaugh's. Letting his hands drop back to the rail, he laughed. "They never coulda burned us outta that stone house. But here's the kicker: we didn't have wood for a fire, so we couldn't cook." Smiling and buoyant in relating the story, he nodded at Garrett, who sat tall and gangly on his big bay. "Then ol' Pat, there, he started cookin' up some meat . . . upwind o' us. When we got scent o' that, the game was up." Billy smiled for the punch line. "So we took a vote and decided to come out for breakfast."

Some of the spectators laughed, and Billy managed to pull off his hat to take a bow. "I sure hope you folks in Las Vegas can serve up something good for us here. You can work up quite a appetite in the back of a rickety old wagon amongst a army o' sour-faced lawmen."

A middle-aged Mexican woman with dark eyes appeared by the side of the wagon. "We will bring you the food you like, Bee-lee."

A portly man in a heavy brown overcoat shouldered past the woman and put a hand on the icy rail of the wagon bed. "Obviously, this rogue has never stolen from you," he snapped over his shoulder, scolding the woman. After giving Billy a cold glare, he picked up his pace toward the front of the parade. "Sheriff Garrett!" he called out, so loud that the crowd quieted to hear what he would say.

Garrett twisted his long skinny body around, one hand on his pistol butt.

"Sheriff, after you get your prisoners settled, you and your deputies come to the plaza," the man invited. "We're going to buy you men drinks at every saloon in town."

219

A grocer yelled from the doorway of his store. "I'll help foot that bill, by God."

From the opposite side of the street, another merchant added his name to the tab. Without replying, Garrett faced forward in his saddle and plodded ahead for the city offices.

Billy raised his manacled hands and laughed. "Well, that don't seem fair! We're the reason these boys wearin' badges are so famous today! Seems to me you oughta be throwin' us a fandango!"

Rudabaugh had been sitting in the wagon bed with his legs pulled up and his head resting on a forearm bridged across his knees. Now he looked up, his face crimped with impatience.

"Shut up, Kid!" he hissed. "Quit drawin' attention to us, for God's sake!"

A citizen walking close to the wagon leaned in and squinted. "That's Rudabaugh!" he exclaimed. Excited, he turned to address anyone who would listen. "They've got the man who killed our jailor!"

Rudabaugh's head went down between his knees again, but the crowd pushed in closer, and the voices around the wagon turned hostile. A volley of projectiles came flying at the wagon—dirt clods, stones, scraps of wood, horse apples, and a tin can or two. Because Billy was chained to Dave, he took as much pummeling as did Rudabaugh.

"Damn, Dave!" Billy laughed. "You've been here only a coupla minutes, and I believe you've already wore out your welcome!"

Garrett wheeled his mare around and walked his horse into the reactionary crowd. "Get back from the wagon and quit your throwin'! Else you'll be sittin' in jail next to these boys."

By the time the wagon rolled up to the county jail, the local law officers were venturing out onto the street, rifles in hand, their cautious eyes fixed on the prisoners. The onlookers had settled down, but their numbers were comprised of an oil and water mix of sentiments. Some continued to curse Rudabaugh. Others poured more accolades on Garrett and his men. Many still joked with Bonney, while a few condemned him for his crimes. But all the citizens seemed to know they were witness to a historical event.

As the prisoners shuffled from the wagon with their new escorts from the local police force, the Mexican boy darted to Billy's side and plucked at the Kid's sleeve. "*¡Te escaparás de esto, Bee-lee!*"

Feigning a concerned look and lowering his head, Billy raised a chained wrist and touched his forefinger to his lips. "Now, don't be lettin' out my secrets, compañero." When he winked, the boy smiled and nodded with the energy of a woodpecker.

The prisoners' cells were dark and dank with a rough floor of chunky flattish stones embedded in hard-packed mud. The cell block felt colder than the street outside. The stale air in these close quarters reeked of urine and sweat. Still chained together, Bonney and Rudabaugh shuffled into the largest cage, followed by the other two prisoners, who shared another set of leg irons.

"You got to be jokin'!" Billy announced for all to hear. He stopped in the middle of the gloomy cell and was tugged to one side when Rudabaugh flopped down on a crude pallet of folded cowhide laid over a frame of wood. Billy turned back to the knot of lawmen crowded around Garrett. "Pat, I wouldn't bury my worst enemy in this wretched cave!"

Garrett ignored the comment, turned to the jailor, and pointed to the cell. "Lock it!"

The man worked the key in the lock and turned to Garrett awaiting further instructions.

"My men need some rest," Garrett said to the jailor. "We leave for Santa Fe tomorrow. If Bonney or any of his friends try to escape, shoot them. Understand?"

The man stood slack jawed in the dim light, his head tilted back to look up at the sheriff who towered over him. "Yes'r, I b'lieve I do, but they don't let me carry a gun, Sher'ff."

Billy conjured up a devilish smile. "Don't you worry, Pat, I wouldn' leave you standin' all alone on the dance floor." His smile widened, the slice of light spreading from the cell block door illuminating his two front teeth that angled slightly askew. "I'll be right here waitin' on you, Pat." Then, all the humor drained from the Kid's face. He shook his head at Garrett. "But I ain't never gonna forgive you for shootin' that horse out at the spring."

Garrett, who had been checking the cell for a potential escape route, now turned an expressionless face to Billy. "That was a good horse, was it?"

"That ain't the point, Pat. You laid that poor beast out right in the doorway."

"You were coaxing that horse inside the building, Billy . . . planning your getaway. Couldn't let you do that."

Billy shook his head. "Nope. Wasn't me. Rudabaugh was tryin' to arrange his own transportation. My horse was inside with me all night. I was ready to skin out o' there like grease poppin' outta the fryin' pan, but you burned up that plan. I couldn't get my mare to jump over that damned dead horse. If I'd tried, I'd'a prob'ly stove my head in on the top o' the door-frame." Billy sneered. "If you hadn'a murdered that horse, I might be halfway to Texas right now."

"Hey, Billy . . . what about Bowdre?" one of the prisoners yelled. "You ain't gonna cuss 'im out for shootin' Charlie?"

Billy scowled and shook his head. "That's diff'rent," he replied. "Charlie knew what he was gettin' into. And he wasn't so big he blocked the way out."

Making no comment, the sheriff turned back to the jailor. "Test that lock!" he ordered.

The man frowned with surprise. "Yes'r." He grabbed the bars of the door and shook it. When he faced Garrett for further instructions, the sheriff turned to one of his own deputies.

"Jim, one of us will always be here in the front office. You take first watch."

When Jim East nodded, Garrett turned his attention to Barney Mason.

"Barney, you'll take over at midnight. I'll send over Cal at sunup. The train pulls out at eleven tomorrow morning. If this crowd outside gets organized, we might have a fight on our hands. They want Rudabaugh for killing their deputy here last year."

Mason shifted his weight from side to side, looked around at his fellow posse men, and then raised his chin to Garrett. "Why don't we let 'em have Rudabaugh, Pat? We've got the Kid. Whatta *we* care?"

Garrett turned hard eyes on Mason. "We leave nobody, understood?"

Mason's face pinched. "Why fight for the likes o' him?" He nodded at Rudabaugh.

Garrett looked at each of his men and settled his gaze back on Mason. "If you want to leave the posse, tell me now, Barney. I've got a job to do, and I aim to do it."

Mason frowned down at the toes of his boots long enough to collect himself. When his head came up, there was a wounded look in his eyes, and the tone of his voice softened.

"I ain't goin' nowhere, Pat."

Billy laughed and applauded, each clap of his hands accompanied by the clinking of the chain hanging between his wrists. "Thatta boy, Barney! I know Pat would agree . . . loyalty is more important than brains. You make a good lap dog, son."

Mason blinked slowly and turreted his head to Billy. Without making a reply, the deputy walked out of the cell block, his bootheels stabbing at the stone floor like a final insult.

"He'll be all right, Pat," said Jim East. "He's just sick o' chasin' after this murderin' bunch and tired o' bein' cold and had enough o' bein' away from his home and his wife."

Garrett made no reply. He turned and walked out of the cell block, his exit a longer and taller version of Mason's departure, his boots ringing with the sound of authority. The other posse men followed him into the front office, leaving only the jailor.

"Poor Barney," Rudabaugh whined in a mocking falsetto. "Maybe he oughta sleep in here with us in this fine pig's sty."

Jangling his ring of keys, the jailor approached the cell and gripped the bars. "There ain't no jail too miserable for you, Rudy-bow" he snarled. When Dirty Dave would not look at the man, the deputy spoke to Billy. "He's the one murdered the jailor who had this job b'fore me."

"Go to hell!" Rudabaugh growled. "Too bad *you* weren't workin' here then."

The jailor spat to one side and turned back to Billy. "And if you're a friend o' that'n, I reckon you belong in here the same as him."

Billy approached until the chain pulled taut and drew a grunt from Rudabaugh. "Don't judge me by that rascal." He nodded back toward Rudabaugh. "We ain't friends . . . more like business associates."

"Hogwash!" the jailor snapped back. "You oughta be more careful choosin' who you do bus'ness with."

Billy let his head sag forward, and he laughed. "Amigo," he said and brought up a big smile, "I believe you just wrapped up my whole story in those few words."

Rudabaugh jerked on the chain, causing Billy to reel. "Kid, will you shut your mouth for a while! I'm tired of hearing your jaw-flappin'!"

Billy turned back to the jailor. "On the day good manners got doled out, I believe ol' Dave was off courtin' the devil's daughter."

The turnkey started for the door but stopped with his hand on the knob. "Mr. Rudy-bow . . . that jailor you kilt . . . he was a good friend o' mine. He was friend to a lotta folks. I'll be surprised if you get outta Las Vegas without you a-gettin' a good view of the plaza from the windmill." In the dim light of the corridor his face broke into the distorted shadows of a smiling gargoyle. "That's where our last lynchin' took place." He laughed with one scratchy exhalation. "Our lawmen watched it from the saloon doors and raised their glasses."

Rudabaugh spoke up from his pallet. "Save it for somebody else, old man. I don't give a mule's ass how I cash outta this miserable world."

After the door closed on the prisoners, for half a minute there was complete quiet in the cell block. Then, rattling his chains, Billy dragged his pallet closer to Rudabaugh to allow for the confinement of their shared tether.

"It's gonna be cold as hell here tonight," Rudabaugh carped. "You reckon they'll give us some blankets?"

One of the boys in the back—Wilson—spoke up. "There's a little wood heater back here outside the cell, but there ain't no fire. Maybe they'll light that up for us."

Billy lay on his bunk and laughed. "Wouldn't count on it, boys. Our jailor don't appear too fond o' ol' Dave here. I reckon we'll all pay for Dave's sins tonight."

"Well, he's gotta bring us some damned blankets, don't he?" Rudabaugh huffed. "They can't just let us freeze back here!"

Billy laughed again. "Dave, he might bring me an' the other boys a pile o' buffalo robes, but I reckon the best you can hope for is a bucket o' snow to wear on your head."

It was a long, cold night that each prisoner endured silently beneath his single blanket that the jailor had at last doled out. The man had even begrudged one to Rudabaugh, though Dave's blanket alone was moth eaten and urine scented. The wood heater stood cold as an insult all night.

With the morning light slanting through the cracks in the east wall, the outlaws lay semi-conscious somewhere between the fatigue from shivering and the haze of sleep that teased them from a frigid distance. The office door opened, and Barney Mason scuffed into the cell block. He was in mid-conversation with a middle-aged man who followed behind him. The visitor wore a tweed overcoat, slouch hat, and wire-rimmed spectacles. In one hand he carried a notebook.

"You got ten minutes," Mason decreed in a tone of voice that brooked no argument. "You want out before then . . . just knock on this door. You want a chair?"

"No," the man responded with a slight bow. "But thank you." Taking off his hat, he looked around for a place to perch it. Finding none, he replaced the hat on his head and smiled into the occupied cell. "Which of you would be Mr. Bonney?"

Billy propped himself up by an elbow. "I might be . . . if you're a good lawyer."

The man offered a perfunctory smile and performed his little bow again. "My name is Koogler. I print the *Gazette* here in Las Vegas. I'm here to interview you."

Billy sat up and yawned. "Well, that all depends if I wanna answer your questions. All the newspapers in the territory have been makin' me out to be like some foamin'-at-the-mouth, crazy, wild animal that needs to be shot on sight. I might talk to you if only you'd write me up like I was at least part human."

The door opened partway, and the familiar face of the local postal agent leaned through the crack. For reasons Billy and the boys could never work out among themselves, this mail carrier had remained on friendly terms with them throughout the Lincoln County War.

"Boys, I just wanted you to know . . . I've brought you all some warm clothes to wear for your trip into Santa Fe."

"That's mighty considerate, Mr. Cosgrove," Billy said. "Gracias, amigo. Good to know we still got some friends around here."

"The deputy out here will have to go through them all first," Cosgrove explained. "But he'll bring them in soon. Good luck, boys."

"Adios," Billy called as Cosgrove exited and shut the door.

"Well," Koogler hummed, "it seems you do have a following of sorts." He cocked his head at an angle. "How is it some despise you and others want to shower you with gifts?"

Billy laughed. "Oh, that's easy enough. The first part is about some o' the men I keep company with." He made a comic face and used his body as a shield to hide the finger he pointed at Rudabaugh. "The second part has prob'ly got to do with my good looks and dancin' skills."

As the newspaperman wrote down the words, his expression turned doubtful. "You're going on trial for two murders, yet you don't appear to be too concerned."

Billy shrugged. "What's the use o' gettin' all morose? The cards turned against me this time, but I could draw a flush any minute."

Koogler looked confused. "You don't think they'll hang you?"

Billy laughed. "Now, see there? You figure there's only one way it can go from here. I find that a confinin' way to look at things. The wind might blow a different way tomorrow."

"Do you mean to say you think they won't get you to Santa Fe?"

Billy's infectious smile was not working on the *Gazette* man, but the Kid kept his spirits high. "You never know how things'll turn out 'til they do."

Koogler offered a patronizing smile and dipped his pen into his ink bottle. "Let's get down to business. How old are you?"

"Twenty-one," replied Billy.

"How tall?"

Billy frowned. "Hell, I don't know. I was a hair taller than Charlie Bowdre." He called back to his comrades. "Hey, boys, anybody know how tall Charlie stood?"

" 'Bout five and a half foot," Wilson answered.

"Well, there you go," Billy said. "Make it five seven."

Koogler nodded as he wrote. Then he looked Billy over from boots to wavy hair.

"I would guess you weigh no more than a hundred-forty pounds?"

"Well, hell," Billy laughed. "It's the middle o' winter. That's a lean time for a man on the scout. I'm prob'ly down from my usual weight."

The door opened, and Mason ushered in a second well-dressed man, this one also carrying a notebook. "Here's another one," the deputy announced.

Koogler lowered his notebook and pen to face the interruption. " 'Another' *what*?!"

Mason gave Koogler the bland expression of insult. "A reporter. I'll start your ten minutes again right now."

"Now wait a minute!" Koogler protested. "I was promised an *exclusive* interview!"

Mason's dead eyes showed nothing. "Ten minutes," the deputy repeated and pointed to Koogler's feet just inches from the cell. "Keep yourself back outta arm's reach, you damned fool." He raised his arm higher to point into the cell. "Think o' those boys in there like a den o' rattlesnakes. If you git bit, don't expect me to come in an' save you from your own ignorance."

Koogler quickly stepped back from the cell door, but his expression remained one of contempt. "Who are *you*?" he demanded of the newcomer.

The smaller man smiled and offered his hand. "I'm a journalist. I write for the *Santa Fe Messenger*. My name is Eustace Raines, sir. How do you do?"

Koogler's hands remained at his sides until he raised his pen and pointed at the door. "You can stand over there until I finish."

Raines lowered his hand and stared in confusion at the Las Vegas editor. "That would not allow me the promised ten minutes, sir. I have no intention of—"

Koogler took a step closer to the younger man and thrust his pen toward the door again. "You'll get your turn when I am done," he commanded.

"Well, that don't hardly seem fair," Billy chimed in with his easy laugh. His smiling eyes fixed on Koogler. "You already had five minutes with us, and now you're gettin' ten more." He gestured with his chained hands toward Raines. "Let's see what kind o' questions he'll come up with? Could be he's better at this than you are, Mr. Kookler."

"It's 'Koogler'!" the man barked.

Raines blinked rapidly as he fidgeted with his notebook and stepped around his rival to stand before Billy. "Thank you, Mister—?"

Billy smiled and stretched the chains as he approached the bars, pulling Rudabaugh's pallet several inches over the rough stones. "I'm William H. Bonney!" Billy said, turning on the charm. "Pleased to make your acquaintance." As he extended one hand through the bars of the door, the chain raked across the metal crossbar with a grating sound.

Hesitating, Raines stared at the offered hand and then brought up apologetic eyes. After a standoff of ten seconds,

Billy withdrew his hand and clapped for his visitor.

"Well, see there, Mr. Kookler?" Billy laughed. "Maybe you *can* learn somethin' from this young man. It's smart to never get too close to a man inside a jail cell, 'cause you got somethin' he wants mighty bad."

Raines opened the front of his coat and looked down at himself. "What do you mean? I don't carry a weapon."

Billy laughed. "*You* got your freedom. *He* don't."

The young journalist's face filled with wrinkles. "How could he take my freedom?"

When one of the boys in back started to chuckle, Raines looked toward the laughter.

"Come back here and shake my hand, and I'll show you," Rudabaugh prodded.

Raines turned his attention back to Billy and tried for an earnest smile. "I have come a long way to talk to you, and I would appreciate an interview with you, if you feel up to it."

Billy's smile widened. "Well, now . . . I believe I have just witnessed a healthy dose of professional courtesy." Billy winked at Raines and turned to Koogler. "Now, you and I didn' start off proper like that, did we? I don't believe you thought to ask for an interview in a civilized way, did you? Maybe I oughta let Mr. Raines handle this interview."

Koogler sniffed. "If you don't want to answer *my* questions, then so be it. That's the way I will write up the interview for my readers." He couldn't resist a smirk. "And then maybe the people can make up their own minds as to whether or not you are human."

Billy laughed and leaned his forearms on the crossbar. "Well, at least we oughta let Mr. Raines catch up on where we were in our conversation, Mr. Kookler. Don't you agree?"

Koogler's brow lowered over his eyes. "I see no reason to do that. It is *my* interview."

Ignoring Koogler's protest, Billy looked up at the ceiling and narrowed his eyes. "Let's see now, we established I am twenty-one years old . . . about five foot seven . . . and a hundred an' forty pounds." Billy laughed and pointed at Raines. "So, tell me, Mr. Santa Fe, what's *your* first question for Billy Bonney?"

After opening his notebook, Eustace Raines licked his fingertips and began leafing through the pages. "I have a list here somewhere. I jotted them down while traveling here on the stage." His face closed down with worry, and his movements began to appear frantic as he searched his notes. "I can't seem to find them right now," he said with a nervous laugh. He closed his eyes and pressed the notebook to his chest with both hands as he tried to calm himself. If he had been laid out flat on his back, he would have looked like a corpse ready for the coffin.

Raines opened his eyes and spoke in a meek voice. "In the hope of interviewing you, I came by here last night, and the deputy on guard duty—a Mr. East—told me that you could have no visitors until this morning. However, he and I did talk for a while, and he told me all about your capture at Stinking Spring."

" 'Capture!' " Billy balked. "Hell, we gave ourselves up outta hunger."

"But weren't there men killed?" Raines asked.

"There was one man executed without warning," Billy explained. "And a poor old horse that never did nobody no harm." Billy shook his head once. "You'll have to interview Pat Garrett about those two. He's the one kilt 'em both."

"What about the men you have killed?" Raines asked. "They say you have murdered a man for every year of your life. Is that correct?"

Billy snorted and let his head hang forward. After shaking his head a few times, he looked up.

"A sheepherder over near Anton Chico fell into an old mine

shaft and died from drinking the water that leaked outta the ground. They say it was arsenic poisonin', and the whole thing got blamed on Billy Bonney. Another man got bit in the neck by a prairie rattler down in the Tularosa Valley. Died in about three minutes, they say." Billy laughed. "Guess who they pointed their finger at for that?" His chains rattled when he poked a thumb at his chest. "They've put my name on murders in places I ain't even been."

Raines chewed on his lip and frowned. "Well, who was the man killed at the spring?"

"Charlie Bowdre," Billy reported. "Shot three times . . . twice in the chest . . . lived only a few minutes. He was a good friend."

Raines seemed at that moment to remember the notebook in his hands. Opening to a blank page he began scribbling with a pencil.

"How old was Mr. Bowdre?" he asked.

"Hell . . . *old*!" Billy said. "Over thirty anyway."

Raines nodded and wrote down the number. "Was he from around here? In New Mexico Territory, I mean?"

"He wasn't a native, but he married one," Billy said. "I ain't sure where he hailed from, tell you the truth."

"Born in Georgia!" came the answer from the back. "But Charlie grew up in Mississippi."

Billy waved at the air. "Don't matter where he came from. He was as good a man as ever come to the New Mexico Territory."

Koogler cleared his throat and took a step closer. "I guess you don't know that Bowdre met secretly with Garrett just two weeks ago, trying to make some kind of deal to get himself off the hook." The newspaperman rocked back on his heels with a snide smile plastered on his face.

" 'Course I knew it," Billy countered. "Charlie tol' me ever'thin' that was said durin' that little rendezvous. He just

232

wanted to get him and his wife outta the fight, and I don't blame 'im for it. It was Manuela who wanted to leave, and so Charlie and her planned to slope on outta the territory just after Christmas. 'Til then, Charlie swore to Pat he was done ridin' with us." Billy shrugged. "Just didn't work out that way. It's hard to say why."

"Is that why Garrett shot him?" Raines asked. "For going back on his word?"

Billy shook his head. "Charlie went out early to check on the horses. Garrett thought it was me, on account o' Charlie and I wore the same kind o' hat. And we're 'bout the same size."

"So Garrett was trying to execute *you!*" Raines said. "There was no attempt at arrest."

Billy shrugged his shoulders. "That's the way it is in a war. We done the same to Sheriff Brady. I guess Pat was just doin' what he thought was good strategy. Get me outta the way, and the boys holed up in the stone house might give up."

"You mean because you are their leader?" Koogler interjected.

Billy laughed and turned his head to call back to his fellow prisoners. "You hear that, boys? This Mr. Kookler thinks I am the head of some outlaw gang." Ignoring the Las Vegas journalist, Billy looked Raines squarely in the eye. "I was never leader o' anythin'. I was always for Billy."

"What about Mr. Bowdre's wife?" Raines asked. "What happens to her now?"

Amused, Billy turned to Koogler. "Are you takin' notes on this young man's professional manner? You might could learn a thing or two from 'im."

Koogler scowled as though he had detected a vile scent in the room. Folding his arms over his chest, he tried to appear above Billy's criticism.

"When they brought us through Fort Sumner after capturing us," Billy went on, "they delivered Charlie's body to his wife. I thought Manuela would kill everyone in the posse. She knocked Jim East over the head with a fire poker and beat on Garrett with her fists until some of those brave posse men pulled her away." Billy's smile faded when he pulled in his lips. "But Pat was a gentleman. He paid for a new set of clothes for Charlie . . . and for the burial."

"Hey, Kid!" yelled Wilson from the back of the cell, "be sure to tell 'em about what Garrett gave *you*."

Billy looked down at the stone floor but not before showing a hint of a smile.

"What did Sheriff Garrett give to you?" Raines asked.

While Billy shook his head, Wilson answered for him. "Garrett give 'im five minutes with—"

"All right!" Billy interrupted "If it's got to be told, I'll be the one to tell it!"

From the pallet behind Bonney, Rudabaugh groaned. "Yeah, and be sure to tell how I got dragged into it. God! I thought I was gonna puke!"

"Were you the best man, Dave?" Wilson joked.

"More like 'worst man,' " Billy muttered and leaned closer to the bars to lower his voice. "I got a sweetheart there at Fort Sumner."

Wilson's voice broke in casually from the back. "And in Anton Chico . . . and San Patricio . . . and La Mesilla . . . and White Sands . . . and Lincoln . . . and Puerto de Luna—"

The Kid couldn't resist a smile. "Yeah, but my best girl is at Fort Sumner."

"Oh . . . Paulita!" came a whispery voice from the back of the cell, the performance full of kitschy drama. "I love you so, Paulita! Forget me not as I go off to jail!" Wilson's presentation ended with a cackle of laughter.

Bonney stood erect as he faced the back of the cell block. "Shut up, Wilson!"

When it appeared that no more performances would be offered from the back of the cell, Billy turned back to the young Santa Fe newspaperman. "There was a little somethin' troublin' my girl, and Garrett let me have some private words with her before we left."

In the quiet that followed, Rudabaugh began to laugh. "If you fellows want to know the details, just ask me. I was there . . . chained to Romeo . . . I heard it all."

Billy turned and jerked the chain so hard, Rudabaugh fell off of the pallet onto his shoulder. On impact he kicked out with one leg and sent the chamber pot clanging across the stone floor toward the far wall, flinging its contents over part of the cell. Wilson rose from his bunk, flinging his hands and wiping his face in the crook of his arm.

"Goddamnit, Rudabaugh!" Wilson growled and delivered a vicious kick, but he slipped on the wet stones, and his boot only glanced off Dave's ribs. Rising, Rudabaugh cranked circles in the air with his elbow, testing the joint where the arm meets the shoulder. Fuming, the two outlaws squared off, crouching, their chains rattling as they hunched their shoulders up around their necks and pumped their fists in the air like pugilists circling in a fighting ring.

The office door opened, and last night's jailor strode in carrying an armload of firewood. Following him was Barney Mason, a shotgun in one hand and a Colt's revolver holstered high on his hip. Rudabaugh and Wilson straightened and stood as quiet and attentive as two children caught in their mischief.

"What the hell did you want to stink up your cell for, you damned fools?" Mason said, wincing at the new stench in the room.

"They're gonna be the ones to clean it up, by God," the jailor ordained and lowered his load of wood to the floor by the stove. Piece by piece he began stacking wood inside the heater.

Rudabaugh shuffled to the bars to scowl at the man kneeling at the stove. "Where the hell was that fire when we needed it last night?"

Without turning, the jailor took his time arranging the wood. "I got some repairs to address in the cell block after you stinkin' devils have cleared out. I don't wanna get chilled." Now he stood and gave Dirty Dave a gloating smile. "I'll light it after you boys start for the train." He strolled up to Mason and stopped. "I ain't cleaning up after a spilt piss bucket. Not for the likes of Rudy-bow. I'll bring soap, water, and some rags, and you can prod 'em with that scattergun to wipe the cell clean."

Mason nodded and turned to the two journalists. "Time's up!" he announced and jerked a thumb toward the door. "You two can take your leave." Insinuating himself between the cell and the reporters, Mason herded them toward the door.

Raines raised an arm and tried to peer over Barney Mason's shoulder at the Kid. "Mr. Bonney, may I talk with you again in Santa Fe?"

"My schedule is a little confining right now," Billy called out. "I'll try to work you in."

Koogler stood his ground before Mason and tried to puff out his narrow chest. "I have not managed a proper interview with this man here interfering." Gesturing toward Raines, he stepped closer to Mason and lowered his voice. "I was promised by our sheriff that—"

Mason halted the spate of protest by putting his face in Koogler's. "These boys are not prisoners of San Miguel County," he informed the newspaperman. "They're Garrett's!" Taking the Las Vegas journalist by the arm, Mason escorted him out of the cell block.

Before the door closed, Garrett entered the room, stooping to clear the lintel even with his hat in his hand. He was dressed for cold weather in his heavy buffalo robe overcoat. Behind him came Jim East, similarly clad in thick layers. Both were dotted with snow, their faces bronzed by the sun, looking as if they were just now returning from another manhunt. Mason returned to the cell block, closed the door, and leaned against the wall.

"Barney," Garrett said in his soft Southern drawl, "let's get these boys into their new clothes. I want to move them to the depot before a crowd can gather outside."

Mason nodded. "One minute, Pat." He pointed with the shotgun at Rudabaugh and Wilson. "These two monkeys have got some cleaning to do."

The cellblock door opened, and the jailor, with a mound of rags draped over one shoulder, toted in a heavy bucket and set it on the stones. Mason pointed the muzzle of the shotgun into the cell.

"Move back against the wall!" Mason ordered. "If you don't wanna go to Santa Fe, this'll be your chance to give me a reason to oblige you."

When the jailor sorted through his keys, Garrett put a hand on the old man's shoulder and gently turned him. "We don't have time for this," he intoned in a flat order. He turned to Mason, whose eyes took on the same hurt look from the night before. "Let's get those clothes on these boys and get moving."

When Mason scuffed into the front office, Rudabaugh approached the cell door and took a grip on the bars. "What about something to eat?" he complained.

Garrett gave him a withering glare. "Rather have a meal or your hide?"

"You could let Dave stay and have breakfast with all his Las Vegas friends," Billy suggested as he approached and gripped the bars. "The rest of us can go on to Santa Fe."

Garrett turned a dour face to Billy's boyish smile and then showed this same expression to the somber men in the rear of the cell. "All of you get dressed. We leave in ten minutes."

Mason returned with a double armload of folded, new clothes and dropped it all on the wet floor in front of the cell. Garrett gave Mason a silent glance of reprimand, turned and walked out of the cellblock with East following close behind him. Barney Mason delayed long enough to kick at the pile of clothes and tumble them over on the soiled floor. Then he, too, left.

The train had been parked on the side rail since its arrival in early morning. At nine o'clock Garrett and his deputies, in a closed wagon, arrived at the depot by a circuitous route. With barely a word spoken, the prisoners and lawmen boarded their assigned car, where half a dozen passengers eyed them with uncertain looks. As soon as the prisoners were seated, all the shades were pulled down over the windows. Three lamps were lighted, and in the muted glow the deputies ran chains through the prisoners' leg irons and seat supports until all were secure.

Fifteen minutes had not passed before Barney Mason came inside the car from his post at the rear coupling landing. "Pat," he called out, "they're on to us. We got a mob outside. They're coming across the plaza now."

Garrett assigned one deputy to guard the front door while he took the rear. The rest took positions at windows, where they peeked around window shades, their rifles at the ready.

"Damn, Pat," Billy laughed, "sounds like a big crowd out there. And all they want is Rudabaugh. That seems a small thing to ask."

The Kid carried his grin to Dirty Dave, but Rudabaugh would not look at him.

Garrett walked to the front of the car, turned, and addressed the few passengers who were not connected to his mission. "There's bound to be a fight here today," he explained in his no-nonsense voice. "I am an officer of the law sworn to deliver these men to Santa Fe. If you don't want to be part of this affair, I suggest you change cars. If you stay, pull out your hardware and give us a hand. It'll be appreciated."

As Garrett walked the length of the car to the rear, several people exited out the front. The few men who remained now held revolvers in their laps. At the backdoor Garrett kept his eyes on the unorganized mob milling around on the tracks. Still wearing his big dark overcoat, he stood in shadow like a tall tree that had taken root just inside the door.

"There may be a lot of them," Garrett told his men, "but they'll have to come in one at a time through these two doors. We'll see if there's a man out there willing to be the first one in."

Outside, where the mob moved among themselves like nervous livestock, one rough voice rose above the others, trying to galvanize the crowd into action. He was a stout, red-nosed man in a sheepskin coat with the collar pulled up around his thick neck. Hatless, he wore his hair slicked back over a balding spot at the crown of his skull. When he began shouting about the town's righteous duty to hang Rudabaugh, Garrett opened his door and planted one boot on the coupling platform, his rifle held next to his hip, the barrel angled down. The crowd quieted.

"All of you, get away from this train. I'm sheriff of Lincoln County and acting as a deputy U.S. marshal. I'm taking *all* these men to Santa Fe. You are obstructing the services of a federal officer in his duty."

"We've got five times your numbers, Garrett!" the red-nosed man challenged. "We can open up on you through the windows." The men around him murmured their agreement, and then all grew quiet to hear Garrett's reply.

Pat Garrett nodded and looked around at the numbers flooding the rail yard. "As to shooting through the windows," he said softly, "there are citizen passengers in here who are not connected with us. Do you want to be responsible for murdering them?"

He waited while a current of conversation passed through the crowd. When they grew quiet to hear more, Garrett could see that some of the citizens' resolve had abandoned them.

"As to your numbers, it's true you've got us over a barrel in that department. But you ain't got the kind of men I got."

"What does that mean?" the hot-headed spokesman said with a scoffing laugh.

Garrett waited for complete silence again. "It means . . . my deputies are battle-hardened and do not yield. They rode through a blizzard to arrest these men, and they have no patience with men like you who want to make a big show of *trying* to take their prisoners. You men have not earned that right." Before anyone could reply, Garrett raised his voice for the first time. "And know this . . . at the first shot fired, I will arm my prisoners." He pivoted his head, looking as many men in the eye as he could manage in the time that he waited for the silence he needed. Fixing his gaze on the spokesman again, he settled his voice back down to its soft Southern timbre. "If you try this, how many of your friends here do you reckon will die today?"

The red-nosed man looked off to one side as though he were expecting to see bad weather looming on the horizon. When he turned back to Garrett, he had nothing to say.

"Leave off on this and go home before anyone gets hurt," Garrett said. "So far, there hasn't been an offense committed. Let me do my job." He stared into the leader's baleful eyes until that man turned and folded back through the crowd. A few others followed, and slowly the momentum to disperse caught on. Garrett went back inside and ordered one of his deputies to make his way up to the front of the train to talk to the engineer.

"What'll I tell 'im?" the deputy asked.

Garrett pointed to the man's Winchester. "Take that with you and tell him to get this damned train started for Santa Fe *now!* If he balks, force him off the train and make his assistant take over."

The deputy hesitated. "Well, what if *he* balks?"

Garrett glared at his deputy. "Can you drive a train?"

The man's worried face tightened more as he shook his head.

"If they both refuse, come get me. I'll drive the damned thing myself if I have to."

When the deputy began moving up through the cars, Garrett leaned to the window beside Bonney, pried open the shade a crack, and checked the crowd outside.

"Hey, Pat," Billy said. "Did you mean that about givin' us our guns?"

Garrett nodded and kept peering out the glass. Billy cocked his head and smiled with a spark of mischief in his eye.

"You know, Pat, sometimes I think you and I ain't all that diff'rent from each other."

When Garrett made no reply, Billy narrowed his eyes at Rudabaugh, who had been quiet throughout the standoff. "You know what, Pat? I think ol' Dave here might be about halfway to soilin' his britches."

Garrett raised the shade on the window and straightened. "Looks like your interviewer is hounding you again." He pointed out the window, and Billy turned to see the *Gazette* reporter standing beside the track looking up at him. Opening the window, Billy stuck out his head and arms and greeted his visitor with his winning smile.

"Mr. Kookler!"

From the front door the deputy called Garrett's name. Holding the arm of Raines—the Santa Fe newspaperman—the deputy let his eyebrows float up with a question.

"He's got a ticket, Pat. Says he's travelin' with us."

"Let him in," Garrett ordered.

As Billy conversed with Koogler, Raines moved down the aisle in a cautious manner, his eyes darting around at the array of guns on display. Stopping before Garrett, the young reporter stood meekly, the top of his head leveling off at the sheriff's chin.

"Sheriff Garrett?" Raines began in a whisper, "I'm going to Santa Fe, too. May I sit with Mr. Bonney to continue my interview? And then, perhaps, I might talk with you, too?"

Garrett considered the journalist for five seconds. "You carrying any weapons?"

"No, sir," Raines replied. "I never do."

The sheriff motioned with the Winchester. "You can sit there with him if you want, but I'm not doing any interviews."

After Raines sat down next to Billy, he pulled out his notebook and waited as the *Gazette* man outside the window fired a volley of questions at the prisoner.

"Were you worried?" Koogler asked. "This was as angry a mob as I've ever seen here!"

"Nah!" Billy said. "These folks were just needin' to put on some show to make 'em feel better 'bout themselves. If I had my Winchester, I coulda licked the whole bunch all by myself."

Garrett used the muzzle of his rifle to tap on Billy's shoulder. "You got a guest, Kid."

Billy turned and laughed in delight at seeing the young Santa Fe reporter seated next to him. Taking Raines's hand, he shook with the gusto of a long-anticipated reunion.

"Well, hello, son. Are you back for more?"

Raines could not help but smile. "Yes, if I may."

Billy held up a forefinger. "Don't go anywhere!" He leaned back out the window. "Sorry, Mr. Kookler, but another journalist is here with me by appointment. And since you made no appointment—" He swept off his hat and waved it through the air.

"I'll say 'adios' to you now."

When Billy turned back to Raines and shook hands again, Garrett tapped the window glass with the muzzle of his rifle. "Close that window and pull down that shade until we're out of town."

When Billy did as asked, Garrett started for the rear door. Billy reached past Raines and tugged at Garrett's sleeve, stopping him.

"Say, Pat, how come you was to do that for Rudabaugh?" Billy asked in an earnest tone. "Why'd you stand up for 'im?" He spoke with complete frankness, as if Rudabaugh and Raines were not present to hear him.

Garrett responded in kind. "When I arrest a man, he becomes my responsibility. I don't care who he is or what he's done, I won't give him up to a bunch of fever-brained vigilantes."

"No matter what he done?" Billy said, intrigued.

Garrett fixed cold eyes on Rudabaugh's surly face. "I guess today proves that, don't it?"

Billy laughed and bumped Rudabaugh's shoulder with the back of his fist. "You hear that, Dave? Somebody actually cares about you."

Garrett waited until Rudabaugh turned to meet his eyes. "But if you snake out of this trial in Santa Fe," the sheriff said in his Alabama voice, "I'll bring you back here to Las Vegas myself to stand trial for murdering that jailor. Once I deliver you, I don't care what they do to you. So, maybe you'll get to meet all these folks again and finish up this little party they started."

The train lurched forward and began a slow buildup of speed. Now jittery, Rudabaugh leaned to the window and peered out through the shade at the depot sliding away from him. The chugging of the engine and the clacking of the rails rang out like a song of salvation.

Billy smiled up at Garrett. "You're a real man o' principles, Pat. You know that?"

When the train got up to speed, the window shades opened on both sides of the aisle, and light flooded into the car, highlighting a galaxy of dust motes stirring in the air. On both sides of the train, the last adobes and jacals of Las Vegas passed by them and gave way to ranches and open country.

Garrett winced, pushing his big moustache up to his nostrils. "You boys smell like a holding pen for sick cattle."

Billy smiled and pointed at Rudabaugh. "That's Dave. He fell all over his slop bucket this morning." He laughed. "I got to admit, Pat, it's one o' the reasons I was hoping you'd come out on the short end o' that little standoff you had back there." He nodded toward the rear of the car. "For my money, those boys coulda taken Rudabaugh, and I'd'a given 'em my blessing."

Garrett almost smiled. "Did you forget the two of you are chained together, Billy?"

Billy smiled. "Well, I figured they'd take pity on me for being paired up with 'im in chains. I reckon they'd'a spared me."

Garrett looked from one to the other, as if studying the differences in the two outlaws before him. "Those are all *what-ifs,*" Garrett said. "That makes them pointless to ponder."

Billy sat forward and pointed at the sheriff. "Now that's where you and I really differ, Pat. It's the what-ifs that keep my pony runnin'." Billy narrowed his eyes and shook his head. "Without the what-ifs, there just ain't no hope, Pat."

Garrett gave Billy a doubtful look. "I wouldn't be putting too much stock in hope, Kid. You got too many indictments against you."

Billy sat back with a smug smile. "I reckon we'll just have to wait an' see, won't we?"

Garrett gazed out the window at the landscape drifting past them. The speed at which they moved made it seem that time had somehow gone haywire and changed the way a man ought to look at the world.

"I reckon so, Billy," he said and, balancing himself by the seat backs, moved off toward the rear of the car, leaving the Kid with his interview.

17
Blessing's Notes
Offices of *The Santa Fe Messenger*
and County Jail
Santa Fe, New Mexico Territory
January 1881

"I can never hope to be like you, could never match your smile
But I know I am a better man to know you this short while."

I usually depart the *Messenger* offices by four thirty on Wednesdays simply because my chorale rehearsals at the church begin at five sharp. Today is different. I sit at my desk pretending to edit my article on the collective works of the late Dostoevsky, but all my faculties are focused on the tongue-lashing that spills out of my editor's office and fills the press room with a sense of dread.

Poor Raines! He has been working as a reporter for less than a month, and already he has incurred a dozen of these scathing critiques concerning his writing. In my eight months as a staff reporter, I received only one of these soul-numbing lectures. It was in my first week on the job, and I am determined never to be its recipient again. When Edmond Pitts's journalistic sensitivities are insulted by inferior writing, he employs the coruscating voice of a prison guard. I well remember my brief introduction to his anger. It was like facing into an August sandstorm with both eyes open.

It is common knowledge in the office that Raines secured the job through his father, who serves as an assistant to the territorial secretary of finances; still, it is difficult not to pity the boy. We all know that Eustace Raines has limited skills in writing, but he is courteous and likeable . . . like the solemn schoolboy who wants to learn his numbers but lacks the capacity to keep them in their proper order.

But there is more to this pall of tension hanging over the office than hearing young Raines being dressed down. I am wondering why Mr. Pitts has asked me to remain after hours and be a witness to the wretched affair. I check my pocketwatch. The harangue has lasted ten minutes, and not once have I heard Raines's voice dare to enter the fray.

"Blessing!" Pitts roars from behind his closed door.

To hear my name yelled with such ferocity brings me to my feet like a soldier called to attention. I march across the room to my editor's door, open it, and see displeasure written all over Pitts's face as he glares at me from behind his desk. Raines stands before him, head down and shoulders sagging. He looks as if he has been beaten down by a hailstorm. I cannot see his face, but his stillness suggests he is a thoroughly chastised man.

Exhaling sharply through his nose, Pitts beckons me to enter with a quick, fluttery motion of his fingers. I close the door and step forward quickly to stand abreast of Raines.

"Blessing, I want you to teach Raines here how to handle obituaries." He scowls at the boy as he speaks, and then his eyes snap back to me. "He'll be in charge of the dead for a while, until he learns something about interviewing the living. Just lay out a format for him that he can follow. Can you do that?"

"Tonight?" I say.

Pitts gives me his malicious smile. "Unless you think people will stop dying because it inconveniences you."

I glance at Raines, but he remains catatonic. I spread my feet and prepare for the coming battle.

"Sir, I have my chorale work to get to. My singers are down at the church now, waiting for me . . . depending on me."

Pitts sits back deeper in his chair, crosses his arms over his rounded belly, and cocks his head as he smiles at me. "Blessing, how much will you be paid for this project at the church?"

I lick my lips and frown. "Sir, this is part of the program for the Festival of—"

"How much!" he interrupts.

I settle my gaze on the floor next to Raines's shoes. "There is no pay, sir."

Pitts sits forward and flops one of his forearms on his desktop, his hand fisted like a judge's gavel. "And how much do I pay you each week?"

Feeling his eyes bear down on me with the weight of his position as my employer, I am quiet for as long as I dare. "Eleven dollars a week, sir."

He pushes his bushy eyebrows higher on his forehead. "Then I would say you are a journalist first. It is your paying work here that allows you to pursue your hobbies, correct?"

In this instant I catch a glimpse of an image of my life tottering on an assayer's scale—rich ore on one side and pyrite on the other. I realize that I am perched upon a watershed moment that will, depending upon my reply, dictate the course of my immediate life for better or for worse. My pride wants to say *I am a musician!* but my bank account begs otherwise.

"I'm a journalist, Mr. Pitts," I say dutifully.

Victorious, Pitts raises his hand and flicks the backs of his fingers toward Raines. "You may go now. You start with obituaries tomorrow." He points at me but lowers his eyes. "Get with Blessing first thing in the morning. I want you up and running on this by ten o'clock."

Relief floods through me. I turn to leave, but Raines is reluctant to go. "Sir," he pleads, "the statistics I used were drawn out by the *Gazette* man. Since he is more experienced than I—"

"Koogler could not accurately report on fresh horse flop!" Pitts decrees. "He writes like a maudlin old woman." With a pained look, he makes a movement as if sweeping Raines from the room with the backs of his hands. When I start my pivot to leave, Pitts levels his forefinger at me as if it were a loaded revolver. "You stay! I have a job for you!"

Hearing Raines exit the front door, I cannot help but envy him. I can only pray that he has the decency to contact the church to let them know I will be late for rehearsal tonight.

Pitts lifts a sheaf of papers from his desk and holds them, poised to read. "Listen to this," he chuckles and makes a vague gesture with one hand for me to sit, which I do. " 'After a standoff in which one outlaw was killed,' " he reads aloud, " 'Billy Bonney and three of his associates were captured by Pat Garrett's posse at Stinking Spring east of Fort Sumner.' " Pitts pushes out his lower lip and dips his head to one side. "Not a bad start," he concedes. *"But—"* He holds up an index finger to keep me in place.

Through the paper I see lines of longhand. "He didn't submit a typed article?" I ask.

Pitts produces a tight smile. "He can't type," he quips and continues to read. " 'This reporter rode the train from Las Vegas to Santa Fe with Bonney. I sat right next to him, and we talked for most of the journey. So enthralled with his adventures in crime was I that I remember nothing of the scenery outside the window. Nor did I think once about the pain in my hip that usually arrives when I sit for too long.' "

Pitts slaps the papers to his desk and glares at me. "You see how quickly this becomes about the interviewer rather than the interviewee?" Shaking his head, he picks up the papers and grudgingly continues. " 'Billy Bonney is not the desperado who I expected.' " Pitts gives me a quick editorial sneer over the improper "who." He sniffs and goes on. " 'He is about my weight and height—one hundred forty pounds and a little over five feet six inches. His handsome face is smooth and youthful with a slight fuzz that shows he does not yet shave. His front teeth are ever so slightly prominent and misaligned, giving him that appeal that mothers respond to in their children. He and I are the same age at twenty-one. The odd thing is this: I sometimes felt I was conversing with someone much older, someone who has experienced so much more than me.' "

Pitts pauses again and arches another editorial eyebrow at the improper pronoun in the comparison. Then he continues in his pedantic drone.

" 'Other times he was like a schoolboy acting up, pulling pranks. For example, during the noon meal on the train one of the deputies expressed an interest in a last wedge of pecan pie. Bonney, though manacled with heavy chains, quick as a cat scooped up the pie and jammed the entire piece into his mouth. He then gave the disappointed deputy a poker face, as the group around these two burst into laughter.

" 'The embarrassed deputy got angry and employed a whirlwind of profanity that cannot be repeated here in ink. Bonney appeared contrite. After drooping his head in shame, he suddenly produced the triangle of pie from his mouth intact, looking no different than it had when he had lifted it from the plate.

" 'At this juncture in the performance, Bonney said, "You're right, Barney, that was thoughtless and greedy of me. I surrender my pie to your authority." The men around these two again roared with laughter.' "

Pitts tosses the papers to my side of the desk. "It goes on and on like this. Fix it! It goes to press tonight. My pressmen will work all night if necessary. We know the *Optic* and the *New Mexican* are running Bonney interviews tomorrow. If we don't run one, we may as well hoist a white flag." He backhands the air in the general direction of the business section of town. "To some people, the capture of this adolescent killer is the biggest news the territory has seen in years. This boy's crimes have cost ranchers a lot of money. And many men who went up against him paid with their lives."

Stepping forward, I pick up the packet of papers. "How long?" I ask.

Pitts shows sharp lines around his mouth as he frowns at the papers in my hand. "That one is much too long. I can give you a half a column under the masthead . . . front page . . . three hundred fifty words. Forget all that malarkey about the pie!"

He selects a dead, half-smoked cigar butt from the cookie tin that serves as an ash tray on his desk. As he strikes a lucifer and lights the disgusting remnant, I look down at Raines's wandering handwriting. But I do not read the words. I am picturing my chorale group sitting around the organ in the nave, wondering where I am. When the cigar smoke wafts my way, I resolve to hold my ground against the repulsive smell.

"Sir," I say, bolstering my courage, "I have choral musicians who are expecting me to—"

Pitts halts my speech with an ink-stained hand flattened at me. "I'll send the clean-up boy to let them know you are not able to attend tonight. Which church is it again?"

I dare to enter an eyeball-to-eyeball standoff with Edmund Pitts. After three heartbeats of peering through the acrid cloud of smoke, I know that I am outmatched.

"Mr. Pitts, in addition to being the choral director, I am the organist. Without me—"

" 'Without you,' " he interrupts, "they can practice . . . what is the word?" He waves the cigar in the air, creating a swirl of smoke. " 'Capa-bella'?" he tries, sounding ridiculous.

I temper my voice to correct him. "*A capella.*"

"*That's* it!" he says and jabs the red tip of the cigar my way. Using the usual sweeping motion with his hand, he dismisses me from his office. "Now go write something we can use! Trump those hacks at the *Optic* and the *New Mexican*! Let's sell some papers tomorrow!"

After he pulls out a mock-up sheet and begins assigning the spaces for articles within the allotted columns, I remain and watch him scratch notes across the page. He works as if I am not present.

"It's the Loretto Chapel," I say.

Pitts looks up, annoyed. "What?"

"Send the boy to the Loretto Chapel. He can tell my choral group we will meet tomorrow."

Pitts taps the cigar on the edge of the tin and gives me a gloating smile. "See? That wasn't so hard, was it? Maybe you *are* a journalist, Blessing." Lifting the bell on his desktop, he rings as if he is calling the territorial legislature to order. "Boy!" he yells.

"His name is Joseph," I remind, but Pitts doesn't hear me. He is at work again.

I walk out of the office and intercept the errand boy as he hurries to answer Pitts's call. His skin shows the olive cast of the Mexican population, but his fearful eyes are the color of green glass, all of which has led me to believe he is a mixed blood of some kind. After instructing him with precise details for my singers, I retire to my desk. Joseph continues to his destination, reports to Pitts, and then jogs past me on his way outside to the church. After laying out my notebook and pen, I wade into the shallow waters of Raines's rejected article.

After an hour and a half of sorting through the usable information in Raines's piece, I have produced a finished product and begin to type it, proofing as I go.

The Notorious "Kid" Captured at Last
by Eustace Raines and John Blessing

Those who do not know William Bonney (alias "Billy the Kid") personally might think him a feral dog scarred with gunshots, riddled with fleas, half starved, and vicious enough to take a bite out of a child's plump leg. But his very appearance belies his outlaw life.

At twenty-one years old, he presents a slim but striking countenance. He wears no facial hair, but this is not a decision about fashion. His smooth cheeks still show the silky sheen of youthful fuzz never touched by a razor, which only seems to promote a paradoxical innocent visage for a man who has killed so freely. His boyish good looks, it is commonly said, endear him to females who want to smother him with motherly love. Children love him, because he takes time to talk to them . . . even to teach them games. At the same time his ever-ready smile tantalizes the señoritas with a more carnal pounding in their hearts.

He has dark-blue eyes, weighs one hundred forty pounds, stands a hair over five feet six inches, and wears a healthy mop of wavy, light-brown hair, but what most women see in him, I am told, is the snap in those eyes. That and his smile. He is, by all accounts, a charmer.

Bonney's hands are small, nearly effeminate, so much so that his slender fingers might, to some, seem out of place wrapped around the handle of a revolver. His slight frame is offset by a certain grace of movement and, when he chooses to employ it, a cat-like quickness.

It is rumored that he has ended the lives of twenty-one men, but he denies it. He will go on trial for two murders—one concerning the death of Andrew "Buckshot" Roberts at Blazer's Mill and the other for Sheriff Brady in Lincoln. He also faces charges of livestock theft.

Now Mr. Bonney resides here in the territorial capital awaiting his court appearance in Lincoln County. His current lodgings
are on Water Street at our fine county jail.

Before going into Pitts's office to deliver the article, I put on
my overcoat, as an overt message that I intend to depart the
premises as soon as possible. I have no intension of laboring
through a rewrite. When I drop my story on his desk, Pitts looks
up from the ledger in which he is writing and pins me with his
I-need-you-to-do-something-else glare.

"I have arranged with the sheriff for you to interview Bonney
tomorrow at three o'clock."

I frown. "When did this come about?"

He closes his book and puts it away in a drawer. "I had the
boy stop by the jail after he ran down to your church."

" 'Three o'clock,' " I repeat, thinking about my five o'clock
rehearsal. I can't imagine spending more than an hour with a
rustler and murderer. "All right, I can do that."

He picks up my typed copy, slumps back in his chair, and,
with thumb and forefinger, squeezes his lower lip into a fleshy
pocket as he reads. I am unsure if I should stay for a critique or
slip out and grasp my freedom while he is occupied. I choose
the less consequential option.

Pitts laughs, just a deep rumble in his chest, but it is the first
time I have heard something humane bubble up from his
dictatorial soul. "That's good!" he says and laughs again as he
taps his finger to a particular paragraph on the paper.

I take a mental picture of the smile he has allowed me to see.
I will want to describe it to a few of my fellow journalists to
know if they have ever witnessed such approval from the old
man. For another minute I watch his amused eyes slide from
side to side as he reads the lines.

"Very good!" he growls and slaps the paper down on the desk

with a flattened hand. He picks up the bell and rings it as he opens another drawer and begins probing and rattling through its contents. When he pulls out a bottle of whiskey, I am startled to think that I might have reached some new plateau of writing acclaim after these months working for the *Messenger*. He bangs the glass bottle down on the desk and laughs again. Apparently, a celebration is in order.

He unscrews the cap and throws back three back-to-back draws of the amber liquid, his throat gulping and pulsating as if he has swallowed a panicked frog. When the bottle strikes down on the desk again, he exhales in a gale of alcoholic fumes. I almost step forward to take my part in the festivities, when he screws down the cap and returns the bottle to its drawer.

"Only after hours," he confides with a sly smile. "It's an editor's commandment that I adhere to."

The boy, Joseph, enters the office and looks from Pitts to me and back to Pitts. "Sir?"

"Take this to the typesetter," Pitts instructs him, but rather than hand him the paper he pulls out a pencil. On the front of my article he scratches out my name to leave Raines as the sole author. Then he smiles at me. "So we don't fall out of grace with the governor's office." Whipping the paper from the desk he extends it to the boy and addresses me.

"We'll need another story that goes inside Bonney's thinking," Pitts ordains. "We'll want to know why he's committed all these crimes . . . how a boy his age can so easily kill . . . that kind of thing." He turns his attention to the errand boy. "How old are you, boy?"

Surprised, Joseph straightens. "Almost thirteen, sir."

"You ever kill anyone, son?"

The boy's eyes widen. "No, sir!"

"Well, what if you had to? *Could* you kill someone?"

"What do you mean?" Joseph asks in a timid voice. "Why

255

would I have to?"

Pitts shrugs. "What if someone was to do harm to your mother? Could you kill then?"

Joseph frowns. "Anybody would do that, sir. Wouldn't you?"

"Too late for me," Pitts says. "My mother died in seventy-four." Pitts snorts a laugh. "Good thing, too. I considered killing her a few times, myself." Getting no comment from either of us, he uses both hands to dismiss the two of us. Joseph leaves, but I stand my ground.

"Mr. Pitts, may I ask who gets credit for the next article I write about Bonney?"

He gives me a dismissive wave. "Oh, don't get your feathers up, Blessing. Politics plays its part in a newspaper, too. Your name will go on all subsequent pieces. Now go!"

And so I do.

After gathering my things, I leave the building and start for the plaza, until someone moves out of the alley to my left and approaches at a fast walk. "Mr. Blessing?"

I recognize Joseph's voice and feel my heart settling back into my chest after trying to climb out of my throat. "Why are you skulking around in the dark? Don't you know you can get shot doing something like that?"

"Sorry if I scared you, sir," the boy whispers and looks back toward the newspaper building as if checking to see if we are being watched. "I need to tell you something before you go to the jail tomorrow."

"All right then. What is it?"

"Bee-lee is not what people say he is. He's a good friend to those who are poor."

I drape the strap of my satchel over my head, widen my stance, and jam my hands into my overcoat pockets. "You know Bonney?"

"Yes, sir. Before I started work here, we lived at Fort Sumner.

We all knew him there."

With my eyes adjusting to the dark, I lean in to study his face. "Are you Hispanic?"

He nods. "My mother is Mexican. I am told my father was an Anglo at Fort Stanton."

"You don't have much of an accent, Joseph."

"No, sir. My mother . . . she raised me to fit into the white world. My true name is José," he explains and gestures toward the newspaper building, "but here I am Joseph."

"So you know Bonney personally? You've talked to him?"

Joseph nods, and by the gleam in his eyes I know he is telling the truth. "Me and my friends used to watch him practice with his pistol. He would line up empty cans and bottles on a fence, then he would stand back and pick them off. He would let us name which target to hit."

"Was he good at it?"

Joseph's eyebrows rise higher on his forehead. "In all the times I watched him, I never saw him miss but once. He was quick, too." He shakes his head slowly. "I have never seen anyone shoot like him. He is not like most men."

"What do you mean by that?"

The boy shrugs. "Like the time he missed. That was when my amigo Julio surprised him and threw a bottle into the air. Bee-lee tried to shoot it, but the bottle was falling fast. Most men would have been angry or made some excuse. Bee-lee laughed and said, 'Well, let's hope some flyin' whiskey bottle is never out to get me.' "

I can't help but laugh. "What is it you would have me write about Mr. Bonney, Joseph? If you could perform the interview, what would *you* ask?"

He props his hands on his hips and looks toward the business section of town. Only the glow from the saloons throws any light out onto the plaza.

"I have only a mother, sir, but that is enough for me. She works hard and provides for me in every way." He nods toward the *Messenger* building. "I took this job because I want to help her buy the things we need."

"Well, that's very good, Joseph. But what is your point?"

He lifts both arms from his sides a few inches and lets them fall back in a muted slap against his clothing. "Bee-lee didn't have anybody . . . not since he was young like me. And he didn't have a place to live. He was on his own. Ask him what that was like. People might think better of him if they read about that."

Fifty yards away, two men exit a bar, both of them laughing in a rowdy manner. Joseph and I watch them stumble across the plaza and enter another lighted doorway, where they are greeted by a whoop from another saloon's patrons.

"I'll keep that in mind, Joseph," I promise, and together we turn for the plaza. When he starts to veer off west beyond the Palace of the Governors, I call out to him. "Is there anything I can tell Mr. Bonney for you, Joseph?"

The boy stops and smiles. "Tell him that José still practices the trick with the three stones. Tell him I am getting better." He waves and begins jogging for home.

At three o'clock sharp I stand like a human crucifix in the county sheriff's office, my arms extended from my sides as a Deputy East runs his hands over my person, searching for weapons. He even checks my private area, his manner as clinical as that of a doctor examining his patient. I suppose such necessities are standard fare to lawmen.

"Billy's already got 'im quite a audience in there," East informs me. "Go on inside. Just remember not to get too close to his cell."

When he opens the door to the cell block, I hear a young voice holding forth beyond the knot of men crowded before the last cell. Though I can see only the backs of their heads, the listeners appear to be rapt. Some are taking notes. I recognize two reporters from other newspapers. Three others are Santa Fe businessmen.

"Most people got no idea how many abandoned mine shafts there are out in that country," the speaker continues. "The wrong step can be a damned calamity. A man can get swallowed up right quick without no one to know the difference for miles around."

Joining the back of the crowd, I rise up on my toes to see a handsome youth behind the bars, his smile revealing two front teeth that are barely misaligned. His eyes dart around as though he wants to look at everyone at once. It is my first view of Billy Bonney, for I have no doubt that this is the famed outlaw. Despite his poor writing, Eustace Raines has described him well.

Behind Bonney are three others stretched out on crude bunks, their backs turned to the crowd, a blanket covering each prisoner from boots to shoulders. In an adjacent cell two rough-looking men sit on their beds with their backs to the wall, their legs stretched out before them. They appear as caught up in the story as the other spectators.

"So there I am," Bonney says, crouching and spreading his hands with the flair of a seasoned raconteur, " 'bout a hundred feet down in the dark a-lookin' up at a patch o' blue sky that seems 'bout the size of a dinner plate." He pauses to show his audience a solemn expression, and then he holds a half-completed shrug as if his muscles have locked up. "I figure I'm a goner. The stone walls are wet and slick as bear grease. No way I can climb outta there."

"But how did you survive the fall, Billy?" someone asks.

Bonney stares down at the floor for a time. "Spiderwebs," he says at last. "Must'a been thousands of 'em. When there's that many, you'd be surprised at what they're capable of."

A murmur of laughter ripples through the crowd.

"So, what'd you do?" a man asks.

"Well, I was damned lucky," Bonney goes on. "Old Barney Mason, there, come along." He points to the heavily armed deputy leaning against the wall to my right, and all heads turn to him. "Yes, sir . . . Barney was my salvation, even though it took two tries to get it right."

The stoic guard ignores Bonney. Under the scrutiny of everyone in the room, he pulls a twist of tobacco from his pocket, bites off a chaw, and works on it with his jaws knotting.

Bonney cups a hand beside his mouth and calls up to the ceiling of his cell. " 'Is that Barney Mason up there?' " he calls out, now reliving the story like a stage actor.

The crowd looks at the guard again, but he remains aloof, chewing, and staring angrily at his boots as if he is enduring a diatribe on police brutality.

"Barney's a little embarrassed, folks," Bonney explains. "You'll understand when I finish relatin' this story."

Raising his head, the deputy fixes the prisoner with a loathsome glare.

"What about it, Deputy?" one of the reporters asks. "Is there any truth to this tale, or are we being hornswoggled?"

Saying nothing, Mason stares at the man and chews in a steady rhythm.

"So there I am at the bottom of the shaft," Bonney continues, "and I yell up to ol' Barn." Again Bonney pretends to call up to the ceiling. " 'Can you help me get outta here?' " Now the Kid changes character. He frowns, puffs out his chest, and props his hands on his hips as he peers down into an imagined mine shaft. Deepening his voice, he adds a raspy texture for his Barney Mason portrayal. " 'Well, whatta ya want me to do, Kid?' " Returning to his own voice, Bonney calls to the ceiling again. " 'Have you got a rope, Barn?' " He lowers his voice and delivers the answer to the floor. " 'Yeah, I got a rope. So what?' "

Bonney smiles and leans into the bars of his cell to deliver a confidential aside to his spectators. "It goes like this for a few exchanges. You see"—Bonney flattens a hand beside his mouth as if to shield his words from Mason, but he whispers loud enough to be heard by everyone in the cell block—"Barney can be a little slow sometimes." Assuming his original storytelling voice, he continues. "It takes a while but I finally convince Barney that throwing a rope to me would be the answer to my prayers."

The prisoner closes his eyes and flattens his hands together, palm to palm before his chin. His wrist chains jangle briefly before settling into a quiet and lazy swing beneath his arms. Then he opens a rascally eye to make sure all are still with him. Breaking from this pose, he props his hands on his hips again.

"So, Barney disappears for a while, and I know he's fetchin' his rope. When he returns to the edge of the shaft he yells down to me, 'I still don't see how this is gonna help you, Kid.' And I say, 'Just throw 'er down, Barn.' And he does! And right away I realize he was right all along. That rope wasn't going to help me a lick."

"Was it too short?" someone asks.

With a sober expression, Bonney shakes his head. "Nope . . . plenty long."

"Too weak?" another man tries. "The kind to break on you?"

Still solemn, Bonney shakes his head again. "Nope . . . felt plenty strong."

"Well, what was wrong with it?" a reporter queries.

Bonney shakes his head as if reliving the predicament right there in his cell. Leaning into the bars of the door, he lowers his voice to draw his listeners in.

"Truth be told, weren't nothin' wrong with that rope."

The crowd went quiet . . . waiting for the riddle to be revealed.

"So," Bonney continues, "I yell up to Barney, 'Barn, you wouldn' have a second rope, would you?' " Now the storyteller assumes a startled expression. "And, by God . . . against all odds . . . he does! So I holler up to him, 'Can you get that one now, Barn?' 'Sure,' he says. He's gone for a few seconds, and then he returns with his second rope. He yells down to me, 'Whatta ya want me to do with this one?' And I say, 'Throw that one down, too.' After pondering over my request, Barney balks, sayin', 'I don't see how this'n will work out any better.' "

Bonney addresses his punch line to the ceiling. " 'This time, Barn, when you throw down the rope . . . could you hold on to one end?' "

The laughter that erupts fills the cell block with an acoustic roar. Everyone looks at the deputy to see his reaction, but the joyless man wears his same dead-eyed glare, apparently sending a private message to his prisoner.

"I'm all outta stories, boys," Bonney says. "Who's got another question for me?"

All arms go up, including my own. The cocky prisoner smiles as he considers selecting one of us. When his eyes settle on me, I feel my face warm as if I have been caught in some mischievous act.

"Let's hear from this young man, why don't we?" Bonney says. "He ain't had a chance to speak up yet." He rises up on his toes to better see me. "Are you a reporter, too?"

When everyone turns to see who has caught the prisoner's attention, I feel sure the color of my face has deepened to that of a setting sun. Looking down at my notebook, I review the questions I had prepared for this meeting. I choose one of these to get my paralyzed tongue working.

"Yes," I answer. "I write for the *Santa Fe Messenger*. I

understand that within the last week you lost two of your best friends to Pat Garrett's posse."

Bonney holds on to his smile, but it no longer appears genuine. In the silence that grips the room, I feel the urgent need to say more, so I blurt out the first thought that comes to mind.

"I would like to ask about those men—Thomas Folliard and Charles Bowdre—for they can no longer speak for themselves. Perhaps you can say something on their behalf for the sake of the people who loved them. Something their families might like to read in the paper."

Billy's face loses all its pretension and showmanship. His blue eyes are as earnest as a dying man uttering his last words. Without his teeth on display, Billy Bonney is indeed a handsome young man. Now that he has turned serious, I sense that he possesses a natural charisma that would make men and women alike feel they could talk to him about anything.

Before he can answer, the cell block door opens, and Deputy Mason stirs from his corpse-like pose and levels his rifle at the office entrance. All the spectators turn to see Deputy East enter the room and give Mason a look that lowers the guard's rifle.

"Time's up, gentlemen," East announces.

I let the others move past me so I can approach East in private. When I stand before him, I have to look up to meet his eyes. He studies me with toleration.

"Mr. East, my editor arranged my interview with the prisoner through the sheriff. My appointment was for three o'clock. As you may remember, I was prompt."

"Hey, Jim," Bonney calls out. "Let 'im stay, would you? He got no show in this confab."

East looks over my head at the prisoner, takes in a deep breath, and turns to Mason.

"I gotta listen to more of Bonney's mouth?" Mason gripes.

When East does not answer, Mason hitches up his rifle in one hand and starts for the door. "I'm goin' to the privy. If you want a guard in here for all this hogwash, you can stay yourself."

After Mason exits the room, East speaks over me to Bonney. "You got water in there, Kid?"

"Well, I'd rather I was wadin' through the waters of the Pecos," Bonney replies, "but . . . yeah . . . I got enough."

East looks down at me and seems to consider my plight. "I want you to stay back five feet from those bars, understand?"

"I do," I assure him.

He purses his lips and checks on the other prisoners, who remain dormant on their bunks. When he faces me again, he lowers his voice to a personable tone.

"I got work to do. You gonna be all right in here alone?"

"Certainly," I say.

He nods, but still he seems reluctant to leave. "You need anything, just knock on the door," he says quietly to me. "Mason should be back directly."

"Thank you so much, Mr. East."

When the deputy closes the door behind him, I turn back to Bonney, who still stands with a loose grip on the bars of his cell. Leaning his forearms on the crossbar, he clasps his manacled hands together outside the bars. I step closer but stop at the recommended distance.

"Tom Folliard was my closest pard," Bonney whispers, his voice filling the space between us like a shared prayer. "Tom was a orphan, too, you know. On his own against the world." He looks to one side as though he can see through the walls at some scene from his past. "And Charlie was as good a man as you'd wanna ride with. We all woulda worked a ranch together somewhere if we coulda got through this war."

After writing this down, I ask, "When did *you* become an orphan, Mr. Bonney?"

Bonney offers a melancholic smile. "Better call me 'Billy.' I might not recognize who you're talkin' to with that 'mister' attached." Billy tilts his head forward to rest on the bars and looks down at the floor. "Let's see. Never knew my real father. He died when I was a baby. I was fourteen when my mother died. My stepfather left when my mother passed."

I think back to my own level of maturity at that age, and I wince. "How did you manage to stay alive?"

Billy laughs, but his eyes are dull. "Any damn way I could." Then his voice turns somber. "Back to Tom," he continues, "he was a damned good soldier. Woulda done anythin' I told 'im. You can't ask for better'n that." A troubled look wrinkles his brow. "After they shot 'im at Fort Sumner, I hear the posse played poker while waitin' for Tom to die."

"That's true," I reply. "The deputy—East—told me after Tom was shot, they brought him inside to a fire so that he could die in a warm place. And, yes, there was a card game. But the sheriff and the deputy were decent to your friend, even as Tom cursed them. East brought your friend water, and Garrett beseeched him to rest easy as he was living the last few minutes of his life, and he ought not go out with such anger in him."

Billy's head comes up, and he stares into my eyes. "Pat said that?"

I nod. "I am told your friend died peacefully, if such a thing is possible with a gunshot."

Billy looks down again at the cold earthen floor of his cell and presses his head into a gap between the bars. His wavy hair is circled by what appears to be a permanent indention from the fit of his hat.

"What was Tom like?" I ask. "Outside of this war, I mean?"

Billy raises his head and allows a tender smile. "He was a tall, Irish, red-headed powder keg who was loyal to his friends. Always first to offer to do a chore. Build a fire. Cook up a meal.

Clean up a fry pan. Picket the horses. He could stand guard all night if need be and live in the saddle for days on end. He was gettin' pretty damn good with his *pistola*, too."

"Sounds like he learned how to take care of himself," I venture.

Billy cracks a crooked smile. "Well, it's either that or go toes up in a unmarked grave somewhere."

"And as for Bowdre?" I prod.

Billy nods. "Charlie and I go way back. Met him when I first come into this country." His eyes glaze over with a memory, and he snorts a laugh. "Charlie tol' me I was a pebble in his boot in those days, but we got to be pals o' the highest order."

One of the other prisoners stirs in his bunk, turning his head to project his voice toward us. "Be sure to tell 'im how your so-called 'friend o' the highest order' had a little midnight chat with Pat Garrett just before we got hemmed in at Stinkin' Spring."

Billy frowns and shakes his head. "Rudabaugh don't know what he's talkin' 'bout. He's just mad 'cause the judge found him guilty this morning. Got nine'y years for robbing the mail. And now he's gotta go back to Las Vegas to stand trial for murderin' the jailor there." He presses his face between the two bars again and lowers his voice to a confidential tone. "Charlie Bowdre never turned against any o' us. He just wanted outta the outlaw life. He had a wife to take care of. He tol' me all about that meetin' with Garrett."

"Then why was he with you at Stinking Spring?" I press.

Billy shrugs. "Just bad timin', I reckon. It was to be his last ride with the Regulators."

"And what will his wife do now?"

Billy's eyes take on a pensive shade of blue. "I reckon she'll just keep on goin'. She's a capable woman." He coughs up a dry laugh and shakes his head once. "When the posse brought

Charlie's body back into Fort Sumner, I thought Manuela would kill Garrett. She tried to beat 'im to death with her fists until some o' the lawmen pulled 'er off 'im." Billy squints one eye and raises a manacled hand to point at me. "I believe if she coulda got her hands on a gun, she'd'a shot ol' Pat, presto-changeo . . . and maybe the deputies, too."

A coarse laugh issues from Rudabaugh's bunk. "Well, somebody oughta kill the long-legged sonovabitch!" Rudabaugh rolls our way on his pallet. "If I could get my hands on a gun, I'd do the job for 'er. Then I'd shoot my way outta this stinkin' place and ride hard for Mexico."

Billy laughs and lowers his voice for me alone. "If I could get *my* hands on a gun, first thing I'd wanna do is shoot Ruda-baugh. He's gettin' pretty ripe to live with."

Looking down at my notebook, I let my hand lie idle on the page. For some reason that I cannot explain, I prefer that the public not read about a threat of murder from Billy Bonney's lips . . . even if his victim would be Dave Rudabaugh.

I summon my most sincere voice. "How does someone so young become so easily inured to killing, Billy?"

He lifts both eyebrows and fills his cheeks with air as he exhales. "I reckon it's like most anything else. If you do it enough, you get used to it."

After I write this down, I study his pensive face. "But you were so young when you started. I don't see how—"

He fixes his eyes on me with an intensity that makes my breath catch. "I bet you never got on the losin' end of a scrape with a bully twice your weight who was tryin' to crack your skull with fists the size of bricks."

I shake my head. "No, I—"

"Well, if you ever do . . . and if he's got you pinned down on the ground so you can't get free . . . and there's a crowd standin' 'round cheerin' the bastard on—" Straightening from the bars, he stands eye to eye with me. "If you could reach a gun, what would you do?"

I swallow and see that he is waiting for an answer. "I'm not sure," I admit.

Billy laughs. "Well, a man who can't make up his mind will not survive." Angry, he looks away from me, and I take the opportunity to study his slight build. I try to imagine him grappling with a larger man, but the picture does not bode well for Billy.

"That's how it started for me," he says in an offhand manner. "When you get outmatched like that, you do whatever it takes. You can't count on somebody else throwin' you a rope. You got to pull yourself out."

He fixes me with a serious gaze, and for a moment I imagine a younger version of him.

"I reckon once you kill a man," he says in a calm voice, "somethin' is different down inside you. I think it ages you a few years . . . presto-changeo! And then, the next time you get in a scrape and got to make some show, that gun just jumps into your hand and knows what to do."

As the Kid watches me write my notes, I feel a cold tingle run down my spine. It's like the trickling of ice water. This is my first conversation with a known killer. Standing just six feet away from him, I am keenly aware that *his* face is the last his victims saw . . . assuming they were shot from the front. When I finish writing I stare at the paper, but I don't read. I do my best to inject a reporter's neutrality into my voice.

"Does it not bother you that you have ended the lives of other men?"

When I look up at him, he is casually shaking his head as if I had asked him about his preference for beef over venison. "The men I killed had writ their own death warrants. Ever' one of 'em had a black heart, due to the fact that they, too, had killed.

Either that or they were tryin' to kill me." Staring at me, he appears to dare me to challenge his logic.

"Does this go back to the murder of Mr. Tunstall? I've heard he was like a father to you."

He shrugs off the question, and I fear I have trespassed into a place too personal. "I reckon you had a good father," Billy says coolly. "Am I right?"

"Yes," I reply. "He was a hard-working man. Loving to my mother." I lower my eyes for a confession I have never before admitted. "I'm afraid I was a bit of a disappointment to him. He did not know how to conceive of a son dedicating his life to writing music."

Billy's face brightens. "You're a musician?!" He claps his hands, and the manacle chains jangle. "I knew there was something 'bout you I liked. Can you serenade me in here sometime?"

I laugh quietly. "I play the organ. There might be a problem getting one in here."

The door opens behind me, and I turn to see Deputy Mason enter, his rifle still attached to his hand as if it is a part of his body. "Chit-chat is over!" Mason announces, directing his cold remark to me. He thrusts a thumb over his shoulder. "You can leave now!"

With a groan, Rudabaugh turns on his bunk. "You came in too quick, Mason. This here dandy newsman was about to play Billy's organ!"

The other prisoners burst out laughing, and my face flushes with warmth. I'm sure I am as bright as an editor's red ink.

"Hey, Mr. Blessing," says Billy, smiling. Extending his arm through the bars, he offers me the courtesy of a handshake. "Good o' you to come by."

"Keep your distance, goddamnit!" Mason orders.

Against all better judgment, I act on a whim of resentment

toward the overbearing deputy, step forward, and take Bonney's hand. His grip is somehow both delicate and firm at the same time. In his deep-blue eyes, I see a certain yearning—like a man scanning a broad empty plain hoping to locate a source of water.

"When you come back to see me," Billy whispers, "would you bring me some paper and a pen? They won't supply me here. I want to write the governor."

"Of course," I promise.

When he releases my hand, I stand in place as he steps back, his arms stiff as he leans on the bars. He smiles and nods at me in such a way that I wonder if I have passed some test of character of his making.

"You goddamned fool!" the deputy snaps from behind me. "I told you to stay back!"

"I almost forgot," I say to Billy. "José—our errand boy at the newspaper—hopes you are faring well. He says to tell you he is still working on the trick you taught him in Fort Sumner. The one with the three stones."

"¡Pequeño José!" Billy sings happily. "¡El brillante! Tell 'im to keep at it. He'll get the hang of it." He snaps his fingers and points at me. "Hey. Use that in your story. Let people see I'm human."

I feel my coat bunched into a knot behind my neck just before I am jerked backward. Spun around by a shoulder, I am just inches from the steely eyes of Deputy Mason.

"You ain't got the sense God give a cross-eyed jackass!" he growls.

Gripping the bars now, Billy smiles at the sight of me dangling in Mason's grip. "Better listen to 'im, Mr. Blessing," he says laughing. "Ol' Barney's 'bout an expert on jackasses."

Mason escorts me rather roughly to the door, speaking over his shoulder as we move. "Keep up your laughin' while you can,

Kid. You got some new misery comin' into your life startin' tomorr'."

"How's that, Barn?" Billy calls out in a lighthearted tone.

Mason turns in the open doorway and delivers a self-satisfied smile. "Me an' the rest o' Garrett's men leave today. We're headin' back to Lincoln, and I won't have to listen to your jaw-flappin' no more." His smile tightens. "You'll have a deputy U.S. marshal checkin' in on you and escortin' you to your trial in La Mesilla."

"Yeah?" Billy chirps, pretending to be interested. "And who would that be?"

Mason's smile spreads up into his spiteful eyes. "Big Bob Olinger." Satisfaction radiates off Mason's face like heat. The deputy hustles me out the door, slams it shut, and locks it.

Now that my arm has been released, I feel the blood run freely again in my vessels. I watch Mason lay his rifle on top of the desk and drop the keys inside a drawer. When he sits and glares at me, it is clear he is disappointed I have not already vacated the premises. I fasten my coat, securing each button carefully, using the act to buy some time.

"Who is Big Bob Olinger?" I ask.

Mason stands, walks around the desk, and opens the front door, where he waits for me to walk out of his life. "Olinger hates the Kid from hell to Sunday," the deputy volunteers.

"Why is that?"

Mason arches one eyebrow. "Bonney's gang kilt a friend o' his. Bob'll be the one just a-waitin' on the Kid to try an' escape." The deputy snorts. "Bob favors a ten-gauge and knows how to use it." He waggles his fingers for me to leave.

I pass through his smug gaze and out the door but turn for a last question. "Who was the friend that was killed?"

Mason steps through the doorway and looks down Water Street as if taking inventory of the businesses lined up along the thoroughfare. "Man named Beckwith," he mumbles.

I rack my brain to pull up that name from the territory's obituaries of late, but no Beckwith comes to mind. "What were the circumstances of Mr. Beckwith's death, if I may ask?"

Mason sniffs and looks anywhere except at me. "Happened in Lincoln. Olinger and Beckwith were in the posse that surrounded the McSween house. Beckwith was shot down like a mad dog whilst tryin' to negotiate with McSween."

I put on my poker face. "You mean the posse that set fire to a home with women and children inside? *That* posse?"

Now Mason turns to me rather quickly. He fixes me with a grim gaze that could ignite kindling. There are wagons and horses and people moving along the street, but the sounds of the plaza seem oddly distant. I realize how alone I am as I stand before this stern-faced officer who loathes Billy Bonney and certainly has no use for me.

"Yeah, that one," he says, walks back into the office, and slams the door.

I start down the street at a fast clip for the chapel, where my singers await me. I check my watch and see that I am already a few minutes late. As I hurry, I know that I should be mentally preparing for my chorale, but instead I am thinking about Billy Bonney. Already my feature article is taking shape in my head as if the story is writing itself.

18
County Courthouse (Old Dolan Store) Lincoln, New Mexico Territory April 1881

"So, they locked you up in heavy chains to pay for all their sins
Then sentenced you to die after they'd killed most of your
friends."

In spite of the blatantly pro-Dolan bias of the presiding judge, the trial in La Mesilla began with a victory for William Bonney. The federal indictment against him for killing Buckshot Roberts was dismissed on a technicality that was cleverly orchestrated by Billy's attorney. But there was little time for celebration. Soon after, the court found Billy guilty in the ambush murder of Sheriff William Brady on the main street of Lincoln. The judge ordered Billy to be held in Lincoln until the second week in May, when the Kid would be hanged in a public execution.

The trip from La Mesilla back to Lincoln was executed in clandestine fashion, taking lesser used roads and traveling by night to avoid any attempts at a rescue of Billy Bonney by his sympathizers . . . or an ambush by his enemies. The long journey chained to the floor of a closed Dougherty wagon was, for Billy, monotonous and cold, made harder still by the treatment of the men in whose charge he had fallen. Several were old enemies, one of whom had been shot by the Kid during his break from the burning McSween house. But none was so abrasive as Big Bob Olinger, who missed no opportunity to prod the Kid with the muzzle of his shotgun. His favorite trick was digging the end of the barrel into the flesh below Billy's chin and forcing the Kid to rise up on the toes of his boots.

Even when the Kid was allowed to wander off into the brush to relieve himself, Olinger accompanied him, taunting Bonney all the while with the images of hangings he had witnessed in his career. For a man who seldom smiled, Olinger seemed happiest when threatening the Kid. Try as he did, the deputy could never crack Billy's mask of indifference. The more Billy held his poker face, the more Olinger poured on his tales of gruesome deaths on the scaffold.

"There was this one weasel," Olinger started up again as Billy squatted in a stand of gama grass. "Name of Kelso . . . a rustler over Tularosa way . . . always smelled like the armpit of some fat whore." The big deputy allowed the deep hollow laugh that rumbled up from his broad chest. "Well, he finally kilt a rancher one night, and we caught 'im over near White Sands holed up in a sheepherder's hut." Olinger shook his head. "This boy had a mouth on 'im . . . a lot like you. And he says to me, 'You can hang me if you want. I don't give a shit!' " Big Bob's laugh rolled like distant thunder. "Remember *that* part. It's what makes this story worth tellin'."

The Kid said nothing.

"So, the day comes for his little comeuppance party, and he's walkin' out to the gallows in his manacles and leg irons, scowlin' at ever'body and scuffin' his boots like he's the toughest son-ovabitch to ever ride outta Texas. Well, he starts to climb those steps and his legs just give out on 'im, and me an' another deputy have to carry 'im the rest o' the way." Big Bob stalled in his story long enough to toss a stone at the place where Billy was hunkered down. "His face was 'bout as white as your scrawny ass, Bonney."

He waited for a comeback from Billy, but there was none.

"So, they put the hood over his head, and the preacher reads from the Book, and then the sheriff asks if there's any last words." Olinger cupped a hand behind his ear as though he were listening to the silence hovering over the desert around them. "But all is quiet. So I say to Kelso real soft like, 'Where's all that cheap courage you was throwin' 'round the other day, you damned, murderin' sonovabitch?'"

When Olinger chuckled, his deep voice was like an empty barrel rolling across a wooden floor. Scrunching up his face, he attempted to deliver the scratchy voice of the condemned man.

" 'I ain't scared o' dyin', by God!' He announces that loud enough for the crowd to hear. So, then the sheriff gives the word to the hangman, but before Kelso drops there comes this terrible growlin' and bubblin' sound. Like a bugler tryin' to sound reveille from underwater. Then comes the stench, and we all realize that this brave desperado has shat his pants as his farewell speech." Now Olinger let go with a hearty laugh that turned the heads of the men waiting on the road.

Billy stood and fastened his trousers, giving the deputy none of his attention. Waddling in his leg irons he weaved his way out of the grass, stopped next to his guard, and stared back at the transport wagon and the posse members, who waited beside their mounts.

"Bob, you wanna know the part o' that story that really disturbs me?"

Olinger bared his teeth when he smiled. "Which part?"

Billy swiveled his head to show the deputy a concerned expression. "That part 'bout you starin' at my ass." He nodded toward the wagon. "Do those boys know that about you?"

Olinger's face turned the color of heated metal. Spinning Billy, he pressed the muzzle of the shotgun between Billy's shoulder blades and pushed hard, causing the Kid to stumble forward and trip on his chains. Billy hit the ground hard, and right away he began laughing. Rolling to his side he looked back at the incensed deputy.

"You're a real brave man, Bob! I wonder how you'd do in a square fight?"

Olinger pulled out a ring of keys from his coat pocket. "We could find out right quick, I imagine. I would love to slap that smart-mouth grin off your face."

Billy pushed up from the ground and brushed the dust from his coat and trousers. "I said 'a fair fight,' Bob. You're twice my size." He narrowed his eyes, as though recalling a memory. "I reckon that's on account o' that rumor I heard over at the Chisum ranch."

Olinger frowned, creasing two deep lines above the bridge of his nose. "What rumor?"

Billy looked off toward the horizon and shrugged. "The one 'bout your mother couplin' with a breeder bull in a stockyard that year before you were born."

Olinger's lips pulled back from his gritted teeth as he jabbed the shotgun into Billy's chest. "You think I won't shoot you, you little sonovabitch?"

"Oh, sure," Billy replied. "Long as I got no gun to defend myself. What about a straight-up duel . . . you and me . . . whatta you say, Bob? Have you got the sand for it?"

Olinger sneered. "I'm going to enjoy watchin' you kick at the end of a rope."

"But you didn't answer my challenge, Bob," the Kid said. "Did I frighten you?" Then he looked surprised and sniffed the air. "Why, Bob! You didn't soil *your* britches, did you?"

Quick as a thought, Olinger reversed the shotgun and drove the butt of the stock toward Billy's midsection, but Billy was faster. Making a sharp pivot, the Kid spun like a bullfighter and made a grab for the stock of the shotgun with his manacled hands, but Olinger was too strong for him. Reversing the weapon, Big Bob planted the stock against his shoulder and put the muzzle just inches from the Kid's face. In the quiet that followed, the sound of the hammers cocking was as sharp as glass cracking in the cold.

"Olinger!" one of the deputies called from the wagon. "Leave off! Let's get moving!"

Big Bob looked toward the stalled caravan and straightened. When he turned back to Billy, he snorted an airy laugh through his nose.

"I just want you to try runnin' off. That's all I need to fill your skinny ass with lead, you damned little sonovabitch."

Billy smiled down at the ground and shook his head. "There you go again, Bob . . . talkin' 'bout my ass." When he looked up at his tormentor, Billy affected a worried look. "I know how lonely it gets out in these hills, Bob, but I just can't see myself satisfyin' your urges. Maybe you should think 'bout partnerin' up with a handsome stud sheep from out near Fort Sumner. There's plenty in that country to choose from."

Before Olinger could react, one of the other deputies appeared with an open canteen in his hand. "What's the problem, Bob?"

"No, problem," Olinger barked and jerked the Kid around with one hand as he prodded him with the shotgun in the other. "Chain his ass back—" Catching himself, Olinger kicked out at Billy's boots and shoved him toward the road. "Chain him back in the wagon. You ride with 'im! I'll sit in a saddle for a while. I'm sick o' listening to 'im."

When they arrived in Lincoln, Billy pushed back the wagon's canvas canopy to gaze out at his old stomping ground. He was surprised when the wagon and its entourage passed by the old pit jail and continued to the west end of town. Stopping in front of "the House"—Jimmy Dolan's longtime mercantile and den of financial iniquities—the posse men dismounted and formed a loose circle around the wagon, their rifles in hand. Billy stretched his chains to their limit to peer out the rear of the wagon at Lincoln's largest building.

"What're you boys plannin' for me?" he laughed. "Are you handin' me over to Dolan?"

Pat Garrett rolled up the canvas at the back of the wagon. "The county bought Dolan's building for a courthouse," he explained. "No jail cells yet, but we got a special room set up for you."

Billy stared at the building and laughed. "Well, ain't that convenient. Dolan is finally goin' broke, and he talks the county into buying his store."

Garrett turned to Olinger. "Take him upstairs. We're not putting him with the other prisoners. He goes in the northeast corner room next to my office."

Olinger nodded and called out to the building. "Hey, Bell! Come 'ere!"

Standing in the front doorway, Deputy J. W. Bell flipped a cigarette into the dirt and walked to the wagon. Pulling the prisoner from the bed of the wagon by his chains, Olinger gave the Kid a vicious jerk, causing him to fall hard on his side in the dusty hardpan.

"No need for that," Garrett said in a quiet reprimand.

Big Bob smiled at Garrett. "Street must be slippery, Sheriff."

Garrett watched Billy sit up and rub his shoulder. "Just get him upstairs," Garrett said, "without killing him."

Olinger pulled Billy to his feet and then took a two-handed grip on his shotgun. "I love a movin' target, Kid. Why don't you try an' make a run for it?"

Billy smirked. "You gotta pick the apple when it's ripe, Bob."

Frowning, Olinger motioned for Bell to lead the way, and then he prodded Billy from behind. Inside, at the back of the building, they climbed a dark narrow flight of stairs. On the second floor they walked a hallway and turned through a door at the northeast corner.

Billy shuffled through an office and, in the few seconds available to him, inventoried the room. An unlighted oil lamp sat upon a desk topped by stacks of papers and a large ledger. The room was illuminated by a single window that looked out over the front balcony.

"Move!" Olinger ordered and pushed the prisoner through the open door to the corner room. There it was brighter with indirect lighting making its way in through two windows, one on the east wall and the other on the north. A simple cot was set up against the east wall. A chamber pot was half hidden in the shadow under the bed. Directly across from the bed at the opposite wall stood a chair and small table. Bell stood by the table and leaned his back against the wall.

"You boys shouldn'a gone to so much trouble for me, Bob," Billy said.

Olinger jabbed the shotgun into the back of Billy's neck and pushed him toward the cot. "Sit down and shut up!"

"Now, Bob," Billy began, turning and smiling for his performance, "I've been a-sittin' all the way from Mesilla. Let me walk out the kinks a little."

Olinger backed away and spoke quietly to Bell, who pushed away from the wall and left the room. Then Olinger propped his shotgun beside the door. When he turned, he saw that Billy's eyes were fixed on the scattergun.

"If you feel lucky, make a play for it, Kid," Olinger dared. He strode up to Billy and shoved him so hard that when he sat down on the cot the back of his head banged against the wall. Big Bob spread his boots and tossed his ring of keys against Billy's chest. Billy made no move to catch them, nor did he flinch. The keys dropped into his lap, but he ignored them.

"Unlock your leg irons, run the chain through that ring, and lock it again." He pointed to the floor where a swivel ring was hinged to a metal plate bolted to the floorboards. "When I check the lock, if it ain't done right, I'll slap you upside the head, you understand?"

Whistling a tune, Billy followed orders, tugged on the lock to show it was tight, and extended the keys to the deputy. "Snug as a bug in a rug, Bob."

Standing back from the cot, Olinger held out a hand palm up. "Toss 'em to me."

Cocking his arm, Billy threw the keys hard at Olinger's chest, exactly as the deputy had done to him. By reflex, Big Bob tried to catch them but missed, and they clattered to the floor.

"Pick 'em up," Olinger ordered. "And *put* 'em in my hand."

In the dead quiet of the building, the two glared at one another. Outside on the street, two men's voices murmured in friendly conversation, giving the standoff in the room a sharper edge.

When Garrett walked into the room, his lowered head just cleared the doorframe. Olinger lowered his hand and kicked Billy's boots aside. Stooping, the deputy snatched up the keys and checked the lock on Billy's chains. Standing by the doorway, Garrett studied guard and prisoner.

"Well, hey, Pat!" Billy sang out. "Ol' Bob here was just about to show me how he could crush my fingers under his boot if I was dumb enough to fall for the old drop-the-keys trick."

Olinger kicked at the Kid's boots again. Pocketing the keys, he lumbered to the other side of the room and retrieved his shotgun. Garrett looked slowly around the room.

"We'll get some water in here for you," the sheriff said in his soft Alabama voice.

"Mighty neighborly of you, Pat," Billy returned. "I could eat somethin', too. Who cooks up the meals here?"

Garrett stepped to the front window and looked across the road and to the east. Without his coat he was like a tall scarecrow propped up against the rectangle of light.

"Normally, we take prisoners over to the hotel, where they sit outside in the alley and eat. If the weather is bad, we bring the food inside here." He strolled back to stand before the Kid. "Normally," he repeated. "But you'll be taking all your meals here." He nodded toward the cot. "We'll fetch you a meal in a coupla hours." Turning, he reached the doorway in three easy strides and stopped to look back at Olinger. "I want to see you and Bell in my office."

"Now?" Olinger said.

"Now," Garrett said and left the room without closing the door.

Olinger walked back to Billy, leaned, and took a grip on the manacle chain. Jerking hard, he almost pulled the Kid off the bed. Billy stiffened and examined his wrists where the edge of the metal had scraped the skin and drawn blood.

"You and me will have plenty of time together, smart-mouth," Olinger said, smiling down at his prisoner. Using the shotgun, he prodded Billy across the bed to the wall. "Then we'll hang you out there in front of the whole town." He pointed out the east window.

Billy smiled. "Guess we'll see 'bout that, Bob."

Olinger sneered, and then his head bounced once with a silent laugh. When he left the room, he slammed the door shut, and two seconds later a key rattled and the lock tripped.

From the next room Billy heard Garrett's gentle Southern voice take on an edge. "Bob, you been at this for a while, but you made some mistakes in there. I don't want mistakes with this prisoner. Do you understand?"

"Bonney ain't goin' nowhere, Sheriff," Olinger's voice returned. "He—"

"You give that boy one blink of an eye," Garrett interrupted, "where you are off guard, and he will kill you before you know what happened."

Olinger started to speak again, but Garrett's voice dominated.

"You were kneeling on the floor within his reach, the keys to his chains right there to take, and your shotgun ten feet away."

There was no reply from Olinger.

"The two of you are assigned to Bonney from right now until the day he hangs. One of you will be with him at all times. After this moment, he will never be in that room—or anywhere else—by himself. You two can work out your shifts. Any questions?"

Bell's raspy voice carried through the wall. "How long are we holdin' 'im?"

"He hangs on the thirteenth of May," Garrett answered.

No one spoke for a time, and, by the sound of it, no one moved.

"No mistakes," Garrett said again. The two deputies mumbled something together so that neither response could be made out. "Now," said Garrett, "one of you get in there."

When the latch clicked and the door opened, Billy was surprised to see both Bell and Olinger enter the room. Big Bob closed the door and handed Bell his shotgun. Crouching four feet from the Kid's bed, Bob dug into his coat pocket and pulled out a stick of chalk. Sidling across the floor in a squat, he grunted as he drew a rough white semicircle three feet from Billy's bed. Rising with a final grunt, he took the shotgun from Bell and, breathing hard, turned to the Kid.

"There's gonna be two rules," Olinger announced, looking from Billy to Bell as if he were making this decree to both men. "One!" he said and flipped up a thick forefinger. "You do everything I say!" He leveled the finger at Billy. "Everything!" Then he pivoted his arm to point at Bell. "Everything *he* says, too."

Olinger stared at Bonney as if daring the boy to speak. Billy pursed his lips in what seemed a contemplative mood.

"Two!" Olinger continued and held up two fingers.

Like a schoolboy asking a question of his teacher, Billy raised his manacled hands and waggled his forefingers at the lawmen, his chains swinging before him. "Now, wait a minute, Bob. That's already two things. Do everything you say . . . and do everything Bell says. It ain't fair to add a third rule like that just 'cause you miscounted."

"Two!" Olinger repeated, this time louder. He cradled the shotgun in one arm and pointed with his free hand at the floor. "You cross that line, and we *will* shoot you. This is your only warning on that count. You cross that line, and we figure you intend to escape. *¿Comprendes?*"

Billy smiled. "Ever'thing except how that was only two rules. I still say it's three. But I understand if you ain't covered your numbers in school yet, Bob."

Olinger took a step toward Billy, but Bell stepped forward and pressed the back of his hand into the bigger deputy's coat front. "Leave 'im be, Bob. He'll hang in three weeks. We'll take our satisfaction from that."

Big Bob snorted, hitched his shotgun in one hand by the forestock, and started for the door. "You can take this watch, J.W.," Olinger growled and pushed the ring of keys onto Bell. "I'm going to get something to eat."

"Whoa, Bob!" Billy called to his back. "I got a question 'bout the rules."

When Olinger stopped, Billy stroked his chin as though he were working out a perplexing problem. Then, pointing at the chalk line, he gave Olinger a look of childlike innocence.

"Do you boys get to cross that line goin' the other way?" He opened his hands in a shrug. "I mean, how do I get my food?"

Without a response, Olinger strode out the door and slammed it behind him. Shaking his head, Bell crossed to the door, locked it, and sat in the chair beside the table. In a slow, calm manner he slid his revolver from its holster and tapped the gun down on the tabletop. Crossing one leg over the other, he tilted the chair against the wall and stared out the north window.

"So how's the food here, Bell?" Billy asked.

Bell held his gaze on the limited view of the mountains outside the window. "Good as any other jail, I reckon."

Though the deputy would not look at him, Billy nodded. With his chains jangling, the Kid slid forward on the bed and set his feet on the floor. Probing the back of his head with his fingertips, he felt for blood but detected none.

Billy laughed. "Ol' Bob's got a bad case o' loathin' for young Billy, don't he?"

When Bell said nothing, Billy looked down at his boots and tapped out a snappy rhythm on the floor. When he looked up again, Bell was rolling a cigarette.

"Wouldn' wanna play some cards, would you?" Billy tried.

Bell ran the filled paper across his tongue and sealed it. Striking a lucifer on the heel of his boot, he cupped the flame with a hand and craned his neck forward to light. In seconds, a cloud of blue-gray smoke hung in the stillness of the room, hovering around the deputy like a wraith. When Bell shook out the flame and dropped the spent lucifer on the table, he exhaled a stream of smoke that cut through the drifting cloud like a river rushing through a breach in a dam. Through this haze, Bell fixed his gaze on Billy.

"I ain't your friend, Kid. I'm here to keep watch on you, and that's what I plan to do."

Billy offered his easy laugh. "Don't mean we can't play some cards, does it?"

Bell had assumed his vigil out the window again as he drew on his cigarette, but now he plucked it from his mouth and studied Bonney with something harder in his eye. "I won't cut the cards with you. You killed a good friend of mine."

Billy frowned. "You mean somebody actually thought of Sheriff Brady as a *good* friend."

"I ain't talkin' about Brady," Bell snapped. "It was Jim Carlyle. You shot a damned good man in the back, and you'll roast in hell for it." Bell looked away again.

The Kid leaned forward, propping his elbows on his knees and threading his fingers together before him. "There's more to that than people know," Billy said.

Turning sharply to the prisoner, the deputy's eyes took on a fierce glow. "I was there!"

Billy frowned and raised his hands palms up. "Well, then you oughta know. Carlyle was shot from the front by your own men, and you boys covered that up."

"Horse shit!" Bell hissed and stared out the window again.

Billy cocked his head. "Did you actually see it?"

After a long silence, Bell exhaled a stream of smoke and shook his head. "I was behind the barn relieving myself." He took another draw and spewed this cloud toward Billy. "I was only gone a coupla minutes."

"Did you examine the wounds?" Billy asked.

Bell took in a long breath and purged it quickly. "No," he admitted. "I didn't want to."

When the deputy crossed one leg over the other and frowned at his cigarette, Billy took this as a cue to continue. "You boys were holdin' Greathouse, who'd left the house to parley on our behalf. Carlyle came inside to balance out a trade. While we negotiated with 'im, somebody outside fired off a shot. One of our boys said your posse must'a killed Greathouse. Carlyle got this pale look on his face. He must'a reasoned he'd be next . . . to even up the score. That's when he crashed through that window. Some o' your men shot 'im but would never own up to it." When Bell glanced at Billy, the Kid raised his eyebrows and nodded once. "Later, I heard they thought it was me tryin' to skin outta there. They didn' recognize Carlyle. They just shot too quick, that's all." Billy lay back on the cot and propped on an elbow.

Bell balanced his cigarette on the edge of the table. Its red coal of tobacco smoldered and sent up a string of smoke that wavered in the air like the slither of a snake.

"I heard that story, too," Bell admitted, gazing at his propped boot. "Guess I didn't want to believe it." His head came up, and he fixed Billy with a solemn gaze. "I want you to tell me the goddamn truth about it. It's in the past now. Ain't nothin' gonna change it. You're gonna hang either way. Just level with me about Carlyle, would you?"

Billy raised one manacled hand, palm out. "I already tol' you. I swear it on my mother's grave."

They stared at one another for half a minute, the only movement in the room the cigarette smoke climbing to the ceiling. Bell dropped his propped boot to the floor and stood.

"Aw hell . . . I'll go see can I find us a deck o' cards."

On the sixth morning of his incarceration in Lincoln, Billy was stretched out in his stockinged feet on the cot. He lay on his back, one leg bent, the knee propped against the wall, and an arm crooked over his face. The room was filled with a cloud of acrid smoke from Bob Olinger's cigar, and Billy—determined not to give the deputy the satisfaction of a complaint—breathed through the fabric of his shirtsleeve and listened to the occasional sounds of traffic out on the street.

A dry crackling of paper caused Billy to lift his arm and turn his head to see the rarity of a genuine smile on Olinger's face. The big deputy folded his newspaper back upon itself and settled it in his lap. Billy covered his eyes again.

"I see where they hanged a horse thief over at Las Cruces,"

Olinger remarked in a jovial tone. "Citizens took 'im outta the jail and strung 'im up from a pulley over a hay loft at the livery." He chuckled and read on silently for a time before continuing. "Listen to this: 'The victim was left hanging for three days until the stable man complained about seeing the dead man twitch and move. It appeared he was trying to come back to life.' "

Olinger's reading style was monotonic and choppy, stringing together the words in a labored fashion. He laughed a single bass note that seemed to rise from a deep well.

"This'll be educational for you, Kid," he said in his brash voice. Continuing to read, he resumed his droning delivery. " 'When the resurrecting man was lowered to the ground, Doctor R. W. Greene knelt to examine the body. Attaching his stethoscope, the good doctor opened up the man's shirt to find that, indeed, life was in evidence.' " After a pause, Olinger burst out laughing. "Oh, this is too good!"

Billy remained motionless on the bed.

"It was a goddamned nest o' rats," Olinger finished and brayed like a mule.

Billy did not have to look at his guard to know that his face would be glowing with sadistic pleasure. But he did look. He watched as Olinger regained his spiteful smirk, unfolded the newspaper, and arranged it for turning a page.

"Your cigar is makin' me sick," Billy said in a flat tone.

Olinger's smile widened enough to show his teeth. Laying the paper on the table next to his shotgun, he took a long draw on the cigar, his plump cheeks indenting ever so slightly as he inhaled deep into his chest. When he released the breath he leaned forward suddenly, spewing a geyser of smoke directly toward Billy.

Billy smiled and inhaled deeply. "Actually I like it. I lied so I could have a little smoke myself. Thanks, Bob."

Olinger's face darkened, and he picked up the paper again.

"If a mob should come for you, Bonney, how much protection would you expect from me?"

Billy crossed one chained leg over the other and smiled at the ceiling. "Oh, I reckon you'd supply the keys to my irons . . . and the rope . . . and the nest o' rats."

Big Bob cracked a sly smile. "Hell, I'd even offer to haul you up on the pulley, hand over hand, give you a good last view of this country." Olinger barked a single laugh. "I love that picture . . . you hangin' by your neck where you can't choke out a single word."

Billy turned to his antagonist. "You know, Bob, if I get to hell before you, I might already have achieved some rank there. So, when you arrive, *I* might be the one in charge of *you*. I already got some ideas on how to introduce you to the devil."

Sneering, Olinger narrowed his eyes. "Whatta you mean *if* you get there ahead o' me? In three weeks, you'll be rotting underground with worms burrowin' into your skull."

Billy propped up on an elbow and threaded his fingers together over his belly. "Now, you may not know it's me, Bob, 'cause they say we leave these bodies behind and we take some other form in death." Billy smiled. "But it'll be me, Bob. I'll see to it with the devil himself."

Olinger snorted. "I reckon you already got connections with him, Kid."

"But in case you don't know it's me, Bob, I'll be sure to give you a signal. Knowing your difficulties with schoolin', I'll keep it simple. How 'bout I just say, 'Hello, Bob! Welcome to hell!' " Billy's face turned serious as a preacher's. "Think you can remember that?"

Olinger occupied himself with folding the newspaper. "I'll be sure to write it down, Kid."

Two knocks sounded on the door, and the sheriff's muffled voice turned Olinger in his chair. "It's Garrett. I'm coming in."

"Come on!" Olinger called back.

The lock tripped, and Pat Garrett bowed his head to enter. In his hand he carried a wooden chair by the top slat of its backrest. When he swung the chair before him, it settled on its four legs on the floor with barely a sound.

"Got your noon meal, Billy," Garrett said and slid the chair right up to the chalk line. "And you got a visitor from Santa Fe."

Olinger sat a little straighter and frowned. "You said no visitors for him."

Garrett looked around the room, examining everything in it. "Governor says different." Turning, he spoke through the open door. "Ham! Send in the boy!"

The olive-skinned boy from the Wortley Hotel entered with a wooden tray that held two large plates, each topped by identical plates inverted as a cover to hold in warmth. Walking the food toward the prisoner, he kept his head bowed and his eyes on the floor. Billy swung his stockinged feet to the floor and sat up.

"Hold up, boy!" Olinger ordered, and the youth stopped just shy of the chalk line.

As Olinger rose, the boy turned to him, awaiting the customary inspection of items brought in from the outside. Big Bob lumbered up to the boy and lifted the top plates. Clacking the dishes together he set them on the table and turned back to examine the food. After jabbing a finger into each serving to probe for contraband, he stuck the finger in his mouth and cleaned it. Then he lifted the plates to check their undersides and the tray beneath.

"*Son tamales, frijoles, arroz y tomates,* señor ," the boy said, his voice a timid whisper.

Big Bob wrinkled his face and glared at the boy.

Garrett started out of the room and spoke over his shoulder. "He says he's brought tamales, rice, beans, and tomatoes, Bob.

Probably ought not to shoot him for that."

Olinger towered over the boy and leaned in to intimidate. "You're in a territory of the United States, son. Speak American!"

The boy recoiled by arching his back. "Know only leetle, señor."

Olinger pointed to the chalk line. "Set the tray down there!"

The boy knelt and placed the meal on the floor with the line bisecting the tray. Stepping back he stared at the prisoner with a blank expression.

"Gracias, José," Billy said in his friendly way. *"Eres un buen hombre para entregar comida caliente."*

Rattling his chains, Billy picked up his meal, settled back on the bed, and propped the tray on his thighs. Dunking a rolled tortilla into a bowl of beans, he took a hearty bite, chewed, and through a mouthful called out to the office.

"So, who's my visitor, Pat?"

When Olinger stepped into the doorway to see who waited in the next room, José turned back to Billy and widened his eyes as if he might speak with some urgency. Billy raised his hand, palm out, to hush the boy.

"So, how's the weather out there, José?" Billy said loud enough to be heard by the others.

José spoke in a rushed whisper. *"Debajo de los periódicos en la letrina . . . mañana."*

Billy stuffed more food into his mouth and held his cool blue eyes on the boy's anxious face. As he chewed, he watched the boy hold a fist to his stomach, where it was hidden from the men entering the room from the office. Extending both forefinger and thumb, José mimicked the shape of a gun pressed flat against his blouse.

"Well," Billy said, "it'll start warmin' up soon enough." He gave the boy a smile and snapped his fingers so quickly that

José blinked. "Things can change mighty quick, presto-changeo," Billy reminded.

Following Garrett, a small, lean man in a brown suit entered the room. Olinger remained by the door and scowled at the newcomer. Removing his hat, the visitor gave Billy a nod.

"I'll be damned," Billy chirped. "You came to Lincoln to see me!"

"There's a chair for you," Garrett said to the visitor. "You've got twenty minutes." He gestured toward Olinger. "My deputy will be here with you all the time." Pointing to the chalk line, Garrett put an edge to his quiet voice. "You are not to go closer to the prisoner than that line."

"Understood, Sheriff."

"Let's go, son," Garrett ordered and placed a hand on the boy's shoulder. As they left the room, Olinger took up his post by the door and held his shotgun in the crook of his arm. John Blessing sat in the chair, set his satchel in his lap, and extracted a notebook and pen.

19

Blessing's Notes
Lincoln County Courthouse
Lincoln, New Mexico Territory
April 27, 1881

"You were just outnumbered in this double-dealing game For every crime across this land they branded with your name."

After an early lunch at the Wortley, I take up my satchel and cross the street for the courthouse, following in the footsteps of a young boy carrying a tray of covered dishes. Before he reaches the courthouse door, I see his reflection in the front window. Tentatively, I call out to him.

"Joseph? Is that you?"

When he turns, I see fear flash in his eyes, but his face relaxes when he recognizes me. As I approach, he checks up and down the street and then bites his lip as he looks me in the eye.

"What are you doing here in Lincoln?" I ask, smiling but curious.

He shrugs with a shy smile. "My mother . . . she moves us here. We live with the Baca family." Holding the tray at the level of his belly, he nods toward the east end of the town, and I assume the Baca house lies in that direction.

"What about your job in Santa Fe? At the *Messenger*?"

Again he nods, this time toward the Wortley. "I work at the hotel now." As evidence he raises the tray a few inches. "I do the odd jobs. I carry the meals to the jail."

My face probably shows some degree of shock. "You mean . . . to Billy Bonney?"

He turns to glance at the closed courthouse door just yards

away. "They don't know about me knowing Bee-lee. If you tell them, I will probably lose my job."

I hold up both my palms. "I see no reason to do that." I examine the stacked plates on his tray. "So, that food is for Billy?"

"*Sí,*" he says, his jade eyes begging for secrecy. "Also, they call me José. They do not know that I understand English so well. Can you also not mention that?" He shrugs. "That way, perhaps, I will hear things that I can report to you for your writing, yes?"

I consider the idea for a moment. "Yes," I admit, "that could be helpful."

Inside the building at the front desk, we check in with an obese deputy, whose name, so he tells us, is Ham. Moving at the aimless speed of bored livestock, he guides us to the back of the building, where we scale a narrow staircase with a right angle turn near the bottom. The climb up the dimly lit stairwell is almost comical as we are forced to ascend at the plodding rate of the overweight man who leads us. His heavy footfall would seem to be a test of the Dolan building's architecture.

On the second story, as instructed, we wait in the hallway as the panting deputy knocks on the open doorframe of a small office where a long, gaunt, gangly, mustachioed man in a black suit sits at a desk and scratches a pen across paper. His freshly starched white blouse glows like moonlit snow between the dark lapels of his coat.

"Sher'ff . . . the boy . . . from the hotel . . . is here . . . with the Kid's . . . midday meal," announces Ham between gasps of breath. The deputy then jabs a stubby thumb my way. "And there's a feller here . . . with a letter . . . says he's s'posed to have . . . a in'erview." He sets my opened letter on the desk. Without touching the paper, the sheriff cocks his head and reads it. When he finishes, he exhales a long breath and lays down his pen. Standing, he ignores the boy and gives me only a glance.

"Have you searched him, Ham?" he inquires of the deputy.

"Who?" the deputy asks. "The boy?"

Garrett gives his man a stern look. "What's the rule?"

The obese deputy shifts his considerable weight from leg to leg, as if he is now mired in mud. The floorboards groan with each tilt of his formidable ballast. Still catching his breath, he points to the letter on the desk.

"Well, that there is signed . . . by somebody in the gov'nor's office, so—" He leaves the sentence unfinished and stares open mouthed at the sheriff like a sheepdog awaiting a command from its master.

"Do it now," Garrett says. "Both of them."

As the clumsy deputy rifles my satchel and runs his clammy hands over my body, the sheriff stands and turns his back to us. With his hands clasped behind him, the tall man gazes out the front windowpanes beyond the outside deck fastened to the face of the building.

"Mr. Blessing," Garrett says, his voice hollow as it echos off the glass, "looks like your editor has some pull with the governor. Are you going to defend the Kid in ink again?"

"Sheriff, I'm only trying to paint the entire picture."

He turns and studies me from a cold distance. "Of a convicted murderer?"

I look down at my shoes long enough to compose a rational reply. "No man is just one thing, Sheriff. Wouldn't you agree?"

Garrett looks deep into my eyes without blinking, just as Pitts, my editor, likes to do. "I reckon that's so," the sheriff admits. "But I read that article you wrote a while back, and I'd say you left out a few things about Billy."

"Oh?" I manage to say without sounding too hurt by his literary critique. "Like what?"

Garrett maintains his stoic stance and turrets his head no more than an inch to look east on the street below. "It was right down there," he says in his soft drawl, "on a nice morning like this one, when Billy hid behind a wall with his gang and killed Sheriff Brady and his deputy as they strolled down the middle of the road."

With an effort, Ham straightens and steps back from me. Then he kneels to search the boy. When he rises he is breathing heavily again. Garrett turns a hard eye on his deputy.

"You check the food?"

The deputy gestures to the closed door to my right. "Bob'll just do it again."

Garrett picks up the letter, folds it, and comes around the desk. He is so tall I have to tilt back my head to meet his eyes. Without a word he hands me the paper and digs a key out of his trouser pocket as he walks past me. Knocking on the door, he raises his voice.

"It's Garrett! I'm coming in!" Inserting a key, he unlocks the door.

From inside the room comes a deep-chested reply. "Come on!"

Garrett hesitates and looks back at Joseph, who lowers his head to gaze upon the dishes he carries. "Hold the boy here a minute," he instructs the deputy. Then the sheriff gives me a look of thinly veiled tolerance. "You wait here, too."

Lifting a nearby chair by its backrest, Garrett enters the room and engages the guard in a low conversation that I cannot decipher. Joseph and I exchange glances but remain quiet.

When Garrett calls for the food, Ham sends in the boy. I hear more conversation, part of which is the boy speaking in his native tongue. When I start to sidestep toward the door to listen, Ham insinuates his rotund personage between me and the prisoner's room.

"You can just wait there till the sheriff calls for you," he says and points to a spot on the floor. I take one step back, where I can still see the occupants of the other room.

When I hear the clatter of dishes, I watch a tall, hefty man poke his finger into the food on the tray. Then Billy Bonney's melodic voice takes over the room as he exchanges pleasantries with the boy, calling him José. In half a minute Garrett reenters the office and stands before me.

"We're not going to have any foolishness this time, Mr. Blessing. There will be no hand-shaking with the prisoner in my jail. No contact. Do you understand?"

Trying for a look of contrition, I meet Garrett's insistent eyes. "I understand, Sheriff."

He jerks his head for me to enter. As I follow him inside, I step into the strong scent of cigar smoke and see the infamous prisoner chewing a mouthful of food as he leans to catch a glimpse of me. It is obvious he recognizes me when he breaks into a smile and laughs.

"I'll be damned! You came to Lincoln to see me!"

I supply a cordial smile, but I feel it fade when I direct it toward the deputy on guard. His broad face appears to be made of polished stone, and his gray eyes narrow to an appraising, suspicious squint. The sheriff gives me instructions on what is expected of me and then escorts the delivery boy out of the room, leaving me with one man elated to see me and the other looking as if he might toss me out a window.

I sit in the straight chair, set my satchel in my lap, and pull out my notebook. "Hello, Billy. I understand things did not go in your favor in La Mesilla."

"Well, not all together," he says. "They threw out my case about shooting Buckshot Roberts. It was a federal warrant, but my lawyer proved the killin' didn't take place on the Mescalero reservation, so—" He laughs. "Besides, I didn't kill Roberts.

Charlie Bowdre did."

"But the court found against you in the murder of Sheriff Brady."

"Well, I never denied that. If anyone ever deserved killin' more, it could only be Jimmy Dolan." He shrugs. "Or maybe ol' Bob Olinger there." Billy nods toward the man on duty.

Olinger glares back at him with a palpable loathing. "If they'd'a tried you for every man you kilt, we'd be hanging you every day for a month," the deputy says with a snide grin. "But once will be plenty for me." His eyes gleam with pleasure. "I can't wait to look into your eyes right before you drop . . . to see all that sass and guff turn to pure terror. I already put down a twenty-dollar bet that you'll cry out for your mama."

Ignoring the deputy, Billy leans forward and looks me in the eye. "They convicted me of stealin' livestock, too," he continues, "but what I took was owed me by John Chisum, who withheld my rightful pay for the time I worked for 'im." He spews air through his lips. "I guess Chisum figured when they started callin' me a outlaw, it absolved him of all debts owed to me."

Olinger begins a sibilant laugh for our benefit, and I turn to him with the intention of asking him to refrain from interrupting my interview. He looks right at me, daring me to speak.

"Poor Bonney," he whines, turning on the sarcasm. "All the world is against him. Nothing is his fault. Every man he's kilt just happened to jump in front o' his bullet."

"Don't mind Bob," Billy says casually. "He's just jealous 'cause no newspaper has ever interviewed him." He flashes a quick grin at the deputy.

Curling his lip into a sneer, Olinger sits in the chair by the table and balances his shotgun across his lap. He stares at us in a most unsettling way. I feel my breathing check when he extends an arm and points a finger directly at me.

"You put anything about me in that goddamn article, and I'll look you up in Santa Fe and shove that writin' quill up your ass."

Billy leans in closer to me to whisper like a stage actor explaining a plot to the audience spread out in a theater. "Bob's somehow got fixed on people's asses. I would advise against an interview with him."

Olinger stands and levels the shotgun at Billy. "Shut your goddamn mouth, Bonney!"

I swivel a quarter turn in my chair, my anger trumping my professional demeanor. "Deputy, I would appreciate it if you would let me conduct my interview uninterrupted." I point at the door that leads to the sheriff's office. "Sheriff Garrett granted me this time . . . officially. Shall I summon him?"

Olinger sits again and does his best to ignore us. I turn back to Billy and lower my voice to a level that keeps our conversation private.

"Is there any hope for an appeal?"

Billy looks down at the floor and shakes his head. "That takes money . . . somethin' I ain't got right now." He shrugs. "Maybe I can get the gov'nor to help me now."

"Wallace is in the East, enjoying the success of his new book. I doubt this territory will see much of him again. I've heard a rumor that he is resigning."

"Well," Billy sighs, "he snookered me once. Before he traipses off to be a famous writer I'd like to give 'im a chance to square things with me."

I hold little hope for that, but I don't want to say anything discouraging. I check my pocketwatch and put it away.

"I have only a short time, Billy. What would you like to say that you'd like people to read in the Santa Fe paper?"

The Kid has not touched his food since we started talking. Now he sets the tray aside on his cot and leans forward, his forearms braced on his thighs.

"There really ain't no point in arguin' my case. People won't believe me. I've been made out to be such a mad dog, people who *don't* know me are gonna believe whatever they already read. And people who *do* know me . . . well, they already know better."

I lay down my pen. "Well, we can just talk about whatever comes to your mind," I suggest. "And if we don't come up with something good today, I'll be back tomorrow."

Billy's face pinches and freezes. Only his eyes move as they dart toward Olinger and then back to me. He leans toward me as far as his chains will allow.

"No, not tomorrow!" he whispers so quietly that I hold my breath to hear him.

I pat the folded paper in my coat pocket. "I brought a letter that will allow me to—"

"No!" he interrupts and fixes me with a stare that makes his eyes hard as blue marbles. "You can't come tomorrow," he whispers. "I don't want you anywhere near this place. You should get out of town tomorrow."

I look behind me to check on Olinger, but he is occupied with a newspaper. When I turn back to Billy, I cock my head and frown.

"But—"

Billy is already shaking his head. "No!" he says, his voice so flat with finality that I know it is useless to negotiate.

"Well, what about the next day? I've come a long way to talk to you, you know."

"We'll see," he says, and his gaze slides to Olinger. When he looks back at me, he winks.

It is difficult to refuse Billy Bonney when he speaks in such a personable way. "All right," I agree. Then I lean forward as far as I dare without trespassing over the chalk line on the floor. "But why?" I ask, quiet as a librarian's whisper.

"I can't answer *all* your questions," Billy says in a conversational tone. Sitting back on the cot he gives me a subtle grin that makes me even more curious about his demand. "How long were you plannin' on stayin' in Lincoln?" he asks, all the warmth back in his voice, as if nothing of import has passed between us.

"I'm not sure," I reply. "I suppose until we've covered everything you would like to say."

"So you weren't expectin' to stay into next month?"

I shrug. "I really don't know. Sometimes these talks can take several sessions." Then I realize what he is asking, and a cold chill passes through me. "You want to know if I plan to be here for your—" I find myself unable to say the word.

"Hangin'," he says for me. He allows a sheepish grin. "I guess I do."

I stare out the east window. It is on those grounds next to the courthouse, I am told, where a gallows will be erected. When I swallow, I feel my dry throat tighten like a sailor's knot. Closing my eyes, I bow my head, so that when I open my eyes I am staring at Billy's stockinged feet. I cannot help but imagine those feet dangling below the trap door of a scaffold. ·

"I could not do that," I admit and look into his clear blue eyes. "I just couldn't."

Billy grins. "They say it's over pretty damned quick." With a rattle of his chains, he snaps the fingers of one hand. "Presto-changeo."

When Billy lowers his hand, the chain coils in his lap, and the silence that settles between us is like a secret room that has opened its door to us. I can hear Olinger behind his newspaper quietly mouthing the words that he reads.

"Are you scared, Billy?" I ask, my words so quiet they float in the air like dust motes.

He leans forward to whisper again, and this time I am reading his lips more than I am hearing him.

"First, they got to hold on to me long enough to hang me."

Giving me a wicked smile, he smacks his manacled hands together and scoots one flattened hand forward like a fish darting through water. His eyes brighten with sparks of blue fire.

When the door opens, I turn to see the tall, imposing figure of Pat Garrett standing just inside the doorway, his steady eyes fixed on me. "Time's up!" he announces.

After gathering my belongings, I stand and hesitate. "Thank you, Billy," I say by way of parting. "Perhaps I will see you in a couple of days?"

Billy narrows his eyes as if I have posed a classic riddle. "You never know."

As I back away from the chalk line, I try one last query. "Is there anything else you would like to tell the people of the territory, Billy?"

Garrett steps up behind me, clasps a big spidery hand on my shoulder, and guides me out. Before the door closes, Billy calls out loud and clear.

"Advise persons not to engage in killin'!"

Inside the sheriff's office, I find myself blocked from the exit door by Garrett himself. Spreading his boots, he slides his hands into his coat pockets and gives me a tired look.

"Your letter says you are to visit as often as you please. Does that mean we will see a lot of you, Mr. Blessing?"

"Well, I *have* come all the way from Santa Fe, Sheriff. My editor expects more articles."

Garrett turns to look out the glass panes of the window to the sun porch. After chewing on something for a moment, he dry-spits it away with a little popping sound.

"How about we skip the rest of today and tomorrow and pick up in a couple of days. I've got to go over to White Oaks on business and will stay over a couple of nights." He points down at the floor between us. "I want to be here whenever you visit. Will that be all right with you?"

I decide on the spot not to divulge that I have already promised Billy I will stay away tomorrow. "That will be fine, Sheriff." For reasons I cannot explain I feel the need to polish off my answer with a white lie. "I was considering a trip out to Fort Stanton tomorrow to talk to a few soldiers. But I hope to continue my interview with Bonney following that."

Garrett nods and steps aside. "We'll expect you in a few days."

In the hallway I hear the slow, heavy shuffle of the obese deputy climbing up the stairwell from the ground floor. I have no choice but to wait. When he appears on the upper landing he is breathing in deep gasps, and his face glistens with a sheen of perspiration. Putting my back to the wall, I let him pass, but then I linger to hear what might be said. Stopping in the sheriff's doorway, Ham wipes a sleeve across his forehead. In one hand he clasps an open sheet of paper, which he holds out to Garrett. I pretend to sort through my satchel, as though I am checking to see that I have all my belongings.

"Acquisition papers, Sheriff," Ham says. "The county didn't approve the amount we asked for. Guess you'll have to talk to them boys down at the mill."

Garrett snatches the paper and reads, his mood dark now. "What do they think I can do? Lower the price of mill-sawn lumber all on my own?"

The deputy has no answer for that.

"We might have to build the damned thing ourselves to cut the cost," Garrett mutters. Then he folds the paper and stuffs it into the breast pocket inside his coat.

"Are you making repairs to the building, Sheriff?" I ask, talking over the deputy's shoulder.

Ignoring me, Garrett takes down his hat from the wall rack and addresses the deputy. "Tell Bell to go down to the livery and get my horse ready. I want to get over to White Oaks before it gets dark."

When Deputy Ham starts away, I turn to follow him until Garrett addresses me again. "We're building a gallows, Mr. Blessing."

Again, a tingling sensation runs down my back, but this time the feeling is like hot steam, as if Old Scratch himself has breathed down the nape of my neck.

20
County Courthouse
Lincoln, New Mexico Territory
April 28, 1881

"But iron bars and prison guards and all the law intends Cannot keep a ghost from slipping through the cracks just like the wind."

When three quiet knocks sounded on the door, Bell set down his coffee mug, sat up straighter in his chair, and gripped the revolver on the table. "What!" he yelled and stared at the door.

After a beat of silence, a timid voice replied. "*Es José. Traigo la comida,* señor."

The deputy stood, his gun leveled at the door. "Where's Ham?" he demanded.

"*Estoy solo,* señor."

Bell turned at the waist to squint at Billy. "What'd he say?"

Billy lay on his side on the cot, his eyes closed and his knees drawn up as far as the chains allowed. His face was clenched like a fist, and one hand lightly pressed to his stomach. When he opened his eyes and spoke, his voice was weak.

"Says he's alone."

Bell turned back to frown at the door, then again twisted to Billy. "Well, do you reckon you can eat anything now? You didn't have no breakfast."

Billy closed his eyes again. "I'm feelin' worse. Why don't you eat it?"

Bell unlocked the door and opened it to find the hotel boy standing with a tray. The deputy holstered his gun and lifted one of the cover plates.

"What we got here?" he asked, talking more to himself than to the boy.

At the sound of the plates clacking, Billy opened his eyes and watched Bell's back as the deputy inspected the food.

"The Kid is sick," Bell said and took the tray from the boy. "But I could eat."

Olinger appeared in the office behind José and spoke to Bell over the boy's head. "I'm takin' the others to the Wortley for their noon meal. You want me to bring you something?"

Bell set the tray on the table. "I plan to eat this here if it ain't filled with hot peppers," he said and frowned. "A damn pepper will burn my stomach like a hot coal." Still standing, he spooned up a sample and chewed, awaiting a verdict.

Olinger clasped the back of the boy's neck and guided him out both doors into the hallway with a push. Then Big Bob walked back into the corner room to assess the prisoner.

"He still bellyachin'?"

Bell spooned up more food and nodded. "Been sick all day," he said around a mouthful.

Olinger snorted an airy laugh and turned to go. "Be back in a hour," he said.

Bell locked the door and sat down to his meal. "Sure you don't want some o' this, Kid?"

Clutching his abdomen, Billy pinched his eyes shut and shook his head. "I'm too mis'rable to eat."

"Well," Bell said, "no reason to let this waste, right?

Outside in the hallway they heard Olinger march the other prisoners toward the stairs, their leg irons sliding and rattling on the bare wood floor. A few minutes later, Olinger was barking orders below the east window, and Billy knew the prisoners were filing across the street toward the hotel. As the sound of their jingling and shuffling faded, he sat up and swung his feet to the floor. With a grim expression set on his face, he began pulling on his boots.

"Bell!" he gasped. "I got to get to the outhouse pronto!"

The deputy froze with a rolled tortilla poised before his mouth. "Use the piss pot, Kid."

Billy hissed air through his teeth. "That pot can't handle what I'm about to do. Feels like my whole insides are comin' out."

Bell set down the tortilla. "Well, damn, Kid, you already been out there once this mornin'."

Billy looked up. "Tell that to my gut." Then he winced and pressed both hands to his stomach. "I got to go *now*, Bell! She's 'bout to blow!"

Bell stood and fumbled for his key. "All right, all right! Hold on, goddamnit!" He unlocked the door and passed through Garrett's office into the hallway. "Ham!" he called down the hall. There was no response. "*Ham!*" he yelled louder. "Where the hell are you?"

The building remained quiet.

"Bell, I ain't got long!" Billy warned.

"Shit!" Bell muttered and hurried back into the room. "Sit back against the wall!" he ordered, extending a stiff arm to point at Billy. The Kid groaned but complied. Kneeling at the floor ring, the deputy unlocked the chains that secured the leg irons. Then he locked the two chains together as one, stepped back, slid his revolver from its scabbard, and motioned with the gun toward the door. "You go first, Kid. I'm right behind you."

Hunched over like an old man, Billy moved stiffly across the room, the chains dragging across the chalk line with him. When he passed through the sheriff's office, he scanned the room for weapons but saw none. Continuing into the hallway he shuffled toward the stairwell, all the while holding his hands to his belly and grunting with each step.

"Lord, I hope I get there in time," he groaned.

Bell stayed back four steps, just as Garrett had ordered. "Well, hurry it up then, damnit!"

Billy pivoted his head a quarter turn. "That might give the wrong outcome, Bell."

When they reached the ground floor, Billy led the way out the back door and started across the open ground toward the privy fifty yards away. Bell came up beside him now, urging him forward, trying to speed up their pace.

Stopping at the outhouse door, Billy turned and held out his wrists. "How 'bout riddin' me of these chains for a bit?"

Bell's face closed down, and he shook his head. "Can't do it, Kid." He bobbed his gun twice toward the privy. "Get on in there and do your business. And don't make me wait all day for you out here."

Billy entered the small shed and let the door slap shut. There was no latch. In the dim light of the enclosure nothing seemed different since his visit here in early morning. It was a simple single-seater with a loose stack of old newspapers piled on the floor. There was nothing else in the room but semi-darkness.

"Better give me some space, Bell. This ain't gonna be pretty."

"I'll be all right," Bell said, his reply touched with sarcasm. But he took two steps back, holstered his gun, and propped his hands on his hips as he studied the lot on the east side of the courthouse where the hanging scaffold would be constructed. He could see old man Gauss working with a hoe in the small garden plot he maintained there.

Without unbuttoning his trousers, Billy sat and began quietly rifling through the papers on the floor. Near the bottom of the pile he felt a lump that made his heart go light. Lifting the papers away he filled his hand with the heft of an old Navy Colt that had been converted for self-contained cartridges. He knew by its weight that the gun was fully loaded.

"José," Billy whispered to the dark. Then he broke into a smile.

"You all right, Kid?" Bell called out.

Without making a sound, Billy stood and pulled his shirttails from his trousers. After securing the gun under his waistband, he let the blouse drape over it in front.

"Just be glad you ain't in here with me, Bell. It's a grim moment for Lincoln County."

With his hands still splayed over his hips and his elbows pointed to either side, Bell paced away a few steps, turned, and walked back to stare at the shed. "How much longer you reckon you'll be?"

Billy sat again and rustled the papers. "Gimme a minute. I'm finishin' up."

When he emerged from the privy, he held his hands to his abdomen and still walked with a little crouch in his spine. Filling his cheeks with air, he exhaled a sigh of relief.

"You gonna make it?" Bell asked.

Billy nodded. "I'm ready to get back. Maybe I can eat somethin' now."

Bell frowned. "Hell, I already et up most of it."

Billy shrugged. "I don't need much. Just a little somethin' to sit in my belly."

As the two men crossed the yard again, Godfrey Gauss leaned on his hoe and watched them. Billy noticed Gauss and nodded to the old man, who had once cooked for Tunstall at the Rio Feliz. Gauss returned the nod, watched the pair for a few more seconds, and then returned to his work.

When guard and prisoner passed through the courthouse door, Bell hung back a few yards and waited as Billy entered the twilit stairwell. At the sharp turn in the stairs, Billy glanced back as the deputy closed the door. Bell's gun was still holstered. As they climbed the steps, Billy's boots scraped on the treads, keeping up a rhythm as steady as a clock. The chains on his legs made a racket that filled the narrow stairwell. Slipping a hand under his blouse he brought out the gun in a smooth unhurried movement and pressed it flat against his stomach. Keeping up his plodding pace, he climbed the last few steps with Bell following four treads behind.

At the top of the flight, when Billy pivoted left into the hallway, he swung all the way to the wall, his back pressed against the boards. Continuing to lift his boots and step in place, he kept up the same tempo with his chains, as if he were still walking.

"Hold up, Billy," Bell called out, his voice relaxed but authoritative.

When Billy heard Bell's footfall approach the top tread, he pivoted and leveled the gun at the deputy's chest. Bell froze, his eyes glassy as they fixed on the gun. When Billy cocked the hammer, the deputy's hands began to levitate until they hovered beside his shoulders.

Bell swallowed. "Don't kill me, Kid . . . please!"

"I don't wanna have to kill you," Billy said and pointed with his free hand at Bell's holstered gun. "Just hand me that shooter . . . real easy now. Do it with your left hand."

For two heartbeats the two men stood unmoving, facing one another, Billy catching the faint light from the north end of the hall and Bell bathed in the dark of the stairwell. The complete silence inside the building made it seem as though death had already staked its claim here in this dim passageway.

Bell slowly rotated his head a few degrees, his eyes remaining glued to Billy's. Swallowing audibly, he began a slow retreat backward.

"I'll just leave through the back door, okay?" Bell bargained. "I'll just go and leave you be, all right?"

"Can't let you do that, Bell," Billy replied. He extended his left hand, palm up. "Just stop where you are and give me that gun."

Bell took another step down. "I'll just go and leave you be," he said again. "I swear it, all right?

Billy crouched and extended the gun to arm's length, sighting on the badge that glinted with light on Bell's dark silhouette. "If you take another step, I'll kill you, Bell."

Bell stopped and breathed through his mouth as he stared up at Billy. His eyes appeared wild and unfocused. Billy snapped the fingers of his empty hand, trying to bring the deputy back to his senses.

"Get up here now!" Billy ordered. "If you don't, I'll kill you!"

Bell's breathing began to escalate, but he continued to stand as stiff as a newel post. In a flash of movement, Billy descended the few steps between them, grabbed Bell by his shirtfront, and jerked him to the upper landing. When Bell went for his gun, Billy raised the Navy Colt and slashed the barrel into the side of the deputy's skull, the gun discharging at impact and spewing a plume of smoke into the stairwell.

The quick blow had been so unexpected that Bell made no effort to counter it. Falling forward, he landed face down, his chest stretching into the hallway and his legs angled downward over the top several steps. His head bled as profusely as if he'd been shot. When Billy knelt to reach for the guard's pistol, Bell started to scramble backward, sliding down the stairs on his belly, until midway down he got his feet beneath him and pushed up to a crouch.

"Don't shoot me, Kid! Don't!"

With his gun trained on the deputy, Billy held out his free hand and curled his fingers in a come-hither gesture. "Just keep your hands empty and walk up here," Billy instructed.

In the dark of the stairwell the whites of Bell's eyes seemed to gather light where there was none to be found. His hands clenched and then opened. The blood running down the side of his head had soaked into his blouse making a dark stain over his shoulder and chest. Darting the tip of his tongue around his lips, the deputy glanced behind him as if getting his bearings.

"Don't do it, Bell!" Billy commanded and cocked the pistol again.

Bell's eyes filled with a panicky desperation. He turned and bolted, his boots clattering on the stairs like a stud horse kicking out at the walls of its stall. Billy fired and watched Bell hit the wall where the stairs took a hard turn. The deputy grunted and pressed the side of his face against the wall, and in that instant Billy could see where his bullet had gouged into one side of the deputy's back.

Billy cocked the Navy Colt but hesitated when Bell's body shuddered and his knees started to buckle. "You were too late for this game," Billy muttered. Straightening, he lowered the hammer on the pistol and watched Bell stumble down the remaining few steps and out of sight. When Billy heard the door fling open and bang against the exterior of the building, he considered going after the dying man to retrieve the keys to his irons, but Bell still had his gun, and time was against Billy.

Hurrying down the south end of the hall he tried the first door he came to. It was locked. After stepping back, he charged the door, putting his hip into the wood just beside the latch. With a loud crack the lock gave, splintering wood and twisting the lock plate askew.

It was a storage room, and the first thing he saw was Olinger's shotgun. Snatching it up he opened the breech and found two fresh loads. Snapping the barrels back in place, he made a quick survey of the shelves and spotted his .44 rolled up in its holster and cartridge belt. He propped the scattergun against the wall, pulled down his personal rig, and flung the Navy Colt to the back of the room. When he buckled on the belt, the familiar fit of the leather endowed him with a surge of confidence. He checked the loads, found the cylinder full, and stuffed the pistol back into the holster. Among the other items stored in the room, he found the self-cocker that Tunstall had given him. This he stuffed behind the buckle of his cartridge belt. Then he secured a Winchester rifle and a box of .44-40 cartridges.

Snatching up the shotgun, he skipped down the hall through Garrett's office, his chains scraping and rattling all the way. Laying the rifle and box of cartridges on his cot, he moved to the east window and raised it. Down below he saw Gauss talking to another man in the garden. Gauss was pointing behind the courthouse, and the other man, seemingly transfixed, stared in that direction. Billy assumed they were talking about Bell, but he couldn't know if the deputy was dead or alive.

"What the hell happened?" came a booming voice from the street. "Did Bell kill the Kid?"

Billy knelt, propped his elbow on the windowsill, planted the stock of the shotgun firmly against his shoulder, and watched Olinger approach the gate that led to the side yard. Big Bob walked with a purposeful stride, his prisoners nowhere in sight. With his thumb Billy cocked back both hammers on the ten gauge and waited.

"The Kid has killed Bell!" Gauss called out and began to approach Olinger.

"What!?" the big man scoffed, the skin on his face tight and lined with doubt. "How—?"

"Hello, Bob!" Billy called down when the deputy was almost at the gate. When Olinger stopped and looked up at the window, Billy hesitated just long enough to see the terror register on the man's face. Then he pulled both triggers. The roar of the shotgun shattered the quiet of the town, its echo spreading down the main street and fading to an indifferent quiet. Big Bob Olinger lay sprawled out in the street on his back, his arms splayed out from his bloody torso, his legs spread and the toes of his boots trying to point east and west.

"Welcome to hell, Bob," Billy said quietly.

Gauss stood unmoving, staring at the gore of Olinger's mutilated chest. Even from the window, Billy could see that the big deputy's face had achieved a peace never witnessed on his living countenance. Big Bob lay so still and bloodied, there could be no doubt that he was dead.

"Hey, Gauss!" Billy called in his friendly way.

The old man looked up at the window, his face distorted into a mask of fear. He took two steps backward but then stopped, his empty hands rising slowly to the level of his ears.

Billy laughed. "Put your hands down, Godfrey. Ain't nobody gonna hurt you." He set the shotgun against the wall and propped his forearms on the sill. "Is Bell dead for sure?"

Gauss slowly lowered his arms and nodded. "Dead as a man can be."

"Any more deputies in town today?"

Gauss frowned and shook his head. "Garrett's gone to White Oaks. Ham is at the fort hospital to see the doctor."

"Can you find me a key for my irons?" Billy said. "Should be one in Bell's pocket."

Gauss's face wrinkled with disgust. "Don't ask me to do that! I can't be searching through a dead man's clothes!"

"Well, I'll need somethin' to bust open these irons," Billy returned. "What have you got down there?"

Gauss turned to survey the grounds until he faced the garden. "Can I walk over there and get something?" he said and pointed.

"Well, I *hope* you can walk," Billy said laughing. "Go get it an' throw 'er up here."

The old man walked stiffly to the garden and sorted through an array of tools lying in the dirt. Returning to the building, he carried a small miner's pick in one hand. When he stood below the window again, he began swinging the pick next to his leg as he looked up at Billy.

"Better step back," Gauss yelled.

It took four tries before the little pickax banged against the window casing and clattered to the floor. Smiling, Billy stepped to the window and clapped with his manacle chains swinging and scraping along the sill.

"Reckon you can saddle me a horse, old boy?" Billy called out.

"What horse?" Gauss replied.

Billy grinned and frowned at the same time, as if he had heard the wrong punch line to a joke. "A damned fast one," he said. "Bring it 'round quick, would you?" When the old man made no move, Billy waved him toward the back lot. "Go on, now! Find me a good one."

As Gauss made his way to the stables, Billy scanned the buildings on the other side of the street. A few townspeople were emerging from the hotel and from the Whelan Store. Several more citizens gathered at the east end of the side yard, where they craned their necks to get a glimpse of the body in the street. Billy gave them all a two-fingered salute from his brow, sweeping his hand upward in a flippant arc.

"Sometimes you gotta *take* what you need!" he yelled and waited to see if there might be a reply. There was none.

Snatching up the Winchester and ammunition, he returned to Garrett's office, threw open the drawers of the desk, and searched for a key that might work for his leg irons and cuffs. Finding none, he peered out the window over the small balcony in front. A crowd had formed directly across the street, every spectator looking expectantly at the courthouse. To his right he saw three young Mexican boys in the street. Like statuettes in a graveyard, they stood unmoving, their attention fixed on Olinger's corpse at the gate.

Billy sat on top of Garrett's desk and, wielding the pickax, began hacking at one of the leg irons. After two minutes of constant pounding, the lock broke. When he started on the left one, he found it difficult to hit the prime breaking spot without banging his shin with the haft of the tool, so he gave it up and tucked the free end of the chain under his cartridge belt.

Picking up the Winchester he walked into the hallway and out the balcony door to smile at his audience, whose numbers had doubled as he had banged away at his restraints. When he leaned one hand on the rail to address the crowd, he caught sight of a thin Anglo merchant in a white shirt and dark trousers hurrying up the street toward the courthouse. The man carried a shotgun at port arms before him, like a soldier walking at double-time. He had not seen Billy, for his eyes darted birdlike from the crowd to Olinger and back to the spectators.

Recognizing the clerk from one of the stores, Billy laughed to himself and levered a round into the rifle's chamber. The ratchety sound stopped the man in his tracks. Billy leaned sidesaddle on the railing, sighted down the rifle, and smiled. The swinging of his wrist chains was the only movement on the balcony. Looking up, the citizen lowered his weapon in a slow, dreamlike surrender until the gun hung at arm's length before his thighs.

"Hold on right there, friend!" Billy called out and freed up one hand to point east down the street. "I want you to turn around and go back where you came from. Take that scattergun with you and store it in a closet somewhere. You don't wanna die today."

The merchant seemed paralyzed, his eyes unblinking and dull as two old coins. Pivoting his head, he looked again at Olinger's body lying face up in the dusty street. Then he scanned the crowd as if someone among the onlookers might suggest his next move.

"Go on!" Billy said. "Do it! I'm standin' pat against the world here, and I ain't got a lotta choices on how I do that."

The man lowered his head and stared down at the ground for a moment. Then he turned and walked away at a faster pace than he had arrived.

"I didn't wanna kill Bell!" Billy announced to the crowd.

Everyone grew quiet and still as they waited for more.

"I begged 'im not to run. But it came down to him or me, and I chose Billy."

Not one person in the crowd moved. Even those who were hurrying up the street to join the spectators slowed and lightened their step as if they might be interrupting some private event.

Billy pointed at Olinger's body. "But that sonovabitch got his due!" he said louder.

The crowd hung on his every word. Then, like a quick change in the weather, Billy smiled, propped the rifle against the baluster rail, and, as if to embrace all who had gathered, spread his arms as much as his wrist chains allowed.

"I guess this is what it feels like to run for gov'nor!" he announced and, laughing, paced back and forth the length of the deck. Stopping, he raised both arms again and smiled. "Who'll vote for Billy?" Lowering his arms, he leaned on the banister. " 'Least I'd be a gov'nor who keeps his word!"

Now the bystanders were talking among themselves, seemingly more relaxed at the arrival of anarchy in their community. One of the Mexican boys called up to Billy and pointed toward the west corner of the courthouse. The Kid leaned out to watch old Gauss lead a spirited bay into the street. Walleyed and chopping the dirt with its hooves, the horse held its head high and ears erect as if sensing danger in the crowd of citizens lining the road.

"You're a good man, Gauss!" Billy called out. "If I get voted into office, I might appoint you the territorial secretary of horses." He picked up the rifle and pointed a finger at the old German. "Stay right there. I'm comin' down." Before turning for the door behind him, Billy swept his finger across the crowd. "Don't nobody think about crossin' me now! I'll kill anybody who stands between me an' tomorrow!"

Hesitating, he hitched up the loose chain that tried to slip from his belt. When he scanned his audience and spoke again, there was a hint of contrition in his voice. "I'll just ride outta Lincoln, an' you folks can go about your day. I don't mean no harm to any o' you long as you afford me the same courtesy."

Billy emerged from the building in a relaxed manner, the Winchester in his left hand, the muzzle pointed down. As he stepped into the street, the leg-iron chain hung from his belt in a loop that scuffed the ground as it swung beside him. When he reached Gauss, he took the reins from the old man and tried to push the rifle deep into the scabbard mounted on the saddle. The nervous horse whinnied and sidestepped, swinging its hind quarters in a wide arc in the middle of the street.

Gauss took hold of the cheek strap on the bay and tried to calm the horse with a litany of mumbled German words. When the animal had settled sufficiently, Billy tamped the rifle in place, booted into the stirrup, and winked at Gauss.

"Thank you, old friend," he said quietly. "Tell the owner I'll send this high-strung jackrabbit back to 'im soon as I can."

As Billy pulled himself up by the pommel, the free end of the chain dropped from his belt and clinked in the hardpan of the street, sending the bay into motion again. Billy had just swung a leg over to gain the saddle when the bay reared and walked backward two steps with its fore hooves clawing at the air. Billy leaned over the withers to maintain his seat, but the horse made a little leap upward, landed on all fours together, and bucked hard, throwing its haunches high in the air as its head lowered almost to the street. Billy sailed over the horse's shoulder and landed on his side with a jarring impact. The bay snorted, claiming its victory in the contest, and then broke into a gallop, making a beeline for the stables behind the courthouse.

For a few seconds no one dared to speak. Then Billy's laughter broke the tension. He propped up on an elbow and smiled at Gauss.

"Well . . . how's that for a getaway?"

A ripple of laughter passed through the crowd. One of the Mexican boys ran after the loose horse, and, when he did, two others followed.

"Would you get 'im for me again, old boy?" Billy said to Gauss.

The old man started for the back of the courthouse in his bent and peculiar walk. Billy stood, dusted himself off, and propped his hands on his hips as he waited.

"What will you do now, Bee-lee?" asked a dark-haired Hispanic woman cradling her baby in her arms.

The Kid smiled down at his boots and pinched the bridge of his nose as he shook his head. When he looked up, he singled out the woman who had called to him.

"Well, if I can remember how to ride a horse, I reckon I'll be as gone as yesterday." Billy forked his hands over his hips and eyed the crowd from left to right. "Shouldn' nobody bother to go lookin' for Billy Bonney this side o' Ireland. You can tell that to Pat Garrett."

Gauss brought the horse around again, took a wide stance on his feeble legs, and gripped the bridle with both hands as he looked the bay in the eyes and spoke to it. The three Mexican boys returned and sat on the porch of the courthouse to watch what might happen next. Billy secured the leg-iron chain under his belt again, toed into the stirrup, and mounted. The bay spun once in a tight circle and settled enough for Billy to address the crowd one last time.

"Adios, boys!" he yelled and flung an arm high as a farewell salute. "Ladies!" he added. *¡Nos vemos en los bailes!*

Before reining his horse around, Billy caught sight of two figures standing back from the crowd under the front awning of the Wortley. A thin man in a brown suit and bowler hat looked back at him. Next to the dandy was a boy dressed in faded white muslin. Billy hid his recognition of the two beneath the smile he had pasted on for his grand exit. The journalist, Blessing, raised a hand in a tentative wave. The boy, José, had turned his head to stare at Olinger. The profile of his face appeared to be carved out of oak—a cameo of misery or regret or some other emotion that haunted the soul.

Billy swept his arm across the crowd, pointing at all who had gathered, letting that finger come to rest on Blessing and the boy. "¡Gracias, amigos!"

Turning the horse west, Billy held the bay to a walk, moving down the street like a man returning home after a day's work. His back shifted in contrapposto rhythm with the easy gait of the horse. Just before angling north toward the river, Billy began to sing in a high tenor.

He sang quietly at first, but as he forded the Bonito and heard the water part around the bay's legs, the lines began to pour out of him like sweet spring water bubbling up from the earth, the music rising and falling effortlessly at his will, declaring his freedom and claiming his place in the world again. Beyond the river, the flat valley bottom opened up to him like an invitation to resurrect himself. Once again life seemed full of possibilities.

The two lives forfeited for his emancipation were behind him now. That was the cost of surviving. It could just as easily have been his blood to soak into the dust of Lincoln today. But none of that mattered now. He had come out the winner of this game. *Someone* had to. And Billy was always good at games.

21
Blessing's Notes
Lincoln and Old Fort Sumner
New Mexico Territory
July 1881

"O, Billy, *el valiente,* you were much too young to die They
killed you out of need to save the gov'nor from his lie."

I have not seen Billy Bonney in over two months since he broke
out of the Lincoln County courthouse. Remaining in town after
the murders of the two deputies, I have been seeking out
interviews with anyone who will talk to me about the Kid, and I
am amassing quite a collection of stories.

Part of me expects to see Billy brought back to Lincoln in
chains, where I will continue my interviews with him. But a
deeper part of me hopes he remains hidden, a sentiment I keep
to myself as I visit the citizens of Lincoln and accumulate my
treasury of anecdotes on Billy the Kid.

It is clear to me that Billy Bonney has ascended to a new
echelon of folklore now that he has pulled off the impossible by
escaping Pat Garrett's custody. As far as the citizens' depth of
relationship with the outlaw is concerned, I am beginning to
suspect that the line between truth and fiction has begun to
blur. Everyone has a "Kid story" and is anxious to relate it . . .
and to see it retold in the newspaper with the source's name
put into print. As usual, in my occupation, celebrity is a power-
ful aphrodisiac.

There are, however, some stories I cannot dismiss. A reporter
gains a sixth sense about the veracity of an interviewee. More
times than not, these are the people who ask that their names
be withheld from any article I might write for the newspaper.

As a case in point, take the aging señora in the Gutiérres family. Upon visiting her modest adobe home, I was treated to a wonderful peach wine and a marvelous story of the generosity of "Billy the Kid." Judging by this elder woman's no-nonsense demeanor, I have no doubts about the truth of every detail.

As the story goes, one of her nephews was riding a mule in the San Andres Mountains above Mesilla as he searched for half a dozen sheep that had strayed from the grassy meadow where they regularly foraged. When the mule shied at the sudden buzz of a rattlesnake between its hooves, the rider took a tumble into the rocky scrub brush, where he had the misfortune to bounce off a boulder into a bed of prickly pear, taking the brunt of the needle-like impalements on his backside.

The rattlesnake, thankfully, slithered away, but so had the mule wandered off. By the time the forlorn boy had extricated himself from the cacti, he had incurred a good many more wounds from the relentless spines. Even worse, one leg was broken. He could not walk and neither could he ride, even if he had an animal to mount. Looking around in every direction he could see no hope for a rescue. He carried no gun with which to fire off a signal round. The nearest abode was seven miles away. All the boy could do was build a fire and make as much smoke as possible. Then he prayed.

Even summer nights in the mountains can be cold, and the hapless shepherd felt an unprecedented gratitude the next morning for the rising of the sun. With great difficulty, he scraped around for more wood and stoked his fire. By midmorning, having run out of wood, he struggled out of his boots and set them on the coals, producing a darker smoke that spiraled upward like a semaphore of distress. But the black cloud dissipated all too quickly in the mountain winds, and the boy lay on his side and began to cry. He had bewailed his fate for less than an hour when a clatter of stones opened his eyes.

"I sure hope that ain't your breakfast you're workin' on there, amigo. It stinks to high heaven and looks a mite overcooked."

The young Anglo speaker wore a sugar-loaf sombrero and simple white muslin trousers and blouse. Sitting atop a sleek but well-muscled blue roan mare, the visitor smiled, establishing instant negotiations for peace. His somewhat crooked front teeth further endeared him to the boy, because the young shepherd's little brother carried a similar trademark smile. With his slender hands and smooth schoolboy face, the stranger appeared not too many years older than the Gutiérres boy, himself.

"Can you help me, señor?" the injured boy pleaded.

The rider laughed. " 'Course I can," he said and dismounted by throwing a leg over the roan's neck and sliding off his saddle on his rump. Landing lightly on his feet, he took off his big hat and hung it on the horn of the saddle. "Looks like you drew the low card, son." He widened his smile. "Name's Billy Bonney."

After splinting the boy's leg with several dry yucca stalks lashed snugly with pigging strings, Billy built a lean-to shelter to shade the boy. Then he rode off to a stand of pines that fringed a low ridge on the west face of the mountains. When he returned, he carried a bundle of dry wood lashed behind the cantle of his saddle. In his hand he carried a curved piece of stone that resembled the bottom of a bowl. On top of the stone was a large glob of gray-brown material speckled with flakes of bark.

"What ees that?" the boy asked.

Billy dismounted and set the rock down for inspection. "Pine sap," he said and loosened the bundle of sticks to fall on the ground. Then he squatted beside the small fire and began adding fuel. "We're gonna heat up some sap on this rock. Then, when it cools enough that you can stand it, we'll press it to your skin. As it cools it'll suck those stickers outta where the sun don't shine."

The boy's forehead tightened and lined like a furrowed field. "Does it hurt?"

Billy frowned. "This is one o' those cases where it don't matter if it hurts. It's got to be done. You got to be able to sit my horse with me to git outta these mountains."

So went the rescue of a young Mexican herder by the outlaw Billy the Kid. That boy never saw Billy again after their chance encounter in the San Andres, but the Gutiérres family never tired of recalling the event.

There is the rancher near White Oaks who had lost his prime breeder bull to a gang of midnight rustlers—cutthroat drifters, he claims, who invaded the Pecos Valley from the Texas panhandle. Unasked, Billy brought the half-ton animal back to the bereft cattleman without so much as a word about a reward. Why Billy chose to help this particular gentleman is not known.

A Lincoln saloon owner swears he witnessed the Kid winning eleven straight hands of poker one night, pulling in over four hundred dollars in a matter of hours. The losers, he claims, were so distraught over their bad luck that Billy divided up his winnings, giving every man—including himself—the same equal share.

There is a young Mexican schoolteacher who holds classes in the church below the Baca house, and she informs me that Billy had joined her students one day for the purpose of demonstrating a variety of dance steps that might be useful to them in a coming Christmas baile. The real gift, she confides, was not so much how to dance but showing the boys that dancing is something a man can do with pride. Billy, she tells me, helped the boys understand that dancing is one way into a woman's heart. As for the girls, they took to Billy with fluttering eyelashes, and each begged to serve as his partner in the demonstrations. Billy's response to his sudden popularity with these girls was to smile at the boys and say, "See there? What'd I tell you?"

Two people remain conspicuously absent from my notes. Pat Garrett will not talk to me. His reputation has taken a hard blow since Billy's escape, and his appearances on the street are infrequent. Not because he is out looking for the Kid. He isn't. He seems to be biding his time, I am told, and while doing that he avoids all socializing.

The other name missing from my notes is José, the hotel boy. I sought him out at the Wortley but was told he had left the hotel's employment. When I tried the Baca house where he and his mother were staying, I discovered they had left for parts unknown. Probably Mexico, if the rumors are correct. Which, of course, makes me wonder about José's part, if any, in Billy's infamous getaway.

On a Monday morning I manage to cross paths with the obese deputy—Ham—at the post office. He seems to hold me in some measure of esteem. This, I suppose, is on account of my letter from the governor's office. After giving me the details of the debacle at the courthouse—a narrative stitched together by Garrett, he informs me—he gives me a fleshy wink and leans in to relate a day from years ago when he had engaged in target practice with the Kid.

As Ham tells the story, he had been collecting taxes at one of the outlying ranches east of town, when a friendly shooting contest had developed among some of the hands as they waited for their employer to return from town. Ham claims to have come in second, beaten only by Billy Bonney, who had shaken his hand and paid the deputy a compliment.

I'd hate to face your steady aim in a square fight, Ham, Billy is supposed to have said.

I smile and nod, not believing a word of it. When he begins another story, I am relieved to see the postal clerk waving two envelopes in the air, trying to get my attention.

"Excuse me," I say to the rotund deputy. "I'm expecting an important letter." I smile and deliver a small bow as I make my escape.

As I move toward the counter, I remind myself that my parting words to the deputy were not entirely a lie. The optimistic side of me half expects a letter of praise from Edmund Pitts, my editor, commending me for my first article on William Bonney, which ran last week.

The clerk cocks his head and squints one eye. "Mr. Blessing, right? The newspaper reporter?"

"That's right," I reply and notice that one of the envelopes is yellow.

"Got two for you today." The clerk's eyebrows rise above the frame of his spectacles. "One is from the governor's office. This other'n is a telegram from your newspaper. It was wired to Las Vegas, and our carrier delivered it here."

Taking this news in stride, I receive the letters as if a missive from the governor is an everyday occurrence for me. I carry my mail outside and stop under a big cottonwood tree by the curb, where I study the inscribed address. The governor must have an accomplished secretary, because my name is rendered in a majestic cursive, complete with baroque flourishes and ruler-straight alignment . . . capped off at the end with a complimentary *Esquire*. Below my name the destination reads: *General Delivery, Lincoln, New Mexico Territory*. At the bottom border of the envelope one more line spans the length of the paper: *If not picked up in five days, forward to the* Santa Fe Messenger.

In the upper left corner, the return address is less specific. It reads: *Office of the Governor*. I turn the envelope over. Nothing is written on the back.

Tearing open the seal I find a scrap of newsprint torn from a mail order catalogue. It is folded once and covered with small print and an illustration of a woman's corset. Opening the fold,

I find the same flowing cursive that addressed the envelope. It is written diagonally over the eight-point type of the corset advertisement. It reads as follows:

I was governor for the day in Lincoln, wasn't I? Come to Fort Sumner. I'll tell you the rest of the story.

Looking west down the main street, I fix my gaze on the courthouse and think of Billy Bonney last April, parading back and forth on the balcony after he had killed two men. He had announced to the town from that lofty perch that he felt as if he were running for governor.

"You *were* the governor of Lincoln *that* day," I whisper under my breath and imagine the boyish smile that endears Billy Bonney to so many. Inserting the paper back into the envelope, I start for the hotel to pack my things. As I walk, I open the yellow envelope and pull out a telegram composed of four words: *Stop writing. Return immediately.* It is signed: *E. P.*

Stopping in the street, I frown at the telegram and again read the curt message from my editor. From the Whelan Store to my right, a very tall man in a dark suit emerges from the front door. Pat Garrett holds his hat in one hand and with the other rotates a big, unlighted cigar in his puckered lips, as if he is screwing the thing in place.

"Wouldn't have a light, would you?" he says.

A cold shiver runs down my back when I stop in front of him. His hair is slicked down and shining wetly, and I can smell pomade emanating from him like nectar wafting from a desert rose. As if reading my mind, he pushes his hat down on his head and fixes his gaze on me.

Crunching the two envelopes in my fist, I manage to smile up at his cold slate eyes. "I might, Sheriff," I say in a voice half an octave above my normal register. "Let me check." Stuffing the crumpled papers into my inside coat pocket, I bring out the small box of lucifers I had used to clean the nib of my pen this morning.

Garrett gives no indication that he recognizes me, but his eyes remain fixed on mine as I strike a flame and hold it up before his face. Leaning down he touches the end of the cigar to the flame, his cheeks sucking into shaded hollows around his moustache as an acrid cloud of smoke billows around us. I cannot help but cough. As he studies my face, his eyes are like two lighted windows seen through a fog. At last, he lowers the burning cigar beside his leg. I shake away the flame of the lucifer and drop the charred stick in the street.

"Haven't heard anything from your friend, have you?" Garrett says in his easy drawl.

A twinge of panic flutters in my heart. The wadded letters in my pocket now feel like a brick bulging under my coat. I'm not sure if he refers to Billy Bonney or José, the hotel boy.

"Who?" I reply and manage to keep my voice from cracking.

Garrett pauses long enough to show me the subtlest of smiles. "The Kid," he says. "Heard any rumors?"

I try for a surprised look. "Bonney? No . . . no rumors," I say, my answer technically true.

Drawing on the cigar, he looks diagonally across the street toward the courthouse where, during his absence, two-thirds of his in-town deputy force was eliminated within the span of five minutes. Following his gaze, my eyes fall upon the stack of lumber piled in the side yard. It has been over two months since the boards were delivered, yet no one has begun the construction of the gallows. I decide not to ask.

"Were you at Fort Stanton that day?" Garrett asks.

I frown. "Pardon?"

The sheriff affords me a look of toleration. "When Bonney escaped. You said you were going to the fort that day."

"No," I say, scrambling to assemble a story. "The interview

327

was cancelled."

Garrett nods and settles his gaze back on the courthouse. "So you were here?"

I look around as if getting my bearings. "Standing right there, Sheriff," I say and point to a spot in front of the hotel porch.

He returns his gaze to the courthouse and inspects the upstairs balcony where Billy had held the town captive with his antics. "So you've seen him kill now," Garrett says in a flat tone.

When I do not reply, he turns to look at me.

"How do you feel about your 'Robin Hood of the Trans-Pecos' now?"

I do my best not to cringe at the phrase I had coined in my newspaper article. Coming from Pat Garrett's lips, the moniker sounds like a child's invention. But I am surprised at my private thoughts. Though I have struggled to remain neutral in my writing, I find my assessment of Billy's murderous deeds that day now leaning toward justification.

If I had been in Billy Bonney's boots that day . . . and if I had been more familiar with firearms . . . and if I knew I was scheduled to be hanged by my neck until either my spinal cord snapped or my last breath was squeezed from my lungs . . . perhaps I would have dispatched *anyone* standing between me and the freedom that I so desperately sought.

I did not witness Deputy Bell's dead body that day, but I most certainly saw Olinger's bloody corpse. His big imposing frame had lain unmoving at the edge of the street for the entire time that Billy had addressed the townfolk who had gathered. Olinger was part of the past, his deep voice never to speak again, his eyes closed into permanent darkness, and his ears deaf to Billy's performance on the balcony. All his future had been snatched away in the flash of one explosive moment.

I had heard the shot as I sat in my room and arranged my notes for a new article. When I went outside following the flow of curious people streaming from the hotel, I saw the bright, glistening red of Olinger's fatal wound shining in the sun like a freshly spilled can of paint.

And yet, even today, I feel no pity . . . no loss . . . no accusatory judgment about the crime. I had seen just enough of Olinger's abuse toward the Kid to feel a tiny spark of wicked satisfaction over the outcome.

Though I have always taken pride in the fact that I could never take another man's life, I now must question that moral stance, wondering if this supposed asset is actually a character deficit of mine. I find myself thinking not about whether I *could* kill . . . but, instead, to save my own life . . . what if I *couldn't* kill? This is the first time I realize that I feel something akin to admiration toward a boy so young as Billy, who could steel himself to the ultimate sin for the sake of his own survival.

Swallowing these thoughts, I concoct a courteous smile for the sheriff and cock my head with a question. "After Bonney depleted your staff of two officers, don't you suppose he has left the territory, Sheriff Garrett?"

He sucks on the cigar again and shakes his head. "No, I don't."

I narrow my eyes and try to appear curious. "Why would he stay in the New Mexico Territory?" I ask, just to hear his theory. "Bonney has everything to lose here and everything to gain by taking up a new life someplace far away from here."

Garrett appears amused. "For that very reason. Everything he has is here. He doesn't want to lose it."

I feel my face wrinkle up, just as it does when my editor critiques my writing. "I'm not sure I follow," I say.

Garrett clamps the cigar in his teeth and talks around it. "That's because you've prob'ly always had a home and a family, Mr. Blessing. Prob'ly born into both. Billy had to earn his." He removes the cigar and points it toward the trees behind the hotel, where the land tilts down to the small, charming river. "For a man accustomed to bein' on the run, Billy's put down some deep roots here. It's the old part of this land that is his home. And the Mexican people who still live on it, work it, reap its bounty, and depend on it. They're his family. Far as I know, there ain't nobody else."

"But he does have a brother," I say, showing off a little.

Garrett is unfazed at this news. "That so?" He swivels his head to look down the street. "Billy never mentioned 'im."

The sheriff calmly draws on his cigar. After he expels a plume of smoke he studies the cigar in his hand as if he is determining its length in centimeters.

"Well, Mr. Blessing, if he did have a brother, I reckon it's a shame Billy didn't stick with 'im and come up with a better life."

The sheriff's compassion and philosophical capacity take me by surprise. As he stares off at the mountains, I look down the length of this long, tall lawman, taking a new measure of the man. Only now do I see that he idly turns a box of lucifers in his left hand. I keep my voice casual.

"Sheriff, you sound like a man who might understand Billy Bonney a little bit."

He looks thoughtful as he fills the air with smoke again. "I might," he admits and meets my eyes. "My wife is Mexican, you know."

"I didn't know," I say. "So, maybe you and Billy have some things in common?"

He removes the cigar from his mouth and glances at me briefly before studying the cigar again. The red ring smoldering on the brown paper wrapping keeps a steady string of smoke rising between us.

"Some maybe," he says and purses his lips. "But only some." He turns and looks across the street at the scene of his deputies' debacle. "Can't say I could shoot a man in cold blood. That might be the difference."

I simply nod and study his face in profile. There is a natural hardness in this man's countenance. I cannot recall a time I have seen him smile. That makes for another difference in the two men in question. Billy's smile is as much a part of him as his dark-blue eyes.

"If you hear something," Garrett says quietly, his gaze now taking in the stores to the east, "let me know." When he looks down into my eyes again, I feel as if he can see into the dark recesses of my soul where my secrets are filed away. "Good day, Mr. Blessing."

When he starts out into the street on his long, gangly legs, I suppress the memory of the telegram in my pocket and summon the courage to speak to Garrett's back. "Sheriff, might you permit an interview for my paper now?"

He turns and studies me as he takes a long draw on the cigar. After easing out a lazy curl of smoke, he bobs the cigar toward me.

"Ain't that what we just had?" he says, his taunting eyes fairly daring me to object.

Before I can say something inane or incompetent, he turns on his heel and crosses the street in his same long, steady stride, leaving a trail of gray smoke hovering behind him as if the very air has been scorched by his presence.

Walking past the hotel, I take the footpath that leads down to the river, where a cushiony patch of grass spreads right to the lip of the stream bank. I sometimes sit here by the water to organize my notes and compose my articles. Today I lower myself to the sandy flat beside the stream and scan the area in all directions. Seeing no one, I kneel, take out the wadded papers from my coat pocket, and set them on the little beach at the water's edge.

Striking another lucifer, I touch the flame to the papers and watch them burn. As the yellow flame builds, the papers darken to a thin shell of black and break apart into weightless flakes that float on the air and touch down on the water where the current carries them away. I stab the spent lucifer into the sand and stand to watch the water flow by for a time . . . long enough to know I will travel northeast to see Billy.

Fort Sumner is a former military compound whose every structure has been converted into a civilian quarters or private business. My assigned room, I am told, was part of the old barracks for the enlisted men. Though empty, it is partitioned off for privacy by an array of blankets hung from sagging ropes that crisscross the building just below the rafters.

Two lighted candles afford enough illumination to study my guest quarters, which is a corner room composed of two bunks with a small table between them at their heads. On the two whitewashed adobe walls I find rows of marks scratched into the paint, quartets of vertical lines, each foursome struck by a diagonal slash—the kind of record-keeping one would expect to see in a prison where an inmate tallies his days.

Sitting on one of the beds I finish polishing up the notes that I jotted down during my long afternoon talk with Billy Bonney. And what a wonderful conversation it was, covering the episodes of his life not known to the general public. When I close my notebook, my eyelids feel heavy, and my weary body sags. I check my watch and find that it is after midnight. After storing my writing accouterments in my satchel, I slide the satchel under the bed, toe off my shoes, and lie down to put my feet up. With my fingers laced behind my head, I stare up at the glow of the candle playing on the rough ceiling. Save the night crickets chirring outside, the past few hours have been quiet, and I am tempted to sleep but for the continuation of the interview that Billy has promised for tonight.

Though my belly is full, I cut a slice from the small block of tasty cheese on the night table. I find myself wishing for a glass of wine, but the mescal donated by the Gutiérres family will have to do.

I expect Billy at any time. He has spent the evening with Paulita and promised to meet me here at midnight, but I fully understand that he might be late, depending upon the nature of their rendezvous. As he described their trysts to me, some are "whirlwinds of passion" and others "cold baths of argument about their future." Personally, I am hoping for him something in between, where the two might decide to leave the territory together to raise their coming child.

When the door opens, right away I hear Billy's friendly laugh as he speaks to someone outside in the plaza. A voice replies to him in Spanish, and both men laugh. Then the door closes, and I hear the familiar, carefree shuffle of Billy's boots approaching my curtained room.

"Anybody home?" Billy calls out.

"Right here," I answer.

I stand and hold one of the draped blankets aside. After ducking in, he tosses his hat on the extra bed and from his waistband removes a pistol, which he drops next to the hat. After inhaling deeply, he purges the breath in a long sigh and sits on the bunk, leaning back on his elbows to smile at me.

"How is Paulita?" I ask.

"Bold and beautiful," he replies, a little flicker of mischief playing across his face. "Have you had some supper?"

I place a hand to my stomach and inflate my cheeks. "Deluvina fed me until I thought I might burst." I sit down on my own bed and face him, my arms stiff and my hands clasping the edge of the mattress.

Billy laughs. "If it's good food you want, you oughta think

'bout marryin' her."

When he sees my startled reaction, he laughs again.

" 'Course you'd have to settle for bein' the runt in that lit-ter," Billy ribs. "She might be short, but I think she's got 'bout sixty pounds on you." Pushing himself up, he begins tugging off his boots, and, one at a time, he drops them to the floor.

"Is Deluvina a sister to Paulita?" I ask.

Billy closes his eyes as he shakes his head. "She's Navajo. Got captured by Apaches as a little girl. Paulita's father traded for her. Presto-changeo! Cost 'im ten good horses, so I hear." Billy bobs his eyebrows and takes on an amused grin. "Ask me, the Apaches got the short end o' that bargain."

I nod. "She is an excellent cook, but I think I prefer to remain a bachelor a while longer."

Billy narrows his eyes and nods, as if I have said something wise.

"Paulita's father was a rich man, wasn't he?" I inquire.

Billy pivots to swing his feet up on the bed and crosses his legs at the ankles. "He was well thought of here. Acquired a lot o' Spanish land grants from the old days and somehow held on to them when the fat-cat politicians in Santa Fe started grabbin' up all they could. With the old man dead, Pete looks after it all now."

"Pete?" I say.

"Pedro . . . Pete Maxwell . . . Paulita's brother." Billy makes a face. "Looks after his sister, too . . . a damned sight too much, if you ask me."

"You're not on good terms?" I ask.

Billy shrugs. "Pete and me go back. We get along all right. He just don't want me for a brother-in-law, that's all." He shrugs again. "Any brother worth his salt is not gonna be too keen on a man who makes his unwed sister heavy with child." Lying back on the bed, Billy smiles up at the ceiling. "Which is why me an'

Paulita slipped out to the peach orchard tonight." He rolls his head to wink at me. "Summer nights . . . under the stars," he says, as though he is spreading the Gospel. "I'm here to tell you: a fellow and his sweetheart can make a fine memory in a orchard on a summer night."

I feel my face warm, and I am certain my skin is as red as the core of one of the overripe peaches lying in the grass out there among the fruit trees. "So you had a good evening?" I venture, knowing fully well it is a stupid thing to say.

"More than good," Billy laughs. Then he surprises me with an expression so earnest and vulnerable that I feel myself go absolutely still to hear whatever he might say. "D'you think I could make a good father?" he asks, his whispery voice so innocent and gentle I feel my heart open to him the same way it would to a child who asks me about Santa Claus. "I mean . . . if I set my mind to it and get us outta the territory?"

Leaning forward, I prop my forearms on my knees and offer my sincerest smile. "I do," I assure him. "I think, as a father, you would give the child everything you missed and longed for when you were a boy."

Billy props up on one elbow and nods with renewed energy, as if I have served up the perfect answer. "That's the same way I was thinkin'." Just as quickly as it had arrived, his enthusiasm disappears. His young face fills with questions. "But what 'bout me an' all my past? What happens when a child finds out his father was once a outlaw?" Embarrassed, he frowns, but, by the steady burn in his eyes, I know he expects good counsel from me.

"I suppose if you go far enough away, the past won't matter. People won't know you. You can just start over . . . be whoever you choose to be." Wanting to lift his spirits, I smile. "Your son—or your daughter—will know only the father who's there every day. The one who provides . . . and works . . . and

plays . . . and teaches them how to dance." I soften my voice.
"And simply loves them."

Billy stares down at his bed cover and idly smooths the
blanket with repetitive strokes of his hand. Even with the
wrinkles ironed out, he continues the motion, seeming to appreciate the feel of the wool. Then his hand stops moving on the
blanket, and he nods.

"Sounds just 'bout right to me." His unguarded eyes roll up
to catch my expression. "I can do all that," he assures me.

I lift my cup of mescal from the table and raise it to him. "I
know you can," I say and drain the remains of my refreshment.

He begins to rub his hand over the blanket again. "You
know . . . I never signed up for this war. Didn' none of us sign
up, except those Seven Rivers boys and the damned Texans that
Dolan hired. This fight was like a swole-up river. If you lived in
this territory, it just washed over you, swallowed you up, no
questions asked." He shakes his head in a tired way. "Once
you're in somethin' like that, you'd better learn how to swim
pronto. Else you'll drown."

We are quiet for a time. Far off in the night a chorus of
coyotes rises from the south. Their yips and howls weave
together and crescendo until the sound is like an army of wailing women warriors, screaming obscenities, taunting the village
to venture out into the dark to face them in battle.

"Full moon tonight," Billy says.

When I merely nod, his dark-blue eyes glaze over as he stares
at the wall behind me.

"I was figurin' on Paulita and me headin' down to Chihuahua. See if I could start up a little cattle ranch there."

"And what about Paulita's brother . . . Pete?"

Billy arches an eyebrow and gives me his crooked grin. "Well,
I wasn't plannin' on askin' *him*."

I nod. "Sounds like a good plan," I say. "When would you leave?"

Billy lies back on the bed, laces his fingers together over his stomach, and studies the rafters with a frown. "Pretty damned soon. I got a feelin' in my bones."

"What do you mean?"

When he closes his eyes and goes quiet, I assume he will not answer my question. But then his eyes open, and the expression on his face is one I have not seen . . . not even in the Lincoln County jail while he was waiting to hang. His light eyebrows push low over his eyes, and he appears to gaze up into the ceiling at some faraway image that haunts him.

"I had this dream," he whispers. Pulling in his lips, he appears to stare harder at his problem. Then he turns his head quickly to look me in the eye. "Thing is . . . I don't usually put much stock in a dream. But when I told Paulita, it scared her."

I feel my face tighten to mirror his look of worry. "Can you tell me about it?"

He spews air and cocks one eyebrow. "I ain't sure I want to. Paulita says—" Interrupting himself, the Kid sits up, sets his feet on the floor, and frowns at the front curtain. His hand seems to move of its own volition to find the handle of his pistol on the blanket.

Sitting up straighter, I face the same direction and try to hear whatever has put him on edge. From outside in the plaza comes the slow steady pace of someone walking. Two men by the sound of it. I can hear no conversation amongst them. The rhythm of the steps sounds natural and without stealth as the passersby continue deeper into the compound. Billy relaxes his grip on the gun, closes his eyes, and rolls his head in a slow circle from shoulder to shoulder, stretching his neck. When he looks at me again, he slaps both flat hands to his belly.

"I ain't et," he says. "I'm 'bout hungry as a toothless badger."

I point to the table. "I've got cheese."

Billy frowns as he eyes the plate. "Which kind? Goat or cow?"

"Goat," I report.

He makes a sour face. "Can't tolerate it." Pushing up from the bed, he grabs the gun, stands in his stocking feet, and slips the pistol into his waistband. "Pete's got a side o' beef hangin' in the cooler. I'll go cut off a piece an' cook 'er up. Only take a few minutes."

Leaning to the table he picks up the small butcher knife and begins wiping it on the cloth napkin folded next to the cheese. He starts out but stops inside the parted blankets and points the knife blade at me. "When I come back, I'll tell you 'bout that dream. Maybe you can translate it to a better meanin' than Paulita did." He flips the knife with a smart flick of his wrist and catches it by the handle. "Presto-changeo," he says and starts to leave.

"Hey, Billy?" I say, stopping him. His face holds all the wonder and anticipation of a young boy gazing through the window of a bakery. I can't help but smile at the unaffected nature of his emotions. "My newspaper hasn't printed another of my articles since that first one came out in April. I think my editor has shut me down. I just want you to know, if that's true, I'm going to write a book about you."

Billy Bonney flashes his inimitable smile, and his eyes catch the glow of the candlelight. "Well, make it a good one. Hell, I might wanna read it myself."

I laugh. "I'll do my best."

"Oh!" Billy says and snaps his fingers. "Maybe I oughta give you this." Stepping back toward me he fingers a rectangular plate from his shirt pocket. When he hands a tintype to me, he shows an embarrassed grin. "It ain't the best likeness, I guess, but I reckon it'll do."

I study a photographer's image of Billy posing for the camera, his rifle in hand with the stock propped on the floor. His pistol holstered, and his frumpy winter clothes give him an overall oval shape, disguising his lean look. By the expression on his face, it appears that he is asking the photographer, *Well? How do I look?*

"Maybe you can use it in the book," he calls out.

When I look up, the curtain is settling, and Billy is gone. In his socks he is so quiet that I know he has left the building only by the soft *click* of the door latch. Alone I listen to the silence settle in around me. Fort Sumner is as peaceful a place as I have visited in the New Mexico Territory. The people here are loving and humble. Almost all are native New Mexicans, and their culture seems better preserved here, without the heavy hand of Anglo influences. I can understand why the village drew Billy back, his bride-to-be, notwithstanding.

Poring over the tintype again, I smile at a treasured gift. In the picture Billy looks a little stiff as if the photographer had positioned him just so. From under my bunk, I drag out my satchel and store away the portrait in a leather pocket. Then I begin to sort my writing accessories on the bed covers.

While Billy's words are fresh in my mind, I want to write down his metaphorical description of being swept up in the Lincoln County War. This is the Billy Bonney I would like people to read about. In my book, I will, of course, have to ascribe these words to my interviews with Billy in Lincoln. I can't have the world knowing I was hiding out in Fort Sumner with the territory's most wanted outlaw.

As I rustle through the pages of my notebook, my fingers stop moving at a sound from outside. It's Billy's voice, coming from a few doors down at the corner building. Straining to hear his words, I can only make them out clearly enough to know that he is using his fluent Spanish. I hold my breath and hear only silence for ten seconds. I exhale with a sense of relief, assuming that Billy was conversing with one of his Hispanic friends.

A gunshot freezes my spine, and the blood in my veins goes cold. Then another shot sends a jolt through me as if the bed has tried to buck me off to the floor. The explosions seem both muted and close at hand at the same time. For some reason, I look across my little curtained room at the bed where Billy had just minutes before been lounging, opening up to me about his feelings. The depression of his weight on the blanket is still discernable, as if a ghost of his same size and weight has taken up residence there. I feel suddenly sick and cup my hand over my mouth, afraid that I might lose my supper.

Now there are several voices speaking in hurried, low tones. These are grown men I am hearing . . . Anglos . . . excited in a self-contained way. I realize that my feet have, of their own accord, pushed into my shoes, and I rise from the bed as if it has lifted me up to my feet.

Pushing through the hanging blankets I hurry to the door, open it, and step out into the stark light of the full moon that hangs high in the desert sky. The plaza glows as if it is giving back a cooler version of the heat of the day. Two doors down, I see three men talking at the corner building. One stands in a long duster, hatless and yet still a head taller than his companions. When he looks my way, I recognize Pat Garrett. His expression is nothing like my last memory of him, when he stopped me to light his cigar. Gone is the steel in his eyes. The hard angles of his lean face are softer. He appears gaunt, uncertain, and restless. When he turns away from me, he rubs his left hand across his mouth and moustache. Only then do I see the gun in his other hand.

A gargling scream tears from a woman's throat, the shriek spilling out from the corner house and spreading across the plaza. The horrid sound makes me think of an enraged female animal protecting her young. A short, heavy figure runs out onto the porch and collides with the three men gathered there, startling them. It is a woman. Two of the men back away as she begins beating Garrett's chest with the pads of her fists. I realize it is Deluvina. She is crying, screaming, and cursing as the sheriff tries to grab the wrists of her flailing arms. When Garrett barks an order, the two men approach tentatively to restrain her, until finally she collapses to her knees and bows her head to sob into her hands.

Stepping into the street I start walking toward the distraught woman. When one of Garrett's men calls out to me, approaches two steps, and pulls his gun from a holster, I raise my hands above my head but keep moving.

Still wailing, Deluvina looks up at me, her face wet and bright in the moonlight, showing nothing but misery. "They keel him!" she moans. "They kill poor Bee-lee!"

The deputy turns me around by the shoulder in a full circle, looking for a weapon, I suppose. In a daze, I rotate in the street like a puppet. Then, ignoring the man, I kneel to Deluvina as she wails in the street. When I flatten my hand between her shoulder blades, her flesh feels thick and warm through her muslin blouse.

"They *keel* him," she whimpers.

The glow of lamps now show in some of the windows of the nearby buildings. Doors open, and inhabitants venture out. Two women hurry toward us from around the corner of the compound, both wrapped in shawls over their nightclothes. As they hover over Deluvina and console her, I recognize the taller one. It is Paulita. Looking back through the doorway of the corner house, I now see light inside the room. By the wavering illumination on the back wall, I know that a candle has been lighted.

A man wearing a nightgown emerges barefooted from the

room and then becomes suddenly animated when he sees the three women huddled together. He hurries off the porch and approaches Paulita, enveloping her in his arms, and speaking in Spanish in low tones between her sobbing gasps.

Without thinking, I walk toward the candlelit room, my legs going into motion as if I am being drawn to the doorway by some unnamed force of nature. Before I reach the fence gate, the second deputy stops me with a hand clasped to my upper arm.

"Let's just stay out here, mister. No one goes inside."

Feeling numb all over, I keep staring at the room.

"Leave 'im be," says a soft Southern voice.

Pivoting my head, I stare up at Garrett, who looks at me with the eyes of a lost child. Neither of us speak. When I feel the deputy loosen his grip on my arm, I approach the doorway and see right away a dark hat lying on the mussed sheets of a bed. I recognize the wide-brimmed haberdashery as Pat Garrett's.

In the shadow of the bed, I make out a body sprawled on the floor, and I feel myself go weightless. As soon as I enter the room my senses are assaulted by the acrid bite of spent gunpowder. The candlelight glows on Billy's young face, lifting off his smooth skin like an aura. His lips are parted slightly, just showing the tips of his front teeth. The serenity of his countenance is very much like the expression I saw just minutes before when we talked in my room about his future with a family. Oddly, all I can think about is the smile that will never return to his face. It is forever gone. Forever . . . except in my memory.

Kneeling, I feel the back of my throat harden like stone. I am not sure I can speak, but the need to say his name impels me to try.

"Billy?" I whisper.

I know he is dead. I knew it when I heard that first gunshot. A small stain of blood wicks into his blouse directly over his heart. Beside him on the floor is the butcher knife. His gun is loosely gripped in his lifeless hand.

I study his face with a strange desperation, as if I fear I may forget his features over time. But my memorization of his face is short-lived. My vision blurs with tears until his image is reduced to a vague, amorphous glow of reflected candlelight.

When a soulful, heart-rending wail rises out on the street, I wipe my eyes with my sleeve and peer out the doorway, where the crowd has doubled in size. I can see Deluvina back on her feet, crying out as she pulls Paulita into an embrace. But Paulita is now stiff, ignoring the older woman as she stares back at me. Her face is hard and grim, set with either acceptance or hate—which one, I cannot determine.

Several women group around Paulita and Deluvina, so that they appear to be holding each other up as they cry each upon the other's shoulder. All but Paulita. She stands as the aloof hub of all this misery, her face as stoic as a brave man climbing the steps of a gallows.

Garrett and his men stand just inside the fence with the man wearing the nightgown. I assume this to be Pete Maxwell, Paulita's brother. Engaged in earnest conversation with Garrett, he appears to be on good terms with the sheriff.

Looking back at Billy, I cup my palm to his cheek. He's still warm, but there is about him the unmistakable feel of death. Suddenly tired, I push off my thighs to stand up and look down on the young outlaw I have come to know and like.

"Goodbye, Billy Bonney," I say as softly as a breath.

When Deluvina accompanies Paulita into the room where I stand, an entourage of older Hispanic women follows, all these mourners whispering prayers in Spanish, crossing themselves with knobby fingers, their teary eyes fixed upon the corpse. A collective murmur of bereavement commences as the women resort to sobbing. Their lamentations are like a blanket offered to Paulita . . . to wrap her in their love. But she remains autonomous and strong, glaring down at Billy as though destiny had long ago prepared her for this.

Trying to be invisible, I back to the wall and listen to their weeping, until I feel like a trespasser in a foreign land. Sidling out the door, I gain the street and walk unnoticed through the crowd of people who are keeping up a constant babbling of anxious conversation. Billy's name is on every tongue.

After a few paces, I hear my name spoken in a soft drawl. Stopping, I turn and see Sheriff Garrett, still hatless and carrying his revolver in his hand, walking slowly toward me on his long, spindly legs. When he stops before me, I can still see uncertainty in his face.

"You saw the gun," Garrett says. "And the knife. I had no choice."

"Really?" I say, tainting the word with as much sarcasm as I can muster. "He was going for something to eat. He planned to cut some beef."

Garrett looks off to one side toward a small group of people hovering in the doorway of one of the residences. He is a laconic man, but now his silence seems awkward, as though he is at a loss for words. When he turns back to me, his eyes are already pleading his case.

"He was the kind you couldn't hesitate with. If you did, he'd kill you."

The night air cools my face where the tears continue to flow. I feel no shame in crying before this man. On the contrary, my emotion feels more like a weapon I can use on him.

"You didn't try to arrest him." I say this not as a question but as an accusation.

Garrett looks down at the few feet of ground separating us. When his head comes up this time, he holds an annoyed look.

"There was no opportunity. It was dark. I was lucky to make the kill."

" 'Lucky'?"

Garrett scowls. "You know what I mean."

Despite the fact that I must look like a blubbering child, I feel immune to his intimidation. "You're a sheriff," I remind the man towering over me. "Your job is not to assassinate but to arrest."

Garrett doesn't flinch. "The governor didn't see it that way."

"I'm sure he didn't. He also didn't know how to keep his word. Getting rid of Bonney would have been a convenience for his conscience, would it not?"

Pat Garrett scrapes up a solitary laugh that sounds like he is trying to clear something from his throat. "Look . . . you liked the Kid. Hell, we all did in some way. But you didn't have to stand on the wrong end of his pistol. He was quick to make up his own law and dispense it."

"Where none other was to be found," I dare to say.

Garrett gives me a hard glare. "It doesn't work that way, Mr. Blessing. Not where we're tryin' to build somethin' out here. You got to have the law."

"And that would be you?" I say.

He nods. "It is. For now it is."

At the corner house a sudden silence falls over the people crowded around the gate that opens to the plaza. When Garrett turns to check on the situation, I look past him to see Paulita, alone, walking slowly from the killing room. Her chin is held high, and she looks straight ahead at nothing, as the people part for her, their scuffling feet like a whisper of condolences. Then she returns down the same way she had arrived, the same smaller woman joining her now, and together they go out of sight around the corner. Garrett faces me again, his eyes hard, reflecting the moonlight like ice.

"It was the law that murdered Billy's employer, Sheriff," I remind. "Sheriff Brady sent a gang of cutthroats to do James Dolan's bidding. That's what started this war."

Garrett looks down again and shakes his head. "That's all done. It's the past." He puts on a countenance of denial and glares at me. "Didn't have nothing to do with me, and ain't nothing I can do about that now."

I begin to feel frustrated. He has an answer for every argument I throw at him.

"You knew him," I press, a sound of pleading slipping into my voice. "Didn't you owe him the chance to surrender?"

The sheriff looks off into the night and runs his fingers back through his hair. "The Kid didn't know quit. There was never going to be another surrender like there was at Stinking Spring. If I owed anything to anybody, it was to me . . . a chance to keep on living." He leans in slightly and speaks personably, as if we are old friends. "It was him or me. I did like anybody else would."

"He was leaving soon, Sheriff." I nod toward the room where a crowd of people now obscure the glow of the candle. "Billy and Paulita were expecting a child. They were going to start over in Mexico."

Garrett straightens at this news. I can see I have hit a nerve. Again I recognize the lost child in his eyes. But the surprise in his face soon hardens to resolve.

"Then they should have left," Garrett asserts. "They waited too damned long." Turning, he walks back toward the crowd gathered at the gate. Pulling back one side of his long coat, he snugs his revolver into the holster belted at his hip.

"Sheriff?" I call out.

Garrett stops and pivots a quarter turn to look back at me.

"What about that difference between you and the Kid? That you could not shoot a man in cold blood? I guess we can strike that one off the list, don't you?"

Garrett continues to stare at me, but he says nothing. Slowly he cocks his elbows upward and rests his hands on his narrow hips. When he pivots his head to look back at the room of mourners, I take the opportunity to leave.

As I walk away to sequester myself in my room, I carry that last image of Garrett's face. It is a mosaic of complex emotions: triumph, guilt, authority, regret, and maybe some shame . . . all this stirred up in a pot and served out under the name of *duty.* Right away I erase this slate of memory. It is not Garrett I want to remember. Nor is it the macabre scene of spectators unexpectedly come together in the middle of the night to witness the aftermath of a killing. I want to carry a picture of Billy Bonney, one more personable than the tintype he gave me.

Rejecting the lifeless form I'd seen lying on the floor by candlelight, I probe deeper, rolling time backward a handful of precious minutes to see him talking with me as we lay on our bunks and explored the idea of his being a husband and a father. I run back the clock until I can see his smile, and—when I do—I ignite the mental flash pan and take the eidetic photograph that burns his image into my brain. A mental tintype to carry with me. A remembrance of a lighthearted boy who had won my friendship from the first time we met. This is the Billy Bonney I want to remember.

In the privacy of my room, the candles still burn, drawing me to my bed like a beacon of light guiding a sinking ship to a sheltered cove. I sit atop the blanket, prop my elbows on my knees, and find myself looking at Billy's hat lying crown down on the other bed. My breathing becomes ragged until soon I break down altogether, wracked with a sense of loss I have never before experienced. I lower my face into my hands. The sound of my crying takes me back to my childhood, and this only unlocks a host of forgotten doors to deepen my misery.

I weep for several minutes before finally straightening my spine and wiping my raw eyes with the sleeve of my shirt. There in front of me next to Billy's hat is the indention of his outline on the other bunk. Like a sculpture in reverse, it adumbrates two shallow trenches from the weight of his legs, a bowl from his hips, and two small pockets where his elbows had pressed into the mattress. I swallow my tears and speak to the depression as if his soul has come back to rest here with me for a time before the long journey to the other side.

"I'll tell your story," I say, squeezing the words through the tightness in my throat. "I will."

Opening my notebook and bottle of ink I begin to write, letting the words follow the music that has been composing itself in my mind over these last months. My hand works with an unexpected energy, as though it has become an independent entity that has no patience with my customary hesitations during the creative process. I write like this for more than an hour, never striking out a phrase to be replaced and never lingering over a choice of words. The Muse has full control. I am merely the life force supplying the mechanics of moving the pen.

When one of the candles burns out, I remove my shoes, blow out the other candle, and stretch out on the bed. Closing my eyes, I pray for the soul of Billy Bonney. Then, surprising myself, I laugh a single breathy note at an unexpected picture that takes shape in my mind: I see Billy sitting down with God, explaining all his earthly deeds, and charming the Heavenly Father with his boyish grin, a ready joke, and his contagious laugh.

Holding this image in my mind, I take in a deep breath, let it ease out, and wait for sleep to deliver me to the light of a new day.

Epilogue
House of Books
540 D Beacon Street
Boston, Massachusetts
December, 1919

"Come ride along beside me when the desert moon is bright
Your ghost is my companion and my song will be your fight."

The hole-in-the-wall bookstore on Beacon Street was one of eight shops partitioned off from the large brick warehouse that had once accommodated the Holtzclaw Carriage Works. Squeezed between the Bunker Hill Haberdashery and the ever popular Bostonian Bakery, the bookshop should have drawn in a good class of clientele, were it not for the daunting state of confusion evident in its shelving system. And in its idiosyncratic proprietor.

Books were sorted by rather arcane themes rather than subject, title, or author. Categories took on names like "sacrifice" and "spiritual windfalls" and "futile aspirations." The only possible way to find a specific book—other than by endless browsing—was to elicit the help of the owner, who was the mastermind behind the unorthodox method of filing. But few wanted to engage this storekeeper—an aging wisp of a man with starkly white hair and a voice so soft, one had to hold his breath and lip read to decipher the words.

Those willing to engage the bookseller's odd ways were, for the most part, children, who adored the old man, his snow-white hair, and the gentle tone of his voice. These young ones loved to be guided through his maze of musty shelves and hear his opinions of the motley titles. The shopkeeper always seemed to know what passage to read aloud to his young customers, as if he had read their minds and knew which paragraphs might best benefit them. It was these returning children who had kept the business afloat in its first years, and then, when they themselves became adults, they continued to patronize the House of Books, eventually bringing their own children to keep the tradition alive.

After a decade and a half of struggling to survive, the book shop had gained a kind of cult status among Bostonians. It never made the list of must-see landmarks for tourists in the Cradle of Liberty City, but business was stable.

On a cold winter morning, with snowflakes the size of silver dollars tumbling down on the city from a rumpled ceiling of overcast gray, a tall, barrel-chested man bundled up in a heavy overcoat, slouch hat, and bright-red knitted scarf kicked his shoes together outside the bookstore entrance. Peering through the glass pane of the door, he brushed away epaulets of snow from his shoulders and then stilled himself to listen. He thought he had heard music. Now there was only the sound of a delivery truck idling in front of the bakery next door. Straightening, he unwrapped his scarf and stuffed it into his coat pocket. Then he took off his hat, slapped it against his leg, and tried the door.

When he entered, a quaint, jingly bell above the doorframe announced his presence to a warm but empty room. Closing the door against the cold, he set off the bell again and then waited until complete silence gathered around him.

"Hello?" he called out.

Getting no reply, he pulled at the fingers of his leather gloves and looked around at the towering shelves of used books. The room itself was a tall, narrow space that appeared to extend forty or fifty feet back into the building. At the center of the open area where he stood, a wood heater threw off a comfortable aura of welcome. Against the right wall was a small rectangular woodbox filled with neatly sawn logs. A pair of canvas gloves lay atop the logs.

To his left stood a check-out counter with a cash register and a lighted lamp perched upon its varnished top. Stepping closer to look behind the counter, all he found was a shaft of winter light streaming in through a window, illuminating a small table and an empty chair with a woven cane seat. An opened book lay page down on the table and drew a quiet, huffing laugh from the visitor's chest. It was a well-worn copy of *Ben Hur* by Lew Wallace.

He looked around the room again. "Is anyone here?"

Hearing nothing, he returned to the radiant warmth of the heater and surveyed the room. Except for the area where he stood, every space in the shop was devoted to the display of books. Thousands upon thousands of them. The visitor stuffed his gloves into his coat pocket and strolled toward one of the dimly lit aisles.

Taking off his overcoat, he angled his head to read the titles of books propped on end. Frowning, he took staggered sidesteps as he tried to make sense of the grouping of the books. Giving up, he turned back to the counter and found himself looking into the pale-gray eyes of a frail man with hair as soft and white as strands of refined cotton.

"Oh . . . hello there . . . my name is Burns," the visitor announced and strode forward, shifting his overcoat to his left arm and extending his right hand. "I am a writer from Chicago. I'm looking for John Blessing."

Ignoring the offer of a handshake, the old man adjusted his spectacles and looked from his guest's fleshy face down to the robust torso fitted with an expensive, brown, three-piece suit. " 'Burns' did you say?"

The visitor's smile widened beneath his prim moustache. With his teeth shining in the twilit room, he gave off the aggressive energy of a Teddy Roosevelt.

"Yes, I'm with the *Inter Ocean* newspaper." He lowered his arm but held onto the smile.

The bookseller stared deep into Burns's eyes. "Walter Noble Burns? 'Books and the Men Who Make Them'?"

Burns's face glowed. "So! You've read my syndicated column?"

The old man nodded. "Not in a long time. Years ago, I sent to you my book to be reviewed."

Burns's smile dissolved. "Oh, dear!" he said. His face sagged to instant contrition. "Was I hard on you?"

A tight smile puckered the old man's mouth, but his eyes showed not a trace of amusement. "You did not review it."

Burns looked down at the floor, raised his eyebrows, and exhaled a long sigh. "Unfortunately, I receive dozens of books each week." He smiled his apology and shrugged. "I can't possibly read them all. I have a staff that culls through the pile even before I see them. I'm sorry if yours was thrown onto the trash heap. What was it about?"

The bookseller's expression was as empty as a blank page. "It went into a trash heap?"

"Are you John Blessing?" Burns asked, trying for some momentum in a new direction.

"I am he," the old man assured the visitor.

Burns pointed an index finger at Blessing's chest. "Everywhere I go I have been hearing your name. Everyone says, 'You need to talk to John Blessing.' "

Blessing was unfazed by the compliment. "What particular book are you looking for?"

Burns laughed to himself. "You won't have it here. First, I have to write it, you see."

Blessing nodded. "Good luck to you, sir. I hope someone will review it favorably." The shopkeeper arched an eyebrow. "Or for that matter, that you get reviewed at all."

Seeing that he had his work cut out for him, Burns laid his overcoat on the counter as if staking a claim here. "I was hoping to interview you, Mr. Blessing. I'd like very much to pick your brain for a while. Perhaps I could take you to lunch? You could name the place."

Blessing pulled a watch from his pocket and opened the cover. After putting the watch away, he reached below the counter and brought up an old leather satchel with a shoulder strap. Setting it on the counter between them, he lifted out a cloth bag from inside the main pocket.

"I bring my lunch," Blessing announced and began laying out small packages wrapped in newspaper.

Burns kept smiling. "Well, then . . . perhaps we could chat while you eat?"

The bookseller leaned below the counter again and brought up a long-handled cook pot with a lid. He opened up the wrapped items and placed two tortillas side by side in the pot. Next to them he shook out a large serving of rice and a baseball-sized helping of cooked beans.

"I usually eat by myself," he said flatly.

Undaunted, Burns reached inside his coat and extracted a leather wallet. Pulling out several bills, he took on the confident smirk of one who knew how the world worked. He laid three bills on the countertop and winked.

"Perhaps I can pay you for your time. I simply want to engage you in conversation."

Blessing eyed the bribe. Two tens and a five. He thought of those weeks when he had anticipated the review of his book in the newspapers. He had bought every copy of *The Boston Post* and *The Globe* for two months before finally writing to Chicago to get the bad news from one of Burns's assistants. Blessing had spent more than twenty-five dollars on newspapers alone.

"They say 'talk is cheap,' Mr. Burns," Blessing said quietly. "I disagree."

Burns dug into the wallet again and slapped down three more bills. Ignoring the contribution to his finances, Blessing leaned over the pot and considered the contents.

"My wife insists on preparing lunches for a man twice my size, so perhaps you will help me make a dent in this."

"So, we *can* talk?" Burns asked, his voice beginning to sound desperate.

Blessing rotated the pot to place the handle before his guest. "If you would be so kind as to place this on the stove, sir."

While the food warmed, Blessing dragged his cane-seat chair from behind the counter and set it by the heater. "There is a stool in back," he said and pointed toward the rear of the shop. "If you wouldn't mind?"

When Burns returned with the stool, he set it down to make a triangle of stool, chair, and heater. "Why is there a piano back there?" he remarked, nodding toward the rear of the shop. "Do you play?"

The old man groaned as he sat. "Occasionally . . . during the slow times in the day. I was once a composer."

"Really!" Burns said with the intensity of a music connoisseur. His face was all-business now as he straddled the stool. "Anything I might have heard?"

Blessing smiled. "Only if you visited the Loretto Chapel in Santa Fe in 1880. Or perhaps you chanced to attend the Festival of the Saints in '79. One of my pieces was performed at the Palace of the Governors that year."

Burns squinted with one eye as he calculated the years. "Afraid not, old boy. I was just a school lad about then . . . in Kentucky."

Blessing raised both his hands palms up. "Well, there you have it. I confess that recognition of my work rarely extended beyond the walls of that church."

Burns pushed a grin to one side of his face. "I might have to debate that point, Mr. Blessing. Your name is widely known in certain circles."

Blessing made no comment. Reaching to the floor he rattled through an old coffee can that held a few pieces of silverware. He selected a fork and used it to pry up and roll the sizzling tortillas inside the pot. When he was satisfied with the arrangement, he covered the pot with the lid and slid it closer to the edge of the heater's top plate.

Burns waited until the old man looked him in the eye. "Mr. Blessing, I am writing a book about Henry McCarty. That is why I have looked you up."

Blessing's watery gray eyes showed nothing. "Lucky you," he muttered under his breath. "I suppose a review for you is a foregone conclusion."

Burns could not resist a restrained laugh. "Usually when I mention that name to someone, I get a blank look at best. I assume you know to whom I am referring."

Blessing nodded. "Indeed, I do." He set the fork back in the can and settled in his chair.

"Henry McCarty," Burns repeated, "who became Henry Antrim . . . who became William H. Bonney." He paused for effect and finished the list with a satisfied snap in his eyes. ". . . Who became Billy the Kid." Pointing at his coat on the counter, he rose. "Would you mind if I made a few notes?"

Blessing smiled at these same words that had spilled from his lips countless times. "Take all the notes you wish."

Burns retrieved his writing pad and pen and returned to the stool. "When you were with the *Santa Fe Messenger,* you penned this article on William Bonney." From his notebook he extracted a folded, yellowed page of newsprint and tapped a column that ran down the left side of the front page. "But this issue was not to be found at the *Messenger*. It was missing in their archives. I ferreted this one out from a library collection. It is brilliant, Mr. Blessing. No one else came close to exposing the complexities of the Lincoln County War." He tapped his finger at the title. "It says here: 'First in a series on Billy the Kid.' But I couldn't find any follow-up pieces."

Blessing's mouth tightened to a humorless smile. "It met with resistance," he explained. "The governor complained, and my editor did not support me. I was given a choice: write a retraction or be fired." Blessing produced a snide smile. "I chose a third option: I quit."

Burns folded the old newspaper and put it away. "So . . . you're a man of principles. Did you go to work for another paper?"

Blessing laughed without a trace of humor. "No paper in the territory would have me. Neither could I secure a job keeping books as an accountant, clerking for a dry-goods store, or even sweeping floors at the railway station, even though each of those positions had been advertised in our newspaper. I found myself with no friends. Even the Hispanics who knew and liked Billy Bonney were afraid to acknowledge me. In short, I became the pariah of Santa Fe."

Burns lowered his brow. "What did you do then?"

"I went to New York, where I studied at the music conservatory for four years. Then I traveled for a while, doing some personal research. Finally, I came to Boston. Here I applied for a staff position at Harvard's School of Music and was accepted. And I secured a job playing organ for the Catholic Church. That led to forming a chorale here, which I conducted for years."

Burns flipped through the pages of his notebook. "But I was told time and again . . . by Paulita Jaramillo, by George Coe, George Kimbrell, and Deluvina Maxwell . . . they all told me you were writing a book about the Kid."

"And so I did," Blessing assured his guest.

Burns's face lit up. "Well, what happened?! Was it published?!"

The old man cracked a sly smile. "Yes. That was the book I sent to you for review."

Burns's mouth opened to reply, but now he seemed to have lost access to his vast reservoir of words. He closed his mouth, and the two men stared at one another as the burning logs popped in the heater. The snow continued to fall outside the window, with only the occasional Model T forging a path through the ten-inch blanket that now covered Beacon Street.

Blessing shrugged one shoulder. "You can ask me whatever you wish to know about Billy Bonney, but I can assure you that everything I learned about him went into that book. It's all there between the covers."

Burns's face flushed with excitement. "Well, how can I get a copy of it?"

Blessing removed the lid from the pot and checked the contents. "There are plates under the register. Would you bring out two?"

Burns hurried behind the counter and returned with two white ceramic plates. His manner and movements were quick and nervous, as if time were running out on him.

"Is the book still in print?"

Blessing shook his head and doled out servings. Then he took another fork from the coffee can and offered it to Burns.

Burns snatched the fork. "What about the publisher? Could I coax a copy from them?"

Shaking his head again, Blessing pointed to Burns's plate. "Try it," he said.

Merely out of courtesy, Burns cut off one end of a tortilla and sampled the food and chewed. Then his face brightened as if a new light had entered the room.

"This tastes authentic. It's delicious!"

Blessing smiled and nodded. "My wife is from Coahuila."

Burns scooped up more food, eating with the gusto of a man who had just crossed a barren plain without supplies. Within minutes he was scraping his fork across his plate, trying to salvage the streaks of sauce remaining there.

"My compliments to your wife. Is she in some way connected to Billy Bonney's story?"

The old man lowered his fork with food still balanced upon the tines. "We won't be talking about her," he ordained in a flat tone. "Keep her out of this."

Burns held up both palms. "Of course. Whatever you say. But what about your book?"

Blessing took in a mouthful and chewed. Raising his fork, he pointed down an aisle that led to the back of the room. "Walk to the back corner and look on the right wall just above eye level. It's in a section labeled 'Misunderstood Martyrs.' You'll find three copies . . . silver letters on gold cloth. It's called *A Last Serenade for Billy Bonney.*"

Burns set his plate on the floor and strode down the aisle, passing through a gauntlet of old books that ordinarily would have teased him with the possibility of a rare find. On this day he kept his eyes on the dimly lit back of the room. Silver letters on gold cloth. Nothing else could grab his attention.

When he returned, his head was down as he began to devour the open book in his hands. "You found Bonney's school teacher from Silver City?" he asked, his voice charged with anticipation. But he did not look up for an answer. He flipped more pages and suddenly stopped walking. "And Fred Waite? You actually ventured into the Indian Territory to talk to him?" Looking up with a worried expression, Burns softened his voice. "He's dead now, you know."

Blessing nodded and set down his plate of unfinished food. "Yes, I know."

Burns sat on the stool again and continued to turn the pages. "What about Garrett? Did you interview him?" He suspended his search through the book to stare at Blessing.

"I spoke to him on several occasions. He was not fond of interviews, but he would tell me what he wanted me to hear."

Burns shook his head and spewed air from tightened lips. "What I would have given to talk with Pat Garrett! He died just a little over a decade ago, you know."

"Yes," Blessing said. "I heard. A rather ignominious exit from life."

Burns paged through the book. "When was the last time you spoke to him?"

Blessing gestured toward the book with a feeble hand. "It's all in there," he muttered, but Burns seemed not to hear him and recommenced leafing through the book. Blessing cleared his throat and added. "It was the night Billy died . . . in Fort Sumner."

Now Burns looked up, his eyes on fire with a question. "You were there?"

"Indeed I was."

"What did Garrett say?"

The old man again waved a hand toward the book. "As I said . . . it's all in there."

Closing the book, Burns studied the front cover and the spine. "I'd like to use this as a primary source," he said. "I will, of course, credit you throughout my book."

Blessing offered a bland smile. "Use it all you like," he said. Then he raised a forefinger and waved it from side to side. "But I don't want my name mentioned in your book."

Burns's face lined with deep wrinkles. "But you invested so much into this!" He shook his head as if a fly were worrying him. "This must have taken you years to compile. And you traveled at your own expense, no doubt."

Blessing chuckled. "That's the way we all traveled in those days . . . unless you were a mail carrier or worked for the sheriff. Deputies kept records of their mileage by horse. Did you know that?"

Burns waved a dismissive hand at the question and turned the front of the book toward his host. "But I assume this is your life work, man! Your *magnum opus!*"

Blessing propped his elbows on the arms of his chair, lifted his hands, and threaded his fingers together below his chin. "And what has it brought me, Mr. Burns?" he said, his calm voice a mix of contempt and self-ridicule. He made a tight, humorless smile and lowered his snowy eyebrows. "My newspaper article on Billy Bonney invoked the wrath of the governor of the New Mexico Territory and labeled me as sympathetic to criminals. I lost my job, my choral group, my friends, my future. No one would hire me . . . not even to sweep the dust out of a railroad depot. And the curse caught up to me here in Boston."

Blessing nodded toward the book in Burns's hand. "The publication of that book ended my work at the church here in Boston . . . and the music classes I taught at Harvard. Neither establishment could allow a self-confessed advocate of a convicted murderer to remain on their staff." Unclasping his fingers, he turned his palms upward and sighed. "And now I am a forgotten composer who sells books inside a dark and dreary hideaway in the city."

Burns set the book in his lap and crossed his wrists over it. "But all that could change for you after *my* book. Forgive my boldness, Mr. Blessing, but I am going to write a hell of a tale to capture America's fancy. It's going to be a bestseller, sir. After reading it, people are going to want to read more about Billy the Kid . . . especially words written by the people who actually knew him."

Blessing eyed the man with no small amount of suspicion. "Will you tell the truth?"

Burns folded his arms over his chest and tilted his head to one side. "The truth comes in varying colors, doesn't it? Everyone has his own version of it. Wouldn't you agree?"

The old man turned his gaze to the wood heater and shook his head. "The truth recognizes only itself. It knows no surrogate."

Burns frowned. "Who said that?"

Blessing turned his head to face Burns. "I did." He nodded toward the book. "You'll find it in the epilogue."

Burns leaned in closer and injected an analytical timbre into his voice. "Look, I expect your book to supply me with truths I could not otherwise know. And, in return, perhaps my story will bring your book to the forefront. I'm sorry I didn't review your book. And I'm sorry it did not do better than it did in sales. Maybe it was a matter of bad timing. That and poor efforts at distribution. That's what happened with Garrett's book, you know. By the time it was in print, nobody cared about Bonney anymore. If anyone was going to read about an outlaw at that time, the subject would have been Jesse James, who had just been killed by one of his own gang in St. Joseph, Missouri."

Blessing's face soured. "James was nothing like Billy Bonney."

"That's beside the point," Burns argued. "They were both celebrities. When a celebrity dies you have this brief window of time to capitalize on their life story." He stiffened his hands before him as if he were trying to squeeze a concertina whose parts had frozen up. "But these things circle back around in time. After enough years pass, they get reshaped and painted with new colors by a new storyteller." Burns tapped a thumb against his chest. "That's going to be me. When *my* book opens the door in a year or two, yours will be poised in the threshold, ready to step through."

When silence wrapped around them, Burns assumed he had made his point . . . one that ought to be well taken by the doddering old man. Lifting the book from his lap, he studied the cover again.

"Why this title?" Burns asked, his voice almost melodic with curiosity. His finger began tapping the silver letters recessed into the book's cover. His hand was like a woodpecker chipping away at a barkless portion of a tree. "That could have been the problem right there!" Without waiting for a response, he jumped headlong into his own analysis. "Maybe the title was too sleepy for a widespread readership." He shook his head and frowned. " 'Serenade' may not be the best choice of a word. And, for that matter, why not 'Billy the Kid'? Most of America does not know the name 'Billy Bonney.' "

Blessing did not have to think long about his answer. "The young man I knew *was* 'Billy Bonney.' He chose that name . . . taking it from the true father he never knew. While I knew Billy, he never called himself by any other name." Blessing paused long enough to take a bite of food. "As for 'serenade' . . . when I began to write about Billy, I was simply working as a newspaper reporter. I had no ambitions to pen a full-length book about anything. At heart, I was a composer of music . . . not an author of the written word. So, once I came to really know Billy . . . to admire him . . . I paid tribute to him in the way I knew best. I wrote a composition. I completed it on the night he was killed. His slain body was sleeping peacefully just a few rooms away, surrounded by candles and a cortege of friends who had come to mourn. A 'serenade' seemed appropriate."

"Was it ever performed?" Burns asked. "Your composition?"

"Only once," Blessing said. "I played it for Billy's schoolteacher, Miss Richards, in her home in Georgetown in 1886."

Burns seemed struck with a fever, as if he were ready to drop to one knee and make a plea. "Would you perform it for me?"

Blessing looked out the front window and shook his head. "It has been a very long time since I played it."

Burns leaned and reached out to touch Blessing's knee. "Please, sir, I want very much to hear it. If it's a matter of more money—"

Blessing snorted a laugh, but as he stared out the window the humor drained from his face. "Keep your wallet in your pocket, Mr. Burns. If you want that badly to hear it—" After pushing himself up from the chair, he pointed at Burns's three-legged stool. "You'll need to bring that. I can't play standing up."

Blessing lighted the lamp on the piano and situated the stool just so. Then he sat. Burns stood at one end of the upright, leaning his forearms on the polished cover of the soundboard.

The keyboard glowed in the lamplight, the ivories white as snow touched by moonlight, the ebony keys dark but throwing off points of light like a starry night. Together—as Blessing had often told his students—this black and white pattern comprised a composer's galaxy of possibilities. His hands levitated from his lap and hovered over the keys in complete stillness. Closing his eyes, Blessing began to drag from memory an image of the sheet music he had so carefully detailed on manuscript paper all those years ago.

In this silence Burns watched the old man's hands the way a magician's apprentice studies his master as he introduces a new trick. When he realized he had stopped breathing, Burns quietly filled his lungs with the dusky air of the bookstore.

" 'A Last Serenade for Billy Bonney,' " Blessing announced in a solemn tone. His fingers began moving on the keys, establishing both the subtle and the strong motifs upon which the piece had been built. After this introduction, he softened his touch, delivering the first verse with spare notes that wafted gently in the still air around them.

When he reached the first chorus, he began to put more energy into the keys, and the music seemed to rise above them like a flock of birds taking flight together. Then he pulled back in a decrescendo to repeat the verse, establishing a contrast in the parts and a spell of harmonic wonder. Then the chorus repeated like a thunderstorm, and one final verse closed the composition like the last raindrops dripping off a roof into a water barrel. By the time Blessing's fingers lifted from the keyboard, Burns's eyes reflected the lamplight from a thick film of tears.

Blessing straightened on the stool and inhaled deeply. "There you have it," he said.

Burns lowered his forehead into the cradle of skin that stretched from thumb to index, his face shielded from view by his hand. In this quiet, he swallowed, the sound of it like a bubble of air breaking at the surface of water. After several seconds, he lowered his arm and looked up at Blessing.

"There are no words, Mr. Blessing." His whispery voice wavered ever so slightly. "I've heard no piece of music more divine in all my life." He wiped his eyes with a handkerchief. "I believe I have now seen the heart and soul of Billy Bonney. There simply are no words."

"Actually," Blessing chuckled, "there are. But I no longer have the voice for it."

Burns's jaw dropped. "Do you mean to say there are lyrics?"

When the composer nodded, Burns's face paled to the dull sheen of candle wax. "I must hear them!" he insisted.

The old bookseller laughed. "My voice is as cracked as old leather, sir. I would not want to put you through the ordeal."

The intensity in Burns's face made the whites of his eyes shine brighter. "But I *must* hear the words! Please, Mr. Blessing!"

Blessing stared at his keyboard with a strange little smile

pulling at his mouth. From somewhere down the street they heard the repetitive scrape of a shovel on cobblestones. Blessing turned, looked far down the dark aisle, and checked the front window. The snowfall was so dense he could no longer make out the shops on the other side of the thoroughfare.

"The lyrics are in the book, Mr. Burns. You'll find them spread throughout, introducing each chapter." Blessing stood, raised the shield on the lamp, and blew out the flame. When he started for the front of the store, Burns followed like a loyal dog.

"I suppose I must close up early today," Blessing said as they approached the counter. "There will be no customers getting out in this weather."

"Of course," Burns said and held up the book. "I'll go to my hotel room and read. I am anxious to get into this." Setting the book on the counter, he unfolded his overcoat and slipped his arms into the sleeves. Looping the scarf around his neck, he crossed its fringed ends against his chest and buttoned the coat over it. Then he worked his hands into the leather gloves.

"Would you do me the honor of being my guest for dinner tonight?" Burns offered. "Your wife, too, of course! The hotel restaurant is quite good."

Dragging his chair back behind the counter, Blessing made a doubtful face and shook his head. "I think it best if you finish my book before we talk further. You need to decide on which side of things you come down concerning the Lincoln County troubles." He began to stuff the newspaper wrappings from lunch into his satchel.

Burns stifled a laugh. "Surely you are not still worried about your reputation, Mr. Blessing. No one in Boston knows me. They would have no idea why we are talking over dinner at a restaurant. And even if they did, why would they care about your connection to an outlaw forty years ago?"

"Perhaps," Blessing replied. "But I am a realist now. I lost everything once. Now I have to take care of myself . . . and my wife." He closed the satchel and looked out the front window. "I do whatever it takes. Just like people have always done to survive in this world. Billy Bonney did what he had to do. Pat Garrett did what he had to do. Now I do the same."

Burns conceded the point with a nod. "What if I come back tomorrow," he pressed. "Would you consider singing the lyrics to the song? I know you will agree that reading lyrics is not the same as hearing them in context with the music."

Blessing shouldered his satchel. "I'll think about it. Maybe after a cup of hot tea with honey, my voice might be bearable."

"I'll bring the tea and honey myself, if that's what it takes," Burns declared. When he got no reply, he picked up the book and gazed lovingly at its cover. "I'm going to savor this!" He hugged the book to his ribs. "Thank you for your time, Mr. Blessing." Fitting his soft-brimmed hat to his head, he backed to the door. "I will call on you tomorrow, if you will allow me."

"As long as I have no customers," Blessing said and took down an overcoat hanging on the wall behind the counter. After pushing his arms through the sleeves, he gripped the soft hat remaining on the wall pegs. This he fit to his head in a slow, gentle movement, as if he were being crowned by the pope.

"Of course," Burns agreed and opened the door, setting off the friendly bell above him. A gust of cold wind carried a flurry of snow into the front of the room. "Thank you, John!"

Blessing leaned forward and flattened his hands on the countertop. "Mr. Burns, *A Last Serenade*?" He nodded at the book pressed into Burns's side. "The price is four dollars."

Burns's face reddened as if he had been slapped. He could not help glancing at the six bills still stacked on the counter.

"Of course," he said, scolding himself. "Forgive me." Closing the door and sounding the bell again, he pulled out his wallet once more. Extracting a five-dollar note, he left the bill beside the others on the counter and held out a flattened palm as he backed to the door. "Consider it a late contribution to your research," he said.

Blessing held a curious smile on his face. "How do you like my hat?"

Burns frowned and studied the unspectacular haberdashery. Its crown appeared lopsided with the peak to one side and the rest sloping like a shed roof.

"Very nice," Burns replied in an offhand manner. His eyes went back to the book in his hand, and blindly he groped for the doorknob. "Oh, I'm going to love this!" he exclaimed and held up the book for Blessing to see his joy in holding it. Owning it.

The insistent bell now took on a comic sound, as if it were mocking the man for his inability to make a deliberate exit. For a brief moment, the wind swirled snow around Burns, spinning a cocoon of white lace around him. Then the overworked bell jingled again, the door clicked shut, and the visitor was gone.

The room was again as quiet and as peaceful as it had been before the Chicago writer had arrived. Blessing slipped his satchel strap over his shoulder and picked up the paper money stacked on the counter. Springing the cash drawer on the register, he deposited the bills without counting them.

Standing before the front door, he watched the falling snow round out the face of the city. All the angles and edges of the business district were now disguised with elegant curves and pristine smoothness.

Automobiles no longer braved the street. The snow had won out in the contest. Drifts had piled up high enough to bury the curb beyond recognition. Only one pedestrian plodded his way along the sidewalk, and his progress was slow as he made his way toward the bay.

Then a clinking and rattling sound approached from the east. Soon a brace of muscular Morgan horses high-stepped into view as they pulled a heavy freight wagon down the snow-covered street. The wagon bed was filled with chunks of black coal, taking its usual route to make deliveries. The team of horses snorted, pluming spurts of gray fog from their nostrils, their hooves silent in the snow. Only the jangling harness and the rattle of the wheels carried through the cold window glass. Bundled up against the weather, the driver spared the horses his whip, for there was no need for one. The wagon and team moved effortlessly through the smooth drifts, as if flaunting the tried-and-true methods of the past.

When the wagon passed in front of him, its bulk darkened the glass, momentarily converting the glass door into a mirror that threw back his reflection. Blessing found himself staring at the silhouette of an infirm man wearing an outdated hat.

"Ha!" he laughed aloud. His wife had fairly begged him to replace the old lopsided fedora with one of the newer styles. She had tried to convince him that there was proper head gear for gentlemen of the twentieth century.

"No, thank you," he whispered in the quiet of the shop.

When the wagon moved out of earshot, Blessing stepped closer to the door, where he felt the frigid breath of winter radiate off the glass and bathe his face like a splash of cool water. The sight of the horse-drawn wagon and the battered hat heartened Blessing. Now that he had accumulated enough years to wax nostalgic, he admitted to himself that he liked the old ways.

Over the last years he had found himself reminiscing more and more about his younger days in New Mexico. As he often told his wife, the present had overlooked him, as if he were no longer relevant to the world. And the future held nothing for him beyond getting more infirm and more forgetful.

The past was his province. It was there that John Blessing chose to live his life. Here among all these old books, he thrived. The old paths of memory were his treasured routes. The old San Patricio Road that ran alongside the Rio Ruidoso. The stage line that connected Lincoln to La Mesilla. The horse trails that spoked into and out of Fort Sumner.

As soon as he pushed through the door into the falling snow, the stillness and the quiet of the desert was left behind. A work crew from the Charleston prison was busy clearing snow from the street, their shovels scraping across the cobblestones and the men grunting and complaining to the guards about the cold. As Blessing walked past them, he fought the subtle smile pulling at one corner of his mouth. He imagined stopping before these workers, looking into their baleful eyes, and making an announcement.

"Gentlemen, you are looking at the hat that was worn by Billy the Kid."

But, of course, he did no such thing. Keeping his head down, he trudged on through the snow, hoping he could make it home before snowmelt could soak through his shoes and threaten his toes with frostbite.

It was days like this one when John Blessing took comfort in knowing that Billy Bonney had not outlived his time in that wild and beautiful territory. It had been a dozen years since New Mexico had achieved statehood, and he wondered if Santa Fe and Lincoln and Fort Sumner, like Boston, had become host to a swarm of foul smelling, bumptious automobiles that cluttered up the streets and endangered the lives of pedestrians.

As Blessing made his way home through the sidewalk drifts, he thought about the celebrated Walter Noble Burns, who had once snubbed his book, now opening his door like a beggar with his hand out. Blessing had even given Burns a glimpse of Billy's hat—the very one the Kid had worn in the only known photograph made of him. But Burns hadn't a clue. His mind had been so preoccupied with winning over Blessing for another interview, the great critic didn't see what was right in front of his eyes.

But wasn't that what Blessing himself had done when he had sought out Billy Bonney's acquaintances? And had not every interviewee, in some way, contributed to his cause? Blessing could not help but put himself in Burns's position and empathize with the man.

"Well, Walter, old boy," he said into the falling flakes of snow, "maybe you can do what I could not."

Stomping his way through the smooth mounds of white, he imagined Burns returning to his store the next day, beseeching him to sing the lyrics of his song. Blessing wasn't even sure he remembered all the lines. Dredging up old lyrics had always been more elusive than recalling musical notes. Music was like indelible ink. Words more like evanescent chalk on a blackboard.

Stopping, he looked up into the large flakes tumbling out of the twilight sky and remembered the night he had composed the words. They had flowed from him as naturally as water finding its way downhill. Looking through his tears that night, he had set down the words in a blur, trying to fill the hole inside his soul by giving birth to something whole and new.

All this . . . sitting only a short distance from where his friend lay dead, never again to feel the wind blow off the desert . . . nor to experience the morning coming alive with dawn and birdsong. Never to dance again. Or smile. All that had ended with a gunshot fired in the dark.

Blessing turned and retraced his footsteps back to the shop, unlocked the door, and entered the warm room. After hanging his coat on the wall peg, he moved down the aisle to the back of the store and sat on the stool at his piano. He did not bother with the lamp. There was just enough scattered light to see the pattern of the black keys contrasted against the white.

Moving with deliberate care, he removed the hat and laid it ceremoniously on the top of the piano. Then he took a deep breath and rubbed his hands on his pant legs.

" 'A Last Serenade for Billy Bonney,' " he said in a whisper. This time, as he announced the song to the darkness gathering around him, he felt a warm wave of pride pass through him, spreading from his chest like the ripples from a stone tossed into a pond. Lifting his hands to the keyboard, he played the introduction just as he had for Burns. Then, when the opening verse came around, he closed his eyes and began to sing, his voice delivering an unexpected rich tenor, the notes as clear as spring water, the words like old friends who had returned from parts unknown to reunite him with the most glorious chapter of his life.

> This country shows no mercy to a young boy on
> his own
> With no one to light a candle in the window of a
> home.
> But if a man lives by his wits and grit and plays
> the cards he's dealt
> He just might have what it takes to make that
> journey by himself.

> "Hold dear your mother's lullaby, it's all that you
> have left,
> She loved you more than life itself until her dying
> breath.
> 'Forget me not, my bonny child, for I will soon
> depart,
> I am crossing to the other side, so hold me in

your heart.'

"O, Billy, take the best of her and hold your head
    up high,
She taught you your good manners, but you'll
    still have to survive.
So, keep one eye upon the trail and one eye
    behind your back,
You can live your life just like a king, but watch
    that one-eyed jack.

"There are men who live for evil and will steal
    away your life
And other men will stand by you and fight until
    they die.
Until you learn the difference you don't have to
    be afraid,
You just keep that pistol loaded, and you'll hold
    the world at bay.

"O, Billy, *mi compañero,* you were always quick to
    smile,
You laughed right in the devil's face and charmed
    him with your guile.
The señoritas danced with you and loved you by
    and by,
As you high-stepped to their music with that
    twinkle in your eye.

"So they locked you up in heavy chains to pay
    for all their sins,
They sentenced you to die after they'd killed

most of your friends.

But iron bars and prison guards and all the law
intends

Cannot keep a ghost from slipping through the
cracks just like the wind.

"O, Billy, *mi amigo,* can your soul be really saved?

They say you killed for pleasure and then spat
upon their graves.

But now I know your story and the justice that
you sought

You may have been the only one whose soul
could not be bought.

"I can never hope to be like you, could never
match your smile,

But I know I am a better man to know you this
short while.

If someone should remember me long after I am
gone,

I pray that it will be because someone still sings
this song.

"O, Billy, *el valiente,* you were much too young to
die,

They killed you out of need to save the governor
from his lie.

Come ride along beside me when the desert
moon is bright,

Your ghost is my companion, and my song will
be your fight.

When the final notes faded from the piano strings, Blessing

opened his eyes and looked straight ahead as if he were seeing some image from his past reenacted at a great distance. His hands fell from the keyboard and clasped together loosely in his lap.

"Goodnight, Billy Bonney," he said, the words whispered as softly as a prayer. Then he stood and made his way to the front of the shop, where he began bundling up again for the walk home.

AUTHOR'S NOTE

For me, the most essential elements needed in writing about an iconic historical figure are understanding that character's personal and ambient history and how it shaped his personality. I need to know how the protagonist thought, how he would have responded to any stimulus, and what drove him.

The known facts of Billy Bonney's life are the gifts of meticulous researchers like Frederick Nolan, Robert Utley, Philip Rasch, Robert Mullin, Paul Hutton, Leon Metz, Michael Wallis, Drew Gomber, Mark Lee Gardner, David G. Thomas, Richard Etulain, Bob Boze Bell, James Mills, Waldo Koop, Jack DeMattos, Roy Young, Kurt House, and many others. To all of these historians I owe a great debt for allowing me to absorb in years what took them decades (or, in some cases, a lifetime) to uncover.

To probe into the character's mind . . . to see what current runs deep in his bones . . . for *that* psychological slant, a writer has his work cut out for him. But I had a windfall in this area. I knew Billy the Kid . . . or, at least, a modern-day version of him.

When I was in the fifth grade my best friend was Jimmy Richardson. He was an orphan who had been adopted by a couple who lived in my hometown neighborhood. Jimmy had light-brown hair, light-blue eyes that twinkled with mischief, and undeniable charm. His smile was an elixir akin to adrenaline. Anyone who talked to him for more than a minute fell

A Last Serenade for Billy Bonney

John Blessing

A Last Serenade for Billy Bonney

John Blessing

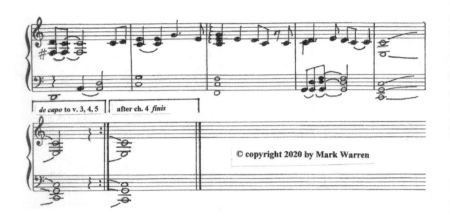

de capo to v. 3, 4, 5   after ch. 4 *finis*

under his spell.

Jimmy had a wild imagination; and, because of that, I could never be certain that everything he claimed about himself was true. But somehow, that didn't matter to me, because, in the way of suburban "blood brothers," I trusted him with my life, and there was no one I would rather be with.

Our most essential common denominator was a thirst for adventure; but, even at our tender age of ten years old, Jimmy was far ahead of me in that department. It was as if he had already lived another life, and now he was picking up where he had left off, this time with me by his side. He pushed the limits on what was acceptable for a couple of grammar school swashbucklers, but his wish list for never-before-done exploits was endless, and so I stuck with him.

Daring Jimmy to try some spine-tingling feat was tantamount to an introduction to his performance of the deed. Always on those occasions, I watched for the quick smile that would crinkle his eyes just before he dove headfirst into the escapade. Then, when he came up for air, I would see that same smile shot my way, announcing that it was my turn to replicate the feat. Because I knew Jimmy so well, over a half century later I was able to slip into the psyche of Billy Bonney with ease.

Gracias, Jimmy the Kid, *mi amigo.*

And, last, my thanks go to Susana Walker, beloved Montessori Spanish teacher, for keeping me on track with Mexican dialect.

ABOUT THE AUTHOR

Mark Warren owns and operates Medicine Bow Wilderness School in the Southern Appalachian Mountains north of Dahlonega, Georgia, where he teaches nature classes and the primitive skills of the Cherokee. Mark began his journey as a Western historian at age seven. He wrote his first musical composition at age fourteen and six decades later penned the eponymous song that serves as the centerpiece of this novel. The author has also written other books of note: *Secrets of the Forest* (four-volume set); *Last of the Pistoleers, Song of the Horseman,* and *A Tale Twice Told.*

The employees of Five Star Publishing hope you have enjoyed this book.

Our Five Star novels explore little-known chapters from America's history, stories told from unique perspectives that will entertain a broad range of readers.

Other Five Star books are available at your local library, bookstore, all major book distributors, and directly from Five Star/Gale.

Connect with Five Star Publishing

Website:
 gale.com/five-star

Facebook:
 facebook.com/FiveStarCengage

Twitter:
 twitter.com/FiveStarCengage

Email:
 FiveStar@cengage.com

For information about titles and placing orders:
 (800) 223-1244
 gale.orders@cengage.com

To share your comments, write to us:
 Five Star Publishing
 Attn: Publisher
 10 Water St., Suite 310
 Waterville, ME 04901